The Warrior's Soul:
A New Birth of Freedom

A Novel by:
Stephen Templeton

Green Ivy Publishing
1 Lincoln Centre
18W140 Butterfield Road
Suite 1500
Oakbrook Terrace IL 60181-4843
www.greenivybooks.com

ISBN: 978-1-944680-56-5

REVISED JULY 2016

Prologue

The sun hung high and heavy in the sky. It beat down without mercy on the warrior and his dwindling band of comrades below.

The warrior stared calmly across the field. The terrible might of an empire was there, a great faceless horde, men plied by gold and driven by the whip intent on breaking through the last thin line that opposed them. They had tried many times to break that line, and each time they had failed. Now, having fully surrounded the position, they were ready to try again. The warrior did not fear what might happen next. He did not fear what might be his fate. All his life, he had trained for this moment, suffering through pain, humiliation, and unimaginable cruelty to build a steely resolve. He knew but two outcomes to battle: victory or death. Both outcomes served their purpose. Both outcomes protected the freedom of his people. Even in death, he and the others would buy time for the rest of the army to gather and prepare a strong defense.

The warrior caught the eye of his king. The King nodded back, a simple acknowledgment that betrayed no emotion. A shared understanding between men who knew of blood and death: nothing else was needed.

Yet for an instant, the King's expression relaxed ever so slightly, the corners of his mouth curling into a crooked half-smile. The smile faded quickly, and iron discipline returned. The King turned and, in unison with the rest of his warriors, raised sword and shield to meet the advancing enemy.

Bodies crashed against shields, and blades flashed. The warrior raised his sword and struck a heavy blow, splitting the skull of an enemy. He knocked down another with his shield and gutted still a third with his sword before returning to finish the first man lying dazed on the ground. Many who dared to break that line fell before the swords and shields of the brave band of warriors, but still the enemy rushed forward as raging flood waters that wash over and eventually sweep away everything in their path.

The King absorbed a flurry of blows, seemingly from all directions at once, and then collapsed on the field. The enemy warriors exulted in their triumph and attempted to drag away the King's body as a trophy of war. The warrior and his band could not, would not allow that to happen and surged forward to re-claim their king. They forced the enemy back, hacking and stabbing with renewed energy, until they had fully surrounded their fallen leader. Whatever happened next would at least happen to all of them together. As the Oracle had foretold, the King and his warriors would perish as one — the Gods demanded a high price for the freedom of an entire people.

Horns sounded across the battlefield, and the enemy horde slowly drew back. It was then that the warrior and his comrades saw the arrows. Earlier in the battle, the enemy had vowed to darken the skies with their arrows. Now they kept that promise. Men, brave and true, fell around the warrior as deadly shafts found their marks. The warrior felt the burning pain of multiple strikes. Still he would not fall.

More arrows came. He struggled. He bled. He stood facing the enemy until at last he was all alone, until his legs could no longer support his own iron will. He slumped to the field; his grip loosened on his sword.

The warrior took one last look at the heavens above, and then darkness.

****

"Captain Miller, Captain Miller. Can you hear me? You have to get up!"

The soldier in green screamed at his fallen officer even as bullets zipped past his own helmet. Explosions tossed sand and seawater high in the air along with the body parts of brave but unfortunate young men. Everywhere the dead and the wounded cluttered the beach, their screams and moans and prayers drowned out by gunfire and the terrifying cacophony of war.

Still the soldier huddled near the captain, begging and pleading once more. Another young man in green, dodging bullets as he struggled forward in the sand, grabbed the soldier by his shirt and yelled, "The captain is dead. You have to leave him and get off this beach!"

A shell landed nearby, throwing sand and other small debris on both men.

Just then, Captain Miller opened his eyes. He did not speak. He did not hear the explosions or the surprised chattering of the two soldiers standing over him. He stared up at the sky, squinting slightly in the early morning sunlight. After a few seconds, he lifted his head just enough to get a good view of the beach. His eyes were wide and blank, seeing nothing and everything all at the same time.

The captain struggled slowly to his feet and stood somewhat unsteady in the loose sand. He looked up and down the beach at terrified soldiers huddled behind any cover they could find. They were not advancing; they just died in place whenever a bullet or artillery shell happened to find its mark. The captain looked back down at his own bloody shirt. A certain look, a particular glow, came to his eyes. The two soldiers in green noticed it too.

It was all clear now to Captain Miller. He realized why he was here, at this place, at this time — and he knew what he had to do. He spoke, quietly at first.

"There are only two types of men on this beach — the dead and the soon to be dead."

The voice grew louder and stronger.

"We have to move forward and get off this beach!"

Quickly and without fear, Captain Miller moved from each knot of huddled soldiers to the next. He exhorted. He grabbed. He pushed. He yelled and screamed. At last men began to move forward again towards the pillboxes and the machine gun nests on the cliffs. Still brave men in green fell, but they edged closer and closer to the enemy.

The captain was at the forefront. He lobbed a grenade into the pillbox and then took out more enemy soldiers with his rifle. At last the machine guns were silent, and the soldiers in green streamed through the break. There was no stopping them now. More enemy soldiers fell or threw down their weapons.

The young soldier reached the top of the cliff. He took one last look back at the wreckage on the beach and grinned from ear to ear. Turning towards the battle in front of him, a battle his army was finally winning, he let out a high pitched howl.

"Captain Miller, we did it! We took this beach."

But the captain did not hear him nor share in the joy of victory. A piece of shrapnel had entered his skull and laid him out on the grassy ground just past the cliff. The brave captain would not rise a second time.

As the summer sun began to peek through the smoke of battle, the people of France tasted freedom for the first time in more than 4 years.

Chapter 1

Simon Anderson strode briskly towards the gleaming office tower up ahead, trying hard to ignore the TV cameras and general commotion around him.

"Trade negotiations are big news, practically the Super Bowl of the modern business world," he quietly admitted. Not that this fact made him any less annoyed as he pushed his way towards the door. He sighed and took a deep breath before he entered. Flashing his TAA identification badge, he moved through security with ease and headed towards the main conference room.

The conference room was on the 10th floor. The elevator ride up gave Simon time to think. The cameras were gone, and he listened casually to the quiet hum of the elevator. He knew why he was here. The Europeans were being difficult. They seemed to cling to past glories from centuries ago and did not fully grasp how they fit into the new world order. That part, most of all, grated on Simon's nerves.

If the Europeans would just be reasonable….

Simon shook his head. The tension was really starting to build up in the back of his neck now. He had hoped that this whole exercise would not be necessary.

The elevator lurched to a sudden halt at the 10th floor. Simon frowned; he expected better from a Class A office tower. No time to complain though. He ran fingers through his thick brown hair, adjusted his silk tie, and patted down the lapels of his tailored suit. Appearance was everything; appearance was power. It was time to put on his game face. Simon's dark eyes were suddenly alert, burning with a well-practiced intensity meant solely to intimidate the competition or anybody else in the way. He flashed a cold, calculating smile and exited the elevator.

The sign above the conference room door was large and professionally simple: "The Trade Association of the Americas welcomes the European Union." Simon barely acknowledged the sign. He flashed his security credentials once more and reached for the door.

He stopped right there. He swallowed hard. For a moment, he considered the plan — and all those people behind that door.

But it was only for a moment, nothing more.

He had a job to do.

Checking his tie one last time, Simon opened the door and moved in to work the room. He smiled. It was his room now. Moving easily from person to person, he spoke warmly, casually. He took time to look people in the eyes. At every opportunity, he pressed the flesh too, sometimes a soft touch to the shoulder, sometimes pumping hands vigorously like a slick backwoods politician.

"Too bad there aren't any babies around to kiss," he mused.

Simon was less jovial, but still coolly professional, when he greeted the French representative and the head of the European Union delegation: "Welcome to the trade talks, Francois."

"I thought your boss would be here," Francois snorted. "Surely these talks are important enough to merit his attention."

"He'll kick off the conference via a live video feed, but he trusts me with running the conference and handling all the details on the ground," Simon replied without missing a beat.

"If we can get everyone seated, we can get started." Simon smiled politely and motioned towards the conference room table.

As if on cue, the large TV screen on the wall began to flicker to life. A familiar face slowly came into view. A face made famous by countless billboards, television appearances, and even postage stamps. A face shaped by delicate features, trim and well groomed, radiating supreme confidence. Simon's boss smiled and began to speak in his polished Latin accent.

"This is Daniel Garcia, CEO of the Trade Association of the Americas. I would like to welcome our friends from the European Union to these important trade negotiations."

The CEO moved on quickly from the introductions. "My friends, the European Union and the Americas are one people sharing the same western culture and values. Yet, we are physically separated by an ocean."

"I am here today," Garcia continued, with more passion now, "and the delegates from the TAA are here today … to bridge that ocean, in a figurative sense, and bring together our two great peoples. Our true destinies are as one, one global economic powerhouse born out of an alliance between the EU and the TAA. I leave the details to my trusted delegates, but I do pray that you will accept our offer and join us. I bid you farewell for now and God speed these negotiations."

With that, the CEO smiled again and abruptly terminated the broadcast.

Simon turned to the delegates surrounding the large oval table and moved quickly into his own opening statements. "We're all here because we have a vital job to do, something that will impact our families and fellow shareholders for generations to come. However, before we get into these discussions, I need to cover some basic ground rules."

"First, only one person talks at a time. As chairperson, I will recognize each speaker. Second, we will stay on track with the agenda. Any new issue not on the current agenda may be moved to a parking lot for us to deal with later or, at my discretion, may be incorporated into the agenda for immediate discussion. And third, it is very important that we stay on a strict break schedule. I believe we can only be productive if we are rested, completely alert, and not worried about biological needs such as food and bathrooms."

Simon brought up the first point on the agenda and then turned over discussion to one of the other TAA delegates. Other people, experts in their fields, could handle the details. His job was to keep the meeting moving and ultimately to secure agreement. He eased back into his chair and tried to relax. Excepting the occasional interruption to recognize a new speaker, Simon was alone with his thoughts. He kept a careful eye on the time as the discussions ground on.

Progress was slow, and frustration mounted. The Europeans were being intransient as Simon had feared. Their current position did not merit such a hard line, but they were too arrogant and too blinded by past glories to realize that. Simon simmered until he could hold back no longer.

"I would think the European Union would share our concern over the recent discussions between the Russian Federation and the Asian Pacific Trade Organization," Simon interjected firmly. "If you thought getting your oil from the Russians was difficult," he added with a hefty dose of sarcasm, "try dealing with the Asians!"

"We share your concern to a point," Francois replied sharply, "but we don't agree that the situation is serious enough to warrant some of the drastic solutions you propose. We have invested heavily in renewable energy over the last several years so we are becoming increasingly less dependent on oil."

The very possibility of needing less oil in the future didn't register with Simon. "If you join us and allow our security forces to move to the border region," he continued, "we will have more strategic options in case the Russians do choose to align with the Asians. We can cross the border quickly and secure the oilfields for ourselves, or at the very least, we can use the big stick to improve our negotiating position for keeping the oil flowing."

The logic of this position was all too obvious to Simon; it should be obvious to anyone who had half a brain he thought. To be successful in global business, you had to move quickly and you had to be ready to kick some ass if needed. Yes, it should have been obvious, simple really.

Unfortunately, it wasn't so clear and simple in the eyes of the Europeans.

"Are you prepared to potentially start World War III?" Francois answered, his voice rising in anger. "Also, to invite your security forces in means that our member countries have to give up their sovereignty."

This last statement cut to the very core of what Simon believed, and he laughed in disbelief. Could the Europeans be that stubborn, or did they really just not have a clue about the global economy?

"National borders are a thing of the past. Constant squabbling among small, independent countries is an inefficient way to manage regional resources and capital assets."

Francois countered with his own hint of sarcasm. "I would think that freedom and independence would still mean something here."

Leaning forward for emphasis, Simon replied calmly and in a very straightforward manner, "Not as much as security and prosperity."

The room was suddenly very quiet, the type of dead quiet that occurs after an argument has been clearly won or after one side of the debate has simply given up and surrendered. Simon smiled and leaned back in his chair. Winning felt good.

Then he remembered.

Simon immediately glanced at his watch, fearing that he might have lost track of time during all the heated discussion. He breathed easier when he noted there were still 15 minutes before the scheduled break.

Still smiling, Simon broke the silence. "We are coming up on our scheduled break so we will need to wrap up this part of the agenda." At just that moment, out of the corner of his eye, he noted a sudden flash of light across the room.

"Oh God no, not…." His voice trailed off as the light exploded into a deafening thunderclap of raw, uncontrollable energy.

The force of the blast rippled across the room, swirling the very air that people might breathe into a fiery vortex of death and destruction. The ground shook beneath Simon's feet, and he felt himself being pulled upward into the churning chaos. Tables, chairs, and body parts were tossed and consumed by the vortex. Anything and everything in its path it destroyed — without cause, without passion, without remorse.

A few terrible seconds, and then it was over.

The air, quiet and still once more, was filled with smoke. Charred papers and other debris fluttered slowly and peacefully to the ground. Simon lay alone in the darkness, cold and unmoving.

Suddenly his eyes opened wide. A burst of air filled his lungs, smoke too; he choked and coughed. For some time, he remained still in the haze, trying to breathe and moving only his head slowly from side to side. He stared blankly at the surrounding chaos and destruction. There was no sound except for the ringing in his ears. Simon struggled to sit up and then rose slowly, painfully to his feet. Still unsure where he was, he lurched forward by instinct alone.

He gradually shook off the ringing noise in his head and began to move tentatively towards muffled sounds rising out of the wreckage, cries of pain and weak pleas for help. He rubbed his eyes; he strained to see. The torn and mangled bodies of the dead lay scattered on the smoldering floor, but here and there were survivors, bloodied and trapped beneath heavy debris. Something clicked in Simon's head, and he immediately understood what he had to do here, no matter that the exact location of the "here" remained fuzzy. There was a fire in his eyes now. He began to move quickly and with purpose.

The shock of the explosion was beginning to wear off. Aid workers mobilized and rushed forward into the wreckage. Simon met them, standing tall amid the smoke and debris despite his own injuries. He began to bark out orders in a calm, clear voice. The rescue teams, incredulous at first, simply tried to treat the bloodied man giving the orders. Simon waved off all treatment, explaining politely but firmly that there were more injured people who needed help. Taking one look at the determination in his eyes, the rescuers moved away to help others or just followed Simon's lead.

Aid workers sweated and prayed in equal measure, desperate to save those who might yet be saved. In the middle of this chaos and madness, Simon was seemingly everywhere at once, helping lift debris off victims or giving words of encouragement to those still trapped. His calm demeanor and personal energy lifted spirits and galvanized the entire rescue effort.

Time itself seemed to move slowly, settling into a certain sad rhythm of people doing what had to be done — the steady, careful removal of the dead; the urgent, though sometimes unsuccessful rescue of the wounded. That there were any successes at all kept them moving and digging.

Simon remained until the last person had been evacuated. It was a young woman, and she was alive, but just barely. Simon touched her hand as they carried her out. He was done. He eased himself down slowly to the floor and then simply collapsed, as much from exhaustion as the lingering effects of his own injuries.

Across town, a wife worried and waited for a phone call that was not going to come. She knew about the explosion at the trade conference from the breaking news splashed all over TV. She also knew her husband had been at that meeting. What she didn't know was if he was hurt or even still alive.

She couldn't reach her husband on his cell phone, and the people she could reach didn't know anything at all. It was frustrating. It was scary. But she couldn't let any of that show. Somehow she had to be strong. Somehow she had to keep telling her young daughter that everything would be okay even if she didn't totally believe that herself.

At last, she heard that survivors were being taken to Wilson Memorial Hospital downtown. The only thing she could do, the thing she had to do, was to go directly to the hospital herself and pray she found her husband alive. She made arrangements with her regular babysitter and then headed downtown.

Chapter 2

The tattered man moved uneasily through the crowded sidewalks downtown. Normally he preferred the anonymity of the crowd. But this crowd was filled with well-dressed professional people, and he feared he would stand out — tangled white hair, a rough growth of beard, and ragged clothes lost in a sea of silk ties and business suits. Still, he wanted to catch the latest news on the terrorist attack at the trade conference, and the nearest large public television screens were in the heart of downtown.

Along the way, he passed a score of large billboards and other gaudy, high-tech outdoor advertisements vying for the attention of passersby. Some of them were filled with bland propaganda. "A better life through better processes" was printed in large white block letters on a simple black background. It was signed by the CEO himself. The tattered man wondered to himself just how many times he had seen that slogan on a billboard. Other ads were more amusing, recalling the old business adage that humor, like sex, "sells". He wasn't so sure of that but enjoyed the change in tone nonetheless.

The next bill boards in line were still bigger and even flashier. He stopped at one in particular. It was hard to miss. He looked up, slowly, intently, all the way to the top just to make sure. There on a 20 foot-tall, high gloss rendering was George Washington, shirtless and ripped with muscles, holding a young and very busty Martha Washington in one arm and a huge sword in the other. It was a new movie being promoted by the entertainment division of the TAA.

The words on the bill board screamed out in bold print: "See the story of the real George Washington. See how the Father of Our Country used to kick colonial ass, and that's no lie."

The tattered man did not remember Washington, the first President, quite that way. He scratched the patch of whiskers on his chin and then patted down something he carried well-hidden in a dirty satchel slung around his shoulder and waist. He dared not pull it out in this huge crowd, but somehow it was comforting just knowing it was still there. At last, he looked away from the bill board and began to move once more with the surging crowd.

The television screen was large enough to be seen clearly from a full city block away. The face of the CEO, looking a little worn around the edges, filled the screen. His expression was grave, and he spoke in a somber tone.

"My fellow shareholders, I regret to inform you that the Trade Association of the Americas has been struck by an act of terrorism. Earlier today, a bomb exploded at trade negotiations between the TAA and the European Union. I am afraid to say that casualties were heavy. The investigation continues, but preliminary evidence suggests that this cowardly act is the work of European Ultra-nationalists bent on sabotaging any potential merger between the TAA and the EU."

His voice rising, the words were direct and more forceful.

"These terrorists do not share our values, nor do they understand our vision of creating a global economic powerhouse through the strategic merger of two great peoples. Like all nationalists, these terrorists live in the past, while we look firmly to the future, a future of security and prosperity. I promise you that cowards with bombs will not prevent us from reaching our goals. I promise you that this act of terrorism and the deaths of innocent people will not go un-avenged."

The CEO concluded his remarks, and the huge screen next filled with various TV talking heads. They were uniformly attractive and uniformly well-dressed. They all uniformly condemned the nationalist terrorists from the European Union and debated what would happen next. They spoke of the casualties not as people, but merely as data which supported their talking points. The tattered man was very sorry that many people had apparently been killed, but he wondered to himself what evidence anyone had that tied the EU to the bombing and why none of the TV journalists were asking that question.

He shook his head in disappointment, slowly and carefully to avoid attracting attention. Then, in an absent-minded way, he patted the object hidden in his satchel once more before turning away from the screen to work his way back through the crowd.

Several blocks away, the scene at Wilson Memorial Hospital was one of controlled, or at least partly controlled, chaos. News people and cameras filled every open spot on the sidewalk just outside the entrance to the ambulance bay. Reporters pushed and jostled with other curious onlookers to catch a glimpse of the bombing victims. Within the bay, however, the process for removing and triaging patients remained calm and coolly efficient. Victims were unloaded; they were examined by nurses or technicians and then quickly assigned a code number dictating the order in which they would be treated.

Ambulances continued to pull into the hospital bay one after another to drop off their patients in a seemingly endless parade of misery. The triage area soon began to swell with the wounded. Difficult, life or death decisions had to be made, and they had to be made right now. A fresh-faced young nurse agonized over the choice between two critically injured victims: a low-level security guard and a TAA manager. Charged with keeping the process moving, the nursing manager quickly intervened.

"All other things being equal," she said calmly, "always go with the better dressed patient." The younger nurse was surprised and frankly a little confused. The nursing manager continued, "The better dressed patient is likely to be more important to the organization and therefore has better insurance. Better insurance means you and I actually get paid."

The younger nurse nodded and then smiled as if a great weight had suddenly been lifted from her shoulders. She tagged the TAA manager to go next and moved on.

The traffic around Wilson Memorial was nearly as clogged as the sidewalk outside the ambulance bay, although there were somewhat fewer cameras in the traffic lines. Holly Anderson tried to be patient as the taxi she was riding in crept slowly forward, but it was difficult. She banged her hands on the back of the driver's seat in frustration, but that didn't make the lines move any faster. It only elicited a rather nasty reaction from the driver.

"What do you expect out of me, lady? I can't drive right over these cars in front of me."

Holly gave up. "How about dropping me here? I'll walk the rest of the way."

"Suit yourself," the driver mumbled. "Try to stay alive when you cross the road through all this traffic," he added with just a hint of sarcasm. "I don't think they have any more room at the hospital."

Holly frowned and thanked the driver for his apparent concern over her safety. The taxi stopped crawling and came to a complete halt; Holly jumped out of the cab straight into the very traffic the driver had warned her about.

"Maybe he wasn't such a jackass after all," Holly murmured to herself, all the while dodging cars and weaving her way through traffic lanes.

At last, she reached the apparent safety of the hospital entrance way. She had to fight her way through tight knots of people, but at least none of these obstructions weighed a ton and could crush the average human being. Holly managed to work her way to the front desk; it still took several minutes to convince the people manning the desk that she was actually a family member of one of the victims, not just another reporter looking for information.

After what seemed like an eternity, Holly's efforts were rewarded. Her husband was at the hospital, and he was alive.

Doctor Johnson was perplexed. He scratched his head and once again examined the digital images from the Cat-scan. With his fingers, he carefully traced the outline of the skull and the pattern of light and dark areas highlighted in the brain. He shook his head and sighed. For all his training and experience, Doctor Johnson just could not understand how a man with these types of injuries could still be alive. He called Doctor Samuels into the room and gestured towards the digital images.

"There has to be a problem with the Cat-scan machine, or some technician has mixed up the scan results and we're really looking at skull images from some poor bastard on ice in the morgue. I cannot believe these are the scan results from a live patient."

Doctor Samuels nodded and replied thoughtfully, "Maybe there are some things that just cannot be explained."

"I believe in science and technology; everything can be explained."

"And yet your patient lives. Maybe you need to quit focusing on a handful of fuzzy pictures and start worrying about how you'll keep him alive. I understand he's a pretty important manager at the TAA." Doctor Samuels smiled at his colleague's obvious frustration.

"Not only that," Doctor Johnson added softly, "I also understand the guy is a hero. He apparently gets up from a fatal injury and then manages to help evacuate the wounded from the bombed out conference room."

Shaking his head once more, Doctor Johnson decided he might just have to accept there were indeed some things that could not be explained.

A nurse walked into the room, interrupting any debate about the limitations of science and technology. "Doctor Johnson, the wife of your patient is here. Can we bring her back?"

"Yes, I don't see why not. I'm sure she doesn't care what medical science thinks. Her husband is alive. That's the bottom line."

The nurse escorted Holly Anderson back through a series of curtains into the examining room area where she could see her husband resting quietly in a bed. Tears welled up in her eyes. She reached forward to touch Simon's hair but pulled back almost immediately. It was terrifying; she didn't know anything at all about the extent of his injuries. Doctor Johnson soon joined her at the bedside.

"Mrs. Anderson, your husband has been gravely injured, but through some sort of medical miracle, he is alive," Doctor Johnson paused.

"… and I believe he will recover."

Holly was stunned. She couldn't speak; she had yet to fully comprehend those words. She looked back down, still struggling with all the emotions, when her husband suddenly opened his eyes.

"Simon, I'm here for you," Holly blurted out.

Simon stared back, smiling slightly. He did not immediately recognize the female face in front of him. "Who are you?" he asked softly. Doctor Johnson leaned forward and shined his penlight into Simon's eyes.

"This really isn't a surprise," the doctor continued. "With this type of head injury, you have to expect some gaps in memory. Hopefully, over time, these memories will come back. I can only advise you to be patient, very patient."

Holly was hurt but didn't want to show it at a time like this. "I understand, doctor. He's alive, and that's all that important right now."

"I can work with this," she quickly added. She sounded confident. Deep down, she wasn't so sure.

Doctor Johnson smiled. "I'm glad to hear that."

"I also need to tell you that your husband is a hero. Despite his own injuries, he was able to assist in the evacuation of the wounded. I even have a message from the CEO himself. He wants me to tell you that the entire TAA is very proud of Simon. He wishes Simon a speedy recovery and looks forward to seeing him back at work."

Holly acknowledged the doctor but was quietly lost in her own thoughts. This morning had started out like any other day; now things had spun wildly out of control. Her husband was alive, a real hero, but right now, he didn't even know who she was. She tried to be optimistic; her husband had to recover quickly. What all this could do for Simon's career was obvious.

What this would do for — or rather do to her marriage remained decidedly unclear.

Chapter 3

It was early morning at the offices of the TAA. The sun had not quite risen above the horizon. All was still except for the steady hum of vacuum cleaners used by the housekeepers, the typical quiet before the storm of activity on a normal workday. The offices were numerous and spacious, befitting an organization of great stature, yet they were decidedly more functional than lavish.

Daniel Garcia entered the office area. He was not always the first to arrive, but he was close. Daniel felt at home in these offices. More importantly, he felt very much in control of things when he was in these offices, and he really didn't like it whenever he felt out of control.

This was particularly true after the events of the day before. Besides his address to all shareholders, Daniel had spent the greater part of the evening doing interviews and answering questions from various news people. The questions were not particularly difficult, and he understood it was part of the job. Still, the lack of sleep was very real, and he was disturbed that he had to answer any questions at all.

On the way into his office, Daniel paused to study some of the value statements and other postings just outside the main conference room. He knew them by heart of course, yet there was something strangely comforting about reading them again. "A better life through better processes" was emblazoned on one posting. He smiled at the thought.

Garcia reached out and touched the adjacent plaque with some reverence, tracing the words with his finger and silently mouthing the guiding principles:

1) All non-value added activity is waste.
2) Waste does not add to bottom-line profits.
3) Eliminate all waste.

He looked around nervously to see if anyone had noticed. It was safe; he was still alone. Yes, it was good to be home Daniel thought.

The CEO settled into his desk and began pouring over the e-mails filling the computer screen. Most of them were about the bombing, requests for more information and questions about the next steps the TAA might take. This was to be expected. Nonetheless, Daniel felt his brief respite in the solitude of familiar surroundings beginning to slip away.

Not long after opening that first e-mail, he heard the front door to the main office area swing open. He clenched his teeth and hung his head; he wasn't alone anymore.

Mary, the administrative assistant, entered the office and chirped, "CEO Garcia, you're in early today. I thought you might take a few hours off after such a busy night."

The CEO managed only a weak smile and mumbled back a reply without ever looking up from his computer screen. "Yes, it would be nice to be in bed still, but there is too much to do here at the office."

"Well, since you're here," Mary continued, "you have several requests for meetings on your calendar. Representatives from both the Class A shareholders council and the Class B shareholders group would like to meet with you to discuss the ongoing investigation surrounding the bombing and any planned response."

"Yeah, just like everybody else," the CEO grumbled under his breath.

"What did you say sir? I'm sorry I must have missed it," Mary dutifully replied.

"Nothing," Daniel Garcia regained his composure and continued in his most business-like tone, "Accept the meeting with the Class A shareholders for this afternoon. Push the Class B shareholders back to later in the week; I'll send a summary e-mail and put out some web-page announcements for them to chew on until then. By the way, I want to move up the meeting with the senior leadership team to 9 am. Please make sure everyone gets the word."

Mary nodded. "Yes sir, I'll take care of that."

As the early morning wore on, a steady stream of employees, some important and some not so important, continued to fill the offices of the TAA. There was the typical burst of energy as the place came to life, but this morning was clearly more than just the beginning of any other busy workday.

The bombing was on everyone's minds. With answers scarce, the office buzzed with a potent combination of gossip, rumors, and shared conversations in the halls. Every employee was involved in some form or fashion, from the highest senior vice-president to the lowliest administrative assistant or security guard. Every employee looked for something, anything, to come out of the senior leadership team meeting.

The CEO entered the main conference room and closed the door behind him. Senior VP's from the various operating divisions and other selected employees surrounded the large conference table. All was perfectly quiet as the leadership team waited for the CEO to speak.

"Ladies and gentlemen, we all know that we have some very serious topics to discuss today. However, we also have to show as a leadership team that terrorists cannot disrupt business. Besides taking aggressive action to punish those behind the bombing, the next best thing we can do to put our shareholders' fears to rest is to demonstrate to them that business, and life, will go on as usual. I therefore request each division head to give his or her regular progress report, but please keep it short so we can devote more time to discussing the next steps on the bombing."

There was genuine surprise around the table, and the executives struggled to hide it, some better than others. No one dared question how the CEO ran the business. After a few uncomfortable minutes, the first division head broke the silence.

"The condo project at Yellowstone is moving ahead of schedule," the Senior VP of Real Estate offered. "We just broke ground on the new gated community around Old Faithful. We are adding special lighting effects to highlight eruptions of the geyser. Our contractor believes this will be a big hit and expects that buyers will pay top dollar."

With that, the Senior VP stopped, nervously waiting for any questions or better yet, a sign of approval from the CEO. When the latter nodded, the executive exhaled in relief and reclined back in his chair to hear reports from the other division heads.

The Senior VP of Healthcare and Human Resources followed this lead and tried to keep things short. "Our containment plan for the flu pandemic has proven effective. No new outbreaks have been reported this month," he stated flatly. Again, the CEO nodded.

Other executives offered their reports, each one keeping their remarks brief and to the point. Sam Johnson, the Senior VP of Entertainment, clearly recognized the pattern and understood the flow of the meeting. Nonetheless, he still could not contain his own excitement, practically bubbling over when he began to update the group on the status of his pet project.

"The Washington picture is on track to be the next blockbuster," he gushed. This elicited a few groans and a great deal of eye rolling around the table. Sam was undeterred by the lack of enthusiasm and continued, "Not only are we projecting big money for opening weekend based on advance buzz and the test screenings, but we're also aggressively riding that market momentum by green-lighting the sequel now."

He ticked off other potential revenue streams: action figures, tie-ins with fast food restaurants, and the like. "And get this," Sam paused for effect. "We are very close to signing the hottest young actor in Hollywood to play the dashing Lafayette, Washington's sidekick in the sequel."

Sam's enthusiasm was greeted with a hefty dose of sarcasm around the table. Someone asked, "If I remember my history correctly, wasn't Lafayette a Frenchman?"

"Yes, I guess he was," Sam responded. "What difference does that make? If anything, the French accent will appeal to teenage girls, a key demographic which buys a lot of tickets to movies."

"Frenchmen are so European," the same naysayer continued. "Do you really think audiences are going to fall for a European hero after a terrorist bombing perpetrated by Europeans?"

By now, the CEO was thoroughly frustrated by the pace of the discussion. He grimaced, rubbing his eyes with his right hand before moving to massage his temple. The group around the table noticed this movement and fell into an uncomfortable silence.

"No, they won't," he answered forcefully. "Make the Lafayette character a Latin American, even if you have to change the name. Remember that entertainment does not need to be historically accurate, just profitable. Now let's move on!"

Sam was deflated but tried not to show it. He nodded in agreement with the other executives as the group turned to focus on the Senior VP of Security, James Wilson.

"Please give the Leadership Team an update on the status of your investigation into the bombing," the CEO requested in a carefully measured tone. The TAA's head of security did not respond directly but instead deferred to the young analyst seated to his left.

"Members of the Leadership Team, let me introduce Chris Smith, the best analyst and investigator I have on my staff. Chris is leading the investigation and will give our report."

The young man swallowed hard, paused as he collected his thoughts, and then began to speak. "There are several things we have learned about the bombing, but I have to tell you there are many things we still don't know."

"First, let me tell you what we do know. We do know what type of device was used, and we can tell where it was planted. The device was likely planted sometime between midnight and 6 am the morning of the bombing. I say that because this time period corresponds to a suspicious 6-hour gap in the security tapes covering that part of the building. The system shows a simple electrical malfunction disabled the cameras in that area. However, I don't believe this downtime was purely a coincidence."

Chris Smith cleared his throat and repositioned himself in his seat before he continued. "Now let me tell you what we don't know yet. We don't know who, and we don't know why."

The Senior VP of Security smiled nervously at his colleagues and then challenged the analyst. "Chris, I think you need to clarify your statement there. I thought we had narrowed this down to one of three known nationalist organizations in Europe; you just had not identified the specific group yet. Is that not correct?"

"No," Smith responded cautiously. "I never said that. So far there is no physical evidence at the site that ties the bombing to any known terrorist organization based anywhere, including Europe. Furthermore, there are no credible proclamations over the internet or any other media source where a particular group is taking credit for the bombing. Right now, there is just not enough data to allow me to pinpoint responsibility for this attack."

"Until I have that data or evidence," the analyst concluded, "I cannot in good conscience report to our shareholders that our investigation is complete, nor can I fully consider possible plans for retaliation."

The room was deathly silent as the group tried to gauge the possible reaction from the CEO. The group did not have long to wait.

"You clearly have missed something here," Daniel Garcia retorted, his voice rising in anger. "There are known nationalist organizations in Europe who have opposed our merger talks with the European Union. They have the motive; they have the technology; they recognized an opportunity." "

"You, unfortunately, have not recognized the obvious."

Chris Smith cleared his throat again; he was in genuine distress now. "I am sorry, sir. It is not about what is obvious; it is about what the data tells us. And right now, the data does not tell us anything conclusive."

The executives around the table let out an audible gasp. James Wilson knew exactly what the CEO was looking for from the analyst, and clearly this answer was not it. Garcia was ready to boil over by now. His eyes became impossibly dark. His mouth tightened into a scowl, and he drew a deep breath, the moment of calm before the storm. The CEO made no effort to conceal his anger as he quickly responded to the young analyst. In fact, he seemed to relish it.

"Do not tell me about data. Data is for analyzing experiments in the lab. This is the real world where real people die. We need a real investigation that gives us real answers and real next steps forward. If you are not the man to give us real answers, then we will find someone else who will. Do you understand me?"

"Yes, sir," Smith answered weakly.

Daniel Garcia was not satisfied. "Do you understand me?"

"Yes, sir," Smith repeated, this time with more conviction.

"Very well, then this meeting is over."

As he rose from the table, the CEO glared at his chief of security. Clearly the young analyst was not the only one who had failed to deliver as expected. The rest of the executives waited until Garcia had left the conference room and then filed quietly, and dutifully, out the door.

The CEO arrived back at his office in a foul mood. The meeting had not given him what he needed; he needed investigative results to legitimize the prevailing theory that European nationalists were responsible for the bombing. Without this, he pondered what to tell the Class A shareholders in his next meeting.

Garcia's thoughts were interrupted by a quiet knock on the door.

Mary poked her head into the office. "I'm sorry sir. Do you have time to see the head of the Class A Shareholders Council? He would like to speak to you privately before the meeting."

Daniel Garcia did not like the thought of speaking with the head of the council. He considered Milton Woods to be a pompous, idealistic fool. Woods profited handsomely from the current system, but somehow he dared to question just how the system worked. Garcia had no use for the man, but at the same time, he knew better than anyone that some people just could not be ignored.

"Yes, I'll see Mr. Woods," the CEO muttered. Mary smiled and slipped back through the door.

Milton Woods appeared at Garcia's office a few moments later. Whatever his private opinions may have been, the CEO was especially charming as he greeted the head of the council. Smiling broadly, he grasped Woods' hand and shook it vigorously.

"Milton, how is the family?"

The head of the Class A Shareholders was decidedly less pleasant. "The family is fine, Daniel. Right now, I'm more interested in what you know about the bombing and what you plan to do about it."

"We believe a nationalist group in Europe is responsible for the bombing," the CEO responded coolly. "We are still trying to pinpoint the exact group. Our options for retaliation remain open at this time. This is exactly what I plan to tell the shareholders' council in our meeting today."

"And there is nothing else to say?"

"Nothing at this time." The CEO smiled again, this time not as warmly as before. It was the type of smile that was both subtle and intimidating, a facial expression which served as a warning not to go any farther.

Milton Woods shifted his body uneasily. Having been a senior leader for many years, he understood this type of unspoken message and so declined to press the issue. "Okay," his voice cracked. "I trust you will keep the shareholders council in the loop as the investigation progresses." Garcia nodded.

The head of the council was only partially satisfied. He could sell his fellow shareholders on the idea that investigations of this magnitude and importance took time. That much was sure. Still he was troubled. He considered what might come next but shuddered as visions of past decisions, of past violence, began to intrude upon the present.

"Will you show restraint when it comes time for retaliation?"

The CEO did not answer.

Perhaps feelings of guilt steeled his nerves or perhaps they made him care less about his own personal welfare. Either way, Milton Woods was not going to accept silence for an answer.

Not this time.

"I want to know how you are going to handle this, and I don't want to see a repeat of your strategy for dealing with the Islamic terrorists!" The head of the council gulped hard and waited. He felt strangely liberated that the past was now on the table.

Daniel Garcia did not share those feelings. "We did what was necessary then," he responded sharply, "and we will do what is necessary now."

"What we did before was horrific! What we did before was immoral!"

"What we did before, my tender-hearted friend, was tremendously effective."

"Was it effective to slaughter innocent women and children?"

The CEO pondered the thought for a minute and then answered, "Yes, I believe it was."

"The former management team, your old government, tried to deal with radical Islam by being too soft. Or when they did fight terrorists at all; they did so with one arm tied behind their backs. My team simply took off all restrictions and applied a new paradigm based on solid research and a deep understanding of basic human nature."

"We used to do our best to avoid hitting non-combatants," countered the head of the council. "You, on the other hand, purposely dragged non-combatants directly into the War on Terror. If a suicide bomber happened to hit our interests, your security forces responded by systematically hunting down and killing every member of the bomber's family."

"We're supposed to be the good guys; we're not supposed to murder innocent people." Milton Woods shook his head and looked down at the floor, struggling with the memories of terrible things his silence had allowed to happen.

"And how many times did we have to make that example before potential suicide bombers got the message?" The CEO became more animated with his gestures. His face flushed with anger; the veins in his neck bulged. "I can answer that," he growled, "not many!"

There was a brief silence as Woods waited for the rage he knew for sure was coming. But then the biggest surprise of all: nothing happened.

Garcia simply smiled, his emotions suddenly back under control. The CEO spoke again, yet in a manner more suited to a lecture on basic business principles rather than a discussion on global terrorism.

"What you have to understand," he began, "is that deep down we are all alike. It doesn't matter whether you are white or black, Asian or Latino, Christian or Muslim. Every mother loves her children. Every father wants to keep his family safe. Islamic terrorists have families too. A man might be willing to sacrifice his own life for his God. But is he really ready to sacrifice the lives of his wife and kids? I think not."

Garcia smiled once more and began to conclude his argument. "All we had to do was clearly demonstrate to the world that being a suicide bomber meant you doomed your family to a horrible death. Sure we killed innocent people, but in the end we stopped the bombings and saved many more innocent people, innocent people who would have otherwise lost their lives in those bombings."

Deep down, Milton Woods was horrified by the perverted mathematics the CEO had just used to justify mass murder. His nerves of steel were faltering, however, and he began to slide back into his old comfort zone of silent acceptance. Yes, he might loathe himself sometimes, but he would be alive and comfortable.

The head of the Class A Shareholders Council turned to leave the CEO's office. Just before reaching the door, he stopped. There was one more thing. It was pretty much standard protocol. He turned his head part way back around, careful though not to make direct eye contact.

"Remember to keep us in the loop as your investigation continues," Woods said softly.

The CEO nodded. "You got it."

Chapter 4

Holly Anderson watched her husband carefully as he napped in the back seat of the taxi taking them home from the hospital. It had been three full days since the bombing, and she was glad the doctors felt comfortable sending Simon home so soon. The doctors were still rather perplexed about the nature and extent of Simon's injuries, but they apparently had decided that it was better to spend their time on other, less fortunate victims who were not doing quite so well. Simon even seemed to be recovering parts of his memory as Doctor Johnson had predicted. Her husband seemed to remember her now, or at least that was what he said.

The wife, however, was not quite so sure she believed him.

The taxi cruised out of the city and into the leafy suburbs, passing upscale shopping centers and well manicured sub-divisions along the way. It was a sunny day, and the trees swayed gently in the breeze. Holly soaked in the warmth of the day through the car window, gradually becoming more relaxed as the ride brought them closer to home.

At length, the taxi pulled into a comfortable neighborhood just off the main road and rolled up to the Anderson house. The screeching of brakes and the sudden halt of the vehicle stirred Simon out of his slumber. Rubbing his eyes and stretching tight muscles, he slowly took in the surroundings while the driver climbed out of the front seat and turned around to open the back passenger door. Simon squinted as he stepped out of the car and into the sunlight. The house was large and well appointed he thought, although not quite as large as the picture in his memory.

Holly hurried to Simon's side and clasped his hand. "Honey, we're home," she whispered. "You're safe now."

She tightened her grip on her husband's hand and escorted him carefully up the sidewalk to the front door, partly because she feared he might be unsteady and partly because she simply needed to feel the touch of his skin. Holly fumbled with the keys for what seemed like an eternity before she finally opened the door. Still holding hands tightly, the couple practically stumbled into the house. Holly laughed. It was a nervous, rather self-conscious laugh. She was keen to notice, however, that Simon did not even crack a smile.

The babysitter, Mrs. Wilson, was waiting patiently for Holly and Simon in the family room. The small child squirming in her arms, on the other hand, was anything but patient. Mrs. Wilson finally gave up the struggle. She smiled and let the little girl go.

"Mommy and Daddy," the child squealed as she launched every pound of her little body towards her parents. Blond curls bouncing on her head, she landed at their feet with an arm wrapped tightly around one leg of each adult.

Almost instinctively, Holly reached down to hug her daughter. "Oh, honey, we missed you a bunch! Have you behaved for Mrs. Wilson?" The child nodded, flashing a mischievous grin that highlighted the gap where her front tooth used to be.

Simon's reaction was more subdued, almost stiff by comparison. He patted the girl lightly on the head and then seemed to withdraw his hand. "Suzy, I missed you too," he added softly. The little girl beamed once more. Holly managed only a weak smile.

"At least he remembers her name," she thought to herself.

That thought was not at all consoling. Holly brushed hair out of her face, then quickly dropped her gaze towards the floor to hide any doubts her eyes might reveal. She wondered whether Simon's memories or feelings would ever be more than just polite name recognition.

Suzy's feelings weren't quite so complicated. All she knew was that her daddy was here; she could see him and touch him. All this meant one thing. "Daddy, daddy, play with me," she pleaded, pouting all the while.

Holly quickly intervened.

"Honey, your daddy just got home from the hospital. I really think he needs to take it easy for awhile." Suzy frowned, while Simon seemed almost relieved. Holly grabbed Suzy's hand and cheerfully offered, "Why don't I take you outside to play?" The little girl accepted the bribe with a smile, apparently satisfied for the moment.

As she played with her daughter in the backyard, Holly could not help stealing glances back at Simon through the glass patio door. He was moving carefully through the family room, looking it over much like a prospective buyer does when visiting an open house. Here and there, he picked up objects, turned them every which way, and then put them back. Holly thought he looked like someone who had only seen these things in pictures and was curious to touch them.

But these were ***their*** things, the little objects or mementos which filled a house and somehow made it feel more like a home. If he couldn't recognize the things he had helped pick out, the things they had bought together....

She finally turned her head away to focus back on Suzy. Holly was already worried, and watching Simon right now did not make her feel any better.

Like most small children, Suzy didn't tire easily, no matter how hard her mother tried. Holly was willing to keep trying for a good while though; it seemed to take her mind off other things. Relaxing maybe, but Holly realized soon enough that relaxing wouldn't put dinner on the table. So she gathered up Suzy, despite her protests, and went back inside to cook dinner. By this time, Simon had settled comfortably into the recliner chair.

"I'm going to make your favorite dinner tonight," Holly said in the most cheerful voice she could muster. She paused for a moment but then decided against asking Simon to guess just exactly what that favorite dinner was.

Simon smiled pleasantly and nodded. Holly nodded back in agreement and then threw herself, mind and body, into the kitchen.

Dinner was rather uneventful. Everyone ate with a healthy appetite. At the same time, the eating was very mechanical, purely to satisfy hunger and without any passion or feeling to it. Small talk passed back and forth between the Andersons with an occasional, lively interruption from Suzy. Holly abruptly broke the routine.

"Oh, I almost forgot to tell you," she said, "You received an official letter of thanks from CEO Garcia. He praised your bravery at the bombing scene and wants you to take as long as you need to fully recover before you go back to work."

Holly studied Simon's reaction carefully. He seemed reluctant to talk about what he remembered from the bombing, but he did seem to appreciate the offer of extra time off. This in itself was a bit of a surprise. The old Simon was a workaholic who never liked to take time off. Maybe, just maybe, the new Simon would have different priorities. Holly smiled as she considered this possibility.

After dinner and dishes, there was the nightly ritual for Suzy: bath time, followed by story time, followed by bedtime. It had been an exciting day for the child and getting her down for the night wasn't so easy.

By the time Suzy gave into pure exhaustion, her parents were near the end of their rope. Holly and Simon collapsed into their own bed without thought of anything other than sleep. Holly reached over to kiss Simon good night. He didn't pull away, but he didn't exactly put much into it either. She decided not to push things just yet, mainly because she was too damned tired herself.

Simon was tired as well, but sleep did not come easily. He tossed. He turned. He tried not to disturb Holly.

When sleep did finally come, it was filled with images, violent, painful images. The carnage of the bombing had been horrific enough, but Simon's nightmares were filled with other, older visions as well — swords and shields and warriors who died in ancient battles — bullets and bodies on sandy beaches. It all seemed so real; he felt the pain of swords, of arrows, of bullets.

At last he could take no more. He cried out in agony and awoke in a sweat. Holly woke up too, startled and a little scared.

She instinctively tried to comfort Simon and reached out to hold him. "Honey, honey, you're just having a nightmare! You're safe at home with your family."

Simon spread the fingers on his right hand and forced them through his thick, damp hair. He blew out a deep breath and leaned back into Holly. She stroked his hair, gently, tenderly. There was something positive to be said about nightmares she thought.

"Are you having flashbacks about the bombing?"

Simon thought for a moment about exactly how much to tell Holly. He ultimately decided that less was more and answered simply, "Yes, but I really don't want to talk about it right now."

"Why don't we try to get back to sleep? I promise I won't wake you up again." Simon began to pull away from the embrace of his wife.

Physically, the movement was ever so slight. Emotionally, it was so much more. Holly sensed it right away and slowly slid back towards her side of the bed.

"Yes, honey, lets get some sleep," she replied, trying hard to hide the disappointment in her voice.

Morning came all too soon after a rough night. Holly awoke at first light anyway, more on instinct and routine than anything else. She lay on her side for a few more minutes, her back stiff, her muscles tight. She yawned and tried to rub the sleep out of her eyes.

Reaching back over to touch Simon, her hand landed on an empty mattress. Holly was suddenly jolted wide awake. She jumped straight up out of bed and headed out through the bedroom door in a panic. Her fears only grew as she swept through the house without finding any sign of her husband.

Holly was nearly ready to call the police when she caught a glimpse of Simon through the sliding glass door. He was in the backyard, and he appeared to be doing push-ups on the dew covered grass. She was confused at first. Simon was in decent shape; the nature of his job required that he look good in fancy suits. Still, he had never been that much into exercise, certainly not enough to work out at the crack of dawn. After completing the push-ups, Simon moved to the swing set and starting doing pull-ups. Holly continued to watch, less confused now but curious still.

There were more surprises to come.

Once the pull-ups were done, Simon picked up a small branch about the size of an old police night stick and began to do a series of intricate movements: parrying and then stabbing; jumping and then slashing down. Holly was downright shocked by now.

Was this some type of martial arts or a fancy yoga routine she wondered? If so, where did he pick this up, or more importantly, who did he pick this up from? Holly considered the number of business trips Simon had taken in recent years and how long he had spent away from his family on these trips. If he was learning these fancy routines, what else was he doing that wasn't really business related?

Shock began to turn to jealousy, and jealousy began to turn to anger.

Despite struggling with this flood of emotions, she could not take her eyes off Simon all the same. The grace of his movements, the force behind his thrusts, the precision with which he handled the stick: these were all somehow mesmerizing. Suddenly he stopped, the routine apparently completed. He took a deep breath, laid down the stick very carefully, and turned around to head back towards the sliding glass door.

Holly panicked. She didn't know what to do: confront Simon now about these strange exercises or play wait and see. Partly because she didn't really know what to say if she did confront him, Holly decided to hurry back to the bedroom before she got caught spying. She hit the bed and covered up, pretending to sleep. Simon was back in the bedroom only a moment later, moving very quietly himself as if he was purposely trying not to wake his wife. This only made Holly more anxious, but she played along for now and kept still in the bed until she heard Simon climb into the shower.

By the time Simon got out of the shower, Holly was sitting up in bed waiting for him. She still didn't know exactly what to do so she kept it simple.

"Honey, I know you didn't sleep well," she cooed. "Did the shower make you feel better?"

"Why yes it did," Simon answered very politely. "You have to forgive me for waking you last night. I'm having strange dreams these days."

"The doctors told me I might have nightmares as bits and pieces of my memory returned. Right now, I feel like I'm reading a book with lots of the pages missing." He shook his head and then continued, "And I don't just find these missing pages. It seems like someone has crumpled them up into lots of paper balls and thrown them all at me. I have to then carefully uncrumple each page and try to make sense out of it"

Holly was touched by the pain and the sincerity in this answer and momentarily put aside her suspicions about the strange exercises she had just seen.

"Why don't you relax and catch the morning news," she said with a smile. "I'll make us some breakfast."

Simon smiled too, seemingly relieved.

The news was filled with updates on the bombing, final casualty figures and little montages on specific victims. The whole thing seemed played for effect, intended to maximize the emotional impact of the event. Here and there, various reporters chimed in with the latest on the investigation. According to confidential sources, multiple nationalist groups within the European Union were involved. No one would say exactly who, just that the terrorist groups were definitely European.

Simon could only take this for a few minutes before he started clicking through the channels looking for something else, anything other than more stories about the bombing.

He finally landed on one of the cable channels which showed nothing but repeats of old TV shows. It was a digital time warp of sorts, a place in the media that was about as far away from the latest news of the day as one could get. It was also mind-numbing in its simplicity and just exactly what Simon was looking for at the moment. He settled comfortably into the chair and casually allowed the action on the TV screen to wash over him, the various images running together one after another into a continuous stream of dull noise.

Every few minutes or so, the flow was interrupted by commercials hawking something new, some new product or some new message.

"Science and technology will lead us to a prosperous future," asserted one particularly animated effort. "New products, new markets through science and technology," the voiceover boomed. "Students, remember to choose careers in science and technology at one of the many fine universities certified by the Trade Association of the Americas."

The camera then cut quickly to CEO Daniel Garcia. Smiling and appearing very professional, the chief executive continued, "I want to personally remind you that our very future depends on science and technology and encourage our young people to choose science and technical careers that add value to our society. Remember our goal is to remain competitive by continually reducing waste in everything we do. Thank you, this has been a public service announcement from the TAA."

The CEO smiled once again, and the commercial ended.

Simon shifted uncomfortably in the chair and decided to turn off the TV entirely. For a moment, he stared off into distant space, pondering certain memories, disturbing memories, which were working their way back into his head.

Just then, Holly announced that breakfast was ready. Simon smelled the aroma of crisp bacon and agreed that he would rather eat than watch TV anyway.

Chapter 5

Daniel Garcia was not a happy man.

It had been more than 2 weeks since the bombing and still there had been no definite announcement from the TAA about the identity of the terrorist bombers. The delay had created a vacuum of information that others were all too eager to fill with their own theories, some downright crazy, some dangerously close to making sense. Either way, the turning and churning in the flow of news threatened to damage the polished, coolly professional image which the TAA had carefully cultivated over the years.

Stability. Control.

These were the watchwords of the organization Daniel Garcia led. He would not tolerate anything which jeopardized that control.

"Mary," the CEO called out sharply from his office, "Please get the people from Security and Public Relations. I want a meeting right now!" His voice was calm but forceful nonetheless, conveying a sense of urgency while clearly struggling to contain the agitation simmering just below the surface.

Mary knew that tone of voice well and hurriedly began to make phone calls. A few minutes later, the Senior VP of Security and the TAA's Public Relations officer appeared at the CEO's office. Chris Smith, the security analyst, was notably absent.

Garcia was quick to pick up on the significance of this absence. "I am guessing that the young Mr. Smith does not have anything new to tell us," he said quietly.

James Wilson smiled uncomfortably. He hesitated for a moment but then nodded in agreement. "Smith has not been able to turn up any additional direct evidence that ties the bombing to a particular nationalist group."

"Not for lack of trying, I might add."

Fidgeting nervously, the PR officer let out a deep sigh when he heard that news.

"I need something more to sell to the people other than the best efforts of our analyst," he interjected. "I have been feeding the media the generic story about European nationalist groups for the last two weeks, stalling for time until the security guys could give me something else. Frankly, the natives are starting to get restless, and I can't continue to hold them off."

The office was silent. The CEO looked down at his desk. The head of security stared out into space lost in thought. With no answer apparently forthcoming, the Public Relations officer was struck with an inspiration of his own.

"I've got it," he blurted out, striking his head in exaggerated fashion with the palm of his hand. "Why don't I just make up a new terrorist group that no one has ever heard of and then blame it on them?"

Daniel Garcia did not answer; he really did not appreciate sarcasm at a time like this. The comment, however preposterous it was, did seem to catch the attention of the Senior VP of Security. His wandering mind suddenly returned to focus on the problem at hand.

"That's it," Wilson said with a tinge of excitement in his voice.

"What's it? I was just joking," the PR man replied rather abruptly. That sarcasm was fading a bit. "You know, better to joke than cry in times of stress."

James Wilson was quite serious. "Don't you see," he began. "The reason we can't find evidence that ties one of the three known nationalist groups to the bombing is simply because one group didn't do it." He paused for effect, trying to pull the others into the flow of his logic.

No one bit so Wilson continued, "One group didn't do it; all three groups did it, working together. Don't you see? It's an entirely new terrorist network that links together all the major nationalist groups in Europe."

"But what proof do we have of this new terror network?" The Public Relations Officer was quickly losing his enthusiasm for the uncomfortable conversation he himself had started.

"We don't need direct proof. It's the logical next step in the story we have been feeding the media. It's so logical that people will simply believe it."

The CEO was interested but not convinced yet. The PR man was at a loss for words.

"It also gives us more strategic options," the Senior VP of Security added. "Once we get the story out there, the Europeans will be forced to respond. If we're lucky, they'll do our dirty work for us. Either they'll serve up one of the existing nationalist groups as a way to save their own skins, or they'll struggle to deny the new terrorist network. It really doesn't matter because the ball will be stuck in their side of the field either way. We won't have to worry about finding the proof anymore; they will. The EU will be forced to play defense, while we can go on the offensive."

For a moment, there was silence once again.

"It makes good business sense." The security chief and the PR officer immediately turned towards the voice of the CEO.

Garcia sat up straight in his chair and smiled. He was convinced by now. "When I was in MBA school, I learned that the future is inherently uncertain. In an uncertain future, the best strategy is the one that gives you the most options. That way, you can still find a way to win no matter what happens tomorrow, next week, or next year."

"Okay, I can run with this," the Public Relations Officer replied with genuine excitement in his voice. "I better start working on the copy to share with the media so I need to leave."

The CEO nodded in agreement. The PR man got up and hurried out of the office, a noticeable bounce in his step.

James Wilson and Daniel Garcia remained in the office. They were satisfied. They had just come up with a new plan, a way out of this mess. Sure it might take a little while to sell the story to shareholders, but the next steps were clear. Now they could move on to planning the retaliation and getting to what the TAA really wanted. Yes, everything was going to work out just fine the CEO thought to himself.

As long as that analyst didn't get in the way....

Garcia ended the moment of revelry. "What are we going to do with Chris Smith? We can't have him in any way disputing the story about the new terrorist network"

"I think he has the good sense to keep quiet," Wilson replied casually. "He has a young family to think of and a wife with a medical condition."

"I'm not totally comfortable with that." The CEO pressed the issue. "I think we need to move him out of your department to a much less visible position where he will not come in contact with the press."

"Do you want to fire him?"

"No, that might attract too much attention. It would look pretty suspicious as well and could generate lots of questions about our new story."

"Do we need to make him disappear?"

Daniel Garcia frowned. "That would be worse. Just de-mote him to an out-of-the-way position where he will be buried so far down in the organization that no one will even think to ask his opinion on anything."

"But keep his pay rate the same," Garcia added quickly. "Remember, the man has a family." The last words were heavy on sarcasm and disdain.

"All of that is supposed to ensure his silence? Smith has a lot professional pride. He might talk anyway if he figures his career is over."

"James, I'm disappointed. You have obviously not learned to understand basic human motivation very well, have you?"

Wilson did not answer. He was a little confused and managed only to weakly shake his head no.

"No matter what Chris Smith thinks of his career," the CEO continued. "He does have a family to take care of and a wife who needs medical insurance. He can't afford to quit so he will stay on the job. He will go to meetings he thinks are pointless. He will do what you tell him to do, no matter how trivial. His co-workers and former friends will try to avoid him, partly because they don't know what to say to him anymore and partly because they think it's dangerous to associate with someone who has obviously gotten on the wrong side of the power structure here. Through all of this, Smith will put up a brave, even cheerful front. On the inside, however, he'll hate himself just a little bit more each day."

Garcia leaned forward across the desk and gestured forcefully with his hands, like a professor marking a point of emphasis in his lecture. "Ah, but he will stay nonetheless. Think what that does to a man inside, just going through the motions, feeling trapped."

The CEO did not wait for an answer or a guess or even an opinion. "I'll tell you what it does; it breaks a man's spirit."

The Senior VP of Security smiled and nodded in agreement. He was beginning to understand after all.

"If we fired young Mr. Smith, he would be wounded, in a figurative sense. Or worse yet, he would be desperate with nothing left to lose." Garcia paused. The smile on his face was cold, calculating. His dark eyes flashed with a wicked intensity that unnerved even the head of security sitting across from him. When he began again, his voice was calm, measured.

"Wounded men are dangerous. Desperate men are dangerous. Men with a broken spirit are not."

Wilson sat quietly for the moment, contemplating the philosophical significance of what he had just heard. Then he was struck by a thought, a potential loose end that had not been discussed.

"What about the junior analysts and others who have worked on the team with Smith? We can't just forget about them," he asked.

"Think of it as a coaching change," the CEO replied. He smiled once again, this time more friendly than before, seemingly pleased with his own analogy. "It happens all the time in the sports world. The team might be surprised at first, but in the end, the team just moves on. Explain to them that Chris is being transferred and that you are taking over on an interim basis. Since this is such a sensitive issue, you alone will control the information flow and share any data on an as needed basis."

"If any of the other team members do give you trouble," Garcia spoke firmly and with emphasis on each word. Still he lingered on the last word, his voice trailing off as he mulled over the options. The emotion drained out of his face, and all other signs of humor vanished.

"Just get rid of them, permanently," he continued. His manner was very straightforward and resolute. "It is not nearly as difficult to explain the disappearance of low level people who are not well known in the first place."

"I guess I know what I have to do." James Wilson stood up and excused himself, careful to wait for acknowledgement from Garcia before turning to leave the office. It was a small gesture for sure, but critical nonetheless. The CEO was big on his subordinates showing proper respect; not showing that respect was dangerous, even for a Senior VP.

Wilson strode down the hall, his pace deliberate though not hurried. He passed offices and co-workers without stopping for idle, friendly conversation. He knew he had to meet with Chris Smith today to deliver the news, but he didn't have to like it. Smith was talented, and he had always been loyal to the organization, which made all of this even harder. Still, Wilson thought to himself, it was far better than the alternative. And he knew, better than most, just how terrible that alternative could be.

As Senior VP of Security, James Wilson was comfortable with the alternative when it was employed under the right circumstances. He believed in it, understood how valuable it was as a tool to achieve business objectives.

He recalled that it had been very effective in settling the Mexican drug wars a few years back. Violent drug wars were bad for business. Indiscriminate murder and mayhem could not be stopped by typical law enforcement or for that matter, by negotiation, unless of course you were dealing with the right people. That's where the TAA's security forces had come in, simply killing off all the wrong people until they got to someone who was willing to negotiate, someone who understood that everyone could make money off a properly controlled drug trade which focused on moving product rather than getting on the news by slaughtering lots of innocent people.

Wilson shook his head. The alternative sure had been effective back then. He really hoped Chris Smith would take things well. He really hoped he wouldn't have to consider the alternative with young Mr. Smith.

Daniel Garcia remained in his office after his security chief had departed, contemplating all that had just transpired. His mood had changed considerably since the beginning of the workday: more relaxed, confident, giddy almost. Most important of all, he felt back in control of things once more. Plans were at last moving forward. His organization was swinging into action, and nothing, and nobody, could stop it.

Garcia smiled as he considered the prospect.

The bombing and its aftermath had been all consuming for the CEO, no matter that he fancied himself a master at multi-tasking. Now, for the first time in over 2 weeks, he finally felt ready to give the other parts of the business more than just obligatory attention. He swiveled around in his chair to face the computer and dove happily into his backlog of e-mails.

Key economic indicators were the first order of business. Housing starts were up for the second month in a row. There were several notable projects listed in the supporting comments, but one in particular caught his attention. Ground had finally been broken on a new project sponsored by the trade association in the major metropolitan area outside the old federal capitol in Washington, DC. Opening up national parkland in the suburbs for development was finally beginning to pay dividends Garcia noted. Besides, he had always thought Bull Run National Battlefield Park was a silly name; he hoped the developers would drop that name when they built the new condos. Manufacturing activity in the Mexican and Latin American provinces of the TAA was increasing to support the new construction; products were flowing out of the factories on schedule and moving up north to major retail outlets. Mining activity and oil production in several former wildlife reserves were also increasing per the master plan.

So far so good thought Garcia until he came across a troubling e-mail concerning a recent salmonella outbreak. Nine people had died in one of the Midwestern provinces from eating contaminated meat served by a local restaurant with a history of poor sanitation practices. The particular restaurant involved was part of a large fast food chain owned by a wealthy shareholder of the TAA. The CEO decided he would speak to the shareholder about improving safety practices; safety lapses like this could harm franchise values if they weren't handled properly. In any event, it was fortunate the deaths had occurred in a small town so it would be relatively easy to kill the story. If the outbreak had occurred in a larger metropolitan area, it would be more difficult to manage, requiring more resources and a little more creativity in the storytelling.

After e-mailing instructions to handle the salmonella issue, Garcia looked forward to better news coming from the quarterly financial reports. The financials were solid thankfully. The new flat tax rate implemented five years ago was still bringing in enough revenue to cover expenditures by the trade association.

The flat tax plan was one of the CEO's proudest achievements. He recalled how powerful critics had once argued that using a single tax rate for everyone was regressive and hurt the poor. However, he had eventually won the day by showing how wasteful and complicated the old federal tax code had been. Process simplification was a core principle of the TAA, and the flat tax embodied it perfectly. In the end, the new tax plan reduced waste and facilitated a drastic reduction in the size of the internal revenue service required to manage collections. Not surprisingly, the plan had proven to be very popular with the people who had previously been in the upper income tax brackets. These were the people who counted most to the leadership of the TAA, and it seemed clear that this particular constituency valued a government with a positive cash flow far more than a government which tried to take care of the poor.

Too bad, Garcia chuckled, that most of those early critics weren't still around to see how wrong they had been about some of their fellow citizens.

The CEO noted in the report that Social Security revenues were still running ahead of the outlays, due in large part to the contributions of all those young workers in the busy factories of the Latin American provinces. He wasn't particularly fond of this old federal program, but it had been too popular to eliminate. So he had done the only thing he could do: bring in more money from younger workers to help pay for current obligations. He wondered if those younger workers would ever benefit from the program themselves, but then he decided that this potential issue would be someone else's problem many years down the road.

The final e-mail to catch his attention was an invitation. The old Julliard School of Music was being re-modeled into the Julliard School of Science and Technology as part of a trade association program to convert former cultural landmarks into more value-added uses. Several art museums had been rehabilitated last year under the same program after their collections had been sold off to private collectors. This was the first major conversion of the current fiscal year. The trustees of the new Julliard School were requesting the pleasure of the CEO's attendance at the opening ceremonies. Garcia enjoyed these types of events immensely as they gave him a public forum to preach the philosophy of the TAA. After checking his calendar, he quickly sent his acceptance and closed the e-mail.

Daniel Garcia leaned back in his chair, satisfied now. Yes, he decided, it had been a very good day after all.

Chapter 6

Holly Anderson sat alone in her kitchen and stared out the bay window at nothing in particular. Not the flowers blooming around the well-manicured backyard. Not the trees bathed in the shimmering glow of golden sunlight. Not the clear blue sky.

She didn't notice any of those things. She didn't care about any of those things.

A single tear welled up in Holly's left eye and then rolled slowly down her cheek. She was not quite ready to break down and cry; still she was close enough that it wouldn't take much to push her over the edge. Only with great effort had she held back the pain. Just below the surface, emotions threatened at any moment, turning and churning — sadness, fear, anger.

There was loneliness too, and that hurt the most.

The phone rang, the stillness, the quiet, suddenly broken. Holly answered the phone and clutched it tightly. Her words were very soft at first, growing stronger and more animated as she spoke.

"Mom, I'm so glad you called me back."

Holly hesitated, not sure exactly how she could put into words what was on her mind. The silence was awkward as she gathered herself.

"Mom, I just don't know if I can trust Simon." There it was. It was out there now, Holly thought to herself. She breathed a sigh of relief.

The voice on the other end of the phone line was calm and supportive. Holly expected as much from her mother. She felt comfortable telling her mother almost anything, even things she could not share with her best girlfriends. Talking about things was better than not talking Holly supposed, but she wondered deep down if all of this would really make her feel any better. She decided to go on anyway.

"Simon has been at home for more than 3 weeks now. Physically he has recovered from any injuries suffered in the bombing. Most of his memory has also come back."

Holly's mother was always quick to seize on the positive aspects in any situation. "Honey, I'm so glad to hear that. I told you he would recover. If Simon is making so much progress you should be happy!"

"You're right. It is good that he is getting his memory back, that he recognizes things around the house, that he knows who his daughter is. In fact, Simon is saying almost all the right things now, but the way he says them is was what really bothers me. Sometimes it seems like he's reciting a prepared speech or even quoting selected passages out of a book."

Holly dipped her head and her voice trailed off until it was soft and quiet once more. "Either way," she continued, "Simon is still very distant from me, both physically and emotionally.'

The mother could tell her child was hurting. She did not know exactly what to say, but she had to try to get Holly to see the bright side. "Maybe this is just another bad side effect of the bombing. Give him some time. I know he'll come around."

"But Mom, it's not just the emotional distance, although that's bad enough by itself. Simon is doing some new and unusual things, things I have never seen him do before. Nearly every night, we struggle with his nightmares; it has grown into some sort of perverted, painful ritual by now. I'm sympathetic, and I do understand how the trauma of the bombing can cause nightmares. Still, I swear that once or twice, I've actually caught Simon giving commands in his sleep. The trouble is —

he's speaking a strange language I've never heard before. When I wake him up, he doesn't seem to recall anything about the unusual words, or at least that's what he says at the time."

"I don't know what to believe now. Maybe I'm the one having the nightmares, and those strange commands are just a figment of my imagination." Holly stopped talking; she was frustrated and exasperated all at the same time.

"Or maybe there's a more logical explanation," her mother replied calmly. "I've heard that serious head injuries can really blur the line between what is real and what is imaginary. Is it possible that Simon's subconscious mind is just reciting something he has heard somewhere in a movie? I know you've been with Simon for a long time, but you can't tell me that you know every movie he has ever seen or every book he has ever read."

"I know that Mom, but there's more. What about all the exercising in the morning and the new marital arts routine, nothing like I have ever seen before? I confronted Simon about the martial arts and all the precision he seemed to put into using a common stick like a sword. He seemed surprised at first that I had been spying on him, but then he simply explained it away as training the TAA offered to all executives who traveled globally."

Holly didn't wait for her mother's response to that one. She just continued, although less animated than before. "At times, it has gotten so bad, so weird, that I've wondered if the man who came back to me after the bombing is really my husband after all. Maybe it's somebody else inhabiting his body, kind of like a body snatcher."

"Or maybe the stress of this whole re-adjustment is just driving me crazy. Yes, that's probably it!"

Holly's mother seemed to agree stress was the main culprit, but she didn't agree that her daughter was going crazy. That did offer some comfort. Once again, Holly appreciated how understanding her mom could really be. The daughter allowed herself a little smile and then hung up the phone after promising she would call back if she needed to talk again. She noticed the blue skies and sunshine streaming through the bay window and thought to herself what a pretty day it was outside.

Simon caught a glimpse of Holly as he passed by the kitchen. She was gazing casually out the bay window. It was somewhat difficult to tell at first glance, but she also appeared to be smiling.

This was unusual. Since coming home from the hospital, he had not seen her smile very often. Over the last two weeks, in fact, "not very often" had turned into "not at all". Simon lingered just outside the kitchen. He was intrigued by the possibility of that smile.

Holly turned around when she sensed Simon's presence. He took note that she was indeed smiling. Somewhat surprisingly, she continued to smile even when facing her husband. It was a pretty smile to be sure, but more than that, it seemed to transform her entire face.

And that very face seemed to transfix Simon right at the moment.

It was soft and inviting with delicate features made more animated by the simple act of smiling. Dark hair, long and curly, flowed around high cheek bones past smooth, pale skin until it landed gently on her shoulders. Her brown eyes glowed with a certain sparkle which could not be denied even as long lashes fluttered with each blink. Full moist lips parted ever so slightly, revealing just a hint of bright white teeth. Her cheeks were flush with the crimson tinge of embarrassment, excitement, possibly a combination of the two.

Simon stood uncomfortably for a moment, shifting his body awkwardly and trying most of all not to stare. A little embarrassed himself, he struggled with exactly what to say next.

"Honey, he finally blurted out, "you look nice today." Simon took a deep breath and looked upwards at the ceiling to hide his frustration.

"Oh my god, what a lame thing to say," he muttered softly.

Holly was a little surprised but tried to show her appreciation for the compliment anyway. "Okay, thanks," she replied cautiously, "I have to go check on Suzy."

She smiled again, although this time it was more forced. She turned and walked briskly down the hall toward her child's room. Simon turned as well and watched her walk away, studying intently the curve of her hips and the bounce in her step. This time he didn't worry about getting caught staring.

Holly thought that this day might just be different from the rest. She took notice that Simon was making an effort to be more talkative. He even seemed to pay more attention to Suzy, and she could swear she saw him smile at least once. Just maybe, the new Simon might not be so bad after all. She pondered that thought for a moment but was still reluctant to allow herself to start buying into any new hopes or dreams. She wondered what the night would bring and hoped she could get through it yet another time.

The day passed quietly into evening, and Holly and Simon prepared for bed. There was still an awkward distance between the couple. They kissed good night, politely, as part of their evening ritual, and then each party crawled to opposite sides of the bed.

Time ticked by until the nightmares returned once more, as they always did. Holly was not surprised, disappointed maybe, but definitely not surprised. She was tired most of all and had really hoped tonight would be different. Still, over the last couple of weeks, she had developed somewhat of a routine for dealing with all of this. Holly slid quickly to the very edge of the bed to stay out of the way while Simon thrashed about. She had learned early on that it was best to wait until the violent twisting and turning was completely over before trying to comfort her husband. A nasty kick to the ribs had taught her that.

Unfortunately, this night was shaping up to be worse than normal. Holly scrambled to get off the bed as Simon lurched violently from one end of the mattress to the other — twisting, turning, sweating profusely. Breaths came in short, rapid gulps. Hands dug deeply into the sheets, clutching them so tightly that knuckles turned white.

Simon shook his head forcefully from side to side and cried out, "No, not yet; no, not yet!"

He repeated the phrase over and over again, each time louder and with more desperation in his voice. Finally, muscles straining and his back arched in the air, he stopped. His eyes opened wide. They were moist with tears.

This was something new that Holly had not seen before. She reached down to stroke Simon's head. He didn't pull away this time. Instead, he reached up and gently pulled her down to him. For the past few weeks, Holly had been the one who needed the touching, the closeness, yet she had also been the one who had been rejected.

Now it was her turn to decide. Should she push Simon away or take advantage of the crack in his steely facade to give him what he now plainly needed, what she herself had wanted for so long? Holly did not immediately commit herself to the embrace; she pondered what it all might mean to her hopes and dreams for the future.

Her hesitation lasted but a few seconds. It only seemed so much longer as Simon pleaded with his eyes. Holly looked deeply into those eyes at the soul of the man behind them and slid slowly down into the arms of her husband.

The rest of the night passed without incident, without any other nightmares. Simon and Holly remained curled together in a soft, comfortable embrace. The couple slept soundly for the first time in weeks. Their bodies were touching, generating friction and heat. Under normal circumstances, these might have been the precursors to passion. But Holly and Simon had clearly not lived under anything resembling normal circumstances for a good while. Simple exhaustion and the allure of a good night's sleep overruled everything else at the moment.

Simon stirred as the first rays of early morning sunlight poked here and there through the blinds covering the bedroom windows. Carefully, reluctantly, he slid away from his wife's embrace and climbed out of bed. He glanced back at Holly still sleeping soundly. His eyes traced the lines of her long, silky legs. Simon was committed to iron discipline alright, but right now he really didn't feel like being quite so disciplined.

After several agonizing minutes mulling over his choices, he let out a heavy sigh and turned away to dress for his morning workout.

Holly didn't hear the bedroom door close, and sometime later she awoke to an empty bed. She was used to this kind of thing by now; still it disappointed her this particular morning. Wrapping herself tightly in her robe, Holly decided to brave the morning chill and go out to watch Simon exercise. At one time, she had considered this spying. Now it seemed oddly comfortable.

The early morning was indeed cold. Simon's lungs ached as he pushed his body to the limit. Muscles burned. Respiration was ragged, drifting out in misty white puffs. Holly approached the sliding glass door and caught a glimpse of her husband. Despite the chill, Simon had removed his shirt. Sweat glistened on his body, beads of moisture rolling slowly down his chest. Holly eyed those droplets carefully. Taking note of every muscle, of every inch of bare skin, she thought to herself how lean and toned Simon had become over the last few weeks. She smiled, deciding right then and there that she very much liked the look and cut of the new Simon.

Holly continued to watch, not so much because she was curious or surprised anymore. She had long grown accustomed to her husband's morning routine. On the contrary, she was quite simply enjoying this show of raw masculinity. She also knew what was going to happen next. Simon retrieved the short stick he kept carefully stored in the bushes and launched into an intricate dance of powerful strokes and thrusts. There was a strange, almost mesmerizing quality to these movements — violent, yet graceful; exciting, definitely exciting. Holly caught herself breathing more rapidly.

The swordplay continued with great precision until suddenly interrupted by the squeals of a child. Holly was shocked to see Suzy dash across the yard towards her father. She was even more shocked to see Simon abruptly drop the stick and scoop up their child into his powerful arms. He swung Suzy around and around, much to her delight. Simon then gently put the child down and waited for her to steady herself before handing her a small stick. Suzy immediately understood and soon joined into a mock sword fight between father and daughter. With each clash of the sticks, Simon and Suzy laughed a little harder.

Holly laughed herself as she watched the playful little battle. Still it was not long before the laughter dissolved into tears. There had been many tears over the last few weeks, but these were different. For the first time in a long time, there was more hope than sadness carried in the tiny streams that trickled down her cheeks. She wiped her eyes and dared to dream again, dared to believe that her family was really coming together.

She also concluded it was time to gather up both her little warriors for breakfast. Before going out into the back yard, however, Holly took time to compose herself. No matter what kind of tears they were, she still didn't want them to intrude on the happiest family moment she had seen in weeks.

The happiness continued through breakfast. There was laughter all around and healthy appetites too. Holly marveled at how much more comfortable Simon now seemed around Suzy. He offered to share a spoonful of his cereal with the child but then quickly pulled it back before she could take a bite. Both father and daughter laughed. Holly laughed as well, trying very hard not to choke on her food.

She kept watching Simon all through breakfast, the light in his eyes, the powerful jaw, even the way he chewed. The time just might be right she thought to herself. She decided to take Suzy next door to the babysitter as soon as everyone finished eating.

"My muscles are pretty sore. I think I'm going to take a nice warm shower," Simon announced. He patted Suzy on the top of the head and turned towards the bedroom.

"Okay, honey. I think that's a great idea," Holly called after him. Flashing a mischievous grin, she put her plan into action and quickly spirited Suzy over to the neighbor's house.

Holly could hear the water running when she returned. Just perfect. She slid out of her nightclothes and then tiptoed towards the shower. The door to the bathroom was open; warm steam drifted out into the bedroom. She could see Simon leaning under the running water, his eyes closed, his back to the door.

Again, just perfect. Holly slipped into the back of the shower undetected and quietly lathered up her hands with soap. Moving forward under the shower spray, she pressed her body firmly against Simon's back and wrapped her arms around his chest.

"I dropped off Suzy next door," Holly cooed into her husband's ear. Her breath was warm, and for added emphasis, she nibbled on the earlobe. Then with soapy hands, she began to slowly, but firmly wash and massage his upper body.

Simon could feel Holly's erect nipples stabbing into his back, her strong fingers digging roughly into the muscles of his chest. It felt good, really good. He could tell it had been a long time for her. Could she ever begin to understand just how long it had been for him? Simon didn't think so.

But he pondered that thought only for a moment as Holly's hands slid steadily down his torso. She finally reached down between his legs and began to stroke vigorously.

Simon was immediately aroused, struggling not to go off right then and there. Still he was eager to face his wife and soak in the fullness of her seething body. As he turned his hips, Holly got the message and released her grip.

The couple faced one another, breathing heavily, each set of eyes eagerly taking in the contours of the opposite form. Hot steam swirled around them, and soapy water trickled down their bodies. It was the most erotic sight each of them could ever remember seeing in their lives. Husband and wife came together in a wet, passionate embrace. They kissed with all the hunger and desperation of two lovers who knew only the moment and were not guaranteed a tomorrow. Simon reached down and grabbed Holly's toned buttocks to pull her in tight; she moaned in delight as their bodies crushed together.

Realizing things could go no further in the confines of the shower, the couple slowly separated and turned off the water. They stepped out onto the bath mat without bothering to reach for towels.

No words were spoken. Deep breaths and droplets of water landing on the bottom of the shower: the only sounds.

Eyes locking together, they immediately embraced. Simon lifted Holly off her feet in the heat of the moment, and she wrapped her slippery legs around his waist in turn. He held her body effortlessly as their lips sought out and ultimately found one another. Holly found it immensely exciting to be supported in arms so strong; this only served to infuse her kisses with greater urgency.

The pair tottered into the bedroom, their kiss unbroken until they reached the very edge of the bed. Simon gently lowered Holly onto the covered mattress. As he followed down upon her, she opened herself wide to receive him. All of the frustration, all of the pent up passions, all of the touching had led to this very moment. Simon plunged deep inside his wife and began to pump furiously. Holly bit her lip and groaned as waves of ecstasy washed over her body. She dug her nails into Simon's back. She wrapped her legs tightly around his thighs. She struggled even to breathe. Time itself seemed to stand still, extending the pleasure to the very limits of her endurance. Finally, just before total collapse, she felt Simon's release and the thundering explosion filling the inside of her body.

Holly relaxed her grip, allowing Simon to roll over onto his back. He was totally spent. She lay perfectly still, no strength left, staring up at the ceiling and pondering everything that had just transpired. It had been rougher than normal. Hell, it had not been anything like normal. And it had also been the most awesome sex she had ever had. Whether it had the staying power to be anything more than that remained to be seen.

Holly laid her head on Simon's chest, listening, really more like feeling his heart beat. He kissed her on the cheek and gently stroked her hair. She allowed herself to smile, but it was subtle, the type of smile a woman keeps all to herself. Holly was cautious by nature. Still, she was really starting to believe now.

"I have an idea," she said softly. "Why don't we take Suzy tomorrow and the three of us go to that park in the city. You know, where we used to go when we were dating in college."

Simon seemed a little startled by the suggestion at first. "Okay, I guess we can," he answered after a brief, but still uncomfortable pause.

Holly frowned. The response had been less than enthusiastic. At the same time though, she did notice that Simon and all of his parts were beginning to stir to life once more. She quickly decided that any small, lingering doubts could wait until tomorrow.

Sporting a devilish grin, Holly mounted her husband's chest and announced, "I want to be on top this time!" Simon nodded and smiled without any hesitation at all.

Chapter 7

Holly Anderson awoke to the new day feeling rested and refreshed. For the first time in the last few weeks, she had slept soundly through the whole night. And for the first time in the last few weeks, there had been no nightmares at all to interrupt that sound sleep. She was thankful for that too.

She looked over at Simon as he remained still in the bed, so comfortable, so peaceful. Holly wondered just how much their physical activities from the evening before had contributed to that peace. Was it simply pure exhaustion, or had they finally turned the corner on the nightmares? Holly didn't know for sure. Either way, the sunlight peaking through window blinds told her it was going to be pretty today, the perfect day for a family trip to the park.

Many miles away from the pleasant suburb where the Andersons lived, the tattered man noticed the same early morning sunlight streaming through the opening in the large cardboard box he called home. He poked his head outside and looked up at the blue sky. It was difficult to make out at first because of black smoke rising from the many trash can fires dotting nearby streets and alleyways. He understood people needed to keep warm, but he didn't have to like the smell or the way heavy smoke threatened to blot out the sun. But today was going to be different. There wasn't a cloud in the sky. The smoke drifted quickly away, and the sunshine lit up the surrounding streets.

Yes, it was going to be a fine day. The tattered man thought to himself that it might be a good day for a walk in the city park, assuming he could get a ticket. The only park admission tickets available to people like him were the free passes sometimes given out at the Catholic Rescue

Mission two blocks over. With any luck, he might be able get something for breakfast as well as one of the tickets.

The possibilities energized him as he quickly pulled together his possessions and scampered out of the box. Having very little and not worrying about his appearance, the whole process took less than a minute. He made a final adjustment to the satchel slung around his shoulder and set off towards the rescue mission with a bounce in his step.

The sun warmed the face of the tattered man as he threaded his way around the rusting hulks of junked cars and the omnipresent smoldering trash cans. He squinted at first in the bright light. But then he closed his eyes completely, if only for a moment, to visualize what the park might look like on a day like today.

Trees would be swaying in the gentle breeze.

The green grass would feel soft as a carpet.

There would be happy people too, happy children walking and playing.

The tattered man smiled. He could see it all so clearly now.

When he opened his eyes again, the picture in his mind vanished completely, and the harsh reality of this place hit him. There were no shade trees in this part of town. The only green vegetation was the occasional weed that might sprout up in a vacant lot between the scattered remains of a collapsed building. The few buildings still standing bore the deep scars of decay — rotting wood, crumbling bricks and mortar.

The bright morning sun only made it all easier to see. He took a deep breath and pressed on.

As he crossed into the next block, the tattered man could see the line beginning to form in front of the rescue mission. Apparently lots of people were hungry this morning. He hoped that not so many were also interested in going to the park.

Drawing still closer, he could see a young mother at the end of the line struggling to keep her little girl in tow. Every so often the child would break free to play among the ruins of the burned out building next to the mission, forcing her mother to step out of line to retrieve her. The child alternately laughed and begged for more time to play. She was dirty and wore rags for clothes but was otherwise quite cheerful. Her mother, on the other hand, was haggard and hollow-eyed and clearly did not want to risk missing a meal for more play time. The tattered man watched the pair for some time, marveling at both the charming innocence and the boundless resiliency of childhood. All the same, he was saddened by the tragedy of circumstance that any child should have to grow up in a place like this and grow accustomed to what went on here.

Just then, as if on some perverted cue, a gunshot echoed off in the distance. That neither mother nor daughter, or for that matter anyone else in line, paid any attention to it only made him feel worse.

Fortunately the line was moving quickly today. Either the Catholic Rescue Mission was getting more efficient at doling out the food or there was less food to dole out in the first place. The tattered man hoped it was the former, not the latter. Stretching out as far as possible without losing his place, he tried to catch a glimpse of the actual serving size. He wasn't quite close enough to answer that question, but he could see Father Christopher at the very front of the line helping to serve meals.

The priest noticed him as well and called out warmly, "Arthur, I'm glad to see that an old man like you is still energetic enough to get up early for breakfast."

"You know it's the most important meal of the day," the tattered man yelled back.

The line continued to move, and Arthur reached the head of the line soon enough. The question he had pondered for the last few minutes was finally answered. To his dismay, the serving size was indeed very small. Still it was better than nothing, much better in fact than the scraps he often scrounged out of trash cans. He smiled with gratitude as Father Christopher filled his bowl.

Steam rising from the bowl drifted slowly away in the early morning chill. Arthur inhaled full and deep, savoring the pleasant aroma of hot food.

"Father, much as I appreciate a good meal, I was wondering if I might also ask for a favor."

The priest stepped out of the serving line and placed his hand reassuringly on the tattered man's shoulder. He leaned forward and responded with all the patience of his profession, "Of course, my friend. What is it?"

Like someone trying to hide a secret, Arthur fidgeted and looked cautiously from side to side before attempting to answer. "I was wondering," he responded quietly. "Do you have any of those free passes to the park? It's such a pretty day. I would really like to see the trees, the flowers, feel green grass beneath my feet. Maybe even hear some birds sing."

Father Christopher was not at all surprised by the request. He knew Arthur was different from the rest of the street people who frequented the rescue mission. Here was a man interested in more than just a meal to fill his stomach. Here was someone who seemed to think about things like trees when most people around here couldn't even remember what one looked like. Here was someone who actually thought about the future, who tried to help others believe in a better tomorrow, when everyone else was just trying to get through today. There did just happen to be a ticket available today, and besides, if anyone deserved a little extra, surely Arthur did.

Still it wouldn't be any fun to give in so easily the priest thought. He hemmed and hawed, all the while resisting the urge to smile. "Maybe there is a ticket; maybe not. If there were such a ticket, what would you be willing to give for it?"

Arthur tried to play along. "I don't know. What do you think you might want in return?" He paused for a moment and then added with some sarcasm, "You know I wear only the finest clothes. I would literally give you the shirt off my back, but I don't think it's your size."

That did it. Father Christopher laughed out loud. "No, my friend, you may keep your shirt," he chortled. "I don't think it would go with my collar."

The tattered man laughed as well. "No, I don't suppose it would. Maybe something else then?"

The mood of the priest suddenly took a more serious turn. "How about you teach some extra classes for me?"

This abrupt change in the tone of the conversation was quite surprising. Truthfully, Arthur was downright concerned that this particular topic was being brought up within easy earshot of so many people — people who didn't understand the value of such classes — people who might sell out these classes and everybody in them just to curry favor with the authorities.

Attempting to recover a bit of his composure, he ventured forth a cautious question in return: "What kind of classes are we talking about?"

Father Christopher was by now quite aware of the consternation his request had caused. "Oh no, you misunderstand me," he quickly replied. "I'm not talking about those classes, not at all. I'm talking about simple reading classes, non-controversial, perfectly legal reading classes. You've done them before. I've got a new batch of little ones who are showing some real interest in learning how to read."

"Of course," Arthur answered with great relief, "I would be glad to do it. Learning to read is the only hope those kids have." He was smiling now.

"And now that we have finished this little negotiation, may I have that ticket please?"

The priest flashed a sly, self-satisfied grin before reaching into his pocket and producing the coveted ticket. "Absolutely, here you go."

Arthur accepted the ticket with gratitude. "Many thanks. As soon as I finish eating, I'll head right off to the park." He stuffed the ticket into his pocket and turned to find a spot to sit down.

"Oh, I almost forgot," the tattered man added, "I may need another small favor from you, Father."

"And what is that?" the priest replied patiently.

"I suppose there is still a checkpoint at the opposite end of the bridge over the railroad tracks."

"Yes, I suppose there is," Father Christopher answered, not quite sure where this was going.

"Makes logical sense, I guess," Arthur continued, his voice trailing off with the last word. He glanced up at the blue sky in an absent-minded way.

By the time Arthur looked back down, his expression was painfully grim, and he spoke in a heavy, listless tone that betrayed an air of resignation bordering on hopelessness.

"Drug dealers and gangs rule the streets here, killing innocent people on a whim. I know the TAA security forces and local police don't come into this neighborhood anymore. They're cutting their losses, giving up on us. These days, they just worry about containment. The checkpoint makes sure all the bad stuff in this place doesn't get out to the nice clean streets downtown and bother the people they do care about."

The priest nodded in agreement. He didn't like it either, but that didn't mean it wasn't true. Two or three gunshots rang out in the distance. No one flinched. No one bothered to keep count.

Arthur sighed. Venting his frustration wasn't helping much; it was time to be more pragmatic.

"I suspect the security forces will frisk me and check me over pretty good even if I have this park pass. And if they do, I don't think they will like what I'm carrying in this satchel." He placed his hand on the satchel, and for emphasis, firmly patted the object hidden there.

"So, Father Christopher, can I please leave this with you while I'm at the park? You're the only one I can really trust."

Father Christopher didn't answer; he just smiled. Arthur smiled as well. He lifted the satchel over his shoulder and then handed it carefully to the priest. The battered clock outside the rescue mission read 9 o'clock.

Things were very different at the Anderson household nestled in the leafy suburbs on the other side of the city. The TAA did care about people like the Andersons and their neighbors. Tree-lined streets were clean, safe, and well patrolled by security forces. Spacious, comfortable homes sat on perfectly manicured lawns. Everything was plentiful here, especially a little thing like breakfast. The biggest worry Holly Anderson had at the moment — which clothes she was going to pick out for Suzy to wear to the park.

Simon Anderson, however, did have concerns other than the trip to the park. He tried watching the news while the women of the family took their time getting ready. The talking heads on the TV were really trying to outdo one another today. The big story of the last few days: the new terrorist network in Europe that had recently been uncovered by the investigation into the trade conference bombing. The evidence was circumstantial at best, and of course the European Union denied the existence of such a network. That didn't seem to bother the various well-groomed network anchors who openly gushed over the new discovery. A military response was the only real option they all editorialized; the size of that projected military response seemed to grow with each network update. Simon just shook his head in disbelief and turned off the TV.

As he dropped the remote to the coffee table, he noticed a small pile of yesterday's mail. The letter on top of that pile caught Simon's attention. He opened the letter and read it carefully, every word twice in fact. He sighed. The letter was from the TAA, and it wasn't good news either.

The CEO wanted him back at the office.

Simon held the letter tightly, contemplating what it would be like to finally step back into the offices of the TAA. His recollections of that place were muddled: way too many gaps in his memory, way too many missing pages from that particular chapter of his life.

What he did remember so far was but a tiny glimpse into the dark recesses of his subconscious, and even that was a little disturbing. What he might find out next, Simon feared, could be a whole hell of a lot worse.

He couldn't recall much about his old job or whether he had been very good at it. Mostly he worried about what they might ask him to do now. Could he do it? Would he even want to? Simon's thoughts bounced back and forth, not answering the questions at all, but certainly succeeding in tying his mind up into a neat mental knot.

The fruitless debate ended suddenly.

Holly and Suzy bounded into the living room. Picnic lunch in hand, they were full of energy and ready to go at last. Simon looked up and smiled.

"Oh screw it," he murmured under his breath.

At the moment, this was one diversion he was more than willing to indulge. It really was a beautiful day outside. It would be a shame, he thought, to ruin the trip to the park by telling Holly about the letter. Daniel Garcia and the TAA would have to wait. He released the letter and allowed it to fall casually down to the table. The clock at the Anderson home read 10:30 am.

Chapter 8

The ride to the park was uneventful. Holly drove. She was slowly coming to terms with the new Simon, but she wasn't nearly ready to let him drive. Simon, for his part, didn't seem to mind or react in any way that told her she had threatened his masculinity. This was all good as far as Holly was concerned.

They finally arrived at the park and quickly found a parking spot. Having a TAA sticker on your car got you into a lot of places, not the least of which was preferred parking. The sun was now high in the still cloudless sky. Holly squinted as she climbed out of the car and unbuckled Suzy. Yes, she thought, it really was the perfect day to visit the park.

Arthur was already sweating under the hot sun as he tramped steadily towards the park entrance now in view. The clock at the gate edged irresistibly towards high noon. It had been a journey over many miles and many city blocks, but he was here at last. He chuckled to himself that at least he wouldn't have to worry about finding a parking spot.

Still, there was the little matter of getting through TAA security before he could actually get into the park. It had not exactly been a pleasant experience passing through security at the bridge over the railroad tracks leading out of the old neighborhood. And Arthur didn't really expect things to be any easier here. He pulled the park pass out of his pocket.

There were two TAA security guards at the gate. The first one, a heavyset man with an unpleasant expression on his face, approached Arthur. "Whoa old fellow, where do you think you're going?"

The tattered man knew the drill by now. Keep your temper in check and show proper respect, lots of respect. "I have a park pass," he responded politely.

The heavyset guard was not easily convinced. "Let me see that! There are lots of counterfeit passes out there. People like you are liable to do anything to get a free ride." He grabbed the pass roughly out of Arthur's out-stretched hand.

"And we can't let just anybody into the park," he continued, "to mingle with all the fine hardworking people whose taxes actually pay for it." The expression on his face grew darker and even more unpleasant.

The guard examined the pass carefully. He read it. He rubbed it with his hand. He turned it over and back and then read it again. He hemmed and hawed. Arthur knew where this was going, unfortunately. He could tell this guard really didn't want to accept the pass.

"Please sir," Arthur implored, "can you give me a break? I walked several miles to get here today. I'm an old man who would just like to watch the breeze blow through the trees. I'm not a threat to anybody."

The heavyset guard still frowned. By now, the other guard at the gate was getting a little impatient. "Come on Frank, give the old guy a break," he interjected. "He can't hurt anybody. Just frisk him and let him go."

"Okay, okay, don't have a hissy fit! I'll let him go." The heavyset guard did not smile, yet he did dutifully, and very roughly, frisk Arthur.

"You're free to go," the guard said with a heavy sigh. He started to hand over the pass but then quickly pulled it back. Somehow he wasn't quite finished.

The scowl returned to the guard's face, and he pushed his finger deep into Arthur's chest. "I'm warning you," he added. "Don't get into any trouble because you won't like what happens next!"

Remember to show proper respect and just a little bit of fear the tattered man thought to himself. He averted his eyes and answered weakly, "Yes. Yes, sir. I understand sir."

The TAA security guard gradually reduced the pressure on his finger before withdrawing his hand altogether. Arthur took a deep breath and looked up, still careful to avoid making direct eye contact. There was an uncomfortable pause as both parties digested the terms of the mutual understanding.

Finally satisfied that he had made his point, the guard at last handed back the pass. Arthur was not one to push his luck. He nodded in agreement and then hurried through the gate.

Trees swayed gently in the breeze. Sunlight bounced from leaf to leaf until it landed neatly on the grass below. The grass itself was a deep shade of green, and Arthur believed it felt as soft as plush carpet beneath his feet. Children played. Joggers jogged. Walkers walked. Here and there, balls and flying disks filled the air. The whole park seemed to buzz with a steady stream of voices, of conversations, of laughter. It was a happy noise Arthur thought. Everything was perfect here. It was all he had hoped it would be when he set out for the park this morning.

At the moment, unfortunately, his aching feet were all too ready to remind him just how long that trip had been. Arthur decided to stretch out underneath one of the large shade trees. He could rest there and simply enjoy watching all the activity from a safe distance. And he knew very well just how important it was to keep a safe distance. His ragged clothes and scruffy white beard might draw unwanted, potentially negative attention from other, more upstanding, more neatly dressed park visitors.

Holly Anderson had by now found a nice spot on the grass for a picnic lunch, and she went to work laying out the spread. Simon and Suzy played nearby. Their little game was something of their own invention, a combination of kickball, hide-and-seek, and possibly bits and pieces of other childhood games. Suzy kicked the ball; Simon caught it and then quickly hid behind a nearby tree. Suzy squealed in delight as she hunted down her father only to run away herself as soon as she found him. There didn't appear to be any rules, and no one seemed to care. Laughter carried the short distance to the picnic spot. Holly chuckled herself as she watched father and daughter play.

Still, lunch was in danger of being spoiled by ants. So much as she hated to break up playtime, she called out to her family, "Lunch is ready. It's time to eat. Come over here now. You two can play some more later." Simon and Suzy seemed to grumble under their breaths but quickly complied anyway.

Arthur had been especially enjoying watching a father and his young daughter play together just a stone's throw away from the shade tree. The two didn't seem to have a care in the world. If only all the children in this city could live the same carefree life. Arthur wished it were so, but deep down he knew it wasn't and never would be. He smiled anyway and was frankly a little disappointed when the mother called the pair in for lunch.

As the family settled in for their picnic, he was near enough to hear their laughter and near enough to smell the food. This just reminded Arthur how empty his belly really was. After awhile, it became more and more difficult to watch the pleasant little picnic without thinking of the food. The tattered man decided it was time to take a stroll through the park.

Simon Anderson wolfed down the last of his lunch and then leaned back on his hands, stretching out and enjoying the fresh air. "Damn, that was good. I'm stuffed. Maybe I should just take a nap out here in the sun."

"Oh, no you don't," Holly replied firmly. She playfully tapped her husband on the head. "You can sleep at home. We're out here to enjoy this lovely day."

"I know! I know," Simon laughed. "I'm just kidding."

He reached over and gently stroked Holly's hair. She smiled. It was a beautiful smile, he thought, a smile accented by the warm glow in her eyes and the sunlight playing off the curls of her hair. Simon smiled as well, but on the inside, he was struggling to enjoy the moment and not think about going back to work for the TAA — a beautiful day, a beautiful wife and child versus the unknown, a potentially dangerous unknown. Maybe a nice long walk around the park would help.

"How about we go for a little walk? It might help us all digest our lunch." Simon gestured towards his stomach.

Holly smirked and rolled her eyes in mock disgust. "Okay," she answered with a slight chuckle, "if that's what you really want?" Simon nodded. Holly took the cue and began to dutifully gather up the trash and pack up the picnic supplies. The rest of the family joined in.

After the area was finally cleared, Simon grabbed Holly with one hand and Suzy with the other. The Andersons set off for a pleasant trip around the park.

Arthur ambled along one of the walking trails, soaking in the simple and unassuming beauty of the landscape on a bright sunny day: the soft rustle of leaves as trees swayed in the breeze, flowers blooming, birds singing. For sure, it meant more walking on already sore feet, but it did take his mind off the hunger pains deep in the pit of his stomach, a good thing since he really didn't know when he might get his next meal. Arthur walked on with a smile, not worrying at all about how bad his feet hurt.

The path abruptly changed direction and veered sharply to the right, breaking through the trees into a small patch of open space hidden away from the crowds. Arthur squinted at first, but he could just make out a statue placed rather haphazardly toward the back of the grassy knoll.

As he drew nearer, Arthur's eyes began to well up with tears. He couldn't believe what he was actually seeing. It was George Washington, a ragged and well-worn version of George Washington, but George Washington nonetheless. The bronze statue leaned slightly to one side and was streaked with corrosive rust. There were some pieces broken off and even a few bullet holes here and there. Still, it was him — George Washington as the first president of the old United States — not modern day action hero.

Arthur gently placed his hand on the statue and bowed his head with sincere reverence. "You don't belong here lost and forgotten among the weeds," he murmured. "You deserve better. Without you, there never would have been a United States of America."

But then the tattered man remembered where he was and more importantly, when he was. "Too bad, nobody remembers that anymore," he added softly.

He couldn't bring himself to say more. Arthur gradually backed away from the statue. He started to choke up, but the sadness soon gave way to genuine anger. Shaking his fist in frustration, he raged at the heavens above for the injustice, for the ignorance. How could they all forget? Deep in his heart, Arthur knew why, but right now he just couldn't accept that cold, hard reality.

Arthur's silent rant was suddenly interrupted by loud voices coming from the direction of the foot path. Five or six casually dressed young men, laughing and jostling one another, bounded towards the statue.

"Hey, look," one yelled, "it's an old statue and an old man. I don't know which one looks worse." He laughed hard at his own joke, and the others soon followed suit.

"It's not just any old statue," another one of the bunch noted as they all got closer. "It says on the name plate that it's George Washington!"

That piece of information seemed to excite, and at the same time, confuse the boisterous group. There arose a tremendous din of laughter, yelling, and cursing as they all tried to talk at once. Pushing and shoving, each one tried to out-do the guy next to him. For the time being at least, they appeared to forget all about Arthur.

"It can't be him. He's not big enough. Where are the fucking muscles? Where is the big ass sword? I don't care what the damn nameplate says!" Several voices roared their approval.

"Maybe this is Washington before he worked out and got all ripped," replied the self-styled leader of the gang. This observation seemed to quell some of the arguments, and murmurs of agreement rippled through the group.

"Yeah, I bet that's why they stuck this old statue back here," another member of the gang piped up. "Washington looks like such a pussy here, nothing like the two-fisted hero who kicked European ass."

That did it for Arthur. For the last few minutes, he had been trying to stay out of the way of these young loudmouths, but he could hold his tongue no longer. If it wasn't exactly smart or even safe to speak up, so be it.

"Young man," he blurted out, "George Washington, the real George Washington was indeed a great hero!"

"The statue here shows the man as he really was, standing nearly 6 feet tall. For the time he lived in, he was a literal giant among men. But he used that physical presence, along with his natural intellect and strong sense of duty, to lead men, to inspire them to endure great sacrifice and be more than they ever thought they could be. He led the rag-tag Colonial Army to victory over the British Empire in the Revolutionary War, beating the finest army in the world at the time and gaining our independence in the process."

"No, the real George Washington didn't beat men into submission like some two-bit action hero in a bad movie." Arthur shook his head.

"The real Washington," the tattered man continued forcefully, "became the first President of the United States of America, gracefully stepping down after two terms in office when some in the country wanted to make him a king. He set the standard for all the men who followed him into the office."

There was a silent pause. All eyes locked on Arthur. He swallowed hard. It felt good to speak up, to tell the truth for once. Yes, it felt damn good. What it would cost him in the end, however, remained to be seen.

The self-styled leader of the gang spoke up. "That's the biggest crock of shit I've ever heard! Everybody knows Washington was a real bad-ass. It says so in the movie."

"Don't believe everything you see on TV or everything you hear from the TAA. If you could only read the history books...."

"What the hell is a history book? Are you calling me stupid, old man?" A fearsome scowl spread across the face of the young thug. He sucked in a deep breath and moved closer to Arthur.

But Arthur stood his ground. "I'm not calling you stupid, just misinformed."

The thug laughed. "Misinformed sounds pretty close to stupid to me!" The rest of the gang joined in, breaking out into a loud combination of laughter and curses.

"I think it's time we teach this old man a lesson in history. Let's kick his ass Washington-style!" The gang quickly surrounded the tattered man and began to kick and throw wild punches at their intended victim.

Fearing something like this might happen, Arthur tried to respond as best he could. There was no point trying to fight back. He collapsed to the ground under a rain of blows and curled up into a fetal position to hopefully protect his vital organs.

Holly Anderson admired the trees as she strolled along the walking trail hand-in-hand with the two most important people in her life. The trees were tall and majestic, providing all the cool shade anyone could want but at the same time allowing in just enough sunlight to keep the atmosphere from becoming dark and gloomy. She glanced to her left at Simon who was sharing a little joke with Suzy. The child squealed in delight and squeezed her father's hand even tighter. Yes, it had truly been a perfect day, and Holly didn't want it to end.

The path ahead veered sharply to the right and seemed to disappear beyond the trees. For the first time all day, Holly felt something other than the simple pleasure of spending time with people she cared about. It wasn't quite fear or even dread — uneasiness, maybe. She started to pull back a little, but Simon and Suzy plowed right on ahead, dragging her along anyway.

As they passed through the trees to an open field, their blissful reverie was suddenly interrupted by yelling and loud voices, harsh, angry sounds that drowned out the laughter of children and the soft melody of birds singing. The Anderson family stopped cold at the edge of the field. There was a big commotion across the way near an old statue, and it looked to be violent.

Arthur had remained on the ground tucked into a protective ball, still clinging to the last shred of hope that his attackers would somehow tire out and lose interest. The minutes dragged on, yet the beating continued with unabated ferocity. Each kick, each punch only served to excite the gang of thugs even more.

It was a savage bloodlust. Like a pack of wild dogs, there was no holding them back from the kill. Arthur choked on the blood in the back of his throat, and he groaned out loud when a particularly well-placed kick caught him square in the stomach. His white hair was stained with crimson. He couldn't feel certain parts of his body anymore. Maybe that was a blessing he thought. In his battered and befuddled state, Arthur wondered if this was really the end and if speaking up for lost history had been worth it all.

"Oh my god," Holly blurted out, "Those young punks are beating that poor old man to death!"

Tears welled up in her eyes. A wave of nausea churned in the pit of her stomach. She tried yelling for help but couldn't get a word out. She tried to look away but couldn't do that either. Instead she broke down into helpless sobs and clutched Suzy tightly to her waist.

For Simon, on the other hand, this was a moment of great clarity, of undeniable purpose. His breathing slowed. His mind was focused, calm. His muscles coiled. He knew why he was here, and he knew exactly what he had to do right now. He had trained for this. The field of battle was straight ahead. It was smaller but otherwise very much the same as he had seen so many times before. He pulled away roughly from Holly and Suzy. Holly dug her nails into his skin as she tried to hold her husband back.

"No, don't go out there by yourself! We'll call the police for help!"

"No time for that," Simon responded tersely. He headed across the field at a brisk pace.

Quickly closing to within a few feet of the brawl, Simon called out in a voice strong and clear, "Hey, stop that! I think the old guy has had enough!"

It was a minor miracle that anyone heard anything at all above the yelling and screaming, but hear it they did. And surprisingly enough, the pack of thugs stopped beating the old man, at least for the moment. Perhaps it was the sudden shock of the interruption. Perhaps it was the simple audacity of a single man standing up against the whole gang.

And for what, they all seemingly wondered, a ragged old man who was hardly worth killing? Either way, the young punks just stood there downright perplexed.

The self-styled leader of the gang soon spoke up. "Look at what we have here," he bellowed, "some sort of do-gooder, some sort of hero!" He laughed, and the rest of the gang joined in. Simon stood his ground, calm, focused, unafraid.

The laughter, however, petered out rather quickly, and the mood turned more threatening. "Mister, I think you just need to move along and stay out of our business. Let us deal with this worthless piece of shit. I wouldn't want to see you get your clothes all messed up, if you know what I mean."

"I can't do that," Simon replied calmly. "You see, I'm going to take this old guy to get medical help, and all of you are going to leave quietly, very quietly."

"And by the way," he continued, "while I appreciate your concern, I can always wash my clothes if they get a little dirty." Simon smiled.

The gang leader didn't smile. He did, however, quickly size up the lone figure standing directly in front of him. Definitely muscular, a far cry from the broken down old man but not so big really. Maybe not so tough either. It was a comforting thought for sure, at least until he looked into the eyes.

The eyes seemed to be a different matter altogether. They were intensely dark, piercing, looking all but ready to burn a hole through something or somebody. And most important of all, they showed absolutely no hint of fear. The gang leader hesitated. He knew he couldn't tolerate this total lack of respect, but deep down he was somehow less confident than he had been a few minutes before. He swallowed hard, careful not to betray any emotion himself.

"Fellas, I think we have to teach this guy a lesson, just like we taught the old man!" The bravado returned to the voice of the gang leader, and the rest of his cohorts murmured their approval.

"Go get him guys," he yelled out. Still, he was careful to step back as the rest of the group surged forward.

For an instant, only an instant, images of ancient warriors, of swords and shields, of blood and death, passed in front of Simon's eyes.

And just as quickly, the images melted away, allowing him to focus back on the very real danger in the here and now. He deftly stepped out of the path of an onrushing thug and then smashed his fist square in the face of the next closest threat. The blow was so powerful that it knocked the young punk completely off his feet and sent him flying backwards into the rest of the gang. Simon immediately turned his attention back to the first attacker and doubled him over with a quick kick to the stomach before finishing him with a crushing two-fisted blow down on the back.

By this time, the remaining gang members on their feet were just about as worried as their self-styled leader. One pulled out a gun from the back of his pants, while another brandished a large knife.

"The hell with this shit!" the guy with the gun yelled. The guy with the knife was ticked he didn't get to say that first.

There ensued a brief, but loud debate over which weapon was actually going to do the killing. Simon took advantage of this hesitation and managed to grab a broken mop handle lying in the tall grass. It was roughly the size of a small spear, and it felt quite natural in his hands.

"A mop handle against a gun," one particularly eloquent thug piped up. "Really? What are you going to do — clean us to death?" The rest of the gang began to laugh.

Simon knew he had to strike quickly before the laughter had a chance to subside. He gripped the makeshift spear with both hands and stepped boldly forward. In one smooth motion, he swung the weapon swiftly to the right, smashing the gun out of the hand of the potential shooter, and then back to the left to likewise disarm the holder of the knife. Crouching down into fighting position, Simon struck the next closest gang member in the stomach and, with the backswing of the spear, easily swept the guy off his feet.

Once again he was but a lone warrior against the many. Still, Simon relished the challenge; he could feel the blood coursing through his veins. Death was always a possibility, but at times like this, he never felt more alive, more powerful.

With a terrible fury, Simon began to wade through his enemies, landing blows with painful precision and sowing great panic among them. He moved with all the power and agility of a finely honed instrument of battle. Stabbing or clubbing with the spear, striking with his fists and feet when necessary, all the while spinning away from danger or return blows. Bodies fell to the ground only to struggle up to get away as quickly as possible. The gang leader himself turned to flee, but Simon caught him by the cuff of the neck.

"Leaving so soon?"

It was strictly a rhetorical question. The now suddenly reluctant leader of the gang was too scared to answer, and Simon was none too interested in what the young loudmouth had to say anyway.

"Since you were so concerned, I just thought you would be happy to know that I did all this without getting my clothes dirty," Simon added with quiet sarcasm.

"I think your friends have learned the lesson that they should respect their elders. How about you?"

Cowering in Simon's firm grip, the gang leader mumbled something that vaguely sounded like agreement and then began to sob uncontrollably. It was hard for Simon to contain his disgust and even harder to resist the urge to beat down the coward.

The rage deep in Simon's soul, in every warrior's soul, was truthfully a powerful weapon in battle; it was not something quite so easy to turn off when the fighting stopped. Most warriors, however, didn't have to fight battles while a wife and young daughter watched in terror. Simon shook his head. With great reluctance, he gave the young man a swift kick in the backside sending him sprawling face first on the hard ground. The self-proclaimed leader of the gang pulled himself up painfully, still sobbing, and was soon scurrying off after his friends.

At last, the field of battle was clear. The enemy had been defeated. Simon raised his arms up towards the sky and let out a great, thunderous war cry to thank the Gods for his victory. The savage roar rolled across the field, startling birds and sending them flying from the trees.

By now, Holly had reached her husband with Suzy in tow. Suzy was in tears. She was too small to comprehend all that she had just seen. Holly was too relieved to cry right now, although she felt like it. She knew much more about violence than her child, but she had never seen anything quite like this.

And what kind of yell or scream or cheer had Simon just let out she wondered. It was both terrifying and fascinating all at the same time.

Holly approached Simon warily, suddenly none too sure about the man in front of her. Was this really her husband? What kind of man could unleash that depth of savagery even if he was trying to defend someone else?

When Simon saw Suzy, however, he no longer felt the rage. He felt something entirely new, something he had never known before. Simon looked back up at the sky and grimaced. It was a dull pain on the inside. He had never felt the sensation, this strange regret, particularly after a great victory.

Now he knew. How could a man, a father, not be moved by the tears of a child? A heartfelt smile spread slowly across Simon's face as he knelt down to comfort Suzy. He reached out to her face and gently wiped away a tear.

"Honey," Simon said softly, "I'm sorry you had to see that. Those were very bad men who were hurting a helpless old man. Please understand. I had to stop them. But don't you worry. I'm okay, and the bad men are all gone now." He hugged Suzy tightly.

"But Daddy," Suzy sobbed, "I was so scared. I was afraid those bad men were going to hurt you and take you away from me. That can't happen because I love you so much." She hugged her father back even tighter.

"I know, honey. I love you too. Don't worry. It's all over now, and everybody's safe." A single tear welled up in Simon's eye and then trickled slowly down his cheek.

Holly wiped the tears out of her eyes as well. Any lingering reservations she may have had about the man in front of her were put aside, for now at least. She waited until Simon had finished comforting Suzy and then jumped impulsively into his powerful arms, smothering him with kisses.

Simon laughed. "I guess you must love me too!"

"You bet I do, and you better not do any more crazy things like this!" Holly smiled. She shook her fist playfully to make her point.

The happy family re-union was suddenly interrupted by the sound of coughing. The old man was by now stirring back to life. He spit out some blood and let out an audible groan as he struggled to get up off the grass.

"Oh my god, please forgive me," Holly explained. Her voice cracked. She was obviously embarrassed and also a little uneasy around the rough looking old man. "I was just so relieved to see that my husband wasn't hurt that I almost forgot about you."

"How bad are you hurt? Can you stand?"

"I think I can stand. No apologies are necessary," Arthur replied gently, trying mightily to ignore the pain in his ribs. He ran his hand through his wild hair and tried to straighten his ragged clothes.

Most of all, Arthur wanted to look presentable in front of this young couple and their little girl. Maybe it was pride. Maybe it was just simple politeness. Either way, he really wanted to look like somebody worth saving right now.

"My name is Arthur. I owe your husband many thanks," the tattered man continued. He bowed his head and spoke with great sincerity. "It was a very near thing. If your husband had not intervened when he did, I think those young punks would have finished me off."

Holly smiled, not one of those polite smiles but a real, genuine smile. "My name is Holly. This is my husband Simon and our daughter Suzy. I'm very glad Simon was able to help." She glanced back at her husband and squeezed his hand.

Simon swallowed hard. He was not very comfortable with praise. Eager to move on to something else, he asked, "Can you tell me how all this started?"

Arthur smiled and winked at Suzy. "I guess we just had a little disagreement about this old statue here."

"A disagreement over a statue of President George Washington?" Simon was a little confused. "I'm not sure I understand."

"You did say President George Washington, didn't you?" Despite his pain, Arthur was eager to follow up on this.

"Yes, I did. George Washington, the first president of the United States of America."

Arthur continued to probe. "You know about President Washington?"

"I guess so. Washington led the Colonial Army through the terrible winter at Valley Forge, crossed the Delaware River, and ultimately defeated the British at Yorktown. That's how the 13 colonies became the first 13 states of the United States of America."

Arthur's eyes lit up. The pain in his ribs was suddenly gone. He knew it would surely come back, but right now, there was something much bigger and more important to consider. Arthur felt like he could jump for joy if that wouldn't have hurt so damn much. He likely would have tried hugging this stranger who had just saved his life, but somehow Simon just didn't seem like the hugging type.

Either way, Arthur settled on a more conservative tactic, figuring it might be best to keep his excitement under control for the time being.

"You seem to be a little young to know so much about early American history," Arthur said calmly and with barely a smile. "If I remember correctly, they started taking history out of the classroom with your generation. I guess they didn't think it was value-added."

"I picked up the history lessons a long time ago, a very long time ago," Simon replied.

"Interesting, very interesting." Arthur was finding it increasingly difficult to contain his excitement. "By the way," he continued, "how much more American history do you know other than the story of George Washington?"

Simon was now getting a little uneasy himself. Answering questions was turning out to be harder work than beating up a whole gang of thugs. "I guess I have a pretty good understanding all the way up to the beginning of World War II."

"Well then...." Arthur started but then quickly paused. Was he getting too carried away with all of this and throwing caution to the wind? Had he taken too many punches to the head? He wondered. He worried. The silence was getting uncomfortable. If you couldn't trust a guy who had just saved your life, then who could you trust?

Finally, Arthur spit out exactly what was on his mind. "Mr. Simon, sir, maybe you should join my American history class!"

There was silence still, but it had suddenly morphed from merely uncomfortable all the way to positively stunned, at least for Simon and Holly.

Arthur was too excited not to fill this gap with more words. "Yes, something like that really exists even in this day and age. I'm a teacher, you see."

The teacher gestured and spoke with a nervous energy that was doing absolutely nothing to make the Andersons feel more comfortable. "I can really help bring you up to speed on everything that has happened since the war!"

Simon didn't answer, but Holly did. It seemed to her that it just might be time to end this conversation and move on. "Arthur," she said ever so politely, "you haven't told us whether or not you need us to get you to a hospital."

Arthur understood what was going on. He was disappointed, but he understood. "No ma'am," he answered softly, "the hospitals don't see people like me."

"No insurance, no cash equals no medical care. Just the way things work I guess." Arthur's voice trailed off, all that nervous energy, all that enthusiasm completely gone. He shrugged his shoulders and looked down towards the ground.

Holly and Simon stood there uncomfortably, unsure of what to do next. Suzy was getting restless; she squirmed and tried to pull away from her parents' hands.

But then Arthur suddenly had an inspiration.

"You know, if it's not too much trouble, maybe you could give me a ride home? I have people there who can fix me up." He waited for a moment and then added for effect, "It's a very long walk when you're as banged up as I am right now."

He waited some more, hoping to play on the young couple's sympathies. At the same time, he also hoped they wouldn't pick up on his ulterior motives.

Holly thought this at least sounded like a plan. Besides, she could only imagine how painful it would be for this poor man to try to walk a long distance in his condition.

"Okay, I guess we can give you a ride." She smiled and looked back to Simon for support. He nodded his head.

"So it's settled then," Holly continued. "Maybe we should make our way back to the car now."

Arthur smiled. "You're very kind. Thank you very much."

Holly and Suzy darted out ahead. Holly wanted to retrieve the picnic supplies she had dropped back at the edge of the field when all the excitement started. Simon hung back to help the old man along if he needed it.

Taking advantage of this momentary separation, Arthur leaned in towards Simon and whispered, "Mr. Simon, despite your youth, you seem to have a very old soul. I can tell these things."

Simon turned sharply and stared at the old man. He didn't say a word.

This unsettled Arthur quite a bit, but he tried not to show it. "Yes, I can see from that reaction you know there's certain amount of truth to what I said."

The old man didn't miss a beat, or an opportunity, and he was clearly very persistent. "You know, Mr. Simon, I still think you would be a good fit for my American history class. You may not see that just yet, but you will. It's just a matter of time."

"The good thing about you giving me a ride home today — you'll know right where to find me when you're ready!"

Simon shook his head. It was hard to see how this crazy old man might fit into the grand scheme of things. Right now, he wasn't in the mood to try to figure it out. Holly and Suzy were up ahead, and he needed to catch up to them.

Chapter 9

Holly wasn't really enjoying the ride back from the park. The Andersons had just reached the part of town the strange old man called home, a place which clearly stretched the definition of the word. Yes, she was glad they were helping someone who obviously needed it, but at the same time, she was appalled by what she was seeing right now.

They seemed to be heading directly towards railroad tracks; the nature of the city skyline changed dramatically on the other side of those tracks. Charred and crumbling buildings stretched across the near horizon, many of them partially obscured by smoke from countless little fires. Junked cars and piles of garbage lined the streets. A gunshot or two could be heard rattling off in the distance. It was all quite a departure from the peaceful, scenic beauty of the park they had just left. Holly was a little ashamed she had never known places like this even existed.

As they neared the railroad tracks, Holly slowed down the car. There was a bridge up ahead. It crossed over the tracks and then, as far as she could tell, disappeared directly into the abyss.

The entrance to the bridge was guarded by TAA security personnel. The far end of the bridge was shrouded in darkness and smoke, looking very much like something right out of a cheap horror movie. The only thing missing, she thought to herself, was the warning sign: "Abandon hope all ye who enter here." Holly chuckled quietly at the absurdity of it all, trying hard to be discrete and polite at the same time.

The whole arrangement was a little surreal, but it did seem to serve a function — keeping this part of town isolated from the rest of the civilized world.

"You can stop and let me out here," Arthur said casually. "I don't think you want to get any closer to those guards; there might be some questions."

Holly agreed that was probably a good idea. Although they remained at the bridge, the guards did seem to be getting a little curious. It was a good bet that cars sporting a TAA sticker didn't show up here very often, and she wasn't looking forward to trying to explain their situation.

As Arthur climbed out of the car, he looked back at Holly and Simon. "Thanks again for all your help. You've been very kind."

Then he nodded to Simon in particular. "I share stories with friends every Tuesday, Wednesday, and Thursday night at the Catholic Rescue Mission. Maybe I'll run into you again sometime."

Holly was a little unsettled by those parting words. Did the old man know something about her husband she didn't? Admittedly, she still did not fully comprehend everything that had happened at the park today. Did they really meet the old man purely by chance Holly wondered, or was this all part of some grand plan she didn't understand either? She glanced over at Simon sitting quietly, seemingly lost in his own thoughts. Thankfully, Suzy was asleep in the back seat.

Turning back around, Holly watched Arthur cross over the bridge after being briefly detained by the guards. She could only imagine what the old man was walking into. Deep down though, she had to admit to herself that she was glad there was something to keep everything bottled up in that place. Maybe this was just being honest, but it only made her feel more ashamed.

Arthur finally disappeared into the gloom at the far end of the bridge. Holly backed the car away and then gunned it towards the main highway. Normally not a speeder, she thought this just might be the time for an exception to the rule. Besides, who out here would care? Other than the guards at the bridge, there didn't seem to be any police or security personnel around to give out tickets.

She drove on into the gathering dusk. The urgent hum of the engine, the steady grinding of the tires on the road: all else was quiet in the car. Holly wondered if this was simply the result of pure exhaustion or something else entirely.

The lights of the highway came into view, and Holly allowed herself to smile once more. Somewhere down that highway, maybe not as far away from here as she used to think before today, lay all the comforts and security of home. Holly was relieved, thankful even, to be heading back to where she and her family belonged.

She tried now to focus on pleasant thoughts of clear skies, of green grass and clean, tree-lined streets. She would have closed her eyes if she could have.

She tried mightily to concentrate on that peaceful vision of home as the miles passed by, but she just couldn't shake it — that hellish place — the burned out buildings, the sound of gunshots, and especially the last words from the old man.

Holly shook her head in frustration and broke the silence. "Honey, what do you make of what Arthur said? Do you really think he expects to see you again?"

Simon didn't answer right away. "I don't know. You can never tell with a crazy old guy like that."

The response was casual, yet carefully worded. Holly wasn't satisfied.

"What do you mean by that?" Her voice suddenly got louder. Again, Simon did not answer right away. This time she didn't wait.

"I can't believe this! Are you really considering going to that history class he mentioned? Or is it storytelling sessions now? You're an executive with the TAA. You can't be that crazy."

"And by the way, how did you find out so much about early American history in the first place?"

Everything was coming in loud and fast now. How much could he tell her? It had been a whole lot easier to beat up thugs at the park Simon thought to himself. Still he knew there had to be an answer, at least a partial answer.

"I picked it up a very long time ago before you knew me," he replied flatly.

It took some time to process that answer before Holly continued, "And do you have any interest in learning more about American history?"

"I can't say. I don't know yet."

"What's there to know? If you go to any of those classes, you'll put both your job and your family at risk!"

Holly was having a hard time believing what she was hearing right now. "As long as I've known you, you've always towed the party line. Live in the present; plan for the future. I don't recall you ever saying anything about the past, other than to forget about it."

"What if there's more to it than that?" Simon was trying very hard to control his emotions. "What if by learning about our past, we gained a greater understanding of our present so we could make a better plan for the future? What if someone wants to know more than just what the TAA tells us?"

Simon looked directly at Holly, the passion rising in his voice. "Don't you want to know where we came from? Don't you want to know how we got here?"

Holly didn't answer. She just drove on.

The silence though was too painfully uncomfortable to last for very long.

"Maybe, I'm still trying to figure out why I'm here," Simon said softly. There was sadness in his voice. He lowered his head.

"Why you're here? Why you're here? That should be obvious! You're here to take care of your family. You're here to take care of and protect our child."

"You're here …" Holly struggled to choke back tears, "to love me forever."

"Oh god, I know that!" Simon suddenly lifted his head. "I would lay down my life for you and Suzy. But maybe, just maybe, there's something more."

"That should be enough!"

There was no point in arguing about this. Simon could tell as much. He reached up and gently stroked Holly's face. She grabbed his hand and held it there. A single tear somehow escaped her best efforts, rolling slowly down her cheek until it disappeared underneath the clasped hands of husband and wife.

All was quiet once more.

"Honey," Simon interrupted the moment with great reluctance, "there's something else I have to tell you. I didn't want to tell you before and risk putting a damper on our day at the park. I got a letter from the CEO yesterday. He wants me back at work tomorrow."

This little revelation landed with a thud. Holly relaxed her grip on Simon's hand, allowing it to fall away from her face. She looked straight ahead and grabbed the steering wheel firmly with both hands.

She didn't say a word. Suzy still slept comfortably, oblivious to anything going on around her.

It was completely dark by the time the Andersons reached their pleasant suburban home, too dark really to enjoy the ambiance of well-trimmed lawns and lovely tree-lined streets. That was too bad Holly thought. She had really been looking forward to it all during the ride home. The day at the park had not quite ended as planned. That was too bad as well.

Tomorrow was another day at work for Simon, and she was just going to have to get used to that routine again. Losing her husband once more to the all-consuming demands of his job was a distinct possibility. Holly Anderson was a very conflicted woman. She appreciated the comfortable and secure life the TAA provided for her family, but sometimes she absolutely hated what they demanded in return.

The darkness closed in on the offices of the TAA, only a short commute away from the suburbs. Nonetheless, there were still many hard at work, particularly Daniel Garcia. It was the best time to catch up on e-mails, he thought, after most everyone else had left for the day.

The e-mail at the top of the inbox referenced the new containment center for the flu pandemic. Garcia was pleased to see that the massive complex had opened on schedule in the fields surrounding some non-descript little town in the old state they used to call Pennsylvania. Gettysburg, it was — the name of the place wasn't immediately familiar. The location didn't matter much to Garcia as long as there was plenty of land and plenty of security to keep it well isolated from the rest of the population.

There was a sharp knock at the door. James Wilson poked his head into the office. The Senior VP of Security looked concerned. "Do you have a minute? I have some questions about the strategy that I need to discuss with you."

The CEO looked up from his desk. "Sure," he replied cordially, "please come in and sit down."

The head of security nodded and slipped quietly into the office. "I understand you're bringing Simon Anderson back into the office. Is this true?"

"Yes, it is. In fact, I'm expecting him to be back in the office tomorrow." Garcia chuckled. "I see that news still travels fast around here."

The laughter lasted only briefly. The eyes of the CEO narrowed, and he looked directly at James Wilson. "Why do you ask? Is this going to be a problem?"

"I don't know, sir," Wilson answered quickly. "Are you sure this is wise?"

It was a rhetorical question. Wilson cleared his throat and continued to lay out his concerns. Having given this some thought, he was choosing his words carefully.

"I know Simon performed very well in his job and was a real team player around here. He was clearly an up-and-comer in the organization. However, all of this was before the bombing and the significant head injuries he suffered there. I realize he's been recuperating at home the last few weeks. Still, do we really know his current mental and physical state? I mean, are we going to get back the same caliber guy we had before? We are rapidly approaching a critical point in the operation, and I'm concerned about the risk of bringing in someone new at this juncture."

Garcia shook his head and raised his hand as a clear signal to stop. He really didn't like anyone questioning his decisions, even if it was a member of the senior executive team. Nonetheless, he was prepared to address the concerns in a calm manner, at least for now. The next time might be different.

"James, I hear what you're saying, but I know Simon Anderson is fully recovered by now. According to reports from his doctor, Simon only spent a couple of days in the hospital. Either this was a medical resurrection of biblical proportions, or just maybe, he wasn't as seriously hurt as initially thought. Remember there was a tremendous amount of chaos during the rescue effort and the first few days of treating survivors. Under these conditions, would it really be so surprising if there were a few errors in the medical charts?"

The CEO paused for effect. He did enjoy showing off his analytical skills. By now, the Senior VP of Security should have been nodding in enthusiastic agreement, praising his boss for seeing what others could not. Unfortunately, it wasn't quite working out that way; Wilson sat still and stared numbly back. Clearly, the security chief wasn't convinced just yet.

Garcia ran his right hand slowly through his thick black hair, trying very hard to contain his rising frustration. "Okay," he snapped. "You know me as someone who likes to keep his options open, right?"

This time Wilson did nod in agreement.

"Okay then! I'm not bringing Simon Anderson back into a direct tactical planning role for the operation. He was a hero during the bombing's aftermath, for god's sake! Even if by chance his brain has turned to mush, it just doesn't matter. All I need is his heroic face on network TV telling everyone how he saved people on that horrible day and how critical it is for the TAA to strike back. Keep in mind that this operation is going to result in casualties, potentially a significant number of casualties. Public support can whither pretty quickly when the bodies of young soldiers start to pile up. That's where Simon comes in. His job is to keep reminding people just how terrible that day was and convince them that vengeance is worth the high cost."

Wilson nodded in agreement once more.

"Now we're finally getting somewhere," the CEO mumbled to himself. He stood up and put his arm around the shoulders of the Senior VP of Security.

"Don't worry my friend. Simon Anderson is just a figurehead."

"Sounds good," Wilson replied with a grin. "But what if Simon doesn't want to play along?"

"Then we do what we always do. We either persuade him, or … we separate him from the organization." Daniel Garcia and James Wilson knew what that meant. They both laughed.

"I think it's about time to go home," the CEO noted after catching his breath. "We have a full day tomorrow."

Both men walked out of the office and turned out the lights behind them.

Chapter 10

"There is a certain, undeniable freedom in driving a car, the freedom to go where you want, when you want!"

Simon didn't really know why that particular phrase suddenly popped into his head. For sure, he couldn't recall where or when he had come across it. Maybe he had heard it in an old commercial or read it in a magazine somewhere.

No matter, because right now, as he sped down the highway behind the wheel for the first time in a long time, Simon believed every last word of it. The sun was shining, and the morning skies were clear. He drove with the windows down, soaking it all in. The car handled smoothly, all the power of that big engine at the fingertips of the driver. The highway was wide and straight and seemed to go on forever; surely it could take a man wherever he wanted to go.

Freedom: driving equaled freedom. Simon could buy into that.

Or not.

Unfortunately, there was only one place this car was going today — the headquarters of the Trade Association of the Americas. It was Simon's first day back at work; he had no other choice. There didn't seem to be much freedom in that, Simon thought.

The whole process of driving suddenly became a whole lot less glamorous. It was now just another morning commute to the office, and to an uncertain reception at that. Holly had suggested Simon drive himself to work since the Anderson home was only a relatively short distance from the TAA building. There was no way he could get lost, she said.

Maybe it really was that easy. Maybe she was just expressing her confidence in how well he had recovered from the bombing. Maybe she didn't want to go to TAA headquarters any more than Simon did.

Simon didn't have long to consider the whole wide range of maybes. His exit was coming up fast. The TAA building was already clearly visible from the highway, stretching high into the clouds, gleaming in the early morning sunlight. Simon steered the car onto the exit ramp and shortly thereafter pulled into the spacious employee parking lot.

He swallowed hard. His palms were a little sweaty. It wasn't fear; he had never felt fear before battle. But then again, this wasn't a simple clash between opposing armies where one could easily tell friend from foe. No, it was much more complex than that and loaded with potentially dangerous unknowns. Nothing in the scattered pages of Simon's memory had prepared him for this.

For more than a minute, he waited. He wondered. He pondered.

But destiny could not be denied or even deferred for much longer. Simon unbuckled the seatbelt and climbed out of the car. He marched resolutely towards the front door.

He wasn't alone. Other workers sprang up from various points in the parking lot. All converged on the citadel of the TAA. The security guard at the entrance hurriedly checked Simon's ID and waved him through without question. Just like that, he was in. No fuss. No drama.

The elevator Simon boarded in the lobby was jam packed with people he didn't recognize. It stopped at several floors on the way up, thinning out the crowd just a little bit more each time. These were the underlings, the worker bees of the trade association. By the time the elevator finally reached the executive floor, Simon was all alone. The doors opened. Mary, the CEO's administrative assistant, was waiting.

She greeted Simon warmly. "Welcome back! I can't tell you how much we've missed you around here," Mary said ever so sweetly. She smiled and gave Simon a big hug. He didn't reciprocate though, standing there rather stiffly.

As Mary gradually pulled away, her hands slid down along Simon's arms. Almost instinctively, she squeezed the bicep muscles.

"Wow! I can tell you've really been working out. You seemed to have recovered very nicely from that horrible bombing."

Simon didn't know what to say.

There was now a little twinkle in Mary's eyes, and she smiled once again. "Having some time away from work must really agree with you," she cooed.

"Yes, I guess it does," Simon replied. He smiled politely.

Mary took a deep breath and slowly shook her head. "Oh well, I guess we have to go," she continued. "The CEO is waiting for you." There was a touch of disappointment in her voice.

The administrative assistant turned around and headed into the main office area. Simon followed. Along the way, the pair bumped into co-workers and other well-wishers who insisted on taking time to welcome back the prodigal son — handshakes, friendly pats on the back, polite small talk. All seemed to agree that he looked great. Some of these faces looked familiar; some didn't. Either way, they were slowing down progress.

Mary tried to hurry things along. She tugged discretely at Simon's sleeve, all the while maintaining an outwardly cheerful smile. Simon understood the signal and followed her lead.

As the pair moved on, Simon noticed things that looked strangely familiar: the over-stuffed leather couch in the reception area, a painting here and there, and the large plaque outside the conference room.

The plaque itself was a hard thing to miss, bronzed and highly ornate, almost more appropriate for a shrine or memorial rather than an office. Neatly chiseled on its face were the guiding principles of the TAA:

1) All non-value added activity is waste.
2) Waste does not add to bottom-line profits.
3) Eliminate all waste.

Simon stopped and read the words slowly, carefully. He definitely recognized the guiding principles. How could he possibly not remember them? If you were part of the TAA, knowing the principles was not only expected; it was more important than knowing your own mother's name. Endless drilling and communication over the years had accomplished leadership's primary goal of binding the organization tightly together around these core principles.

Yes, the words were absolutely clear to Simon. He closed his eyes but could see them still. Yet there was something undeniably different about those words now. The bombing had changed everything. Maybe, just maybe, the exact meaning behind the words wasn't quite so clear anymore.

Simon lingered at the plaque. Mary smiled and waited. She didn't try to rush him away. Reading the guiding principles was probably very comforting, she assumed. Simon was deep in thought, though not necessarily comforted. He understood what value-added meant. He just wondered who got to decide exactly what was value-added and what was not.

Now was not the time to contemplate that question. The CEO approached with his hand outstretched.

Daniel Garcia was smiling. But it wasn't the cool, polite smile which business associates were used to seeing. It seemed so much more genuine than that, more like a grin really, with lots of teeth showing. He grabbed Simon's hand and shook it with all the charm and enthusiasm of an old backwoods politician trying to buy a vote. For good measure, he threw in a couple of jovial pats on Simon's shoulder with his free hand. With the exception of a heartfelt hug, which would have gone well beyond the bounds of professional decorum, it was in all other respects the type of greeting usually reserved for a long-lost friend. The CEO clearly wanted Simon to feel welcome.

"It's great to have you back, Simon," the chief executive said, still smiling and still holding firmly onto the handshake. "Whoa, that's some grip you have there! Be careful not to break my hand!" He chuckled at his own joke, feigning pain for added effect. Mary laughed as well.

"Well, you seem to have made a full recovery from your injuries," Garcia continued. "And I can see that you're obviously in great shape. Time off and home cooking must really be working for you. Maybe I need to try it!" He laughed again.

"I almost hate to bring you back to work and take you away from all that!"

Simon was cautious. Something wasn't quite right. His memories of this place may have been muddled, but there were some things he did recall — and this didn't look like any of them.

All of this friendliness seemed a little out of place for the headquarters of the trade association. The TAA he did remember was much more conservative, strait-laced almost to the point of being downright cold. Either he was crazy, or something just didn't fit. After a brief hesitation, Simon decided to keep it simple and polite. He returned the smile.

"Thank you, sir. It feels good to be back."

"Ah, I notice you're reading our guiding principles." The CEO gestured towards the plaque. "I'm sure they look familiar, don't they. I know if I had lost part of my memory, I'm betting that one of the first things to come back to me would be those principles. I'm guessing the same for you."

Garcia didn't wait for any type of answer but continued to ramble on in an absent-minded sort of way, as if no one else was in the room. This was clearly something he enjoyed talking about. It didn't really matter if somebody was around to hear it or not.

"Yes, those principles really tie us all together," he mused. "I still remember writing those words many years ago and then reading them to the senior leadership team for the very first time. Back then, no one believed me when I told them that we were going to run the entire organization based on those principles."

His voice rising, the CEO became more animated, more passionate. "No one believed me when I said that every member of the TAA would soon know those words by heart. No one believed me when I said that every decision we make, every action we take, everything we say each and every day, would be guided by those principles."

"Yes, no one believed me back then, but look at us now!"

Daniel Garcia balled his hand up into a fist and shook it, raging against non-believers and the very heavens above. "Eliminate all waste; eliminate everything that is not value-added!"

And then it stopped. The CEO suddenly became very quiet. He smiled and looked over at Simon.

The emotional outburst did nothing to relieve the uneasiness the younger executive was feeling right now. Simon simply, and very cautiously, nodded. The question of exactly who got to decide what was value-added might just have been answered.

The CEO nodded as well. "Well then," he said abruptly. "We have much to discuss, Mr. Anderson. Please, let's go into my office." He waved Mary away, and she dutifully departed.

Simon was almost sorry to see Mary go. It was time to get down to serious business, and this was the part he dreaded most of all.

The office of the CEO, despite its somewhat modest surroundings, could be an intimidating, even awe-inspiring place. It was not just the seat of power for the TAA; it was the very heartbeat of the organization and the billions of people who lived, toiled, and died within trade association territory. Simon stepped through the office doors.

Almost immediately he felt overwhelmed by a crushing pressure from something he couldn't see or touch: a great weight pressing squarely on his chest, threatening to take his breath away. Simon lumbered ahead unsteadily, all the while trying to suck in enough air to re-fill his lungs. His heart raced, straining under the labor, and he could feel his own ear drums vibrate with each pounding beat. He touched both hands together; they were cold and clammy.

One thing, however, was now perfectly clear. He had been in this office before.

Memories stirred. Simon stood — just barely. Everything around him, everything he could see faded to black. Scattered images flashed in his head and then just as quickly flickered out. In a brief burst of light, he saw this same place in another time. He saw himself there, sitting with the CEO. He could only make out bits and pieces of conversation before they too were gone.

Simon's mind tried to process what it could.

There had been meetings in this office prior to the bombing. Simon had been at these meetings. He was sure of that now, but not much more. Meetings about the upcoming trade conference? Negotiating strategies? Something about the need to be tough with the European Union? It was all too much to comprehend.

The CEO noticed Simon's distress. "Mr. Anderson, are you alright?"

Simon didn't answer.

The CEO repeated the question, this time louder. "Mr. Anderson, I'm asking you! Are you alright?"

Words finally began to break through the haze, the confusion. Simon turned slowly towards the voice.

"Sorry, sir, I'm just a little light-headed."

Daniel Garcia eyed the younger executive with some suspicion. He wasn't ready to buy into that explanation just yet. Still, there was business to take care of, and nothing got in the way of business.

"Okay Simon, please sit down," the CEO replied cautiously. "I don't want you to overexert yourself the first day back." He motioned towards the couch.

Simon sat down. He was glad to be off his feet.

Garcia smiled once again. But this time, it was decidedly less friendly than before. It was cool and very business-like, the face of a man ready to begin a serious negotiation. Daniel Garcia looked straight into Simon's eyes.

"Tell me, Mr. Anderson," he probed, "just how much do you remember about the bombing? I don't mean to make you re-live that horrible day, but the success of your next assignment may well depend on how much you remember."

There was an uncomfortable silence. Simon's mind had returned to that day, to that dark and terrible place. Fire and wreckage. Screams and blood. Mangled bodies and shattered faces with cold, lifeless stares.

It was with some difficulty that Simon pulled himself out of that place and back to the here and now.

"I remember the bombing," he said quietly. "Not so much about things before the bombing, but I very clearly remember the aftermath."

There was a hint of anger in Simon's voice. He sat up straight on the couch and wiped a tear from his eye.

"Why do you ask?"

This time the CEO was the one who hesitated. He studied Simon carefully, the body language, the look in his eyes. Garcia could see the obvious pain in those eyes. But there was something else as well — a smoldering intensity, a pent-up rage which seemed ready to explode at any time. It was all a little bit unnerving, even for the chief executive of the TAA. He swallowed hard and pondered the next move.

Whatever he saw in those eyes, Garcia decided finally, it was definitely genuine. And it would make very interesting television.

It was probably better that Anderson didn't remember much before the bombing, the CEO thought. It would certainly make things less complicated.

"Simon, it's quite simple really. We need you to tell the story of the bombing's aftermath, the terrible circumstances under which you and the other rescuers worked. You're a genuine hero. You saved many lives that day. You embody the best values of the TAA. People will be inspired by your example."

For just a moment, the CEO paused to allow his introduction, his hook, to sink in. He then moved in to close the sale.

"Simon, you can help our people, our shareholders, by telling that story on the major network news shows. If you're willing and able, I have arranged for you to do a series of interviews with important television personalities. It will all be tastefully done and with the utmost respect, of course. We won't be turning the story of this tragedy into a circus."

There was another pause. A good sales pitch was not something to be rushed.

"If you do accept this assignment, I'm sure your family will be very proud, and it will certainly be a big boost for your career." Garcia hoped Simon had not lost any of his old ambitions. In fact, he was counting on it.

Simon really didn't know what to say at first. "A big boost for his career…." Those words hit home, and they hit hard. He had heard the CEO tell him that before. And the last time, he now seemed to remember, the benefits for his family were also part of the deal.

This was a little too surreal, bits and pieces of information floating around in his head with nothing fitting together at all. There was only one thing which seemed to make sense in this jumbled, god-awful mess — family. He had to take care of his family, and that was enough for now.

"I'm not sure I can talk about the horrors of that day," Simon replied quietly.

The CEO was oddly sympathetic. He leaned forward and placed his hand gently on Simon's shoulder.

"I know. I know." The voice was quiet, reassuring. "It's a horrible thing. If I were in your place, I'm not sure I could talk about it either."

Once again, Daniel Garcia was patient. He stopped and simply waited, allowing time for his words to sink in and soften up any resistance. After a few, painfully long seconds, he continued, his tone more energetic, more forceful now.

"But I'm not in your place," he said rather abruptly, "and I can't share your burden. I am sure, however, that our shareholders, and you family, need to hear that story. And I can't think of anyone better to tell it than you."

Simon heard the word "family" loud and clear. That was it. "Okay," he answered almost immediately, "I'll give it a try."

"Good, very good, I know your family will be proud of you."

There was really nothing else to say. Simon simply nodded.

"I'll set up the first interview for tomorrow. Now why don't you go settle into your office and try to relax. I'm sure you will need time to catch up and gradually work your way back into the swing of things."

Simon rose from the couch, somewhat unsteadily at first. He took a deep breath and then headed slowly towards the office door.

The CEO smiled. He was very satisfied.

With the door closing behind him, Simon suddenly felt much better. The pressure on his chest was gone, and he could feel the air moving freely into his lungs once again. Now he just had to remember where he put that office.

It wasn't necessarily going to be easy either: finding a non-descript office in a big building full of non-descript offices. Nonetheless, anything seemed better than staying put. Simon quickly scanned the four corners of his mental compass and then set off resolutely in the most promising direction.

Walking freely through the sprawling headquarters of the TAA didn't quite compare to driving the car down the open highway with the windows down, but it sure beat the hell out of suffocating in the CEO's office. Simon strolled down the hallways. He wandered through a maze of cubicles. He peeked through doorways. Everywhere he went, he glanced at name plates and titles, discretely of course. And everywhere he went, he ran into more well-wishers. He smiled politely, made small talk, and then moved on. No one seemed to question where Simon was going. No one commented on his apparent confusion. Maybe they didn't notice. Maybe they were just being polite.

Either way, Simon was downright relieved when he finally found his name on the door of a darkened office tucked away on yet another seemingly endless hallway. This was the place. Simon smiled. He couldn't help it really. There was an almost childlike satisfaction in finding what he had been looking for long and hard. It was a moment to savor success of a sort, very nearly like digging up a buried treasure except that a name plate marked the spot instead of a big red X on an old map.

But for all that, the giddiness really didn't last long. Simon lingered there in the hall. He wasn't ready to go into that office just yet. It was physically a distance of only a few steps, but in his conflicted mind, it was one giant leap forward to a place he wasn't sure he wanted to go. Walking through that door meant that he was really back, body and soul, back at work — and back in the fold of the TAA.

After the disconcerting episode in the CEO's office, Simon didn't know if this was a good thing or a bad thing. Would there be more flashbacks, more nightmares, if he walked through that door? Would he find out more about the activities of the trade association, and perhaps, his own part in them? Would he finally remember what went on during his previous meetings with the CEO?

Simon continued to eye the closed door cautiously, warily, reluctant to even touch the doorknob. There were surely many things to consider, but at the same time, he knew he couldn't stand outside of his own office all day. One way or another, he had to make a move. Maybe all he needed was a push from someone, anyone to show up, maybe just the mere threat of embarrassment if he had to try to explain what he was doing to someone else.

Out of the corner of his eye, he noticed a potential someone walking towards him from far down the hallway. Another well-wisher, perhaps? Simon secretly hoped not. He wasn't prepared to go into a detailed explanation of exactly what he was waiting on. All he needed was that push, short and sweet; no big friendly conversation required.

The approaching figure was a little shadowy at a distance, but he did seem different from the rest of the jovial, glad-handed co-workers Simon had run into today. The body language was clearly more subdued. Head hanging low, the individual trudged forward without energy and seemingly without purpose. Simon wasn't quite sure at first, but the face did look familiar. Smith, James Smith maybe — no, Chris Smith — yes, that was it! Still he checked the name tag on the man's vest to make sure.

Simon was more than a little pleased with himself, but puzzled all the same. Each recovered memory, each new detail brought him one step closer to understanding this place and what he might need to do next. This Chris Smith, however, was very different from the man Simon remembered. The vest, the downtrodden manner didn't really fit with someone who held an important position with the TAA.

Chris Smith soon cleared up any confusion.

Smith had arrived in front of Simon and the office door. He raised his head and stared blankly at Simon, not so much looking at him as looking through him at something, at anything, in the far off distance.

"I'm checking all the computer connections on this floor," Smith said softly. "You're not having any problems with your computer, are you?"

Simon paused to collect his thoughts and then answered carefully, "I don't think I'm having any problems. How about I check things out myself? I'll call you if I run into anything." It was clear things had changed significantly for Chris Smith.

Smith nodded, turned away slowly, and then shuffled on down the hall. Truthfully, Simon was glad to see him go.

There was still the matter of that office door. Simon again faced his nemesis. He reached towards the knob. He had received his push alright. It may have been a little stranger than he expected, but it was a push nonetheless. He opened the door and walked bravely into the office.

Chris Smith was left to continue his slow, melancholy journey through the hallways and cubicles of the trade association. He stopped many times, repeating the same question each time: "I'm checking all the computer connections on this floor. Are you having any trouble with your computer?"

Most of the time, people replied very quickly with a "no" and then went back to what they were doing. On the rare occasion someone actually agreed to have him check the computer, there was no friendly conversation at all, no jokes to kill the time while the diagnostic work ran its course — only an uneasy silence. Smith could feel that silence bearing down on him like a crushing weight, and he was quick to notice that his co-worker made every effort to avoid eye contact. It was almost a relief for both parties when Smith had finally completed the work and moved on.

Yes, things had definitely changed for Chris Smith. Not so long ago, he had been the top security analyst in the organization. Now, he was a simple I.T. technician. It was clearly not the type of career trajectory anyone would logically plan for. The move had happened without warning and without explanation, although Smith thought he knew why. He often wondered, during those long quiet walks down the halls, would he have done things differently back then if he had known this might happen. Somehow he could never quite bring himself to answer that one, and it didn't make a difference now anyway.

Today was just like all the other days since the job change. The former analyst was alone in the crowd, a man without status — a man who had been demoted but not fired. He was a rare case indeed, and his co-workers all avoided him like he had the black plague. People feared him. They didn't know what he had done. They just assumed it must have been bad, and they didn't want any part of it. Smith knew that, understood it perhaps. That didn't make it hurt any less or keep it from killing him on the inside just a little bit more each day.

And the walking really didn't help.

Smith stopped cold in the middle of the hallway, sweating now, his heart beating faster, wondering just how much more of this he could take. He would walk right out of this place if he could, but he had a family to support, and that made all the difference in the world. It was hopeless; he knew it. He was trapped here by his commitments. He drew in a deep breath slowly, painfully, a terrible conflict raging inside which threatened to poison his very soul. Deep down, Smith was learning to hate the TAA. Some days, on the really bad days, he also had to fight off feelings of resentment towards the people he cared about the most. Today was unfortunately one of those days.

Others simply walked by and around Chris Smith much like party guests casually avoiding a heavy piece of furniture misplaced in the middle of the floor. They had places to go; their lives would go on as normal today, tomorrow, and every day after that. The man in the middle of the hallway, whose life was now anything but normal, was simply invisible to them. Smith knew it all too well.

Perhaps the stark reality of this fact snapped him out of the trance. Perhaps it was the realization that he did love his family with all his heart and would do anything in the world for them, even suffer through yet another day here. Either way, Smith pulled himself back together and set off once again on his lonely trek through the halls of the Trade Association of the Americas.

James Wilson was quite the contrast with the former analyst as he made his own journey down those same hallways. The VP of Security walked with pride, with purpose. He was on his way to the CEO's office. He knew he was important here; his job gave him that internal sense of value as a human being. Along the way, he passed right by the downtrodden Smith.

Wilson noticed of course, but was careful not to make direct eye contact with his one-time subordinate. He recalled that Smith had been a very capable analyst. Too bad Smith had not been smart enough to go along with the plan. Just too damn bad! Wilson shook his head and sighed. For a moment, he felt genuine remorse, but it passed quickly. He had just reached the office of the CEO, and there was important business to take care of.

The VP of Security practically burst into Daniel Garcia's office, so impatient that he didn't even consider knocking first. Normally this would have been treated as a most serious breach of professional etiquette. Under the circumstances, however, Daniel Garcia had expected as much. The CEO was in fact somewhat amused by the near total exasperation of his executive team member.

"I know you spoke to Simon Anderson," Wilson said breathlessly. "I heard it from Mary. How did it go?"

"It went very well," Garcia replied. He nearly chuckled at first, but then took a more analytical tone.

"After spending some time with Mr. Anderson, I'm not totally convinced he isn't a basket case. James, your initial assessment may have been correct. The horrors of the bombing and its aftermath have definitely played havoc in the man's head. You can see it in his eyes."

The CEO cleared his throat. "All that being said," he continued, "there are clearly some very big positives here. For one, the guy physically looks great. The female demographic is really going to fall for his handsome face on camera. Also, the pain so obvious in his eyes can really work to our advantage. It makes him seem more genuine, more sympathetic. "

Daniel Garcia paused. He recalled what else he had seen in Simon's eyes besides that pain — an intensity which simmered so uneasily just below the surface, an intensity some might choose to describe as half-crazed. The thought of it still unnerved the chief executive just a little. It was something that could make things unpredictable and potentially very dangerous.

Wilson was all too quick to pick up on any sign of uneasiness on the part of his superior. It only served to reinforce his own lingering doubts about bringing someone so potentially "damaged" into this project, in any capacity at all.

"Do you think we can really trust this guy? How will we control him?"

The questions were not well received. The blood rushed to the CEO's face, and the mood in the office suddenly turned very dark. Daniel Garcia had absolutely no intention of allowing this conversation to get off track.

"I can control Simon Anderson," he replied firmly. "The man has a family. He will play along with us, or he won't play at all!"

That was it. James Wilson was smart enough to recognize when to drop something.

"Okay, I see you have it all under control. What do you need me to do?"

"Nothing really," Garcia answered casually. "The interviews are all set up. The first one is tomorrow in fact." The color in his face was quickly returning to normal. He liked it very much when subordinates recognized that he was in complete control of things.

"It won't take long before Simon's handsome, sympathetic face will be all over the media, saying exactly what we want him to say. I expect that Mr. Anderson will play his role perfectly: the hero tortured by the memories of a tragedy. It will make great television."

The CEO relaxed back into the comfort of his plush chair and smiled with confidence.

The VP of Security smiled as well, really more to hide what he was thinking rather than to signify agreement. He wasn't quite as confident about things as his boss.

Chapter 11

Simon tried to settle into his office, but that was proving increasingly difficult.

There were no nightmarish visions or even disconcerting memories, at least not yet; he was honestly thankful for the temporary reprieve. Still there wasn't any semblance of comfort or familiarity here either. Not that he really expected his office to feel like home, but the whole place seemed rather sterile, as if it had been wiped clean from top to bottom. Hell, the desk chair wasn't even comfortable. He felt like an absolute stranger in his own office.

There was one silver lining in all this, Simon thought. Maybe it was a good thing he didn't feel comfortable here. Maybe that meant he wasn't really back in the fold; he wasn't in the clutches of the TAA just yet. Maybe that meant he still had a choice. It was a longshot to be sure, but it was all he had right now. It gave him hope. Simon took another long look around the blank walls and smiled — precisely because this place didn't seem anything at all like home.

Nonetheless, there was much to do. Simon needed to find out as much as he could about his past activities at the TAA.

First, there was the office. His memories weren't exactly clear on the subject, namely whether he had purposely kept his office this sparse or whether someone had actually cleaned it out while he had been away. Simon suspected the latter. If he was right about that, however, there might not be anything left to help him. On the outside chance the cleaners had missed something, he turned to his computer. Apparently he had not been very creative with his password so it only took a few tries, with some very simple number patterns, before he got in.

Simon dived right into his e-mails. There were plenty of them too, mostly about non-descript topics from equally non-descript people. It was noteworthy that there were exactly zero e-mails from the CEO. Based on the friendly greeting he had received earlier, Simon might have expected to find something from Daniel Garcia.

No dice.

Clearly there had been meetings too, several meetings about the trade conference in fact. Simon wasn't at all surprised that there were no e-mails about the trade conference either.

The final place to look then was the deleted e-mail folder, the last refuge of discarded messages before they disappeared forever into the dark depths of cyberspace. Maybe, just maybe, the cleaners had forgotten to empty it. Simon peered cautiously into that folder. Sure enough it wasn't empty; the janitor had been either too lazy or too clueless to dump the last electronic wastebasket. Either way, Simon eagerly scanned down the list until at last he found what he had been looking for. It was an e-mail titled "Trade Conference", and it had been sent by the CEO.

"I am very pleased that you decided to accept this assignment," the message opened. "Assignments like this don't come along very often. They are inherently very risky. However, for those who are bold enough to grab opportunity with both hands and to do what it takes, these assignments can greatly advance your career."

"The European Union clings to an outdated sense of freedom and national borders which don't fit into the new world economy. They will be stubborn in the upcoming trade conference, but you must be more stubborn. You must make them see our point of view. You must make them understand that their best hope, their only hope, is to align with us."

"We will take a hard stance in negotiations with the EU, and we must be prepared to use any leverage necessary to get what we want out of this conference. Simon, I have every confidence in your ability to execute the plan we discussed in the time frame required. Your family and the entire Trade Association of the Americas will be very proud of you once these negotiations are successfully concluded."

The e-mail was signed: "Respectfully, Daniel Garcia."

The message was formal, yet with a personal touch, and it had clearly been meant to inspire Simon. There were no other e-mails, no other clues, nothing else at all. Simon was confused. Many thoughts, many questions were running through his head all at the same time. So there had been some sort of plan. He realized that now. They had discussed the plan, most likely in the CEO's office. Maybe that's what all the flashbacks were about. At least something was beginning to make sense.

The only problem was Simon didn't remember anything else about that plan. And just exactly what was the time frame required, he wondered. Simon took a deep breath and ran the fingers of his left hand forcefully through his thick hair. His head was beginning to hurt.

The rest of the day passed slowly, painfully, and with no great revelations. Simon's head continued to hurt. Additional well-wishers popped into the office from time to time, but they didn't stay long. Simon was thankful for that; he wanted to be alone. It showed on his face too. Maybe it was the forced smile when guests entered.

Or the short, halting answers to any questions.

Or the stern, penetrating look in the eyes.

Regardless, the intruders seemed to get the message in due course and scurried back out of the office.

The hour hit five o'clock at long last, and Simon joined the relative anonymity of the crowd streaming out of the headquarters of the TAA. As soon as he hit the open air of the parking lot, Simon found that his head suddenly stopped hurting. The slight breeze and the late afternoon sun on his face were refreshing. He breathed in and then exhaled slowly. Despite the rumble of cars starting up and pulling out of their spaces, a quiet calm settled over his entire body. He was oddly at peace with the world again; he was free from the grip of the TAA — at least until tomorrow morning.

Simon's first day back at the office had been eventful, and downright disturbing. It was true he had discovered some things about his past with the trade association, but there were still way too many questions. Standing alone and somewhat dumbstruck in the middle of a parking lot wasn't going to answer those questions. Simon opened his car door and climbed into the seat before his head started to hurt again. Only a few moments later, he was speeding down the highway towards home and family.

It was late in the afternoon yet still very pleasant. Simon cruised down the road with the windows down, enjoying some of the very same freedom he had initially felt during the morning drive. At the time, he had been blissfully ignorant of what being back at the office really meant. He knew better now. Nonetheless, Simon tried very hard to lose himself in the rippling breeze and the quiet hum of the tires riding on the pavement. He tried very hard to act as if he didn't have a care in the world.

But there was no such luck. Not today. Something from Daniel Garcia's e-mail was stuck in his head like one of those annoying songs that played over and over again.

"… in the time frame required," Simon muttered to himself.

What did that really mean, he wondered, and why couldn't he get it out of his mind? How much time was required? Would there be enough time? No! Somehow, he didn't quite know how, but the little voice in his head kept saying there wouldn't be enough time.

"Not enough time. Not enough time," the voice repeated. "No, not yet...." Simon clutched the steering wheel tightly, his knuckles turning white.

"Not enough time. Not yet."

Simon released one hand from the wheel and wiped the sweat from his brow. He was trying desperately to focus on the road and the ride home.

Holly Anderson looked up at the clock. She expected Simon home any minute now. Surely, the TAA wouldn't require him to work late on his very first day back. Surely not!

Then again, she didn't know exactly what to expect, and she was none too happy about that. She huffed and puffed, a few ringlets of curly hair bouncing with every heavy breath. Holly tried to tidy up, but it didn't help very much. Every time she picked something up, she had to fight off the irresistible urge to throw it against the wall. It wasn't easy. Finally, after giving serious consideration to the pros of working out anger by breaking things versus the cons of having to pick up the pieces afterwards, she just gave up and plopped down on the couch.

The only thing left to do, Holly realized, was to wait — and fume.

The minutes passed slowly; they seemed like hours. The house was completely silent, almost painfully so. Suzy was next door with the babysitter, and Holly was all alone. The patience she had only grudgingly accepted was now being sorely tested. At long last, however, that fragile sliver of tolerance was finally rewarded. She heard the sound of a car pulling into the driveway.

Simon hit the brakes hard. The car lurched to a sudden halt just in time to avoid bumping into the closed garage door. It wasn't exactly the prettiest job of parking, but he was home, and he was happy about that. In truth, relieved may actually have been a better description. Simon relaxed his death grip on the steering wheel, allowing the blood and the color to rush back into his fingers. He exhaled slowly and turned off the engine.

Everything was a bit hazy for Simon. The little voice in his head was still echoing the same words he had been hearing all through the ride home, just not quite as loudly as before. The words had been hammered into his memory by now. Even so, they were words he didn't fully comprehend. He climbed out of the car and walked unsteadily towards the front door, moving along more by instinct rather than conscious thought. He didn't have to open the door. Holly took care of that.

"I see you finally made it home," Holly said coolly.

"Yes, I guess I did," Simon replied as he stepped gingerly through the doorway. There was a strong sense of relief in the tone of his voice. Holly didn't pick up on that or simply chose to ignore it if she did.

"This was only your first day back," she continued without missing a beat. "What do you think you're doing working a full day? It's too much too soon. Don't you realize that you have a family at home who needs you?"

Simon understood full well how much his family needed him. Of all the convoluted thoughts and emotions floating around in his head right now, that was the one thing which was pretty clear to him. He didn't feel he needed to be reminded of it either. He wished Holly could understand just how much he was really prepared to sacrifice for his family.

"Well?" Holly crossed her arms and tapped her foot slowly but impatiently. She was waiting for some sort of answer, any answer, even though she wasn't quite sure what kind of answer she was really looking for.

In all his previous experiences, Simon had never been one to mindlessly rush into the fray without first understanding the lay of the land. He now applied that training, that tactical patience, to the current situation, prudently holding back an answer until he could choose the words carefully. Maybe this wasn't exactly a pitched battle, at least not yet, but Simon knew it all could change rather quickly if he blurted out the wrong thing. Words could cut just as deeply as swords.

Holly stood in the foyer waiting. Simon looked deeply into her eyes, the most beautiful brown eyes he had ever seen. It wasn't burning or even smoldering anger that he saw. It was more a curious combination of fear and sadness, a look of uncomfortable resignation. It was the look of someone struggling to deal with real or impending loss. Holly sighed and glanced down at her feet.

"What does the TAA have you doing now that is so important they can't wait for you to slowly work back to a normal schedule?"

"What's so important," she added softly, "that they have to take you away from me again so soon?" Her voice trailed away to a faint whisper. Her eyes remained fixed in a downward, fitful gaze which seemed to wander back and forth from her shoes to nothing in particular on the floor.

Simon didn't answer. He simply reached forward and wrapped his arms around Holly. She didn't pull away, but she didn't really reciprocate the hug either. Her arms hung limp at her side, and she didn't bother to look up. Seemingly intent on avoiding Simon's eyes, she raised her face only enough to reposition her forehead more comfortably on his shoulder.

Still, her husband was undeterred and firmly, but very gently, renewed the embrace. He held Holly in close, not so much to control her as to remind her that he was still there. They stood that way, together, not a word spoken, not a sound, save the soft rhythm of breathing in and breathing out. The silence was punctuated only by an occasional sob which Holly very quickly choked out.

Simon leaned in and whispered into Holly's ear. "Honey, don't worry, I'm here to take care of you and Suzy," He leaned back but kept his arms around his wife.

"It was just the first day," he continued softly, calmly. "It took some time to get re-acquainted with everything. The only assignment they've given me is to do some interviews about the aftermath of the bombing. Nothing else of consequence so far."

Speaking in a strictly matter of fact manner, Simon was very much trying to hide how he really felt about things. After the flashbacks and other nightmares he had experienced earlier today, he wasn't so sure he could make it through a full televised interview without having some sort of meltdown.

Bits and pieces of memories were indeed falling into place, yet the puzzle was far from complete. In truth, even what Simon had figured out up to now wasn't exactly comforting. Deep down, maybe he didn't want to find out anything more. Maybe it would be better for his family if he just didn't know. Maybe wasn't an option for Simon though. He had to know, and he had to know sooner rather than later — because he had to know what to do next. Surely, Simon considered for the moment, he couldn't tell Holly all of that.

"Believe me, I'm not back into the grind at the TAA. I honestly don't know if I will ever be back into that grind again." He paused to collect his thoughts.

"There's still a lot to figure out," Simon said carefully, "but I know my family comes first now."

He tried to sound re-assuring while at the same time battling self-doubt and everything else going on in his head. He knew it was important to stress family commitment, but it was also important not to say too much. It didn't seem, however, that Holly was going to be convinced so easily. She said nothing, and her face remained buried in Simon's shoulder.

Holly was dealing with her own issues. She heard Simon's words, but they were only words, so much noise really. She wasn't ready to believe them or anything else just yet. She knew her husband had to go back to work. She accepted it and hated it all the same. Work had consumed him once before, and she wondered if it would take him away from their family once again. Simon was a different man since the bombing. Holly knew that or at least she thought she knew that. He was more caring, stronger yet more gentle, a much better lover. But now that he was actually back in the office of the TAA....

The anger continued to build in the pit of Holly's stomach. She wasn't even sure exactly who or what she was angry at. She just didn't know what was going to happen next. Would Simon turn out to be the man, the husband, the father she had always hoped he could be? Or would he go back to being the self-centered son of a bitch who chased every promotion at the office and didn't give a damn about his family. Part of her wanted to wrap her arms around Simon and smother him with kisses. Part of her wanted to haul off and deck him. It was a real struggle to determine which part would win out. Holly couldn't bring herself to return her husband's embrace. Not yet. Her arms fidgeted, but they stayed firmly down at her side.

Simon took in a long deep breath, savoring the scent of Holly's perfume for a few seconds more. He relaxed his arms and slowly, regretfully, backed away from his wife.

"What's for supper? I'm absolutely starving," Simon said casually. He had decided it was best to try changing subjects. That, plus he really was hungry.

"Baked chicken," Holly replied in an equally nonchalant manner. She turned and headed towards the kitchen without saying another word.

Simon shook his head and smiled. Changing subjects probably wasn't going to help, he concluded. At least he might get dinner out of the deal. That was worth something. He followed Holly towards the smell of food.

Dinner was filling but otherwise uneventful. Suzy had returned home from the babysitter's house. She chattered incessantly, full of a child's boundless energy and oblivious to any tension or problems around her. Simon and Holly couldn't say the same.

In fact they didn't say much at all, at least not to each other. Mother and father dutifully answered every question from their child with a smile because that's what parents are supposed to do. There wasn't much else other than those smiles. No one wanted to talk about work. No one wanted to talk about how the day had gone. No one, except for Suzy that is, wanted to talk about anything at all. Simon didn't know exactly what to say, and Holly wasn't really sure she wanted to hear anything he did say. So the child talked, and the rest of the Anderson family simply ate dinner.

The chill between Simon and Holly didn't end after the dinner dishes were cleared. It followed them up the stairs as they tucked Suzy in for the night. It followed them into their own bedroom where they faced each other across the broad expanse of an empty king-sized mattress, pondering as two armies might the veritable no-man's land in between the trenches. They exchanged polite pleasantries and evening wishes, nothing more. Simon and Holly each crawled into opposite sides of the bed, careful to maintain their distance from one another. The lights were turned off. Neither party made a move in the darkness to cross over no-man's land and close the gap between them. Husband and wife drifted off to a restless, lonely sleep.

Holly tossed and turned on her side of the bed though she was still careful not to roll over into Simon. Part of her did want to feel the closeness of touching her husband, but the other part, the more dominant part right now, just couldn't get past the anger and the deep fear of losing him to his job once again. So for the time being, she did her best to stay put. And she did her best to sleep alone. She dozed only in short bursts, nodding off into the blackness for a few moments before waking up suddenly, eyes wide open, to stare at the glowing numbers on the alarm clock.

It was during one of those brief periods of sleep that Holly suddenly felt the kick in the small of her back. In her befuddled state, she might have mistaken it for the unpleasant side effects of a bad dream, but the pain was all too real. She opened her eyes and groaned softly. Holly knew what this was. It was real-life, a real-life nightmare. As she slid quickly out of bed and out of harm's way, she looked back over at her husband who was by now thrashing about the mattress. Holly shook her head. Simon's nightmares were back, and with a vengeance this time.

Simon dug his fingers deeply into the bed and twisted the sheets into knots. Sweating, with muscles straining, his face contorted into a painful, twisted caricature of itself. Visions flashed in his head. Images of light and dark interspersed with words which he couldn't quite make out. He was sitting at the trade conference once again. That much was clear. Everyone was still alive. The bomb had not exploded yet. Simon could see himself looking over at something in the corner of the conference room and then back at his watch. He didn't understand exactly why, but it played over and over and over again in his head.

"Not enough time," Simon mumbled. "Not enough time."

His eyes were still closed; the nightmare refused to let him go. Suddenly there was another image, a sharp burst of light which caught the corner of his eye and then quickly covered his entire field of vision. It was all so real, so bright that it was blinding, so powerful that it seemed to consume everything in its path.

He screamed, "No, not yet!"

And then total darkness, the deepest and most suffocating black of night. Absolute silence too, not even the sound of breathing. Simon jolted upright in bed and forced his eyes to open at last. He wasn't at the conference anymore. He was in his own bedroom now, at least that's where he seemed to be. It was still dark, and he was having difficulty seeing anything at all. He reached out for something or someone. He didn't want to be alone.

"Holly! Holly, honey, are you there?"

Simon patted the side of the bed where he thought his wife should be. Finding only an empty mattress, he groped around in the darkness. His eyes were still having difficulty adjusting so he moved along almost totally blind. The light he had seen in his nightmare had been shockingly realistic and so terrible in its fury that it was still affecting his sight. Simon breathed in deep and exhaled slowly, trying hard to bring everything into focus.

It didn't work. He was starting to worry now.

The room was still all black and all quiet, and Simon was struggling at the moment to distinguish between what was real and what was not, to know where the nightmare ended and the real world began.

"Holly, where are you?"

Again, there was a sudden light which drew Simon's attention away from the darkness. Only this time it was much smaller and less threatening. It was a tiny orb that grew slowly, rising like the sun on the dawn to a hopeful new day. Simon smiled as the room gradually came into view. He finally heard his wife's voice. Holly had turned on the light on the nightstand. She spoke reassuringly.

"I'm here, honey. I'm right here."

Holly wrapped her arms around her husband without hesitation this time. She held him close. She held him tight. She held him like she wanted to hold him forever. At least for the moment, Holly had come to terms with the conflict that had thrown her head and her heart into chaos. She couldn't go on worrying that Simon might be taken away from her again somewhere down the road. She knew she couldn't control the future. Simon needed her right here, right now. That had to be enough.

Relaxing her grip only slightly, Holly pulled back so she could look directly into Simon's eyes. She brought one hand up to Simon's face and stroked it gently.

"Don't worry honey. I'll always be here," Holly said softly. She meant every word.

His vision clear by now, Simon looked deeply into Holly's eyes. They were still the most beautiful eyes he had ever seen.

"I know that, and believe me, I'll always be here for you," Simon replied firmly. He meant every word as well.

Holly believed him. There was a definite sincerity, a real glow in Simon's eyes that she had only noticed since the bombing. If one's eyes were truly the window to the soul, then she clearly liked what she saw. It made her feel safe. It made her want to believe, to trust once again. She smiled and wiped a tear from the corner of her eye.

Simon leaned forward and kissed his wife with a tenderness which seemed meant to last for a lifetime. Holly felt the soft lips, the controlled but undeniable passion. She felt the heat. Her heart raced. Holly backed away from the kiss for only a moment. She slowly lifted her nightgown over her head and then, with a wicked smile on her face, quickly tossed it aside. There was a fiery glow, a definite hunger in her eyes now. She moved back towards her husband and eagerly rejoined the kiss.

Chapter 12

Simon woke up the next morning with a smile on his face. The evening before had started off fairly rough, and he really wasn't well rested even now. Otherwise, it had been one hell of a night. It almost made him forget about the interviews scheduled for today.

Almost.

He looked over at Holly still tucked snugly under the covers and smiled once again. He leaned down, nudged his wife gently, and then blew into her ear. Holly began to stir.

"Stop that," she giggled. "It tickles." She reached up and wrapped her arms around Simon's neck. She didn't really want him to stop.

Simon didn't want to stop either. He loved looking into those bright eyes, touching the soft curls of her hair, caressing every inch of her body. It truly would be a pleasure to do this all day, he thought. But then he noticed the time on the clock.

"Damnit!" Simon shook his head. He knew he couldn't be late for the first interview.

Holly noted the time as well. She feigned a pout of displeasure for a few seconds, but then she smiled and released her husband.

"I'll make you a quick breakfast before you have to leave."

As she climbed out of bed, Holly took time to stretch out every muscle in her lean, nude figure. She cupped her breasts with one arm and looked back at Simon seductively.

"I just want you to know what you're coming back to tonight."

Shaking his head once again, Simon regretfully decided it was time to get dressed.

Simon was still smiling as he sped down the highway towards the headquarters of the TAA. Breakfast had been quick but still much more enjoyable than dinner last night. Holly had been especially pleasant this time, supportive even. Somehow she didn't seem to blame him anymore for going to work and doing what he had to do. Her send-off, the kiss good-bye, had clearly been intended to give Simon something to think about all day. It was the coup de grace of the subtle negotiation initiated when she had taken her time climbing out of bed this morning. If there had been any doubt left, the kiss sealed the deal.

Holly wanted to make absolutely sure her husband had every reason to come home this evening. Simon thought that it just might work too.

Nevertheless, there were interviews to do. The headquarters building was rapidly coming into view through the windshield now. Simon knew that it was time to start focusing and steeling his resolve to make it through whatever they might throw at him. It was important to hold it all together during the interview. It was important to keep the CEO happy right now in order to protect his family. It was important to buy time to fully understand what he needed to do here.

But first, he had to get to the office on time. As he hit the exit ramp, Simon hardly slowed down. Everything from that point on happened nearly as fast. It was all somewhat of a blur really: parking the car, moving through security at the entrance to TAA headquarters, riding the elevator up to the executive floor. Mary was waiting for him when the elevator doors opened.

"I'm glad to see you," Mary said with obvious relief in her voice. "You really had me worried there for a minute."

"Even so," she continued, "you're really cutting things close now. The network anchor will be meeting with you in your office in exactly 15 minutes. You better hurry so you can settle into your office and get ready. Believe me; it's very important that everyone on TV sees you back to work at the TAA."

Simon simply nodded and headed straight for his office.

Mary called after him, "By the way, you look great!" She smiled.

Turning around only briefly, Simon didn't say a word, but he did politely return the smile.

After a brisk walk through endless hallways and tightly packed office cubicles, Simon finally reached his destination. It was fortunate he was in such good shape; otherwise he might have been out of breath. And that wouldn't have gone over very well on network television. Simon understood the game he was being forced to play here. He didn't like it, but he understood it. Before attempting to settle into the uncomfortable chair behind his desk, he looked around the office once again. The surrounding four walls, almost totally empty, were still as sterile and coolly professional as they had been yesterday.

"Definitely, nothing like home," Simon chuckled to himself. He knew deep down that this was probably a good thing too.

There was a sharp knock at the door. Before Simon had a chance to acknowledge the knock, Chris Smith poked his head into the office.

Smith was very straightforward. "I'm here to check out the connections so the TV crew can stream their video live though our system. It's a pretty important interview, I guess."

Simon nodded in agreement and motioned for the I.T. technician to come in.

"You're cutting it pretty close," Smith continued, looking up at the clock on the wall.

"But don't worry. I'll get this done pretty fast, almost as fast as the time it takes for an embarrassing picture to circle the globe on the internet." It was meant to be a joke of course, the type of simple banter and camaraderie which colleagues typically enjoy in the workplace. It was exactly the type of camaraderie Chris Smith had been missing since his demotion a few weeks ago.

There was a moment of silence as the words sank in, but then Simon laughed. "That must be very fast then," he replied with a smile. "I know I wish I could take back some of the pictures of my college years that are still floating around in cyberspace."

The I.T. technician couldn't believe what he had just heard.

It had only been a few words to be sure. Still, it meant everything to a man who had lost so much. It was a simple recognition, an act of kindness, a small measure of respect — all wrapped up together into something sweet which could feed the soul of a starving, desperate man.

In the space of a few seconds, the I.T. technician ran through every one of his emotions. He kept working to hide any visible signs of his reaction to Simon's response.

"There. That does it. You're all ready to go now." The I.T. technician stood up, backing away from the wall connection as he did.

"Thank you very much." Simon smiled again.

Chris Smith just nodded. He turned around and then headed out of the office. He was beaming. It was going to be a good day after all. He was sure of it now.

Barely two minutes later, at exactly the top of the hour, there was another knock on the office door. Simon knew who it was.

"Come in," he called out. He felt strong. He felt ready.

A striking woman, tall and blonde and smartly dressed, immediately opened the door and strode briskly into Simon's office. The visitor projected a cool, confident aura that was matched perfectly by the intensity of her eyes, a pale shade of blue which appeared to have been cut directly from Artic ice. Her platinum hair had a silky glow to it and cascaded effortlessly down to the shoulders with not a single strand out of place. The hair itself framed a face that was soft, unblemished, and accented by full lips covered in shimmering red lipstick. She stood there perched comfortably atop a pair of long, lean legs which seemed to go on forever, from the bottom of her short hemline all the way down to stiletto high-heeled shoes.

At first she didn't say a word; she seemed more intent on exploring unfamiliar surroundings. As she moved about the office studying the walls and anything else which caught her fancy, her form-fitting dress highlighted an abundance of everything any man, or a major television network, could ever desire in a woman. Simon couldn't help but notice. He swallowed hard, and a disconcerting thought crossed his mind. Maybe he wasn't quite as ready for this as he had supposed.

"Not much for office decorations, are you?" The woman turned and looked directly at Simon. The pale blue eyes narrowed as she carefully scrutinized the body of the man directly in front of her. "This office is crap for a background, not nearly enough touches of home."

"But you on the other hand," she said with a sly grin, "you'll do just fine."

Never breaking eye contact, the woman sauntered around to the back of the desk and placed her hands lightly on Simon's shoulders.

"I can see that you work out," she continued, "and with very fine results I might add. That's good, very good. It will translate well on camera." She leaned in close and began rubbing Simon's back and shoulders more aggressively. Her warm sweet breath tickled his earlobe.

Simon didn't speak. For the moment, he was unable to pull any words out of the mess of conflicting, yet still pleasurable emotions playing around in his head. The woman smiled. She was used to having this kind of effect on men, and she really liked the power it gave her. It was power she could turn on and turn off whenever she pleased. And it was just about time to turn it off, she decided.

Quite suddenly, she stopped rubbing Simon's shoulders.

"Oh, you must forgive me," the woman said ever so politely. "I haven't even introduced myself yet!" She circled back around to the front of the desk and extended her hand to Simon. "I'm Sally Knox, the Evening News Anchor on Channel 7." She smiled again.

Simon accepted her outstretched hand, still without saying a word. He had experienced a temptress once before, ages ago in a very different time and a very different place. It was never safe to trust one, especially when she was smiling. In truth, he was relieved that Ms. Knox had stopped rubbing his back; it would be easier to resist her charms.

"Hi, I'm Simon Anderson," Simon replied cautiously. "It's a pleasure to meet you." He politely shook the TV anchor's hand, much like any formal greeting to a standard business meeting.

Perhaps sensing a certain amount of unease, Sally Knox was by now also more businesslike. She was always keen to use whatever worked, whatever got her what she wanted.

"Don't worry, Mr. Anderson," she said reassuringly, "this is all going to go very smoothly. It'll take a while for my crew to get up here and set up. In the meantime, you and I can get better acquainted. You can tell me about your family and your time here at the TAA."

This served to relax Simon only a little. He did talk about his family but stayed away from any mention of the trade association. Though dutifully pretending to be interested in the activities of the Anderson family, Sally Knox kept pushing for more details about the

TAA, and Simon was just as persistent in avoiding the subject. This wasn't going to be easy, the anchor admitted to herself, although she kept smiling politely anyway.

There was a knock once again on the office door; it was the TV crew. They were lugging cameras, sound equipment, the works. This time, it was Ms. Knox's turn to feel relieved.

"Oh, my crew is here now," she blurted out. "Looks like it's time to get ready."

The TV anchor pulled her golden hair tightly back into a bun and retrieved a pair of glasses from her purse. She noticed the surprised look on Simon's face.

"You know what," she laughed and pointed to the glasses, "these aren't even real glasses, just a set of clear plastic lens in a fancy frame! The network believes the glasses give me more credibility with the audience."

Sally Knox leaned in toward Simon and placed her hand on his arm. "And according to some of my fans," she said with a mischievous grin and a definite twinkle in her eye, "they make me look smart and sexy all at the same time."

Daniel Garcia paced back and forth in his office. As each minute passed, as each footstep pounded the carpet, the chief executive was getting more and more impatient for the interview to start. He was gambling quite a bit on the success of this interview, an interview with a man who might have a scrambled brain, a man he wasn't even sure he could trust. Garcia shook his head and looked up at the clock on the wall once more. There were still several minutes to go; he knew the network had to keep to its schedule.

Watching the clock or pacing wasn't going to make the time pass any faster, he finally decided. With a heavy sigh, he sat down at his computer and opened his e-mail directory.

The CEO casually panned down the list of e-mails. He wasn't worried about prioritizing. This wasn't part of the normal business routine. Simply trying to kill some time, he opened anything interesting enough to catch his eye.

The first e-mail was from Sam Johnson, V.P. of Entertainment. Normally Daniel Garcia considered Mr. Johnson to be a bit of a buffoon, but the title of the e-mail suggested good news — and Garcia was clearly in the mood for some good news. The blockbuster action movie about George Washington was still raking in the cash at the box office. Recasting the Lafayette character with a handsome Latin American actor had paid off; no one seemed to notice or care that the real Lafayette had been French. The CEO recalled an old adage that the winners got to write the history. He wasn't quite sure he agreed with that. It seemed to him that the people with the most money actually got to write, or more precisely, re-write the history. No matter. He had been right about the re-casting, and he really enjoyed being right.

The next e-mail was from the Trustees of the new Julliard School of Science and Technology. It began by expressing appreciation for the speech Garcia had made at the school's opening ceremony. The CEO also noted in the text of the message that enrollment was ahead of the original first-year projection, certainly a positive development. At the bottom of the e-mail was the school's new motto: "Achievement in science and technology, music for the soul of the next generation." Daniel Garcia smiled as he considered those words. The motto was forward thinking with just enough homage to the past. He thought it was absolutely perfect.

Focusing only on good or interesting news was proving to be a most pleasant diversion for the chief executive. It was a lot more fun than dealing in the real world with real problems. Daniel Garcia understood this was only temporary of course. He exhaled slowly and stiffened in his chair. He knew how to deal with real problems. He knew how to shoulder the burden of leadership. Sometimes he just wished the shareholders of the TAA could fully appreciate all that he did for them. In the meantime, there was still more time to kill, and there were still a few more pleasant looking e-mails to kill it with.

The Gettysburg Containment Center, according to the next message, was now fully operational and accepting patients impacted by the flu pandemic. Again, that was good news. The Senior V.P. of Healthcare and Human Resources had personally managed the project. The CEO was especially pleased with hands-on work from a trusted subordinate. He liked the way the Senior V.P. got things done: on-time and with very little fanfare. The new containment center had been justified as a necessary expansion of the organization's reach in order to better maintain health, stability, and security. Garcia knew that was especially critical in times like these. Still, the less said about the center, the better, he thought.

The roll on good news had to come to an end sometime, and so it did with an e-mail from James Wilson. Shifting uncomfortably in his chair, Daniel Garcia read the text carefully. There were pockets of dissent in the northern suburbs of the city according to the head of security, people who still did not buy into the official story about European involvement in the bombing. Garcia knew this was something which had to be dealt with quickly, and he prided himself on being decisive. He quickly replied to the e-mail, thanking Wilson for being proactive.

Without further hesitation, he also typed a message to the Senior V.P. of Healthcare and Human Resources alerting him to potential flu outbreaks in the northern suburbs.

Daniel Garcia closed down his e-mail log and backed away from his desk. He looked up at the clock on the office wall. It was just about time for the interview to begin.

The final seconds ticked down in Simon's office. Sally Knox noted the red light on the camera and picked up the countdown signal from her producer. She swiveled around in her chair until she was looking directly into the camera.

In a most formal and official sounding voice, she addressed the audience, "Welcome to all our viewers across the Trade Association of the Americas. This is Sally Knox, and I have the honor of bringing you a very special interview today."

"Now, many of you may not immediately recognize the face or the name of our guest," the TV anchor continued, "but I feel sure many of you know what he did on that dark day a few weeks ago when European terrorists bombed our trade conference. Out of the destruction, out of the chaos, a hero emerged. Here was a man who stood tall amid the rubble and took charge during the rescue operation despite his own life-threatening injuries. Many lives were saved that day because of his quick thinking. Yes, many of you know the story. Now I want to introduce you to the man who lived that story."

"His name is Simon Anderson, an executive with the TAA, and he's here with us today."

Sally Knox turned towards Simon in lockstep with the camera as it slowly panned over to include both interviewer and interviewee in the picture. The TV anchor, her eyes glowing with an intensity which easily pierced the fake glasses, was cool and businesslike in front of the camera; it was everything she lived for. Simon, for his part, was anything but comfortable. He sat rather stiffly in his chair, eyeing the camera with some suspicion. He had faced down danger before. He had faced fierce warriors, men of flesh and blood. But the camera didn't flinch. It didn't blink. It didn't show fear.

The TV anchor continued without missing a beat. "Simon, I know this may be difficult, but please tell us about the day of the bombing. Can you start at the beginning and set the stage for us? I know it was a busy day of tough negotiations at the trade conference, and I know nothing could have prepared you for what would happen next."

Her voice was polished and sounded sincere. Simon didn't know if it was an act or not, but she was certainly good at it if it was. Either way, he couldn't show any fear in front of her or that camera. He straightened himself in the chair.

"Well, Sally, it had been a tough day of negotiations with our counterparts at the European Union," Simon replied calmly. "I can see their faces even now."

The trouble was that was literally true. Simon could see their faces clearly. He had not been able to recall their faces before. They had been something lost in the blackness and the haze. Now they were suddenly here, Francois and the rest, so close he could almost touch them. It was all so real, so damn disturbing. Blinking his eyes forcefully, he tried to clear away the images, as best he could, and refocus. He took in a quick breath and let it slowly escape.

"I can see their faces even now," Simon repeated. "Sure they could be difficult sometimes. But they were good people, people who made a strong case for what they believed in."

He looked down and away from the camera. "People who didn't deserve to die," he said quietly. His voice trailed off with the last word.

Sally waited patiently over the next few seconds. A little hesitation was not a problem for her. She didn't want to ruin great television by butting in with a few ill-chosen words. Yes, she was far too good for that.

"It was right before the break," Simon began again. Sally smiled discretely and settled back into her chair.

"I was watching the time," he continued, "to make sure I hit the break just right." And there he just stopped.

Dead silence. The TV anchor was a little surprised but didn't show it.

A jumble of images flashed quickly in Simon's mind, a powerful vision which suddenly transported him back in time to that horrible day in the last agonizing moments before the explosion. It was a nightmare from the past playing out in his head while the rest of his body was wide awake in the here and now. Simon knew what was coming next but just couldn't do anything to stop it. He was powerless.

There he was once more at the conference table with all the delegates, looking first at his watch and then over at something in the corner of the room. It played over and over again, each time ending with a blast of blinding white light. His body shuddered, and his face tightened. He grimaced at the pain from injuries that simply weren't there, a pain though which felt all too real.

It was time now, Sally knew from her professional experience, to take firm control over the interview. She leaned forward, placing her hand gently on Simon's sleeve, and looked directly into his eyes.

"I know this is very tough for you," she said softly. "It would be tough for anyone who has experienced the horrors you have. Now take your time and please try to tell us what happened. We're all here for you."

The words from the TV anchor were heard at first as only the faintest of whispers in Simon's muddled head. They seemed to come from beyond the horrible white light and were distinctly different from everything else that was part of the nightmare. Simon seized on the words, not so much for their meaning, but for the very sounds which might serve as a beacon he could follow all the way back to the real world. The sounds became gradually louder. The bright light dimmed. The pain disappeared. An office desk came into view, and it was from there that Simon looked back into the pale blue eyes of Sally Knox.

"I think I'm okay now," Simon replied. He wiped some beads of sweat from his forehead. Knox smiled once again, although this time with much less self-assurance.

"The bomb exploded," he continued in a carefully measured tone. "I don't remember much about that except for a flash of white light followed by total darkness. When I woke up, I don't know how much later, all was quiet, and there was very little light to speak of. Smoke and debris filled the air. I stood up slowly. It took a couple of minutes to steady myself and get rid of the ringing in my ears. I couldn't see anybody else at first. Then, from somewhere off in the distance, I started to hear moans and what seemed like a weak cry for help. I knew there were other survivors out there now so I followed the sound as best I could."

"Body parts were here and there, everywhere. God help me, but I recognized some of them by the wrist watches still on the arms. There was so much blood and wreckage on the floor it was difficult to move around without falling. I honestly wanted to stop and throw up. It was absolutely horrible … all those poor, innocent people."

Simon cringed as haunting images of torn bodies, of blood and gore, flashed in front of his eyes yet again. He paused to choke back the emotion of it all. Still, a tear welled up in the corner of one eye; he quickly wiped it away.

"But I knew I needed to keep going, and I finally reached the sound of the moaning." The words were precise, the voice clear but now a little unsteady. "It was one of the EU delegates. He was trapped under a pile of debris, and his right leg had been completely blown off from the knee down. It was the strangest thing. I'm not sure he even realized his leg was gone yet. He was so busy trying to dig himself out of that pile, just trying to stay alive."

Simon sniffed and wiped away another tear. The camera zoomed in close to capture every detail.

"In any case, I helped dig the guy out and then applied a tourniquet to stop the bleeding. About that time, the rescue team reached the conference room so I began helping them remove the rest of the injured. And that's about it!" Simon seemed anxious to be finished with telling the story.

"Mr. Anderson, like most true heroes," Sally Knox interjected, "I believe you are much too humble. I think you are leaving some significant details out of the story — such as your own serious head injuries. According to the doctors I spoke with, you shouldn't even have been able to stand up with your injuries, let alone actively assist with the rescue and evacuation of the wounded. And in truth, I also believe it is

a significant understatement to describe what you did that day as simply
assisting with the rescue."

The TV anchor looked directly into the camera and personally
addressed her audience. "No, what Simon Anderson did on that horrible
day was absolutely heroic! This man, a dedicated employee of the TAA,
stood tall amid the wreckage and the carnage and calmly directed
rescuers to the most critically wounded. He refused medical attention
for himself until all those who could still be saved had been rescued. Like
a sea captain of old, he was the last man out."

At the end of her little speech, Sally Knox paused for effect
while still maintaining direct eye contact with the camera. This was a
moment of professional triumph for her, and she wanted to enjoy every
minute of it. Her face had a certain glow to it now. She was very pleased
with her own words and surely would have smiled had she not been so
constrained by professional decorum. With some reluctance then, she
turned slowly back around to face her subject. The camera was smooth
in following her every movement.

"Simon, there are many people out there who owe you their very
lives! How does that make you feel?"

"I'm happy I could save some," Simon answered quietly, "but
there were way too many I couldn't save."

"I understand you may feel that way. However, I want to put all
of this in perspective for you. I want you to see just how many people
you did save, how many families you spared from the loss of their loved
ones."

Knox reached into a folder and produced a computer print-out
which she then waved in front of the camera.

"What I have here is the entry log for the conference building. It
lists the names of everyone who entered the building on the day of the
trade conference. It lists the names of all those conference delegates. I've
highlighted on this print-out the names of the people who survived the

bombing, many of them due solely to your efforts. Mr. Anderson, I want you to read the names of all those you saved." She pushed the entry log across the desk towards Simon.

Simon casually scanned down the print-out. He didn't understand how this was going to make him feel any better. There were indeed several names highlighted on the list, but there were many more that were not. And each of those names not highlighted represented someone he couldn't save, someone who had died needlessly. He noticed Francois's name on the print-out; it wasn't highlighted.

"Please read the names," the TV anchor requested. She seemed anxious but was trying very hard to be polite

Simon didn't answer. There was an awkward silence in front of the camera.

"Please read the names," Sally Knox repeated with greater urgency in her voice. "These are real people. I think our audience needs to hear who they are!" She sensed ratings gold here and didn't have time to be patient. It was, after all, live TV.

Shaking his head, Simon sighed and looked back down at the log. He began to read the highlighted names as instructed, "Sam Hill, survivor, Melinda Green, survivor…."

It only took a short time to complete the list. Simon knew it wouldn't take long, and it didn't make him feel better or somehow more heroic. It only served to satisfy Sally Knox and her bosses at the network. To them, both the living and the dead were little more than pawns in a high-stakes ratings game that played itself out every night during the primetime hours. Mix in a few of the former with a lot of the latter and win the time slot. Simon understood how the game was played and hated the very thought of it.

Muscles tightened. Anger churned in the pit of his stomach. Perhaps it affected his judgment, perhaps not. Either way, Simon decided to give the people behind the camera more of what he knew they wanted. He started to read out the names on the log that were not highlighted.

"Michelle Hinault, dead, David Smith, dead…." This took quite a bit longer than the previous list. His voice seemed to rise with each name read, the anger and frustration boiling over. The TV anchor relaxed back into her chair. She had no intentions of stopping him.

"… Francois Darlan, dead!" Simon breathed in deep and forcefully exhaled. That was the last of the names from the day of the bombing.

Still, the log continued. There were more names listed, names of people who had entered the building in the two days prior to the trade conference. He could have ignored the remaining names, probably should have. After all, he had fulfilled his requirements for the interview and given the boys behind the camera their money's worth. Yet something, reflexes perhaps, or something much more complicated, kept him reading down the list.

Simon had no idea what he was looking for until he finally saw it hidden among the jumble of letters on the computer print-out. It was his name — there in black and white, there for all to see.

If Sally Knox were a real investigative reporter, she might have asked why Simon had been in the conference building the night before the bombing. She wasn't going to do that, however, and risk messing up her made-for-TV spectacle. Simon knew that, yet it did absolutely nothing to quell the sick feeling growing in the pit of his stomach.

It only got worse as the cameras kept rolling. Simon's heart began to race, and beads of sweat formed on his forehead. He searched through his memories. He had to know about the night before the bombing even if the TV anchor wasn't particularly interested. He just had to know.

It was hard at first. There were secrets, deep and dark, which the subconscious didn't want to give up easily. It was hard, but Simon was strong, determined.

It started first as a trickle, but then it all came rushing back, hard and fast, with all the power and deadly force of raging flood waters. Random images crashed through Simon's head, disappeared briefly beneath the waves, and then resurfaced in some sort of sequence. It made order out of chaos, and a story began to emerge out of images, visions, and conversations that had once been totally disconnected. The story made sense, perfectly horrible sense, and now Simon knew everything whether he liked it or not.

More than a minute had passed, barely long enough for all that had transpired in Simon's head but an absolute eternity in TV time. There were no words spoken, no action, save the uncomfortable movements of a tortured soul in full view of a silent, unflinching camera. Sally Knox appreciated Simon's troubled state at first. She thought it made for more compelling television. Still, TV anchors were not known for their infinite patience, and Knox was no exception. It was live TV after all.

"Mr. Anderson?" The interruption did not immediately produce the desired result. There was silence still.

"Mr. Anderson," Sally Knox repeated in a more forceful voice. "Are you okay?" She couldn't let this go on any longer.

"Mr. Anderson, you need to tell us what's going on. You need to tell us how you're feeling right now." She waited then to see what might happen next. If there was any chance of a big emotional finale to this interview, Sally Knox intended to get it.

Simon didn't say a word. He looked up slowly, painfully. His eyes were red and wet with tears. But there was not despair in those eyes, only frustration and a terrible rage that he struggled mightily to contain.

"I pray for the continued recovery of all the survivors," he responded finally. "I weep for the dead. They must not be forgotten!" Simon looked straight into the camera without blinking, without fear.

Sally Knox had done many interviews over the years. She thought she had seen it all. She thought she could handle it all. She looked deep into Simon's eyes. She now realized just how wrong she had been.

"And they will never be forgotten," the TV anchor added nervously. With the first spoken word, the camera quickly swiveled over to focus on her face. She glanced back over at Simon who was still staring straight ahead.

"This is Sally Knox signing off for Channel 7 News!" She gave the cut signal to the camera crew.

"Thanks for the interview," Knox said quietly. "I hope things work out for you, Mr. Anderson." She wasn't sure that Simon had heard anything she said, and right now she didn't care. She quickly gathered up her materials and scurried out of the office, followed soon by her camera crew.

Simon didn't hear the door close nor take note of the abrupt departure of his guests. He was absorbed in his own thoughts. The whole tragic story played out in his head once more from start to finish. It was painful, but it got the point across just in case there had ever been any doubt.

The visions in his head were gone now, but what remained was guilt, sadness, and rage all stirred together into a terribly volatile mix. Simon stood up straight and slammed his fist down on the desk several times. He didn't feel any real pain no matter how much he may have wanted to. He could do no more. Slowly and reluctantly, he slid back into his chair; he began to sob uncontrollably. This was an entirely new feeling for Simon. He had been in battle many times before, yet had never shed tears for fallen comrades. Those warriors, brave and true, had known the risks before ever setting foot on the field. The bombing had killed people who weren't warriors or soldiers or anything at all. They had never known about the risks, and that made all the difference in the world.

Daniel Garcia clicked off the video screen in his office. He was satisfied, not entirely happy, but satisfied still. He had watched the whole interview. As a network production, the interview had been a little uneven and almost entirely unpredictable. Nonetheless, that raw, unscripted quality also made it very entertaining television. Sally Knox had looked as cool and sexy as ever, he thought. The rating numbers wouldn't be out for some time, but Garcia expected them to be good. Clearly, high viewership would keep the horrors of the bombing in front of the general populace during this critical juncture in the retaliation operation. That was good. He also thought Simon Anderson had made a compelling character for the TV audience: handsome, brave, tragically tortured by memories of the bombing.

The conclusion of the interview, however, gave the CEO reason to pause. He did like that Simon had closed with the statement about needing to remember the victims. With a little work by the TAA spin-masters, this could be built into a genuine rallying cry for revenge. The part of the interview where Simon appeared to have zoned out, on the other hand, was altogether a different matter. Watching Simon stare directly into the camera, no blinking, no emotion, but intense, scary intense: that had been truly disturbing. Daniel Garcia had seen that look in Simon's eyes before, and he didn't like it at all. He wasn't quite sure what the TV audience might think. He also knew James Wilson would renew his objections over using a potentially unstable employee as the operation's inspirational front man.

The security chief, Garcia mused, was paid to worry about stuff like that, just as it was the CEO's job to make all the big decisions. And Daniel Garcia never second-guessed one of his own decisions. He knew how to adjust to changing conditions when necessary and would deal with Simon Anderson if the time came. Still, he prided himself on sticking to the basic game plan when others might panic. That's exactly why he was the CEO — and everyone else was not.

The interview had accomplished most of his goals, Daniel Garcia finally decided. He settled back into his chair and smiled.

"Mary," he called out, "please go and give Simon a message from me. Thank him for handling such a difficult interview and tell him to take the rest of the day off with my compliments!"

The executive assistant responded cheerfully and headed off to Simon's office.

By the time Mary arrived, Simon had managed to pull himself back together. Tearful eyes dried. Desk straightened back up. Rage contained. He acknowledged the CEO's gratitude and even managed a weak smile. The executive assistant didn't stay long. She seemed to sense that Simon wanted to be alone. It was true of course. Simon had other things on his mind.

Knowing the whole ugly truth about the bombing was one thing. Doing anything about it was quite another.

The office was quiet, maybe too quiet, as Simon considered his options. Not that many immediately came to mind. He sat at his desk for some time deep in thought, staring grimly ahead at something out there just beyond his sight, something that pulled him, called to him. It was far off in the distance, past the office doors and building walls, something in a dark, forbidding place which he had only seen from the outside. Simon blinked and raised his eyes. He knew what was there, and he knew now he had to get inside that dark place. If it wasn't exactly the answer, at least it was a starting point.

It was time, Simon had finally decided, to go see an old history teacher.

Chapter 13

The sun was high in the sky when Simon left the headquarters of the TAA. It was warm at mid-day, and he wiped a small bead of sweat from his brow as he hurried towards the parking lot.

Leaving work so early was an unusual sensation, to be sure. Then again, Simon supposed, after the interview this morning, nothing about this place could ever be considered usual again. He climbed into the car and forced the key into the ignition with some urgency. The engine started on the first turn, roaring to life due in large part to the extra heavy foot on the gas. Simon was ready. There was someplace to go, someone to see, and both were about as far away from the gleaming headquarters of the trade association as one could possibly imagine.

Simon hit the highway at full speed and simply drove. He drove without enjoying the sunlight and the clear blue sky above. He drove without any thoughts or real feelings at all. He knew exactly where he was going. Beyond that, nothing else was important right now. Simon had no earthly idea what awaited him at his destination. It was a risk he accepted, and he wasn't going to waste time pondering the unknown. Everything would work out, he decided, one way or another when he got there.

The tires riding on smooth pavement made a steady hum. Miles passed by quickly, and there was a decided change in the scenery just outside the car windows. Leafy suburbs transitioned smoothly to a shiny, modern city center which in turn gave way to something older and more run-down, something which seemed mostly forgotten. Trees and perfectly-manicured boulevards had disappeared by now, replaced by long lines of dingy grey buildings one right after another. Simon knew he was getting close. Just over the horizon, black smoke drifted at the mercy of the prevailing winds. As the car crested the hill, the smoke became thicker, and he could just make out the bridge up ahead.

Simon pulled up and stopped before reaching the TAA security guards at the entrance to the bridge. He climbed out of the car and looked around. He very quickly noticed the sky was not nearly as sunny or blue. Even the air, so tainted by the acrid smell of smoldering fires, seemed more difficult to breathe.

The approaches to the bridge were lined with still more charmless buildings, most of them medium-sized apartment towers, all of them a bit worse for the wear. The whole area was covered in the various incarnations of concrete, functional though absolutely dreary, with hardly a speck of green foliage or any other decorative touches. It was not at all nice and homey by the standards of modern suburbia. But it was housing nonetheless, and it did provide some minimum level of shelter and safety.

What lay at the far end of that bridge, however, appeared to be something else entirely. Heavy smoke and haze obscured much from view. Buildings that could be seen at all were scarred and crumbling. In other places, large piles of brick and broken concrete marked where a home or office or store once stood. Random gunshots could be heard echoing off in the distance. Every now and then, one of those shots was followed by the faint sound of screams.

The place seemed more dangerous, more terrible now that Simon saw it in the full light of day. It was all very much like some hellish landscape from an old war movie, a town caught between two great and powerful armies who didn't give a damn about the civilians caught in the middle. The people living on this side of the bridge, Simon thought for sure, most likely looked over at that dark place beyond and comforted themselves with the very real notion that things could be a whole lot worse.

There was a small but steady stream of traffic on the bridge, and it was going in both directions surprisingly enough. It seemed like a rather routine process, very much different from the flood of refugees one might naturally expect from the looks of the place. Dingy, haggard looking people dutifully checked in or out as appropriate with the guards at the entrance. They were a wretched lot, but they shuffled past without any apparent panic or anger. They moved along numbly, aimlessly, as a people beaten down time and again until they had finally resigned themselves to accept their station in life.

It was going to be pretty much impossible to just blend in with the crowd. Simon knew that. It didn't make a difference. He had to get across to that dark place. He had to find the history teacher. For good measure though, he took off his coat and tie before walking towards the bridge. The guards watched with quiet amusement as Simon approached.

"Hey fella," one of the guards called out. "Are you lost? We don't see many people dressed like you trying to cross this here bridge. Even without the coat and tie, we don't think you're going to fit in over there!" The guards chuckled and poked at each other in jest.

It must be pretty boring duty out here, Simon thought to himself. The men who pulled this detail probably weren't at the top of their class either. He decided to play along.

"I'm not lost, guys," Simon answered with a sly smile. "I need to cross this bridge so I can judge the first fashion show they've ever had over there. You know, I have to pick the man and woman who wear their dirty rags with the most personal style. It's all the latest rage really."

Simon's answer wasn't exactly what the guards had expected. For a moment, they didn't say anything at all. They just stood there, trading puzzled looks back and forth.

"Oh, I get it," one of them finally replied. "You're making a joke, aren't you? I don't know if we like smartasses around here." Their manner was suddenly much more threatening.

"Yes, you're right fellas. I am just making a joke. No harm intended," Simon said politely. The guards seemed to loosen up a bit, but they still eyed him cautiously.

"Actually, I'm here on TAA business." Simon flashed his identification quickly. He wanted the guards to see that it was official while not paying too much attention to his name.

"The CEO wants me to investigate potential subversive elements in this part of town," Simon continued, his voice confident, authoritative. "It's all very hush, hush, you know." The guards had that puzzled look on their faces once again, this time tinged with just a little bit of fear. They moved aside quietly and allowed Simon to pass.

"Thank you, gentlemen," Simon acknowledged as he walked onto the bridge. After a few steps, he turned around and spoke pointedly to the guards, "Oh, by the way, you didn't see me here today. Understand?" The men from TAA Security simply nodded.

The guards watched as Simon continued across the bridge directly into the heart of the dark unknown. They shrugged their shoulders. "It's his funeral," one of them said calmly.

By the time he reached the other side, Simon was beginning to have his own doubts. The choking smoke was even worse here, and the buildings, at least the ones that still stood, didn't look any better up close.

No more than a few feet ahead, there was the burned out hulk of a car. The driver's side door was filled with bullet holes. It sat silent in the middle of the road, still pointed towards the bridge and the way out. A failed escape maybe? Simon wondered. Whoever had been in the car most likely never made it to the bridge. He was pretty sure of that. The rusting wreck was a tragic monument of sorts, the perfect picture of death frozen in time and metal. Simon looked away from the car and started down the road through the rubble and the haze. With each and every step, he wondered to himself just how he was going to locate the history teacher in this god-forsaken place. It wasn't as if he had a map, and by the looks of everything around here, he wasn't so sure a map would do any good.

Asking for directions wasn't much of an option either. The few people Simon had seen so far averted their eyes and scurried away as soon as he got close. There was, however, a group of 3 men who didn't seem to be afraid of his presence, and they were walking towards him now. They were dressed very differently from the rest: clean, bright-colored shirts and pants instead of rags. They also walked with a definite swagger. Simon figured out pretty quickly this wasn't exactly a welcoming committee.

"Look at what we have here," one of the men yelled out while the other two snorted in amusement. "Mister, we know you're not from around here because we know everybody who is anybody around here, and we don't know you!"

The man doing the talking grinned, flashing a shiny gold tooth in the process. He pointed directly at Simon. His comrades, the muscle of the group, took up position on either side.

Simon could tell these thugs were more experienced and more dangerous than the young punks at the park. He looked them over carefully and didn't say anything at first.

"What's the matter? Cat got your tongue," the pointing man asked, no longer smiling. He didn't wait long before answering his own question. "The way I see it, you must be lost or really stupid. No-one who doesn't belong here will even get close enough to this place to get lost. So that must mean you're stupid. You're stupid because you came here to horn in on our business. You're stupid because you came here alone and without any protection."

Simon didn't respond right away. He breathed in deep and exhaled slowly, calmly. His muscles tightened. He could feel the blood coursing through his veins, the rage building in the very depths of his soul. Simon had very quickly decided on a plan of action. There was absolutely no way these 3 men, or however many more there might be, were going to stand in the way of finding what he sought here. If he had to fight his way through them, so be it.

"I don't need any protection," Simon replied with his own smile now. "I've got everything I need right here!"

Before the man with the gold tooth could say another word, Simon had smashed a powerful right hand into his face, sending him sprawling backwards. The gold tooth fell to the street a full three feet away from where its owner landed.

The two remaining thugs, stunned by the power and savagery of the blow to their comrade, did nothing for a precious few seconds. Simon made the most of that hesitation. Knotting his hands together into a mighty club, he swung forcefully to his left, catching one of the big men square on the jaw. The man staggered. Simon quickly followed up with a right hook that dropped him cold.

By this time, the last thug standing had been roused to action. He came up from behind and wrapped his massive arms around Simon in a crushing bear hug. The man was not only big but awesomely powerful, like some terrible giant of old. The pressure was overwhelming. Simon could feel his ribs giving way and all the air being squeezed out of his lungs. He couldn't breathe. He struggled mightily but couldn't break the hold.

The seconds passed by slowly, painfully. His strength faltered, and darkness threatened to close over his field of vision.

For a brief moment then, Simon was transported back across the ages to an ancient battlefield where he stood alongside proud, brave men with bronze shields and bright red tunics. He saw the fire in their eyes. He knew in his heart he could never let such men down, not then, not now — not ever.

As the forces of time and nature pulled him all the way back to the present, Simon felt something rising up from the deep, dark place where rage mixes freely with honor and courage, the place where a warrior goes in his most desperate hour. It flowed out of that secret place in every drop of blood through every artery to every aching muscle.

A great renewed strength it was, the very power of the Gods.

The crushing pressure on his ribs continued without respite. It was now or never. Simon suddenly threw his head backward with terrific force, striking his assailant just under the chin. The thick legs of the giant buckled. With a burst of strength and a blood-curdling war cry, Simon broke the hold at last. He turned without hesitation and struck the giant two more powerful blows to the head, first with one fist and then the other. The man collapsed to the ground with a heavy thud.

The leader of the group remained down in the street spitting out blood, his initial bravado having gone the way of the shiny gold tooth. He looked with great surprise from one side to the other at each of his big men laid out on the deck like beaten prize fighters. He shook his head and then motioned back to other men who were rapidly approaching the scene. The reinforcements were carrying guns. They stopped at a respectful distance and pointed their weapons directly at the man who had just clobbered 3 of their friends.

Simon considered his options for a moment. His blood was up. His muscles were ready. He desperately wanted to push through this new obstacle. Still, naked fists and raw courage were no match for guns and bullets, and Simon knew that. He continued to stand his ground defiantly but was nonetheless careful to remain still in front of those gun barrels.

The leader struggled back to his feet. He did bend down, however, to pick up the gold tooth. "I don't know who the hell you are," he said calmly, "but you only get to surprise me once."

He spit out some more blood and started to laugh — a sick, menacing laugh filled with equal parts psychotic rage and a wicked streak of bravery backed up now by bullets. It went on for some time and echoed across the empty streets. The men holding the guns looked back and forth at each other and then began to laugh as well. They were holding all the cards; they could afford to laugh.

Simon wasn't laughing, and soon enough the bloodied leader wasn't laughing anymore either. He stepped forward with a renewed swagger and poked his finger sharply into Simon's chest.

"Boy," he said with a dreadful scowl, "I'm going to break you from sucking eggs!"

There was a brief moment of silence. Both Simon and the men with the guns were a little confused by the reference, but the sound of it was threatening enough to get the idea across. And the idea itself was anything but friendly. Guns had a funny way of doing that, Simon thought to himself; they sure took the friendliness right out of any social situation.

"When I finish with you," the man with the gold tooth continued, "you're not going to be able to surprise me or anybody else ever again!" He poked his finger into Simon's chest a second time to make the point. Simon managed, with great effort, to resist the urge to break off that finger.

The leader stepped back away from Simon and carefully examined the bloody gold tooth in his hand. He kept his eyes on Simon but spoke directly to the gunmen.

"Gentlemen, I want you to shoot this piece of shit full of holes, but I want you to do it slow like. I want one hole at a time, starting with each leg so he can't move. Then move to each arm. After that, start putting holes in the chest, and then finish with the big blast to the head."

"Okay, boss, whatever you want," the gunmen replied cheerfully as they began to chamber rounds in their weapons. Their boss simply smiled.

Over the next few seconds, time itself seemed to slow down right in front of Simon's eyes. Like some slow-motion special effect in a cheap action movie, the movements of the boss and his gun-toting henchmen inched forward with great precision, bit by bit, frame by frame. Small details were ever so clear. Simon could see the blood trickle out of the corner of the boss man's mouth as he smiled in anticipation of the impending execution. Simon's own heartbeat slowed, and he could feel every single beat throbbing in his ears.

It was a funny trick of the mind, the subconscious processing things much faster than anything could ever happen in the real world. Simon understood that, but it did give him just an instant to consider his options. He knew that he wasn't about to stand there and get shot to pieces. Dying outright in a heroic, but doomed, frontal assault would be preferable to that.

It was an easy decision. Simon took a step forward towards the gunmen.

Suddenly, there was the loud crack of gunshots ringing out from the left side of the street. Time, and everything else in this place, abruptly lurched back to normal speed.

The gunmen dropped their weapons, blood spurting from their hands. They grimaced in pain and squeezed their wounds tightly to stem the bleeding. They suddenly had no interest at all in shooting Simon. After shaking off his initial surprise, their boss did make a move for one of the guns on the ground, but he was quickly driven back by another perfect shot that blasted the weapon far out of reach.

The sound of gunfire died away slowly amid the empty streets and crumbling pillars of brick and mortar. All the members of the gang stayed still in their positions. Simon did as well. There was no way of knowing exactly what was going to happen next, and he didn't want to take any chances.

Discounting what was plainly obvious to the senses, everything else about those gunshots was a mystery. Who was the shooter? Why had this individual just saved Simon's life? In the smoky haze, it wasn't even clear exactly where the bullets had come from.

Everything had happened so fast up until now. Now, the pace of things was decidedly different. Now, the anxious seconds ticked by like hours. Simon strained to see until he could just make out two figures in mottled green fatigues approaching from his left. They were well-equipped and moved forward through the rubble with all the ease and cool precision of professional soldiers.

The distance closed quickly, and the two soldiers were soon face-to-face with Simon and his assailants. Both men were solidly built, clean-shaven with close cropped blond hair. One was quite a bit older than the other, yet they clearly shared certain facial features. A father and son, Simon guessed. Their fatigues were well-worn but had a distinct patch of red and white stripes surrounding a field of blue dotted with white stars.

Simon recognized the patch although he doubted his adversaries did. It brought back memories, memories of a different time and place. He had seen it many years ago on a nightmarish, shell-torn beach littered with the bodies of brave young men. He remembered other brave young men who finally made it off that bloody beach and moved forward to victory before everything had abruptly faded back into darkness. He wondered if these men wearing the patch were like those brave men of old.

The answer was swift. Simon was immediately relieved as the soldiers pointed their guns at the man with the gold tooth and the rest of his henchmen.

"Smiling Bob, we have to quit meeting like this," the older soldier said with a chuckle.

It was now clear that the soldiers knew the man with the gold tooth and the rest of his gang. It was also obvious by the sullen look on Smiling Bob's face that he didn't much like staring down the business end of an AK-47 assault weapon. For his part, Simon very much appreciated the sudden role reversal.

"You know I'm going to kill you one day," Smiling Bob replied, still trying to appear brave and menacing despite his huge disadvantage. He spit out some more blood for good effect. It was all for show of course, the absolute triumph of ego and insanity over brains and rational thought.

"Yeah, but today ain't that day," the old soldier added, somewhat amused by the bravado. "Now, Mr. Smiling Bob, take your thugs and your gold tooth and get the hell out of here before I suddenly start to lose my sense of humor!" He motioned with his weapon to push things along.

It took a minute or two for Smiling Bob to gather up his collection of muscle-bound thugs and wounded gunmen. He didn't dare try to pick up any of the weapons scattered on the ground this time. There were some lessons which even a man like Smiling Bob learned pretty quickly. Once all together, the gang limped away to nurse their wounds.

"We'll meet again," Smiling Bob yelled back, "and next time, things will be different!"

"Don't count on it," the old soldier replied tightly, by this time at the very end of his patience. He fired off another round in the general direction of Smiling Bob and his cohorts to make his point. The gang seemed to pretty well understand the basic concept of how to influence others with bullets. They were still limping, but they were now limping away a whole lot faster.

The old soldier turned and looked back at Simon. His chiseled features softened into a friendly smile.

"I guess it's time to make a few introductions," he said. "I'm Gunnery Sergeant Russell White, United States Marine Corps, and this is my son Nathan." The sergeant motioned towards the younger man who cheerfully acknowledged the greeting with a simple smile.

"I'm Simon Anderson, and I sure am glad to see you guys." Simon reached out to shake the sergeant's hand. "Semper Fi," he said nearly automatically. It was something said very naturally but without really thinking, and Simon regretted it almost immediately.

"I'm sorry, but I didn't think the Marine Corps existed anymore," Simon added after a short pause, this time with much less comfort in his manner. His words seemed to trail off to a quiet nothing. He was a little concerned that he might have inadvertently overstepped his bounds with a certain amount of assumed familiarity.

The sergeant was somewhat startled to hear those words right out of the blue and didn't respond right away.

"We don't exist … officially," he continued finally, "but you know what they say, once a Marine, always a Marine. We're still the few, the very few now, and the proud. Hell, Nathan here is an honorary Marine. I trained him myself!"

"Mind me asking, Mr. Anderson," the old Marine inquired warily, "was your father a Marine?" He looked Simon up and down, trying to get an accurate read on the strange young man who knew those sacred words.

"No, sir, he wasn't," Simon replied carefully. "I just happened to meet a few Marines in one of my previous experiences. They were tough men, sergeant, men who knew how to fight, men who knew how to have a good time."

It was Simon's turn now to study the expressions and body language of the old soldier. There was no smile, no signs of approval just yet. Simon threw out the only other thing he could think of right at the moment.

"I'm not nearly as young as you might think I am, sergeant."

Still nothing.

Sergeant White took in a deep breath and exhaled slowly. He wasn't so sure about that first answer. Besides, he still had a few more questions to ask.

"You know," he continued in a friendly but firm tone, "I did enjoy seeing you kick the crap out of Smiling Bob and his flunkies. I really did. That's mostly why we saved your ass."

"Still," the old soldier paused while Simon squirmed just a little, "I need to know who you're working for, and I need to understand exactly what the hell you're doing here." He wanted to be absolutely clear on this point. He didn't exactly point his weapon at Simon, but he did purposely move his finger over the trigger.

"I'm not working for anybody but myself," Simon replied in a clear, confident voice. He stood up straight and proud. "I'm here to see Arthur, the history teacher. The guy with the gold tooth, the one you call Smiling Bob, just happened to get in my way. I'm not afraid to go over or even through obstacles if I have to." He looked the sergeant straight in the eye.

That did it. Sergeant Russell White smiled and moved his finger away from the trigger.

"Outstanding answer, Mr. Anderson," the sergeant boomed. The old soldier was suddenly reminded of better times in years gone by, when the Marines were still the Marines, when everything was loud and proud. It brought a tear to his eye. He lowered his weapon and slapped Simon on the back with his free hand.

"Yes sir, I like the way you think, Mr. Anderson! Coming into this hell-hole alone and unarmed and then taking on a bunch of thugs because they're in your fucking way. Goddamnit, that's what a Marine would do! It warms the heart of an old warrior to see another young man with the right stuff."

Finally, there were no more guns pointed at him. Simon felt an obvious sense of relief.

But there was more — more than simple gratitude to men who had just saved his life. It was something very basic, primitive really, something dating back to the days when cavemen first shook hands to prove they weren't hiding any weapons and could be trusted. Mutual respect, some might have called it. Honor answering honor, others had more eloquently described it on later battlefields. Simon knew it well, and he felt it now. It was an odd kinship with the old soldier and his son, the bond between all fighting men no matter the generation, something only those who have seen blood and death can truly appreciate. Simon looked again into the eyes of Sergeant White and smiled himself. Yes, it was clear they understood each other very well.

"You're in luck, Mr. Anderson," the sergeant added. "We do know Arthur, and we can take you to him." He gestured to his son to gather up any usable weapons from the street first. The young man understood immediately and moved quickly.

"It's this way. Let's go." Sergeant White pointed off into the smoke and haze, ever deeper into the hellish place. Simon didn't hesitate. He followed the two Marines as they moved on down the street.

Hector Gonzalez had heard the gunshots outside the window of his 3rd floor apartment. It was a real window, a symbol of normalcy in a place that had long ago lost all sense of normal, and it was in perfect condition as well, no cracks or bullet holes or pieces of cardboard covering broken panes. The glass itself was a luxury in this part of town, not only a symbol of relative prosperity but a barrier of sorts between home inside and the misery of the world outside.

For sure, Gonzalez appreciated every aspect of that barrier. He could look through the glass at the outside world in comparative safety. See without being seen. Hear without being heard. Ignore what he wanted to ignore. Hector had watched part of the commotion down in the street through that very window. But that was as far as he went. He knew very well who Smiling Bob and his cohorts were. He didn't much like them, but he had to tolerate them in his line of work. Then again, this wasn't work right now, at least not from his perspective. If Smiling

Bob and his friends had picked a fight out in the street with the wrong guy, then that was their problem, not his.

There was a noise Hector suddenly heard coming from behind. He turned to find his young son bounding into the room. The child smiled at his father with all the innocence of those who are young enough to see only the beauty and promise in each and every day and none of the potential dangers. Hector looked into his son's eyes and thanked God for that bright light. Still, he knew it was a father's job to nurture it, to protect it, and that made him appreciate even more his barrier to the outside world.

"Daddy, come away from that window and play with me!" The child bubbled with excitement.

Hector smiled. "Of course son, I always have time to play with you." He glanced back at the window one last time before turning his full attention to the child. "There's nothing out there for me to worry about anyway."

Chapter 14

Simon and his armed escort continued down the street. No-one said anything. Simon figured there wasn't much to talk about in a place like this. Social conversation just didn't seem to fit in very well with guns and the parts of town where men had to carry them. Either that or the sergeant was simply a man of few words.

The group moved at a relaxed, almost leisurely pace, but there was definitely no mistaking it for a comfortable walk in the park. Not here. Smoke and haze obscured the blue sky above. Piles of rubble and debris were more numerous than standing buildings. And still, as far as Simon could tell, not a single working car among the rusting wrecks which intermittently lined the road. There was absolutely no charm to the place, Simon concluded grimly, and it obviously didn't get any better the further you went. He scanned back and forth between both sides of the street, wondering just how anyone could live, or more accurately, survive here.

As the distance passed by underfoot, Simon did begin to notice something distinctly different, something that stood out amongst the general misery of the place. There were a few people moving through the rubble or on the street. They still looked ragged, hungry, but they weren't running away in fear as Simon and the Marines approached. These wretched, hollow-eyed creatures somehow seemed to understand on a primal level who the good guys were. Simon could see it in their faces. He wasn't sure if any of them remembered the Marines and what the Corps had once stood for. Maybe they had just learned not to fear the guys who carried guns but didn't shoot at them. Simon was sure there were plenty of other guys who carried guns they did fear. These people, however, understood the distinction. A uniform, well-worn though it might be, was a symbol perhaps, of safety, of trust, and that just might make all the difference in the world.

The Marines stopped suddenly and pointed. "There," the sergeant said simply. "You'll find the teacher there."

There was a battered building just up ahead, one of the few among the piles of shattered bricks and stone that still had enough of a structure to rightfully be called a building. The sign at the top was worn but could clearly be read.

"Catholic Rescue Mission," Simon repeated the words under his breath. It was close to dinnertime, and the rescue mission was a real beehive of activity. People stood in line patiently waiting for soup and a small piece of bread. Others served the food or washed bowls as needed. Here and there, individuals entered and exited the building as they attended to other affairs. The place seemed to be a genuine going concern, the first real sign of life and normal routine Simon had encountered since crossing the bridge.

Simon had to walk past the soup line in order to get to the front door. His approach did not go unnoticed. The serving stopped. Everything stopped. No words, not a sound, not a gasp, only uncertain stares from the ragged people in line. Simon kept moving. He wasn't really surprised. His clothes weren't torn; he was well-fed: these were not common sights around here. And those individuals who did fit this mold were, based on the experience with Smiling Bob and his cohorts, the bad guys more often than not. Simon understood the cruel reality of this place. It made him uncomfortable and self-conscious all the same.

In fact, without the Marines currently at his side, Simon wondered if he otherwise would have been dealing with something much more serious than simple discomfort. He glanced back and forth between Sergeant White and his son, glad he didn't have to worry about that right now.

The old wooden door to the Catholic Rescue Mission was heavy and required some genuine effort to swing it open. Rusty hinges groaned painfully as Simon and the Marines passed through the entranceway. The air inside the building was stale and thick with a damp musty smell. It struck Simon's nose as equal parts old plaster walls, worn, soiled carpet, and stagnant water. The foul liquid collected in buckets placed here and there to apparently catch whatever leaked in from the roof. It was the undeniable smell of poverty and decay, and it clung to everything inside the door: walls, furniture, and people too.

Only, the people didn't seem to notice. While everyone else in the mission was oblivious to the odor, Simon discretely cleared his throat and tried to suck in only what he absolutely needed to keep the lungs working. He figured the smell was something an individual might get used to over time. Either that, or the residents here had simply decided a little mold and mildew was a small price to pay for 4 standing walls and a roof overhead.

Father Christopher was used to seeing all sorts of people, lost souls really, drift through the rescue mission. Some came for the more obvious reasons: food and shelter. Others came looking for just a little bit of normalcy, a little bit of what they had once known in a better time and a better place. All of them were ragged and worn down. They were his flock, nonetheless, and he took it as his sacred duty to minister to them, to give them hope in their darkest hours. And if there wasn't really hope in their current lives, at least he could offer them hope for the afterlife. For sure, the priest thought he had seen them all come and go over the years.

Then again, as he peered across the room to the bustling area near the entranceway, Father Christopher decided to re-consider that somewhat comforting thought. He had not quite seen anything like the well-dressed young man standing with Sergeant White and his son, at least not for many, many years, and never in a place like this. He approached the strange young man and his escorts, though he was as perplexed as everyone else about the appearance of the newcomer.

"Sergeant White and son, welcome as always!" Father Christopher reached forward and shook the old Marine's hand with genuine enthusiasm. He patted the son on the shoulder for good measure.

"And who do we have here with you today?" The priest was trying very hard to be pleasant and polite while struggling to contain his own burning curiosity. It wasn't working so well. He tried, without much success, to avoid staring at the newcomer's clothes.

Simon understood very clearly what was going on. Without waiting for his Marine escorts to make the introduction, he piped up, "Father, please let me introduce myself. My name is Simon Anderson, and I'm a friend of Arthur, the teacher." He smiled and extended his hand to the priest.

Father Christopher was momentarily speechless. He did not immediately accept Simon's hand. The Marines simply nodded in agreement. Sergeant White chuckled quietly.

There was an uncomfortable silence, only a few seconds maybe. It seemed much longer.

"Why yes, young man," the priest stammered finally. He grasped and shook the offered hand. "It's a pleasure to meet you, Mr. Anderson. Any friend of Arthur's is certainly welcome here."

Yes, that was certainly polite enough, Father Christopher thought to himself. He was guarded still and continued carefully, "And if I might ask, Mr. Anderson, how do you know Arthur?"

"We met in the park the other day," Simon immediately replied. "I was fortunate enough to be able to help out Arthur when he needed it. We talked for a bit, and he invited me to his history class."

Looking directly into the eyes of the priest, Simon paused and took in a deep breath of stale, damp air. Somewhat surprisingly, he managed to continue without coughing.

"Long story short; here I am."

"Yes, I see that you are." A smile, ever so slight, cracked the tense facade of Father Christopher. Arthur had told him about the brawl at the park and the young man who had saved his skin. If this was indeed the man, the priest considered quietly, he could truly be an interesting addition to the history class.

Sergeant White also knew about Arthur's experience in the park.

"Goddamnit, I knew there was something I liked about this guy," he interjected with a hearty laugh. The laughter stopped abruptly, however, as soon as he noticed the frown on Father Christopher's face.

"Sorry, Father," the old Marine added rather sheepishly, "I know I need to watch my language around here."

"But you have to understand," he continued, his voice again swelling with excitement, "we picked up Mr. Anderson here after he had just cleaned the clocks of Smiling Bob and his flunkies. He did it with his bare hands too, only needed our help when the bad guys pulled out guns. And now — and now we find out he's also the guy who saved Arthur. That's just goddamn outstanding!"

The Marine didn't bother looking at the priest this time. He knew what to do.

"Sorry, Father," he repeated quietly.

The language was colorful, at the very least, and the repeated apologies were downright futile. Nonetheless, the sergeant's enthusiastic re-telling of his story was actually making Father Christopher feel a little better about things. It all seemed to validate what the priest was thinking himself, that they just might be able to trust this Simon Anderson after all. Deep down in his gut, he hoped it was true. He prayed to God it was true.

"Well, I guess if Mr. Anderson came all this way on an invitation, it would be pretty rude if we didn't take him to see Arthur. Please follow me this way." The priest smiled and motioned towards the back of the mission. Simon nodded his acknowledgement and then followed his Marine escorts in the general direction indicated.

The mission building, it seemed to Simon, was a lot larger than it had originally appeared from the outside. The whole back section of the building was a veritable maze of dimly lit hallways spreading out in every direction like tunnels winding through an underground cavern. Simon hoped that Father Christopher knew where he was going. Sergeant White and his son, for their part, were much more confident.

Without hesitation then, the group advanced firmly down one of the long hallways. The dark corridor was empty, silent save for the sound of their heavy footsteps. Hidden little rooms were scattered here and there, tucked around corners or seemingly scraped out of otherwise blank walls. Simon dutifully followed the priest and the Marines as they worked their way through this labyrinth and moved deeper into the bowels of the mission, far away from the soup-line crowd at the front door, out of sight and hidden from prying eyes.

And yet there was no getting away from the damp musty smell no matter how far they went. Simon found he was actually getting used to that smell by now. Maybe he was beginning to understand how people really felt around this place. Some things just couldn't be changed, he surmised, so they weren't worth worrying about.

Sounds coming from one of those little rooms caught Simon's attention. Laughing, screaming, crying, everything all at once: it was the sound of children, loud and unmistakable. Simon had not seen any children since crossing over the bridge. That wasn't so much of a surprise though. Based on what he had already seen or run into outside of the mission walls, he figured it was a good idea to keep them hidden away here.

Maybe it was just plain curiosity, or a father's natural instinct, or a little bit of both, but Simon felt drawn to that sound. He stopped and peeked into the room. It was tiny, cramped, and filled nearly to overflowing with small children — short ones, tall ones, all skinny and dirty. They moved and played with great energy despite their physical condition, clearly frustrating a worn and haggard looking young woman attempting to be their caretaker. Simon was amused and saddened at the same time. He thought of his daughter Suzy. He saw her bright smile in some of their dirty faces. He saw the same childhood exuberance, the same innocence.

But there was one very big difference, and he understood it well. Suzy had all the family support and financial means to secure her future; these children most definitely did not. What would happen to them tomorrow was anyone's guess. Simon looked again at all the playful action going on in the here and now. He smiled, thankful these children were too young to understand all that.

Simon felt a hand on his shoulder. "Those are the lucky ones, you know," Father Christopher said quietly. "They've shown some interest in reading, and we're trying to teach them, to give them a real chance out there. No surprise, but your friend Arthur is our best reading teacher as well. He sure could use some help though."

The priest let out an audible sigh. He patted Simon on the shoulder and motioned that they needed to move along. Simon took one last glance back at the children and then rejoined the rest of the group.

They had not gone too much farther down the corridor when Simon heard more voices, clearly adult voices this time. Father Christopher smiled and pointed towards a non-descript wooden door set along a blank concrete wall. The group halted, and Sergeant White opened the door.

"The 13th amendment to the constitution was passed by the northern states during the civil war. It formally abolished slavery, but most people had considered slavery effectively dead since President Lincoln issued the Emancipation Proclamation after the battle … of Antietam."

His voice trailing off with the last words, Arthur looked up from the book at the sudden interruption of the door opening. It was difficult in the dim light to make out the shadowy figures entering the classroom. He could tell, however, that at least some of them were carrying guns. For an instant, a terrible thought raced through his head. Arthur knew visitors to the history class were a rarity, and these were definitely armed. Was this some sort of raid, by the TAA or the criminal element in the neighborhood, he wondered?

Arthur couldn't afford to take chances; he had to protect the book. It was the only one left as far he knew. He closed the book quickly, gently patted the well-worn cover, and then stuffed it down into his satchel.

The sound of footsteps drew still closer. In the space of these few anxious seconds, Arthur had quite prepared himself to flee with the book. Now he heard a familiar voice which just as quickly changed everything.

"Hello, Arthur. It's just me," Father Christopher called out. "I've brought some friends with me."

The old teacher squinted hard to see as the priest and the rest of the little group approached through the receding darkness and gloom. Simon stepped forward into the light and spoke up clearly.

"Hi, Arthur, it's me. I guess I decided to take you up on your invitation. I think it's time for me to sit in on your class and maybe learn something."

Arthur smiled and exhaled the final remnants of a very deep breath he had unconsciously been holding in. He immediately felt better, and it was more than just a breath of fresh air, more than just a genuine sigh of relief. It was so much more — so sudden, bone-jarring even, something boiling up from the pit of his stomach and spreading through every last fiber of his being.

Hope, faith, optimism: whatever one called it, it was truly a scarce commodity in these parts. It had been such a very long time; Arthur had almost forgotten the sensation. But now....

Now he felt it once more, and it felt so damn good. For sure, he knew this Simon Anderson as the man who had rescued him from a beating in the park and most likely saved his life in the process. But the teacher saw so much more than just a man who was good with his fists. He saw the burning intensity in the eyes, the look of a man who was here to do something important. Whatever that was, Arthur didn't really know, and it didn't matter right now. He saw something different, something very special in Simon Anderson. It was a skill all good teachers have, and on this particular day, it gave Arthur a tantalizing glimpse of a brighter tomorrow.

"Welcome, Mr. Anderson, welcome to our class," Arthur said in a voice tight with emotion. "Class, it gives me great pleasure to introduce you to Simon Anderson, a man I met in the park the other day, a man who seems to be quite a student of history himself."

There were no words of hearty welcome, only a quiet murmur among the other members of the class. Simon still stood, rather uncomfortably now, in the center of the light. Arthur was too absorbed in the excitement of the moment to notice. The teacher eagerly dug back into his satchel and retrieved the book. The title on the cover had faded through the years, but today, in Arthur's eager eyes, it seemed to stand out proudly as never before: *The Complete Book of United States History, 2nd edition*.

He opened the book and without looking up continued, "Simon, please find a place to sit down, and we'll let some of our other class members introduce themselves before we get started again!"

No-one jumped right up to take the teacher's offer. It was quiet still, punctuated by a cough here and there. Simon had not yet decided where to sit. There were many eyes looking at him, and they weren't exactly friendly. They weren't necessarily unfriendly either, really more like perplexed. But perplexed meant alert, Simon noticed, and this was distinctly different from the sunken, blank look in the eyes of the poor wretches he had seen sifting through the rubble outside. The awkward silence dragged on, however. Simon was beginning to wonder if he had made a mistake coming to this place.

And then someone broke the ice.

A young woman, her red hair pulled back tightly into a bun, spoke first. "Hi, I'm Jan Carson. I'm here with my son, Matt." She stood up and motioned towards a sullen teenager slumped in the chair beside her. The young man nodded half-heartedly without saying a word.

Carson sighed but then continued with some genuine pride in her voice, "I'm editor of the local newspaper around here!"

"Hah," another voice chimed in. "That's a real joke. You think that 2-page collection of nonsense you pass out is a real newspaper. Hell, most people around here wipe their ass with it!"

"Yes, but only after they read it first," Carson responded defiantly.

The brief exchange elicited quite a few chuckles. Simon caught himself to keep from laughing. He was positively sure that much of what was said was true. He was also somewhat pleased not to be the sole focus of attention for the time being. The general hubbub soon caused Arthur to look up from his book; his expression was stern. Without a word said, the class seemed to get the point pretty quickly. Just as things began to die down, however, someone else joined the discussion.

"Come on Bill, why don't you just leave her alone." The tone was gentle but firm.

The speaker, Simon observed, was a neatly dressed older man. He was a rather formal looking fellow for a place like this, Simon thought, most likely a professional man in another time and place. The clothes, for sure, were not nearly in as good a shape as Simon's; they couldn't possibly be. Not here. Still, he had the definite air of a man who cared very much about his appearance and tried hard to make the most of what he had to work with.

The older man stood up and brushed back his thinning hair. He spoke in a deliberate, carefully measured manner, "I think it's a very positive thing Jan is doing. It's only two pages of news. That may be true, but that's two more pages than anyone else is putting out right now. And she's making every effort to get the truth out, something that isn't very common these days. We just talked about freedom of the press, one of the constitutional amendments Arthur has been teaching us. Ms. Carson is the best example of freedom of the press I know of. In fact, she's probably the last real journalist anywhere around."

There was no laughter this time. Satisfied his point had been made, the man adjusted his collar, cleared his throat, and then sat back down.

"Thank you very much, Richard," Jan Carson added gratefully.

The one called Bill grumbled something under his breath. Simon could tell from the twisted expression on Bill's face that he wasn't very happy. Unlike his more clean-cut antagonist, Bill wore the ragged facial stubble of a man who cared little for shaving and even less for grooming a beard. He forced his palm roughly through the hair on his face, an absent-minded sort of motion which didn't do anything to immediately improve his appearance. The clothes were typical of most of the people Simon had seen around the rescue mission. They weren't quite rags, but they certainly had a few ventilation holes here and there. Bill fumed in his seat for a few seconds more. He then struggled to stand up, taking a few tries before he made it. When he finally did, he walked away from the group with a straight-legged limp. It was then that Simon realized Bill had an artificial leg.

"Oh don't worry, he'll come back. Always does." Simon looked towards the sound of the voice.

The owner of that voice smiled and winked back at Simon. His appearance was rather eye-catching even in less than ideal lighting: long black curly hair with a full beard and wearing a bright red flowered shirt. The eyes, colored pale blue and intense; Simon could swear he saw a twinkle in those eyes.

"Hi, my name is Alexander," the brightly colored man cheerfully introduced himself.

Though still quiet, the rest of the class members were by now just beginning to re-focus their attention on Simon. Simon noticed all those other eyes as well. He was once again alone in the spotlight and a bit uncomfortable about it.

Simon found himself curious to hear more from Alexander, but the brightly colored man didn't immediately oblige. He appeared distracted by a sudden burst of a nervous energy, shuffling his body back and forth in his chair to find some comfortable place where he could finally force himself to sit still. The struggle lasted for a few seconds until Alexander had achieved some sort of success, at least temporarily. He looked straight at Simon and continued in a somewhat grandiose fashion.

"They call me the man of a thousand ideas!"

"Yeah, and not a single one of them works," Bill called out sarcastically from the back of the room.

Alex, the Idea Man, was unperturbed. His face slowly spread into a broad grin which flashed lots of surprisingly white teeth through his thick beard. "All in good time, my man," he chuckled.

"All in good time."

Simon waited in his lonely spotlight. The rest of the class continued to stare, but they didn't seem inclined to say much beyond a few short, desultory greetings. Simon decided it was probably safe to sit down. Not quite ready to make any new friends though, he picked a chair which was in the circle yet not quite so close to any particular person.

Arthur looked up again from his book. "Good, I see you found a seat, Mr. Anderson." The teacher smiled; Simon nodded back.

There was a new and undeniable energy in the air now. Arthur could feel it, could almost taste it, and it excited him very much. It was quiet for the moment, the class waiting for what would happen next. Arthur looked around the room. He had not felt this way since he first began teaching all those years ago — back when he really believed he could make a difference. He lived, had really kept living through all the dark years, for an opportunity like this, and he knew he had to deliver.

"Ladies and gentlemen," Arthur said with a grin, "let's get started. We've been talking about emancipation of the slaves and the amendment to the constitution that finally made freedom of all men the law of the land. I want to continue in that same vein and tell you about one of the most famous speeches ever made in American history."

The teacher closed his book and strolled away from the podium. It wasn't enough to simply lecture from the book, he thought. No, not on a day like today. He wanted to reach out and grab each and every member of the class. He didn't want them to ever forget this. Arthur cleared his throat and began to speak.

"Four score and seven years ago...."

The words sounded familiar to Simon. He had heard them a very long time ago. He didn't know exactly where, but he had definitely heard them. And now here they were again, bubbling up from the deep recesses where that memory had been buried. Yes, he knew this speech. He knew it well in fact.

"... we take increased devotion to that cause for which they gave the last full measure of devotion — that we here highly resolve that these dead shall not have died in vain — that this nation under God, shall have a new birth of freedom — and that government of the people, by the people, for the people, shall not perish from the earth."

His voice swelling with emotion, Arthur finished the speech with a flourish. It had been a little over two minutes, just about the length of the original. He had recited it totally by memory too, and that made him very proud. He took a deep breath and scanned the room for reactions from the class. Then he waited.

Richard smiled to himself. He knew the speech as well. Older than most of the other people in the class, he had a little more of a background in old American history. Even so, it had been ages since he had heard or talked about this stuff. It just wasn't part of the life he had known before ending up in this place. Richard tried not to think too much about the past, about his old life. That was then, and this was now. Wishing wouldn't bring everything back either. He had figured out pretty quickly that he could feel sorry for himself and die here, or he could go on living.

And if he was going to go on living, he felt he had to make some sort of contribution. Maybe now was one of those times, he thought. Since the younger people in the class seemed to be struggling with this one, Richard decided to raise his hand and give the answer.

Someone beat him to it.

"That's the Gettysburg Address. President Lincoln gave this speech in November of 1863 at the dedication of the National Soldiers' Cemetery where the Union dead from the battle had been re-buried."

The entire class, including Arthur, looked straight at Simon, who was a little surprised himself that he had spit out the answer so quickly and almost without thinking about it. Arthur was just about the only one not surprised.

Squirming a little in his seat, Simon responded to all those staring eyes with the first thing that popped into his head: "Believe me guys, I'm a lot older than I look." Again, Arthur didn't seem surprised.

The classroom was still once more. Simon wondered if perhaps it was going to take some time for things to sink in. The silence, however, didn't last quite as long as he had expected, and it was broken by the most unlikely of individuals.

"What's the big deal about all this freedom stuff?"

The teenage son of Jan Carson had suddenly stirred from his lethargic state and now threw his question right out to the group. In his mind, he was only asking the obvious. It had been bothering him since he heard the word emancipation. It puzzled him that much more when he realized someone had actually made an address about the men who died fighting for it. Now it sure felt good to get everything off his chest, and he waited for some sort of response.

And then he waited some more.

But there wasn't any immediate attempt at answering his question, only the hushed, uncomfortable murmur of people whispering back and forth. The adults in the class were either confused or not amused, or just a little bit of both.

"At least he was listening to something," his mother mumbled under her breath. She counted among those who were absolutely not amused.

"I mean if freedom was so great back then," Matt Carson continued, "that men were willing to die for it, why don't we hear about it or talk about it today?"

"And amendments to some piece of paper which was supposed to guarantee these freedoms? A whole government and country run according to that piece of paper? Please, give me a break! The only freedom guaranteed to me is the freedom to scrounge through garbage cans or wait in soup lines for food. That is, if I don't get shot first."

There were still no answers. Those sitting in the circle of chairs simply dropped their heads; they didn't know what to say.

The teenager wasn't finished yet. "If the United States of America was so wonderful, then what the hell happened to it?"

Arthur shook his head. "Out of the mouth of babes," he thought to himself.

Not that he was really surprised. To the younger generation, the history of the place he once called home was no more than a myth. Why would anyone Matt's age believe that things had ever been any different? Arthur was saddened, yes, but he was challenged all the same. He was a teacher, and he could do more than just recite great speeches from memory. He could teach.

"Matt, I'll answer your question," Arthur spoke up firmly. All eyes turned toward the teacher, Simon included.

"We, Americans — it's been a long time since I've used that word. We simply lost faith in what the brave men at Gettysburg, and the brave men and women in all the wars that followed, had died to defend. It came to a point where we were no longer willing to fight for our own freedom, our own country; other things had become more important to us."

Chapter 15

A look of great sadness gripped Arthur's face, and for a moment he remained silent. He breathed in deep, exhaled slowly, and then repeated the cycle two more times. The third time, he pushed, really forced out the air with much more authority.

"Now, you may ask," he continued finally, "how did we get to that point? Greed, fear, ignorance, apathy: it was all of these. But mostly, it was one thing, and one thing above all else — inability to compromise."

"In order to explain all of this, I'm going to have to fast forward through quite a bit of American history. We can go back later and fill in some of the details, I guess." Arthur looked all around the room, checking for some acknowledgement, some sort of agreement in the faces of his students. He was met with a mixture of nods and blank stares. Satisfied that this was as good as it was going to get, he moved on.

"Okay, the battle of Gettysburg wasn't exactly the end of the Civil War, but it did signify that the tide had turned. The Union would survive; the United States would survive. The fighting did last two more bloody years, killing countless thousands and devastating the rebellious southern states. Still, by the end of the war, what had emerged out of this ordeal by fire was a stronger, more unified country, a country that believed in the greatness of its own destiny. The necessities of wartime production had also given birth to an industrial powerhouse. The United States used this awesome power and restless energy to expand ever westward, gobbling up great swaths of territory in the process. It wasn't always pretty, or fair, particularly for native peoples who were forced off their land, but it was effective in the end. An American empire, of sorts, had been created on the North American continent."

"Through the first half of the 20th century then, this empire continued to expand and flex its muscle on the world stage. The United States and its allies fought and won two world wars, defeating the forces of evil in Europe and the Pacific. Millions died in those wars, but freedom was secured in at least parts of the world. As a result, the United States emerged as a global economic and military superpower, a beacon of hope for some, an object of fear and envy for others. Back home, things were good in America; jobs were plentiful. American industry produced goods that were shipped all over the globe."

"But being a military superpower trying to police the world and protect freedom for all peoples cost lots and lots of money. Starting in the last 20 years of the 20th century, the U.S. government began taking on massive amounts of debt to finance its obligations both domestically and abroad. It wasn't sustainable over the long term, but nobody seemed to worry about it much at the time. We lived for the present. The future, most people just figured, would somehow take care of itself."

"In a sense, we were trying to re-make the world over in our own image, and in a way, we were successful. There was always the draw of democracy and the fundamental individual freedoms it guaranteed. Yet there was also the awesome economic engine of capitalism, the freedom to make and spend as much money as you could get your hands on, the freedom to consume anything and everything today without any real regard for tomorrow. Some called it greed; others called it the American Dream. It was our way of life, and we flaunted it. Hell, sometimes we even tried to export it through trade agreements favorable to other countries."

"Yeah," Arthur said with a deliberate drawl, injecting just a bit of showmanship, and sarcasm, into his effort. "Everybody wanted some part of that way of life," he quickly added. "And so we ended up with lots of competition around the world, particularly for scarce natural resources like oil. Other countries decided they wanted to have lots of cars too, and they wanted to drive their cars as much as we drove ours.

It was all part of the good life they had learned from us. There wasn't enough gas to go around, unfortunately, so prices skyrocketed. Suddenly we didn't have all that cheap gas anymore, and we certainly didn't like having to share."

"But that wasn't the only nasty surprise we got. We also found there was plenty of competition for the jobs we relied upon to feed our families. "

"Over the years, we steadily lost good-paying manufacturing jobs to people overseas who would simply work for less. That didn't seem to bother us at first. We could let others do the hard, dirty work of building things; we would simply move those things around and buy and sell them. It was cleaner that way for us, made us feel like we were using our brains instead of our brawn. There was only one problem with all that, however: the new service jobs we gained didn't pay nearly as well as the old manufacturing jobs we lost. Those manufacturing jobs had not only built a country. They had also fueled the growth of a large American middle class, people who were neither rich nor poor, people who had just enough to be satisfied they had made it and secured their own little piece of the American Dream. The loss of manufacturing jobs put the squeeze on the middle class."

"The middle class had always been the key to the success and stability of the United States. As long as these people were happy, the country as a whole was happy. Now these people were no longer happy; many of them could no longer afford the lifestyle they had once known or thought they deserved. They were simply unable to compete under the new rules of the global economy. Many thought the American Dream had lost some of its luster. It was inevitable, I guess; the rest of the world had caught up to us."

"It was painfully hard for some to adjust to that new reality, not so painful for others though. The rich and powerful, always very good at taking care of themselves, were better positioned to take advantage of the dwindling opportunities. No surprise then. The rich got richer. At the other extreme, more people fell from the middle class into the ranks of the poor, and those already there got poorer still. The wealth and income gap between the haves and the have-nots got only bigger."

"Economic recessions and chaos in financial markets across the globe only made things worse. More and more jobs were lost. Fear swept across the land, and tensions increased between the various classes of American society. It was a volatile mix which the American political system seemed wholly unprepared to deal with."

"From the Civil War onward, the United States had been governed by two competing political parties. There had always been some level of disagreement between the two parties over what the government should and shouldn't do, or how much the government should tax and spend. As budget deficits continued to grow over the years, however, the debate grew more heated, fueled in part by political commentators who got higher ratings selling conflict instead of compromise. Television and other media seemed much more interested in what made us different or drove us apart rather than what held us together as a country."

"There was middle ground in the debate over the size and effectiveness of government. We just couldn't seem to find it. Maybe a mixture of budget cuts with some tax increases would've worked. Who knows? We'll never know, I guess. The environment just wasn't right for that type of deal."

"American politics increasingly became a winner-take-all proposition; one party had to win, while the other party had to lose. The winners then tried to force through their legislative agenda, while the losers simply tried to obstruct or block everything in the hope that their party could re-take control in the next election cycle. Loyalty to the party seemed to matter more than doing what was right for the country."

"A divided government to some; a dysfunctional government to many others. But it wasn't just the politicians. Ordinary Americans split along party lines into what were essentially two armed camps. We could no longer be civil to one another over our differences in opinion. We tended to demonize those who didn't agree with us. We even booed our elected leaders at supposedly friendly community parades if they weren't from the party we supported. Athletes refused to visit the White House to celebrate championships won because they didn't want to appear to support the President politically. No matter that championship teams had been going to the White House for as long as anyone could remember. It was no longer that simple. Politics, it seemed, was everywhere, and it colored or poisoned everything we did. Compromise, the hallmark of our great democracy, was all but dead!"

"It was a stalemate, pure and simple. Congress couldn't or wouldn't pass anything. Or if they did pass something, it was merely intended to provoke a fight with a President who was a member of the opposing party. Government could not govern; it could not do for people what government had done for many generations."

The teacher bowed his head and sighed. "And then it happened," he said softly. "Those who believed in the power of the government to do good; those who believed the government could and should level the playing field to help people reach their full potential grew frustrated and simply gave up."

Arthur sighed once again. "That tipped the balance," he continued, "in favor of those who just wanted the government to get out of the way. Government couldn't help solve problems, they believed. In their eyes — the government was the problem. If they didn't benefit personally from something the government did, they couldn't see a reason for the government to do it. If they could afford to pay for private schools or didn't have children at all, they didn't understand why government paid for public schools. If they had enough to eat themselves, they sure as hell didn't want their taxes going towards any program which helped poor people put food on the table. They defined the world in very narrow terms; community extended only so far as their immediate family and friends."

"What they didn't need, they didn't want. So they cut government, and they cut it hard. It wasn't just a matter of bringing deficits under control in the most humane, equitable way possible. It was really more of an ideology, a process of dismantling government entirely."

"And we did nothing," Arthur said sadly.

"There was money to be made. They didn't want a government that invested in people; they wanted a government that invested in the business of making money. One of the first things they did was legislate most unions out of existence. Not many people were in unions anymore so there wasn't a big uproar. But these same people didn't realize that the mere threat of unions had been an effective deterrent over the years in preventing management from taking advantage of its workers. Now that deterrent was gone. Regulations requiring overtime pay for working more than 40 hours in a week were relaxed almost immediately; whole industries were exempted entirely. Next they eliminated the minimum wage across the board. That was supposed to help keep us competitive globally and give business the incentive to hire more cheap workers."

"And we did nothing," Arthur said once again.

"They shut down the Environmental Protection Agency and repealed laws that protected endangered animals or lands. These were hailed as landmark decisions to make our government more business friendly and responsive to the rapidly changing needs of the global economy. There were profits to be made in the here and now. Who was going waste time worrying about the future?"

"And we did nothing," Arthur said tightly. "We were scared. If you were lucky enough to have a job, that's all you really cared about. The people in charge knew that all too well."

"Laws which had once protected small businessmen from the predatory practices of large monopolistic corporations were routinely ignored. Congress didn't even bother repealing those. Personal freedoms and civil rights were no longer absolutely protected, particularly if they were inconvenient or got in the way of making money. The American court system, long the last refuge for the little man seeking justice, became a mockery. Owing their allegiance to the people who appointed them, judges ignored two hundred years of legal precedents and ruled in favor of the rich and powerful."

"And still we did nothing." Arthur said each word slowly and with emphasis, the frustration building in his voice.

"How could we? The majority party in charge had so rigged the process through control of the judicial branch that it became virtually impossible to mount an effective challenge. Voting rules were changed to make it more difficult for the poor to vote. Redrawing of voting districts in the states was handled by the party and blessed by their judges who could choose to interpret the Constitution anyway they wished. Opposition candidates were often forced to run against each other, thus minimizing the number of seats they could ever hope to capture. Even when an opposition candidate did run against the party, the big money pumped into the campaign by business interests simply crushed the challenger."

"Then they decided we no longer needed to vote at all."

"At least they got that part right," Arthur chuckled bitterly. "Voter turnout had declined steadily for years. Nothing seemed to change no matter how people voted so people began to lose interest in the process itself, even those who benefitted the most from the current system."

"There was also the matter of the surging economic powerhouse in the Far East."

"The government had been worried for some time about the Chinese and how quickly they made decisions to move their economy in one direction or another. China was not burdened with all the bureaucracy that came with democratic government. The Chinese leadership made a decision and then the people executed it. It was simple, and the Chinese people seemed genuinely happy and duly proud of their economy. This was an attractive idea to an American government trying to save every dollar possible while still working to turn around a battered economy. Elections were a hugely expensive exercise which took real time away from managing day-to-day operations of the government. I guess they figured the American people would be happy to give up the headaches of regular elections if it meant more jobs and a more competitive economy."

"It was all settled rather quickly and without any real public discourse. To achieve greater efficiency then, the Congress simply voted itself out of existence and turned over decision-making power to a joint business-government board of directors with the President as some sort of CEO. Many a Senator or Congressman took some position under the new arrangement to help, as they liked to say, facilitate the transition."

"There were some dissenting votes in this whole sorry episode, most notable among them a young Congressman with strong ties to the majority party. His grandfather had been a long-serving Senator back in the old days when the two political parties actually tried to work together. The young man believed in the concept of limited government himself but didn't like how far things had really gone. And he certainly didn't feel the American people would be better served without any representative government at all. He spoke out against the dissolution vote on the floor of Congress. It was courageous and all very eloquent, but it was also very futile."

"If only there had been a lot more like him," Arthur said almost wistfully. He paused, thinking back to a time long ago when Congress still met to debate the affairs of the day and America was still America.

"Yes, that Congressman's grandfather had been a bit of a rebel in his day as well," the teacher added with a smile. "The old man was kind of a hero to me when I was a kid, a Senator who defied his own party for the good of the Congress and the country. I didn't realize just how truly special and rare that was until many years later."

Arthur shook his head. "You know that Congressman kind of disappeared from public view after the vote. And I never really found out what happened to him either." The last few words trailed off slowly into that quiet dark place where a man sometimes struggles to distinguish between the past and the present. It was an awkward silence.

Most of the class knew the story wasn't finished just yet, but not a one of them had any idea what to say next. So they said nothing and waited in their chairs, somewhat uncomfortably at that.

And then he was back — as if he had never left.

In any event," Arthur continued with a sudden burst of energy, "things didn't quite work out as planned. The economy was fundamentally weaker than anyone wanted to admit. The manufacturing sector had never really recovered, and it wasn't strong enough to carry all those service and retail jobs. In other words, government spending had been cut, but the private sector wasn't exactly coming to the rescue. More drastic action was needed, and yet another unthinkable was about to happen."

"America the beautiful, the land of the free, the home of the brave — went looking for a merger partner just like any other nearly bankrupt company. They found multiple partners actually: resource-rich Canada to the north and the low cost manufacturing economies of Mexico and Central America to the south. The original American empire had stretched from sea to shining sea. Now there was another global powerhouse which covered the entire North American continent."

"Only this wasn't the United States of America anymore. It was now the Trade Association of the Americas."

"But it sure seemed like America at first. The powers that be made certain of that. They kept the old American President around as CEO for the first couple of years. That appealed to our vanity; made us feel like we were still in charge. Only we weren't, and it wasn't going to be long before most everybody figured that out. Those first two years were nothing more than a corporate transition, a way of easing out the old and replacing it with the new. The American President retired soon enough and was succeeded by an ambitious young executive from one of the former countries of Central America. His name was Daniel Garcia."

"CEO Daniel Garcia had a vision. He also had the advantage, in this new environment, of having a background in business rather than politics. He did what he wanted to do, and he didn't give a damn about pleasing people. It was all very simple to him, really. He treated the United States just like any company that had been taken over via merger. The old logos had to go; the old culture had to go. So down came the Stars and Stripes, and out went the history books. It was more efficient to have a uniform, standardized set of values across the entire Trade Association of the Americas. No matter that we had once been Americans, Canadians, Mexicans, or even Columbians; we were all assimilated into a new corporate culture based on shared science and technology."

"This was intended, of course, to keep us competitive in the global economy. History was just not value-added, as Daniel Garcia put it, unless the TAA could make money on it. Our own American history, the very record of our lives and the lives of our forefathers, was either erased entirely or bastardized to provide cheap entertainment for the masses."

"And we did absolutely nothing!" Arthur pounded his fist hard on the podium. His face grew flushed, veins bulging on the side of his forehead.

"Oh sure, some people weren't happy," he continued hotly. "But it was way too late by then. The genie had already been let out of the bottle, and he wasn't going back in. People who complained too loudly had a funny way of disappearing, if you know what I mean. Besides, the economy was improving, at least for those with the means or connections to take advantage of it. These were the people the TAA seemed to care about the most anyway. To many of them, it was really all about security and prosperity so they kept quiet. Fighting for personal freedoms, particularly for the freedoms of other people, just wasn't a very appealing option anymore."

Taking a deep breath, Arthur paused. "You know I try not to judge them," he said, his tone now more subdued. "If I'd had the choice, I honestly don't know exactly what I would've done myself. Would I really have been willing to sacrifice everything to fight for freedoms lost?" His words were introspective and at the same time, tinged with a certain amount of shame.

"I guess it doesn't matter," he added, "because I didn't even have the choice; history teachers weren't valued anymore in the new scheme of things. Like many of you here, I fell into the ranks of the nameless, faceless poor — the great underclass of society where we were left entirely to fend for ourselves. It wasn't so much fair or unfair anymore; it just was. Hell, we were thankful to feed from the scraps of the table. And just trying to survive from one day to the next didn't give us a whole lot of time to worry about abstract concepts like freedom either."

The teacher fell silent. The story was over. There were coughs here and there, nothing more. Young Matt Carson had listened to it all and didn't know what to say. Simon had listened as well. He just wanted more time to digest everything.

Arthur finally broke the silence himself. "I've just told you about some of the things America did wrong there at the end."

"Now," he said with a big smile, "let me tell you about all the things America did right!"

Chapter 16

Arthur was true to his word. Over the next hour and a half, the teacher illuminated the class on several of the more positive milestones in American history. He seemed very determined, desperate almost, to prove something to everyone in the room — that his old country, his home, had value once; that there were certain ideals worth keeping alive.

Matt Carson was still listening, as was Simon sitting in a chair not far away. The two of them made an odd pair, a lost member of the younger generation alongside one who was impossibly old. They learned much. They learned about laws passed in the early 20th century which broke up the monopolies of the great robber barons and gave the little man the chance to compete. They learned about the Great Depression and the New Deal when the government first said, loud and clear, that it really cared. They learned about the Berlin Airlift after World War II when the United States had the compassion to feed its former enemies and help keep them free. Simon was especially glad to hear about that. It somehow seemed to give meaning to the bloody sacrifice on the sandy beaches of France. Finally, they learned about the Civil Rights Movement along with the court cases and the legislation which ended racial segregation and ultimately moved the country past the lingering horrors of slavery.

"It had been more than 100 years since the Emancipation Proclamation by the time that legislation passed," Arthur said solemnly, "and it cost many lives, from non-violent protesters all the way up to leading politicians. It took a long, long time, but America finally decided that it was no longer okay to treat some citizens differently just because of the color of their skin."

"We hold these truths to be self-evident, that all men are created equal...."

"Yes, the Civil Rights Act of 1964 fulfilled those words from the Declaration of Independence, outlawing discrimination by race, color, or creed. It was still a struggle even after that; not everybody could or would change. Nonetheless, as Abraham Lincoln once put it, the better angels of our nature had prevailed, and we ended government sponsored discrimination at the local, state, and Federal levels. Schools and jobs opened to people of all races, even the grandchildren and great grandchildren of former slaves."

"But the schools weren't just a symbol of the end of segregation; they were a symbol of opportunity for all Americans. There were public universities, community colleges, and trade schools. There were also student loans and grants to help poor kids get a college education. Everyone — everyone, no matter what your name was or who your parents were, had a chance to make it here. The America I once knew cared about this equal access to opportunity, this fundamental sense of fairness."

"The Trade Association of the Americas doesn't quite see things the same way," Arthur continued, his tone sharper than before. "The TAA views society in much harsher terms, more like survival of the fittest — or at least, the most well connected. Wealth and power begets more wealth and power. Poverty begets only more poverty."

The teacher halted on purpose and then smiled. "Well, I don't intend to stand here and tell you what most of you already know. My goal is to teach you how things were really different once and, God willing, how things might be different again in the future. I believe. I have to believe. I just want all of you to believe as well." Arthur looked straight at Simon. For some reason, that didn't make Simon feel uncomfortable at all.

"In any event," Arthur summed things up as he gazed out across the whole class, "we're done for today. Next time I'll tell you how

America won the space race and put the first man on the moon. We'll also talk about the end of the Cold War and the fall of the Berlin Wall."

With that, the teacher carefully closed the history book. The air still tingled with a positive energy, and there was a general, not so quiet, hub-bub of activity as the class slowly began to file out of the room. Not that Arthur noticed much. His hand lingered over the well-worn cover. Skipping around and covering as much ground as he did, he had not really followed the book very well today.

"Some teacher I am," Arthur mumbled softly to himself. He laughed a little too, at a joke which suddenly crossed his mind. He was physically and emotionally spent, but in a good sort of way. It had truly been a very special day. Maybe he hadn't followed the book, but he had done something so much more important: he had pulled the history right off the pages and made it real to the very people who needed to hear it. And that felt damn good.

Arthur smiled and looked up from the podium, just in time to catch Simon looking back as he followed his Marine escorts towards the classroom door. The teacher had resisted the urge of chasing down his new student, partly because of the rubbery feel in his old, tired legs. Mainly though, he felt like he already had some kind of unspoken understanding with this young man, a connection he had felt since their first meeting in the park. This was no time then to be over-anxious, he thought. The two, teacher and student, seemed to study one another from afar for a few more seconds. Simon smiled and nodded back to the teacher, who then returned the gesture before the younger man disappeared completely outside the doorway.

Yes, Arthur was definitely sure of it now. Simon Anderson would be back.

Stepping down from that podium, Arthur felt a little of the spring returning to those old rubbery legs. The priest was waiting for him. "You know, Father," the teacher motioned towards the door, "I believe that young man was sent from above to help us."

Father Christopher looked sharply at his friend. "Aren't you jumping the gun just a little bit? It's only been one class after all," he said with a certain amount of respectful, yet firm disapproval. "Saviors just don't show up in a place like this from out of the blue, especially well-dressed ones at that. I'm a realist. I consider my prayers answered if we are able to save a few and help the rest make their peace with the Creator before they leave this earth."

Arthur smiled and put his arm around the shoulders of the priest. "You must have more faith in what is possible my realistic friend. Remember, after all, that the Lord works in mysterious ways."

It was almost laughable, Father Christopher thought for a moment, hearing his own words used against him. But he wasn't laughing right now. He admitted it was good to see Arthur so positive about something again. Still he didn't want everyone to get their hopes up, only to see their dreams dashed like they had so many times before. It was tough enough living here anyway. No need to add disappointment to all those other problems. Slowly shaking his head, the priest managed only a weak smile. Not exactly an endorsement, but clearly not an outright rejection either.

That was apparently enough for Arthur who slapped the priest on the back with a hearty chuckle. The pair headed together out of the classroom, one man suddenly filled with hope for a brighter tomorrow, the other not so sure.

Simon dutifully followed his Marine escorts back towards the front of the rescue mission, retracing the same path they had previously taken, moving past peeling paint and familiar darkened rooms. Everything about the place looked the same to Simon, but something was distinctly different nonetheless. Somehow breathing in the same stale, damp air didn't seem quite so bad anymore. Somehow his eyes had adjusted to the dim lighting as well. Somehow there was something here more important, more perceptible than the overwhelming smell or the suffocating darkness. Things had definitely changed.

Deep down inside, Simon was glad he had come to Arthur's class. He now had a better understanding of how the United States had fallen from superpower status all the way down to the point of being absorbed by the TAA. For sure, the class had helped to explain some things, put other things into perspective too. It was really more than that for Simon though; something just felt so right about being in this place. It clearly wasn't the pleasant ambiance. It was really something he felt more in the pit of his stomach, something he had been struggling with over the last few weeks. He now understood why he was here, what he had to do — he had a purpose. He was going to help these people.

He just didn't know exactly how yet.

But figuring out that part would have to come later. Simon and his Marine escorts had reached the front entranceway to the mission building. It was time to go. Sergeant White and his son graciously offered to provide a safe escort back to the bridge. As Simon nodded his acceptance of that offer, something just barely visible in the corner of his eye suddenly caught his attention.

It was only a glimpse, a shadow which might otherwise be ignored, but not this time.

It was a woman.

Simon had seen many women here; this one was different. She was just ahead, past the busy soup line, and she stood out from the crowd for all the wrong reasons. In a place where pain and suffering seemed to know no bounds — among people who saw little hope — she appeared to be pretty much at the bottom of the misery scale. She was pale and worn. Painfully gaunt too, really more bones than flesh, with ragged clothes that barely hung on at all. How she was still standing, Simon didn't exactly know. And there was the look in those eyes: dark eyes sunken back into her skull, entirely lacking any spark. It was the look of defeat, total and absolute. It was the look of utter hopelessness. She had given up. Simon had no doubt of it.

He continued to watch her, though he didn't know exactly why. An awkward combination of curiosity and pity churned in his gut, and that made him feel a little queasy. Still he could not turn away. It wasn't really a surprise to Simon when she abruptly collapsed to the street. She lay there quietly for a few seconds before reaching her hands slowly to the heavens as if pleading for some final salvation which was never going to come. Her arms then fell limp to her side. She was there alone, not dead just yet, but clearly ready — and absolutely no-one around her seemed to care. People continued to come and go. Those who were hungry simply stepped over her prone body on their way to the soup line, without stopping, without noticing anything at all. They were careful only not to trip.

Perhaps it was just the brutal nature of this hellish place. Perhaps it was the breakdown of society. Simon didn't know which, and it didn't matter. He could see now a little of what Arthur had been talking about. He could see the harsh law of nature in action. He could see that survival of the fittest, the core philosophy of the TAA, applied here as well. He watched, and he watched until he could watch no more.

Simon surprised the Marines when he broke away without warning and headed directly towards the fallen woman. His escorts weren't the only ones surprised. People halted in their tracks. The soup line stopped doing business. Suddenly all eyes were on Simon. He didn't care. He knelt down by the woman and gently brushed the hair back from her face. He couldn't tell exactly how old she was. He guessed late twenties, early thirties, but the lines and marks etched into her skin made her look much older. Life had been hard for her, Simon could tell that.

She was unresponsive at first. Simon touched her cheek, and she began to stir. Slowly, very slowly, she opened her eyes. He noticed they were brown, just like Holly's. It took a few seconds before those brown eyes were able to focus, then a few seconds more while their owner struggled to comprehend exactly what she was seeing. She reached up to touch the face bent over her just to make sure Simon was made of flesh and blood. At first contact, her hand recoiled. Simon smiled, grasped her hand, and held it to his face. Everything was real. She knew that now.

She smiled back, a pretty smile he thought, and her eyes welled up with tears.

Releasing her hand, Simon carefully slid his own hands underneath her frail body and scooped her up into his powerful arms. She wrapped her arms loosely around Simon's neck and rested her head on his chest. She could feel the peaceful rhythm of Simon breathing in and out. It all felt so natural to her, so relaxing, so very different from how she lived every day. It had been such a long time since she had known any real human contact or compassion. Now, if only for the moment, she felt safe and secure again.

There wasn't a sound, not a stir, as Simon carried the woman to the front of the soup line. An awed stillness it was, very nearly like the passing of the dead.

Except the woman wasn't dead yet, and Simon intended to keep it that way. He motioned for a bowl of soup. As the server complied, Simon positioned his charge upright on the table and grabbed the bowl. Slowly and carefully, he fed soup to the woman. She eagerly swallowed each spoonful, and her eyes lit up. It was more than just the nourishment of course, although she needed that desperately; it was a simple act of kindness that had restored her faith. Her prayers had been answered. Once again, she could believe in something — in someone. She wanted to live.

The bowl was empty soon enough. The woman didn't say a word; she just smiled. Looking deep into her eyes, Simon understood. He put the bowl down on the table.

Father Christopher and Arthur had been drawn outside the mission building by the sudden and absolute silence. They had seen Simon and the woman together. They had been watching in quiet wonder like the rest. Now the priest tasted a surprising dryness in his mouth and noticed something stirring inside which he had not really felt for some time. It was strangely exhilarating. He couldn't really explain it any better than that, but it, this feeling, made him immediately step forward to the soup table. He put his hand gently on the woman's shoulder and offered her a piece of bread; she accepted it gratefully. He looked over at Simon. Both men nodded. Nothing was said or apparently needed.

Simon touched the woman on the cheek one last time and then turned to rejoin the Marines. All was still, hushed. Father Christopher and Arthur watched Simon and the Marines go until they had finally disappeared from sight. The priest shook his head and smiled. Arthur noticed that too. He laughed and slapped his friend on the back once more.

Sergeant White and his son didn't say much as they guided Simon back to the bridge. No different than before. Still, every now and then, when he glanced back at the pair, Simon could swear the old Marine was grinning. That was a bit of a surprise, but it made Simon smile too. He just tried not to be too obvious about it.

They reached the bridge in short order. There were no emotional goodbyes. They were men, men of an old code. They were men with the blood of warriors. They simply shook hands and made arrangements to meet up for the next class. Simon wasn't overly sentimental, but he was practical. He did appreciate having an armed escort in a place like this.

The TAA security guards at the bridge were more than a little surprised to see Simon again. They had figured him for dead. It seemed like a pretty good bet considering all the gunshots they had heard. Now they were curious. As Simon crossed over the bridge, however, the guards noticed the bruising on his knuckles. Then they saw the dark look in Simon's eyes, a forbidding stare oddly reminiscent of what they once knew from drill instructors at basic training. Those guys used to have bruises on their knuckles too, they recalled. It wasn't a pleasant memory.

The security guards looked at each other and quickly reached an unspoken agreement. Sometimes it just wasn't worth asking. They let Simon go without any questioning.

Simon climbed into his car and sped away. The drive home was just long enough to ponder some things, but it wasn't long enough to come up with any real solutions. He still didn't know how he was going to help those people on the other side of the bridge. Of more immediate concern though, he didn't know exactly how he was going to explain to Holly the bruising on his hands from the run-in with Smiling Bob and his thugs. The marks on his knuckles were clearly obvious; they had helped scare off the guards on the bridge. That had been a good thing, very convenient actually. How Holly would react to those bruises might be much more problematic.

The miles passed by quickly. Leafy suburban streets came into view again. By the time Simon pulled the car into his own driveway, he had not completely thought through the story he was going to tell his wife. Now it was too late. Holly and Suzy were waiting for him at the door. Simon stepped out of the car and was immediately tackled around the waist by an energetic little girl with bouncing curls. In truth, the force of the blow hurt just a little, but Simon chuckled; it was a good kind of hurt. He reached down and wrapped his arms around the child.

"Daddy, I missed you!"

"Hey kid, I missed you too." Simon gave his daughter a final squeeze before letting her go. Suzy reached up to hold her father's hand and pull him towards the door. Simon grimaced without realizing it, but then quickly recovered his smile. Holly was laughing at the little spectacle until she noticed Simon's knuckles.

"Oh my god, honey," Holly said excitedly, "what happened to your hands?" Her facial expression was equal parts shock and concern. She grabbed Simon's free hand and gently ran her fingers over the bruises. Her touch was soft and Simon had to admit it felt pretty damn good.

For a moment, Simon simply enjoyed the silky caress of his wife's hands and the sweet smell of her perfume wafting through the air. He didn't respond right away. That was a mistake.

"Well?" Holly used only the single word to essentially repeat her question. It just seemed more direct that way. Her expression was still a combination of shock and concern; only now, the tell-tale signs of anger were also beginning to creep into the mix.

Her husband got the point. With a rather sudden burst of inspiration, he spoke, "Look that interview today was pretty rough. It brought up all sorts of demons. I just felt like I had to blow off some steam so I went to the downtown gym and beat on the body bag for a while. Unfortunately, I forgot to tape my fists."

Simon gently, reluctantly, pulled his hand away from Holly. He turned the hand over palm side down and balled it into a fist, grimacing on purpose and for added effect this time.

"I guess that'll teach me," he said softly.

Holly had seen the interview. It had been painful for her to watch too — the powerful, raw emotions in Simon's face and eyes as he answered one gut-wrenching question after another. She had seen it all, and she never wanted her husband to hurt like that again. Maybe she could understand why he had needed to blow off steam. Maybe she could understand why he had to beat on something so hard. Maybe, but she didn't realize Simon even belonged to a gym downtown.

As Holly quietly pondered that along with a few other maybes, she looked deeply into Simon's eyes. It was puzzling. She saw everything and nothing all at the same time. She saw the glow, the sincerity which attracted her so much. She also saw some things in those eyes she didn't fully understand and probably never would. She pondered some more until she had finally convinced herself. Maybe she just didn't really want to know after all.

Holly reached up and wrapped her arms around Simon's neck. She hugged him tightly to her body. That immediately made her feel much better. She did notice, but firmly decided to ignore, a faint moldy odor on Simon's clothes.

Simon enjoyed the hug as well. He gently stroked the hair on the back of Holly's head and felt the warmth from the whole of her body. He hated lying to the woman he loved with all his heart. But he had to protect his family, and that's what mattered most right now.

"Dinner is ready," Holly whispered into Simon's ear. He pretended like he didn't hear anything, and neither party made a move to break the embrace. "The food is going to get cold if we stay out here too much longer," she continued, stating only the facts, not necessarily what she really wanted to do.

"I'm hungry," Suzy finally added. She had a much simpler view of things. It was time to eat after all. Reluctantly, her parents agreed. They laughed, somewhat awkwardly at that, and then slowly separated, holding onto each other's hands until the very last possible moment. Holly looked back into her partner's eyes and smiled. Simon did the same. It really was time to go. They scooped up their little girl and headed into the house.

A pleasant aroma, almost as stimulating as his wife's perfume, tickled Simon's nose as they crossed over the doorway threshold. It drifted out from the direction of the kitchen and quickly reminded him where he was now compared to where he had been a few hours before. There was no mold or mildew here, only hot food and plenty of it. Plates were filled, and the family dived right in. Suzy was happy to be eating. Holly was happy everyone was together at the dinner table.

Simon was really trying to enjoy the meal himself, but he also realized everything was a bit more complicated now that he had seen what was on the other side of the bridge. For one, Simon knew he appreciated food more than he had before — as long as it wasn't soup. Soup wasn't real food he had decided, merely the illusion of food; water with a little bit of taste sprinkled in. After today, he just couldn't think of soup in the same way ever again. Seeing desperate, starving people up close had a funny way of changing the way a man thought about food, among other things.

Those other things weren't nearly as simple as food. Things which dug and clawed at a man's conscience never were. The guilt of plenty, inescapable it was, the guilt of having when others had not. He was eating all he wanted over here, safe at home with his family, while they were literally dying in the streets over there — and no-one gave a damn. It just didn't seem fair. Simon knew he had to help those people, though he still didn't know exactly how. While pondering that thought, he slowly chewed the last few bites of a nicely cooked chicken breast. Somehow, it didn't taste quite so good anymore.

Holly watched Simon eat. She knew it wasn't her cooking. She tried not to think about what it might really be.

Supper done. Dishes washed. Bath and bedtime for Suzy, story included. Everything on a schedule: Holly liked it that way. It kept her mind busy, and it kept her from worrying so much. Simon and Holly tucked their daughter in and then strolled hand in hand to their own bedroom.

At last they were all alone. Simon reached over and pulled his wife close. He looked into the most beautiful brown eyes he knew, and for the moment, nothing else in the world mattered: bombings, soup lines, the TAA, absolutely nothing. He savored the smell of her perfume. He marveled at the softness of her skin. This time, he knew he didn't have to let her go. Holly smiled and touched Simon's cheek. She didn't want him to let her go either. They kissed, and time itself seemed to stand still.

Afterwards, as they lay together wrapped in each other's arms, Holly traced her hand slowly along the contours of Simon's chest. She felt his body gently rise and fall with each breath. She listened to the beat of his heart. She could swear it matched her own, beat for beat. Two hearts, two lovers, two souls joined together as one. She believed it. She felt it. She reveled in that moment so safe and secure in Simon's strong arms. Her worries, all the things she did not understand about her husband, were pushed aside and tucked neatly away in the warm afterglow. Holly had never felt closer to a man than she did right now, and she wanted it to last forever. Before she drifted off to sleep, she quietly said a prayer.

Simon had heard part of Holly's prayer. He smiled to himself as he watched her sleep, her head resting peacefully on his chest. He too wanted this to last forever. He said his own prayer to his own Gods.

Simon didn't expect an answer right away; he just hoped the Higher Power was listening to someone's prayers. He closed his eyes, and it wasn't too long before he fell asleep as well, still holding Holly close.

The hours passed by quietly, peacefully, with Holly and Simon snuggled tightly together. It was close. It was comfortable. It was simple and pure, everything two lovers wanted. Simon slept there, his mind at rest and completely blank, until visions invaded his thoughts once again. He stirred almost immediately, releasing his grasp on Holly at the same time. His body moved and muscles tensed by reflex, as if they knew by now how to react to all too frequent nightmares.

But this time, this night, was different. The visions weren't of exploding bombs or torn and bloody bodies. They were from another time, another life: great factories pumping out tons of goods to feed a massive war effort, the proud workers who kept those factories running. He saw a nation's strength and freedom. He saw too simple images of home and dinner on the table. It was hope and prosperity.

And then the images faded slowly away to empty blackness.

Simon suddenly sat straight up in bed. Holly began to stir as well. It had been an abrupt journey back from the world of dreams to the here and now — with a few bumps along the way. He regretted disturbing his wife though and almost instinctively patted her gently on the thigh. Simon's eyes were wide open, and he stared straight ahead. There were no lights on in a darkened room; still he could see it all so clearly now.

He had an idea.

Chapter 17

The distant shore was dark, a pitch black mass against the night-time sky, punctuated only by the whitecaps of waves crashing ashore. Lieutenant-Commander Paul Thompson stood on the deck of the submarine and eyed the beach ahead with some concern. The waters in the channel were choppy, not really a surprise, but still not ideal for a smooth run-in and landing. Thompson shook his head and sniffed the salty air. He understood his role very well. He followed orders. If the TAA directed him to do something, they weren't going to ask his opinion; they simply told him when and where. Thompson looked at the water again. Yes, he knew what he had to do, but it didn't mean he had to like it.

"Ladies, get a move on and pile into the boats!" Thompson yelled at a small group of shadowy figures working feverishly at the far end of the deck. His voice was loud and threatening, just like normal, and didn't betray a shred of doubt.

"We have a job to do."

Almost an hour later, Lieutenant-Commander Thompson and his team had finally reached the beach. Thompson was the first man out of the boats, the first boots on the ground. It was the way he chose to lead; it was the same for every mission. Soaking wet and covered with sand, the commander was not a happy man this time. He stared angrily back out to sea, cursing under his breath. The run-in to the beach had cost him one man lost overboard. That would make the mission more difficult. But there was no time to grieve, and he knew it.

Especially since they were running late. The original plan had been to hit the beach under the cover of darkness. Now, because of the rough seas, they had lost that advantage. The first rays of sunlight were just beginning to break through the mist and heavy grey clouds.

Thompson spit sand out of his mouth. "Goddamn waves!"

The rest of the team stumbled out of the boats. They were just as wet.

"Hurry up ladies," Thompson barked. He motioned towards bluffs which rose abruptly at the far end of the sandy expanse. Here and there, ruined concrete bunkers dotted the rugged high ground. He examined those positions with the keen eyes of a trained military man. Good thing, Thompson thought to himself, they didn't have to cross this beach under fire.

"We have a job to do," the commander said flatly. The team gathered the rest of the gear and trudged towards the objective.

It was hard work for water-logged men, lugging their equipment while carrying a few pounds of seawater along for the ride. But they were young and strong, and very eager. Thompson knew that, and it worried him all the same. He spit out more sand. The sun, though still partially hidden by grey clouds, was fully up above the horizon now. They were falling further behind schedule. There was simply no time to indulge any doubts — just like there had been no time to mourn dead men. No goddamn time at all, Thompson thought. He gritted his teeth and yelled out another order.

The young men got the point and moved out across the beach with a renewed sense of urgency. Not that it made things any easier. Loose sand quickly gave way under the weight of a man only to cling stubbornly to his boots as he lifted first one leg and then the other. Each step forward was a struggle, in itself a little battle which had to be won just as surely as any feat of arms. There was lots of sand to cross, all of it seemingly quite prepared to resist the advance.

Slow and messy. The advance, as it were, took more time than planned, but the bluffs were finally reached.

The going didn't get much better as the team began to work its way up the high ground. Walking paths offered more solid ground than the wet sand below, but they were still rutted and uneven. The equipment each man hauled had not gotten any lighter since leaving the beach either. There were also interruptions, or minor detours, as curious young men stopped to get a quick look inside one of the old concrete bunkers. The breakdown in discipline naturally infuriated Commander Thompson who barked out a few choice expletives.

"Aye, aye sir," they responded in unison. Forward progress continued.

A shadowy man met the team at the top of the bluffs. "You're late," he said with clear disdain. His accent was thick, strange, and only added to the unpleasantness in his voice.

The commander shook his head and almost defiantly spit the last bits of sand out of his mouth. He held his tongue.

The last of the grey clouds had drifted away by this time, and the morning sun dutifully began to light up the new day. The landscape leading directly away from the top of the bluff was a dramatic departure from the beach they had just landed on. This time Commander Thompson couldn't help but notice himself.

Rays of sunlight reflected off the dew on well-trimmed blades of green grass, and neat white tombstones, laid out in perfect row after perfect row, spread out as far as the eye could see. A large flagpole towered over this manmade sea of green and white. The pole was topped by a flag of stars and stripes, of red, white, and blue. It floated peacefully in the early morning breeze.

"I'll be damned," Thompson muttered quietly to himself.

For a moment, the commander relaxed some little measure of self-control and allowed a restrained, but very definite smile to disturb the razor stubble on his face. For a moment, he was no longer soaking wet and covered in sand. For a moment, his mind drifted back to another time and place. He recognized the flag from his youth back when things used to be different, when that flag used to be everywhere. That was before the trade association took over, and things changed. He had not seen the flag in the many years since then, and in truth, had nearly forgotten all about it. Now he was here on this beach, on this assignment, and he was looking at that flag once again. He could almost swear he heard, somewhere off in the distance, the sound of a trumpet marching in the Independence Day parade. That had been a perfect sunny day too, he seemed to recall.

There were no more Independence Day parades. The TAA wasn't very big on remembering things it considered to be ancient history, particularly for a country which didn't officially exist anymore. And Lieutenant-Commander Paul Thompson did work for the TAA. The smile on the commander's face, barely noticeable though it had been, disappeared completely.

Thompson's young charges had no clue about the flag; they were mesmerized by the endless rows of tombstones lining the almost boundless expanse of green lawn. It was worse than the ruined concrete bunker. They broke formation again and quickly spread out among the rows. Thompson didn't say a word this time. Chatting excitedly, individuals stopped here and there to trace the letters of a particular name etched in white granite. The names were different, but everything else looked so much the same.

Same letter styles. Same tombstone. Same perfectly green grass. A vast cemetery of uniformity.

These were soldiers. The young men could tell that. They couldn't understand much else.

"Captain John Miller, U.S. Army Ranger. Died June 6, 1944."

"A lot of these guys died on June 6, 1944. What's so special about that date?"

"It was D-day," Thompson answered softly. He wasn't sure any of his men heard him, but he didn't bother to repeat it either. It didn't really matter, he decided. They were just too damn young, too damn young to comprehend the enormity of such sacrifice, too damn young to appreciate special places of honor like this. Thompson bowed his head. He tried to say a little prayer but struggled to come up with one.

Back then, men died for something. Thompson turned and looked out towards the sea. These days, he admitted sadly, men just died. Period.

"You know it's not getting any earlier," the shadowy man sneered, looking directly at Thompson. That fact wasn't entirely lost on the commander, though he really didn't appreciate the sarcasm. The strange accent only made everything sound more annoying than it already was.

"Okay ladies," Thompson yelled. He had concluded that annoying didn't necessarily mean wrong.

"It's time to go. We've got a job to do."

It took a minute or two before young men, young soldiers, began to drift back in from the cemetery. For sure, it wasn't perfect discipline. Thompson waited quietly. He just wasn't in the mood to crack the whip right now.

"Americans. Oh thank God, the Americans are here!"

It was that strange accent again, only it wasn't coming from the shadowy man this time. Thompson turned sharply in the direction of the voice. A frail old woman, stooped and bundled tightly in her coat, pointed her finger excitedly back at the commander and his team. She was accompanied by a young man trying mightily to control her.

He wasn't having very much success.

"You see there," she pointed again. "I told you they would be back. I told you the Americans would come again!" A tear rolled down her cheek. Her eyes were moist but otherwise bright and cheerful.

"Oh thank God. Thank God."

"But Grand-mama," the young man protested, "these are not the Americans you remember."

"Please excuse my great-grandmother," the young man continued sheepishly, speaking directly to Commander Thompson. "She is very old and very confused. She was just a young girl all those years ago when the Americans came ashore on this very beach and freed us from the Nazis."

"But she remembers them still. She likes to come here to this cemetery, to this place, as often as she can to honor these brave dead men."

"We are very sorry to have disturbed you." The young man bowed his head. "We will move on and get out of your way." He turned and grabbed the old woman by the arm. Over her rather energetic protests, he gently but firmly began to lead her away.

Two quick shots ended it all. The old woman and her great-grandson collapsed to the ground without a sound; they never knew what hit them. Commander Thompson spun back around to face his team. One of his men was calmly stuffing his pistol back under his coat.

"It seemed like the thing to do, Commander. I was concerned that the two of them would talk and blow our mission."

The young soldier smiled with all the innocence and charm of a child seeking out some sort of approval. That this something happened to be his first kill hardly seemed to matter. He didn't have to wait long either. There were quick slaps on the back and words of congratulation from his teammates. Even the shadowy man managed something resembling a smile.

"Hey," one of the well-wishers blurted out, "who the hell were the Nazis anyway?"

Thompson didn't smile. He didn't say a word. He sure as hell didn't feel like trying to explain who the Nazis were. He just stared straight ahead without any emotion at all. Deep down inside, in a place safely hidden away from his men and the outside world, he was absolutely horrified. He felt queasy in the pit of his stomach, and his mouth suddenly tasted very dry and scratchy. Any thoughts of old Independence Day parades were long gone by now. There was no honor in this; he knew that.

At the same time, however, the commander knew all too well just exactly who he worked for. The operative phrase really was "worked for" because he sure didn't feel like he was fighting for them. Either way, they didn't pay him to deal with moral quandaries.

After clearing his throat, twice even, the commander spoke quietly but firmly, "Go drag the bodies over behind that large monument and stuff them under the hedges."

"Aye, aye sir!"

"We've got a job to do," Thompson added flatly. It was straightforward and to the point. Nothing more could be said. Nothing more was needed.

As he watched his men drag away the bodies, Commander Thompson could swear the old woman still had a smile on her face. He noticed that queasy feeling in his stomach again.

Across the ocean, well away from windswept beaches and old cemeteries filled with long forgotten soldiers, Simon Anderson awoke to the new day realizing he had a job to do as well. Simon had never met Commander Thompson and was totally unaware of the Commander's mission, which was just the way CEO Garcia had planned it all along. Simon was the face-man for the TV audience, an attractive figurehead whose sole purpose was to remind people why the missions were necessary. Professional soldiers like Thompson, on the other hand, didn't have to worry about the why; they simply did what they were told — without passion, without prejudice. It was the perfect arrangement for the Trade Association of the Americas; it got messy things done, and it got them done fast.

Speed had always been essential to winning in the global economy, and this time was no different. The TAA intended to win fast. It didn't matter how many people died. The TAA didn't care. It was all just a game, a great big global strategic game. Simon Anderson and Commander Thompson were simply the pawns — in different positions on the very same chessboard. Deep down, both men understood the game and knew they were being used by it. Both men also questioned, at times, if the game might be entirely too big for any one individual to influence or change.

By the most fundamental and truest definition of the word, each man just worked for the trade association. No heart and soul commitment to the company cause, only compensation for services rendered. That compensation, reward and burden both, money which was desperately needed and could be put to good use but which otherwise trapped a man and bound him to the organization.

Blood money, some might have called it.

Simon preferred not to think about such things as he drove into work. For sure, he didn't want to be in that office. He didn't want to do any more interviews. He just didn't. Then he thought about his wife and those beautiful brown eyes and his daughter and her bouncing blond curls. He thought about the things he loved, and those things kept him heading straight down the highway to the office building of the TAA.

It didn't take long for Simon to hear about matters once he got into the office. Chris Smith made a special effort to seek out Simon and tell him about the missions led by Commander Thompson and others. Without knocking and without waiting for a formal invitation, he burst through Simon's office door.

"You know what they're doing, don't you?" The I.T. technician asked the question before he had even closed the door. He seemed unusually animated.

Simon shook his head. He didn't know and right now wasn't so sure he really wanted to know. Still, it was hard to ignore the obvious energy in Smith's voice.

"It's started! Do you understand me? It's all started!"

Smith looked straight at Simon who responded back with nothing more than a puzzled look. It wasn't quite the reaction the I.T. technician had been looking for.

More exasperated now, Smith continued, "The retribution has started. The TAA has landed special ops teams in the territory of the European Union." The words came quickly, and the urgency was clearly evident.

Simon was no longer puzzled. He knew what all this meant, and he knew it wasn't good. He didn't say a word though. Sometimes, finding just the right words was not an easy thing. Saying too much too soon only seemed to make things worse. Simon had learned that lesson painfully well over the last few weeks.

The continued silence did nothing to ease the impatience of Chris Smith who was too excited to wait very long for some sort of answer anyway.

"The teams are targeting major public services," the I.T. technician blurted out, "like power plants — destroying, disabling, disrupting! They strike quickly and then get out."

Smith took a deep breath. He was suddenly much calmer. After a delay of only a second or two, he spoke again. The tone and pacing of the words were more measured this time, more deliberate, analytical almost.

"It's an organized campaign of military terror, no better than the people who blow up trade conferences. But of course, the TAA doesn't see it that way. To the CEO, this is really just the next logical step. He likes to call it negotiating at the end of a gun. He'll keep up the pressure until the EU gives in. If they don't give in, who knows what?"

The I.T. technician paused once more. He wasn't really waiting for an answer from Simon. For the moment, he was lost in his own thoughts, back wrestling with his own inner demons. He remembered his old job. He recalled how the TAA handled the potential security problems he once analyzed. It wasn't pretty, and Smith remembered it all now in painfully excruciating detail. Image after image flashed quickly in his head, each new one somehow worse than the previous. Everything seemed so real, so very close — the blood; the cold, lifeless stare of death. There were too many faces to count, every single one a potential problem eliminated, every single one a potential problem he had identified in the first place. Maybe he had not actually pulled the trigger himself.

Maybe but....

Maybe that subtle distinction wasn't quite so important anymore. Maybe, as the former security analyst reflected, he had simply been too good at his old job. The brutal truth of it made Smith cringe suddenly, and there was a definite tightness in his throat now. For sure, he knew the answer to his own question; somehow he just couldn't bring himself to say it.

"Innocent civilians will die over there," Chris Smith said quietly, stating the obvious rather than dwelling on a pointless question. "And no-one over here will even care. They may be happy actually. It's revenge pure and simple. The trade association has sold everybody on the idea that all this amounts to long overdue justice for the people who died in the bombing."

He looked directly at Simon. "You know the European Union didn't have anything to do with that bombing, don't you?" This time the I.T. technician really was looking for an answer from someone other than himself.

He didn't get it.

What he got back from Simon was a stare, not the blank, thoughtless variety, but something colder, harder, and downright threatening. Smith had seen the interview on TV, just like everybody else. And just like everybody else, he had seen the look in Simon's eyes at the end of that interview. It had unnerved him somewhat then, and it really didn't make the I.T. technician feel any better right now to be facing those same eyes and that same look. He felt it in the very pit of his stomach. There was a great and terrible rage behind Simon's stare, Smith thought.

A very quiet, and very uncomfortable, few seconds passed. It seemed much longer to the I.T. technician. Maybe, he considered for the moment, he had been too eager to talk to someone, anyone really, and had crossed the line with a man he barely knew. Based on the look in Simon's eyes, Smith thought that was a line a rational man probably shouldn't try to cross. Maybe, just maybe, getting an answer to the burning question of the day wasn't quite so important after all.

The I.T. technician had thoroughly convinced himself. He cleared his throat, feigned a polite smile, and then turned to walk away.

"I know."

The words coming from the man behind those threatening eyes were quiet but firm. Smith stopped dead in his tracks when he heard them.

"I know the E.U. didn't have anything to do with that bombing," Simon continued. He looked down at the floor and exhaled the last remnants of a breath he had been holding in for some time. It felt better somehow to say that out loud. He took in another deep breath and let it back out, casually, freely, without any hesitation at all. When Simon raised his head, the stare was gone; the eyes were decidedly softer, less threatening.

Having turned back around by now, the I.T. technician noticed the difference immediately. He didn't say a word though. He didn't have to, didn't need to. Simon's words were everything he needed to hear. Smith just smiled, this time a real genuine smile. He spun on his heels and then turned to walk away once more. There was a certain bounce in his step.

Simon watched the I.T. technician walk away. When the office was all quiet again, he took his first look at the calendar for the day. He already knew what was there. The next interview was scheduled for the top of the hour. He had 30 minutes.

Not that it really mattered. He didn't need the time to consider what he was going to do.

That decision had already been made; there was no choice. Simon had a family to take care of, to protect. He had an idea how to help those poor people across the bridge. There was just so much for him to do, so many people depending on him. He thought of the beauty in Holly's smile, the soft touch of her skin. He remembered the faint spark of hope in the eyes of the starving woman when he gave her bread.

Simon shook his head. He knew now that he could give more people hope. This was his true purpose here he believed — not fighting the big, bad Trade Association of the Americas — though in truth, part of him ached to do just that.

This time, this place: it wasn't as simple as drawing a sword and charging forward. He understood that now. He had to find another way, a smarter way to fight the battle. If he had to play their game, at least to a certain extent, then so be it. All he had to do, Simon had decided, was stay out of the way of the TAA and the CEO long enough so he could accomplish what he really needed to do.

He had convinced himself. Simon stood up from his desk and headed towards the door. He couldn't afford to be late for the interview.

He had a job to do.

Chapter 18

It was a few minutes before noon, and CEO Daniel Garcia was satisfied, very satisfied actually. He was not exactly happy; very satisfied was about as good as it got. A man in his position, Garcia thought, could not afford the luxury of actually being happy. To be happy was to lose focus. To lose focus was to lose the flexibility to react quickly as the situation changed. The CEO prided himself on his ability to see what others could not see and to adjust strategy as circumstances dictated.

Things were definitely moving quickly in the European Union now, and Garcia understood that he was going to have to be on the top of his game. But that was really no more than he expected of himself every day. The thrill of competition — deep down, Daniel Garcia knew he lusted for it, savored it. It wasn't enough for the TAA to be successful. It wasn't enough just to win. The other side had to admit absolute defeat; they had to surrender directly to him in front of the whole wide world and the very heavens above. Begging for mercy was optional but definitely preferred. Garcia smiled at the thought.

At least that was the plan. It had worked before.

It would work again.

Yes, the CEO was very satisfied. Everything seemed to be going according to plan, his plan. His special ops teams were causing chaos across the EU, inflicting maximum damage and maximum terror for minimum dollars. It was one hell of a return on investment, he had concluded.

Garcia leaned back in his chair and smiled again. A long time ago, if he remembered correctly, someone had landed an army of a million men on the beaches of France to liberate the continent. For a moment, he tried to calculate in his head just how much that would have cost. Numbers didn't hold his interest for long though; he had never cared much for accounting. He decided rather quickly that the exact figure, whatever it was, must have been enormously large even for back then.

"What a waste," Garcia chuckled to himself, "Spending all that money to set people free." Free to do what, he wondered. Free to worship somebody's flag? That wasn't his idea of freedom.

The CEO had a different idea entirely. He was using a more focused and much more cost effective military model, and he certainly wasn't interested in using military force, and spending money, to protect the freedom to wave a silly old flag. He had people to convince, and this was simply the means to do it. The Europeans, Garcia knew, would truly be better off with the TAA. Maybe they just didn't know it yet.

And if they didn't figure it out soon....

If they didn't figure it out soon, more people would get hurt than really needed to. People were dying right now in the current, surgical attacks on the EU. Somehow that didn't bother Daniel Garcia very much. He knew that people died in military operations. It was unavoidable. Again, if he recalled correctly, the invasion of France in the last great World War killed lots of innocent people — all in the name of freedom. If everything continued to go according to plan, the CEO would give the people of France and the rest of Europe something better this time around: the security of being part of the Trade Association of the Americas. A better deal clearly, and one achieved for a much more reasonable number of innocent people killed.

If everyone was just smart enough to understand all of this, Garcia thought, they would see just how big of a humanitarian he really was.

Simon Anderson had a part in the plan too. The CEO had just finished watching the interview today. Whatever one called it, it had been more stage performance than interview, and it had been far from perfect. Simon's answers were not polished one bit, and there had been a strong undercurrent of raw emotion, anger even. If Garcia had not expected as much, he might have been upset himself. As it were, he rather enjoyed the unevenness, the sheer unpredictability of the interview. It made everything seem so unrehearsed, so deliciously real; it made for great television. He had never intended for Simon Anderson to merely be a pretty-boy spokes model. Damaged, tortured, and ruggedly handsome hero worked so much better for the purpose at hand.

Oh sure, Garcia knew he would hear the same old concerns from his head of security about the dangers of using someone as unpredictable as Mr. Anderson. But, as the CEO saw things, that was the fun in it really. He could deal with Simon Anderson if he needed to; he was in total control — as always. It was all part of his plan, and everything was going according to plan right now. Yes, Daniel Garcia was very satisfied.

The CEO turned in his chair and switched off the TV. He faced his computer screen with some resolve. He wanted the afternoon to be productive. There were simply more pressing matters right now, he decided, than worrying about the mental state of a particular subordinate.

Unlike the trade association's chief executive, Simon was not quite so satisfied with the interview. He had told his story once more, as difficult as that was, and had somehow managed to avoid a direct endorsement of the current military actions in the EU. It was surely a very tight line to walk, yet he had managed to do it — this time at least. Under the circumstances, that was a victory of sorts.

For most people, that would have been enough. Any victory had a right to be savored, even a temporary one which only promised the winner a chance to fight another day.

Simon wasn't most people, and he sure didn't feel like celebrating. Everything felt wrong, so terribly wrong. He knew the whole ugly truth about the bombing, and part of him wanted to yell it out loud from the highest mountain in the land. He couldn't do that though, not right now, maybe never. He had obligations to people he loved, something he had never truly known before. As he closed his eyes and tried very hard to think of home and family, he knew down deep he was still helping to perpetuate a lie.

To a man who knew of blood and death and sacrifice on fields of honor, Simon understood the difference between those times and what he was doing now. There was no honor in this. He tried again to console himself that all of this was for the greater good.

It did help, but only a little. Simon shook his head purposely from side to side, working hard against tight neck muscles. He clenched his fists without really thinking. Somehow, he resisted the urge to pound the top of his desk. That wouldn't help things, he knew.

But he did have a pretty good idea what would. He had to get away; he had to get out of the headquarters of the TAA.

It was early afternoon when Simon finally made good his escape. By then, he was pretty sure the CEO wouldn't be looking for him the rest of the day. Still it was a bit of a calculated risk. There would be consequences if he wasn't in the office when the leadership needed him. Simon understood as much and frankly didn't care. The very element of danger, small though it might realistically be, appealed very much to his inner nature. In his own way, Simon was resisting the awesome power of the trade association. It wasn't much, for sure, but it was all he could do right now; it was something he had to do to maintain his own sanity.

The drive away from the office was relaxing. The further away Simon drove, the more relaxing it got — a small, yet very sweet taste of freedom. He rolled down the window and took notice of the sun high in the clear blue sky. He enjoyed the warmth on his face even as the scenery changed outside the car window, even as green trees gave way to dingy grey buildings, even as the battered bridge came into view and black smoke rose once again from the other side. It wasn't pretty, but it wasn't quite so fearsome, so horrific as it had seemed only the day before. Simon thought for sure he saw bright rays of sunlight piercing the smoke too, as if some great power was ready almost to drive off the blackness for good.

Almost....

Right now, he thought to himself, almost had to be good enough; almost meant hope. For the first time all day, Simon smiled. He knew he had to get back over that bridge.

He had a job to do.

Getting across the bridge was easier this time. No questions from the guards. No trouble at all. They just waved Simon across. He figured the guards remembered him from yesterday, but he was still a little surprised. After all, he didn't even have to mention the name of the CEO. Maybe the guards had seen him on TV, Simon wondered. It was possible; the ratings had certainly been good enough. Either way, he was enjoying a certain measure of respect typically reserved for important people within the trade association.

He had known that type of respect once, back in his old job, back when he seemed to crave it so much. That was all in the past now, a faint image only, something buried deep among a host of more important, more useful memories. What was truly important at the moment was getting over the bridge. If that meant taking advantage of the respect given to an organization he didn't want to be part of — then so be it. Simon laughed to himself. Maybe he had finally found some small advantage to doing those damn interviews.

As he walked across that dark span, Simon acknowledged the guards with a courteous nod. They immediately returned the gesture. Simple as that. No words needed. Simon recognized it for what it was. Obedience, so effortless and so very efficient: it was what everyone who worked for the TAA was really good at.

Simon reached the other side and checked his watch. He was early. If he remembered the plan correctly, Sergeant White and his son wouldn't be at the meeting point for a while yet.

Being alone and out in the open could be very dangerous around a place like this. Simon realized that too. There were no standing buildings nearby for easy cover, but there was a tall berm at the edge of the street which looked almost like a man-made fortification. It was more like a big pile actually, not so out of place in this landscape, composed of equal parts building rubble and burned out car. It was also the largest and therefore most attractive option in the immediate area. Simon moved in quickly and took up position behind the pile where he could keep an eye on the street ahead without being so easily seen himself.

It was the smart thing to do for sure, just not something he probably would have done before. Waiting patiently and quietly had never been Simon's style. It was a challenge to control himself, to control the aggressive spirit which had always made him who he was. But that was then; this was now. Warriors were different now. Fighting was different. Planning and patience were required. Today was not the day to fight his battle. Not here. Not yet. Simon knew as much, and he also knew he had to stay alive long enough to accomplish what he really needed to do. He had learned some things in this strange new world.

So he stayed put and waited — patiently, for the most part. Simon paced back and forth along the full length of the berm, always keeping a look-out, always ready. There was a restless energy in his footsteps, and he moved very much like a caged tiger exploring the limits of his confines. He checked his watch several times along the well-worn path. Each time the clock seemed to move slower still. Simon let out an audible sigh. Patience, he finally had to admit, was a work in progress.

As he made yet another turn at the far end of the berm, Simon caught sight of two camouflaged men picking their way carefully through the rubble. He recognized them immediately.

"You're late," Simon called out with a smile.

"You're early," Sergeant White replied calmly. He never joked about something as important as synchronized timing on a mission.

"I guess we'll have to work on that." Simon extended his hand. The sergeant grasped the hand and shook it heartily.

"I'm goddamn glad to see you! I was wondering if you were going to show up." This time the old Marine was grinning himself.

"You know me," Simon paused for effect, "I try to never disappoint." He was smooth, self-assured. It seemed to come so natural to him.

"I see," Sergeant White chuckled. "You're full of shit, Mr. Anderson." He stopped quite abruptly, and his facial expression hardened. The joke seemed to stop right there too. It was the sergeant's turn to pause for effect — or something else entirely.

Simon squirmed just a little. He began to wonder if he had assumed too much familiarity and crossed some sort of line with the old Marine.

"Fortunately," White continued dryly, "I like people who are full of shit." He pointed up the street.

"Let's go."

There was a sly grin on the sergeant's face no one was really meant to see. Simon noticed but didn't let on that he did. He simply nodded and moved off in the desired direction followed closely by Sergeant White and his son. Simon suddenly felt much better.

Even with armed escorts, the streets were still a very dangerous place. Simon and the Marines were fully on their guard as they moved. They had to be ready if Smiling Bob and his thugs showed up again. There was black smoke on the far horizon, and Simon heard the sound of gunshots off in the distance. It was a sad fact of life — and death here. Simon understood that. For the moment, however, he felt fortunate things didn't seem to be getting any closer. They might just get lucky this time, he thought, and not have to fight their way through to the rescue mission.

The group continued to pick their way among the ruins, edging closer to their objective. Simon took no note of the devastation surrounding him. The shock value had clearly worn off by now. Still, he did notice the residents of this terrible place as they drifted back and forth between rubble-strewn streets and lonely walls remaining here and there, the last vestiges of buildings which had collapsed long ago. These ragged souls seemed to notice Simon as well. They didn't run away this time. The fear was gone, replaced with curiosity maybe. Simon couldn't tell for sure. He did see some of them talk together in groups as he walked by, but he was too far away to hear anything. Even more surprising, Simon thought for sure he saw a few of these people actually smiling. That was a big change from the day before, and it caused Simon to crack a bit of a smile himself.

There were even more people clustered around the Catholic Rescue Mission as the place came into view at last. It was a welcome sight for sore eyes. Sergeant White and his son relaxed their trigger fingers, and their precious cargo breathed a small sigh of relief himself. Like the day before, the mission was a real hub of activity. Simon could sense a buzz in the air as he and his escorts mixed freely with the crowd. Again, there were people talking and pointing and smiling. Simon knew they were talking about him, and that didn't bother him one bit.

"It is good to see you again, my son." Father Christopher met the trio just outside the door to the mission. He reached up and patted Simon warmly on the shoulder. He was smiling as well.

"It's good to be back." Simon replied as he reached over and shook the priest's free hand. He said it without hesitation. He meant it too. What might have once seemed unthinkable was now....

"What a difference a day makes," Simon mumbled under his breath.

Father Christopher opened the door and motioned for the group to enter. Just before they disappeared into the mission, Simon turned and took one last look around at the crowd outside. He still felt the weight of all those eyes.

One set in particular stood out from the rest. Simon looked straight ahead and into the deep brown eyes of the frail woman he had helped the day before. She was at the table helping to dole out the soup herself now. Her hands were thin. Her skin was pale, yet there was a distinct sparkle in her eyes. It was a far cry from yesterday. She seemed better, Simon thought, more alive somehow. She looked back at the man who had likely saved her life only the day before and nodded warmly, politely, as if today were just like any other day. There were no words spoken between them, and Simon wondered if there ever would be.

Yes, she was definitely better; it was all right there in her eyes. Simon thought back to his earlier comment, but couldn't bring himself to say it again out loud.

"What a difference a day makes."

Simon shook his head and then followed the priest into the mission. The frail woman immediately turned her attention back to the job of serving the soup.

Chapter 19

Arthur paced from one end of the classroom to the other, checking his watch at the turn and stealing a quick glance back at the doorway. He was trying not to be quite so obvious.

It wasn't working very well. The rest of the class fidgeted uncomfortably in their chairs as Arthur spun sharply on his heels to make yet another lap. Walking did help, but it used up only a tiny bit of nervous energy, not nearly enough to slow down his racing thoughts or clear a terribly muddled mind.

Yesterday had changed everything. There was so much more to worry about now than the day's lesson plan. Every few seconds, the teacher alternated back and forth between the polar opposites of absolute certainty: positively sure that his prized student would show back up today and then just equally as sure that he would not. Arthur scratched his head and sighed heavily.

After one more check of the time, he decided he really couldn't wait any longer.

"Today," Arthur began, "we're going to talk about the space race between the Soviet Union and the United States." Still he paused and took one last long look at the door.

The rest of the class almost instinctively followed their teacher's eyes toward the doorway. They had clearly recognized the obvious by now. Arthur, for his part, wasn't even concerned with the pretense anymore. He stared long. He stared hard. He wondered if looking at the space where something was supposed to be long enough would somehow make it magically appear. He could only hope.

More time passed, a few seconds only. It seemed so much longer. The room was unnaturally quiet, disturbed only by a random cough here and there. The air itself seemed more stagnant than normal as if, like everything else, it was paused in anticipation of some momentous conclusion. And then....

Hope was finally rewarded.

Simon and his Marine escorts appeared at the doorway. With a just a hint of a smile, Simon nodded at the teacher who simply returned the gesture in turn. No cheers. No clapping. No hearty words of welcome. No nothing at all. Simon casually moved a few chairs around until he found one which seemed to suit him. He sat down quietly and prepared to listen. That was it, a simple resolution, more starkly efficient rather than anything approaching momentous.

Whatever it was, no matter how small and outwardly insignificant it seemed, it worked for Arthur. He took a deep breath and began again, "The space race between the Soviet Union and the United States. Short story, really; the Soviets won."

"There was Sputnik in 1957," the teacher continued, "which carried a small dog into orbit. They followed that up in 1961 with the first manned space flight piloted by cosmonaut Yuri Gagarin. It took the United States until 1962 to put the first American, John Glenn, into orbit around the earth. Hell, the Russians even put the first woman into space in 1963, something Americans wouldn't do for another 20 years."

Arthur paused once again. This time it had absolutely nothing to do with waiting for a particular someone to come through the door. It was all for effect, all about the simple thrill of teaching. Arthur knew exactly what he was going to say next, but he wasn't going to say it just yet. First, he wanted to see how the class was going to react to what he had already said. That was the fun in it.

The reaction was swift and didn't surprise the teacher one bit, given the person who was doing the reacting.

"I thought this history class was supposed to inspire us." Matt Carson broke the silence. He wasn't going to wait for someone else to do it, and he wasn't making any attempt to hide the sarcasm in his voice.

His mother shook her head and tried to bury her face in her hands. A muffled groan loud enough to be heard rippled through the classroom. Jan Carson found herself contributing to that collective expression of exasperation almost as much as the rest of the adults in the class.

"The old United States of America lost," the teenager continued. "How is that supposed to inspire us? How does a country that was supposedly so great lose the race?"

"How?"

"I'll tell you how — maybe because it wasn't so great in the first place."

Matt Carson was very sure of himself. He couldn't wait to hear how all the so-called adults would answer his indisputable logic.

"Maybe we should be talking about the Russians instead." There. He'd said it now. Point made.

Arthur chuckled. This was going exactly the way he had hoped. He could always count on young Mr. Carson to bring up the most negative point possible at just the right time. It was what surly teenagers did. God bless them, Arthur thought to himself. He realized Mr. Carson's mother was none too happy right now, but it was going to be a perfect set-up for the rest of his lecture.

"Oh, my poor young friend," Arthur responded with a smile. There was a gleam in the old teacher's eye. "You just don't understand, but how could you really? You're not of the proper generation."

"You don't know, as an old radio personality from my day used to say, the rest of the story."

If there had been a musical soundtrack available, this would have been the perfect time for an inspirational crescendo. Arthur mused about the possibility. In his opinion, great movies, even those about something as potentially mundane as teaching, always had great soundtracks. Words, actions, and the like somehow didn't seem as real, as powerful without the proper musical chords. He thought briefly about whistling a tune himself, something from memory maybe, but then he decided against it.

Arthur shook his head and smiled. He couldn't remember the last time he had actually seen a movie. As it were, he was going to have to continue sans any grand theatrics.

"You see, in the midst of all this success by the Russians, President John F. Kennedy issued an extraordinary, yet very straightforward challenge to all Americans. At a special joint meeting of Congress in May of 1961, President Kennedy first told the nation that the United States of America would put a man on the moon by the end of the decade. He asked Congress for the resources to build new rockets powered by new types of fuel, to fly a lunar vehicle which had not even been invented yet."

"In 1962, President Kennedy spoke about the importance of the space race to a roaring crowd at Rice University." Arthur looked down at a particularly well-worn page in his history book and read aloud an excerpt from that speech:

"We choose to go to the moon. We choose to go to the moon in this decade and do the other things, not because they are easy, but because they are hard, because that goal will serve to organize and measure the best of our energies and skills, because that challenge is one that we are willing to accept, one we are unwilling to postpone, and one which we intend to win, and the others, too."

Arthur loved quoting the words of great figures from American history. It made him feel so much more alive as a teacher. If he could only pass on to his students such powerful words and ideas, Arthur truly believed, then the history itself would never die — and the ideals of the nation which that history represented might somehow live on. It was a lofty goal to be sure and a tall order for anyone, let alone an anonymous teacher holding class in a dilapidated classroom located somewhere just north of hell itself. But on days like this, so bright, so full of hope and promise, Arthur felt like he was up to the task.

"This was the birth of NASA, the National Aeronautics and Space Administration," the teacher said with a certain amount of pride. It was both a conclusion to the introduction and the beginning of, as Arthur had promised, the rest of the story.

Simon Anderson and the other members of the class listened intently as Arthur regaled them with tales of brave test pilots in supersonic jets, of astronauts who died in terrible fires, of Project Mercury, and the Apollo Program.

"Tragically, President Kennedy would not live to see the mission, his vision, fulfilled. He was felled by an assassin's bullet in 1963." Arthur suddenly choked up and almost immediately looked back down at the pages in the history book. A tear welled up in the corner of one eye; he was intent on hiding that from the class.

Arthur lingered for a moment on a particular picture, his finger tracing the words of the caption over and over again, as if re-reading the story would somehow change the end result. It didn't. It never did. That was the funny thing about the past.

"But Kennedy had truly inspired the nation with his vision," the teacher continued, his voice still tight with emotion, "and that inspiration endured long after his death. In July of 1969, the mission was finally completed when the United States landed the first man on the moon."

"As Astronaut Neil Armstrong took his first steps on the moon, he made one of the most enduring statements in all of American history, simple but powerful words that were transmitted live back to earth to millions of people glued to their TV's." Arthur didn't have to look at the book this time. He knew this one by heart.

"That's one small step for man, one giant leap for mankind."

Young Matt Carson was at a loss for words. The rest of the class didn't say much either. Richard leaned back in his chair with a comfortable grin on his face.

"The moon landing was just that," Arthur declared, "a giant technological leap forward for all mankind!"

"Can you just imagine," he asked the class, "what it really takes to send a man all the way to the moon and bring him back to earth safely? Think about it. It seems impossible, doesn't it? But it isn't. The United States of America did it. The best and the brightest, everybody working together on a single national goal did it!"

"If you can send a man to the moon, then nothing is impossible."

Simon smiled. He understood exactly what Arthur was talking about.

Bill reached down to scratch the only part of his left leg that was still all him. The well-worn prosthetic, which had cost him a full 3 days' worth of food, was irritating the hell out of his stump. It wasn't much better than a pirate's old peg leg, he realized, but it was also the only thing keeping him upright. And that was worth something.

He had kept his silence until now. Maybe because he had kind of been enjoying Arthur's space stories. Maybe because he sometimes preferred to let stupid teenagers do all the talking. Maybe, but no more.

"Are you really trying to tell me that nothing is impossible? Absolutely fucking nothing," Bill asked with special emphasis on the expletive, "are you sure?"

"Absolutely yes," Arthur replied firmly.

"Really?" Bill's face tightened into something midway between a grin and a scowl. Whatever it was, it was decidedly unfriendly.

"No disrespect teacher, but I don't see how the hell you can say that! Is it possible that all of us are going to get out of this hellhole? Or is it possible that we're all going to work together and somehow make this hellhole a paradise?"

"Do you really think anything is possible?" Rotating slowly on his good leg, Bill tried to point to each and every member of the class. "Do you? Do you?" Every time he repeated that simple question, his voice got a little bit louder, his anger boiled a little bit closer to the surface.

No-one in the class answered. Finally Bill stopped asking.

"You see teacher," he turned back towards Arthur, "I hate to disappoint you, but we're not among the best and the brightest here. Most of us," Bill stared down at his left leg for a moment, "are just rejects from the trade association."

"Or," as he looked young Matt Carson straight in the eye, "poor little bastards the TAA never wanted in the first place."

By the time he reached the very last word, Bill's voice had trailed off almost to a whisper. His anger seemed to ebb away at just about the same rate. He took a deep breath, satisfied that he had made his point, though in truth he really wasn't very happy about it. Bill took one last look around the room and then limped back slowly to his seat.

There was a nearly perfect, yet very uncomfortable silence in the classroom, as if every last bit of air had been sucked out of the space. No words. No coughing. No breathing — almost.

"Nothing is impossible."

This time it wasn't coming from Arthur.

Simon stood up straight and said it again, "Nothing is impossible."

Arthur smiled. So did Richard.

"I don't know if we can ever make this place a paradise," Simon added rather stiffly. He had faced arrows and bullets and men in battle. He had faced death without fear. This was different. He had the soul of a warrior, the deadly skills of a warrior. But now he had to do more than just battle the evil in men; somehow he had to speak to the very best in them as well. Words — his words — had to be stronger than cold hard steel.

"But we can certainly make it a better place." Simon's voice was confident, firm.

The classroom was quiet once again, though it seemed to be a very different type of quiet. No deflating, all encompassing, silence this time. The room buzzed with a steady rumble of hushed conversations springing up all over. There was a real and tangible sense of anticipation in the air. Someone just needed to speak up first.

"How? Just how are we going to do that?" It was Jan Carson. It was a real question. It was what good journalist's did. And Jan was trying to be just that, even in this place, even if other people didn't seem to care about such things anymore.

Simon had a ready answer. "We're going to make stuff. We're going to make stuff just like previous generations of Americans did. We're going to make stuff like American factories did to supply the army and navy that won World War II. We're going to make stuff and then sell it or trade it to get the things we need to make this a better place."

"We're not going to wait for somebody to help us because we know nobody's going to come. We have to help ourselves!" Simon smiled, and there was light in his eye.

"It all sounds great," Jan Carson replied, "but I have to ask again how are we going to do this?"

Again Simon had an answer. "There's a small factory building down the street from the mission. All four walls are still standing, and it looks like most of the roof is intact as well. There's wood and metal in all this wreckage around here. We can salvage some of it. We can use it to the repair the building. We can use it as raw materials to build stuff."

It was an answer, not a perfect answer, but an answer nonetheless. Simon had the idea, but even now he didn't have all the answers. He was going to need help from others.

At first, he didn't get it.

"This is absolute fucking craziness," Bill interjected. He had heard just about enough. "We can't do any of this! Nobody can. It's impossible."

"Nothing is impossible," Arthur repeated.

"Bullshit! Just repeating the same thing over and over again doesn't make it true." Bill wasn't much interested in the subtleties of open debate.

"I know," Arthur replied, "because it's been done before — multiple times in fact. In World War II, during the battle of Stalingrad, the city was literally flattened by months of German artillery and aerial bombardment, but the Russians wouldn't give in no matter what. They fought back from the rubble; more than a million soldiers and civilians died. They kept factories running in that rubble, and they finally won that battle. It turned the tide of the war."

"Or, if you want an example closer to home, I can give you one from the American space program we've just been talking about."

"You see," Arthur continued, "there were other missions to the moon after the initial moon landing. One of them, Apollo 13, had a serious malfunction, an explosion, in space. They couldn't land on the moon, but the astronauts on board and the engineers on the ground managed to nurse that crippled spacecraft safely back to earth against all odds."

"At one point during that harrowing ordeal, they had to change the oxygen filter in order to keep the air on the ship breathable. Engineers had to figure out a way to make a square filter fit into a round hole using only things they had on the spacecraft. And somehow they did it. An accident which should have ended in death and disaster instead turned into NASA's finest hour."

Bill didn't say anything else. He just shook his head.

"You'll need some electricity." Alex, the Idea Man, stroked his beard. "I can make that happen," he said with a grin.

"Okay, now, how are you going to do that?" Jan Carson was becoming more and more comfortable with the journalist thing.

"It's very simple really," the Idea Man replied without any hesitation at all. "All we need is a good stiff breeze. We build a small windmill to harness the power of the wind. And the best thing — it's all free!"

"Small windmill?" Jan blurted out. She had forgotten, for the moment, every last bit of journalistic decorum. "I thought windmills had to be big and tall to be useful. Kind of like those massive wind farms you sometimes see pictures of."

"That's exactly what the TAA said," the Idea Man huffed. "They were wrong back then just like you, my dear friend, are wrong right now. Windmills don't have to be that large if they can rotate in both directions and capture the wind no matter which way it blows in. It's very efficient."

Alex huffed once again, somewhat indignant that no-one had yet recognized his true genius. He quietly scanned the classroom looking for support, approval, anything.

"It will work," he added with deliberate emphasis on the final word. He didn't have to convince himself, but it sure felt like he was going to have to sell everybody else on the idea.

There was a momentary pause in the discussion, though the hushed murmur of various side conversations continued unabated.

Richard stood straight up from his seat. He carefully adjusted his shirt and straightened the creases in his pants. "If Alex can get us some electricity," he said calmly, "I think I may be able to get some of those machines going. And once I do, I'm sure Alex here can help us with some simple new product ideas."

The Idea Man smiled.

"I know. I know," Richard chuckled. "You're going to ask me how. It's just part of your job, isn't it?" He was looking straight at Jan Carson who quickly nodded in the affirmative.

"I used to run factories for the trade association, and I know there are people around here with some mechanical ability. I believe, with a little elbow grease, that this plan has a chance."

Jan Carson was just about to ask another question, the most obvious question, when Richard beat her to the punch.

"I know you are all curious how come I'm not still working for the TAA. It was very straightforward really. I guess I'm one of those rejects from the trade association that Bill mentioned earlier."

"They didn't much want me anymore after I was diagnosed with cancer. They fired me, immediately cut off my insurance and pension. That was pretty much it. There weren't many options after that — other than dying of course." Richard's voice never wavered, never cracked, never betrayed even the slightest hint of anger. It was all very matter of fact.

"But you see, of course, I'm not ready to die," Richard continued, casually brushing back his thinning hair. "So I ended up here."

He drew in a deep breath and let it out naturally. He was very comfortable with his own reality even if some others in the room were not. Jan Carson wiped a tear from her eye. Sometimes she really didn't like being a journalist, or even attempting to be a journalist.

Taking note of a few moist eyes, Richard shook his finger back and forth as if gently admonishing a small child for something he shouldn't be doing.

"I came to this class because I think it's important to stay involved. As long as I get out every day, working or doing something else, I'm not just preparing to die. I'm still living. I'm still very much a going concern."

"And I guess I'm asking this class to do the same thing right now." Richard looked around the room until he had made eye contact with every single person. "We need to take advantage of this opportunity, as far-fetched as it may seem to some of you, because we need to keep on living. We need to do it ourselves, for ourselves — no matter what the hell the trade association thinks!"

Jan Carson smiled and wiped another tear from her eye, this time for an entirely different reason. Richard turned and stared back at Simon.

"Nothing is impossible."

Chapter 20

Russell White watched the sun rise through the upper right hand corner of the window. It was the only window pane which happened to be all glass, the remaining panes being fully covered by cardboard or wooden blocks meticulously cut and sized for this very purpose. Sergeant White squinted at the first rays of sunlight peeking into his room. A lot of things had changed around this place since the arrival of their new friend or whatever one chose to call him. One of those changes was the square of clear, unbroken glass perched high and safe in its corner. Not so long ago, that particular space used to be filled by a worn piece of cardboard just like all the rest.

It had been nearly a month since Simon Anderson, that new friend, had made the suggestion to re-open the old factory. Since then, amazingly enough, Alex, the Idea Man, and Richard had delivered on everything they said they would. The roof had been repaired; it wasn't pretty, but it was functional. And the factory had working electricity thanks to Alex's weird little windmill that caught wind blowing in from any direction. Richard found a local man who had some natural mechanical ability, and the two of them working together had managed to get a single punch press machine operating.

That punch press was now producing a variety of simple tools, things like bottle openers or small wrenches. These were small enough that they could be smuggled across the bridge and then traded for goods or food on the other side. It had proven, so far at least, to be a pretty smooth operation, just big enough to be somewhat effective yet still small enough to stay under the radar of the guards at the bridge.

Sergeant White stretched high on his toes to get a good look out of the glass window pane. The sun was bright, and he had to partially shield his eyes. Still from there, he could see some of the results of all that trading. He could see activity. He could see life. He could see work going on to clear space for a new garden and people digging holes for seeds and small plants. He could see minor repairs being made to the mission building itself: patching holes in the roof, covering or replacing broken windows. He could even see some of the trash being carried off; he couldn't remember the last time that had actually happened.

The area immediately surrounding the Catholic Rescue Mission was surely changing. It still looked like hell in White's opinion. Marines, even old Marines, had very high standards for such things. But it no longer looked like Hell with the capital H. It was a significant distinction. The place did look better, and the people living there seemed to feel better about it. He saw smiles on faces and what looked almost like laughter, although he really couldn't say for sure. For God's sake, Sergeant White thought for a moment, it was almost beginning to look like a normal street down there.

This was progress: the quality of life improving just a little bit each and every day. He could see that clearly enough. He also knew just how terribly fragile everything really was in a place like this — with the kinds of neighbors they had. This wasn't a comfortable upscale suburb. There were no nice cul-de-sacs and pot luck suppers here. These neighbors had guns, lots of them, and would likely frown on anything which might even remotely interfere with the narcotics trade they controlled. How they would react to this perceived threat, however, was anybody's guess. The drug dealers might choose the path of least resistance and simply work around the rescue mission, or they could just as well try using overwhelming force to flatten anything and everything in their way. If he were a betting man, White definitely knew where he would put his money.

This much he was sure about: For the progress to continue, for the people and the rescue mission to survive, this place, this ground — had to be defended.

And it was his job to do the defending. Or really his job and his son's job and the job of a few other dedicated men with guns. They had to keep Smiling Bob and his goons at arm's length. There had been some skirmishing, but nothing serious so far. It just meant they had to stay alert and on guard. Sergeant Russell White smiled. He liked having something real to defend again.

"Nothing is impossible," he said softly. No-one was around to hear him. Not that he really cared if someone did anyway. White sighed and looked away from the window. He was proud of what was going on down there on the street. He was proud that he was holding the line right here, right now. It was what good Marines did.

He only wished his older brother was still around to see all of this.

There was a battered chest of drawers in the corner of the room only a few steps away from the window. That chest contained nearly everything of value the sergeant still owned. White approached the chest slowly now and with some reluctance. He opened the second drawer from the top and carefully rummaged through the contents until he found what he was looking for. The package was right there, still in its place. It was wrapped tightly into a triangular shape. As he gently placed his hand on top of the package, a single tear welled up in the corner of the old Marine's eye.

"That's Uncle Frank's, isn't it?" Russell White's son had entered the room almost completely unnoticed.

"Yes, it is," the father replied quietly.

"What are you doing with it?"

"I'm thinking of taking it down to the rescue mission with me."

"Why?"

"Because … I'm just beginning to think the time may be right," the father continued thoughtfully. "And because I think your Uncle Frank would have wanted it this way."

The young man shrugged his shoulders; the look on his face was still puzzled. Sergeant White chuckled. He had not really expected his son to understand.

"You let me worry about such things. You're a young man. Right now, I just want you worrying about how to keep your head down when we're out on the streets." The old Sergeant laughed and gave his son a hearty slap on the back.

"Now, let's you and I head on down to the mission. I think it's going to be a pretty nice day today."

He tucked the package under his arm before the two of them headed out the door.

Not more than a few blocks away from the Catholic Rescue Mission, someone else looked out of his window and saw the same bright morning sun. But he seemed to be coming away with an entirely different assessment of the day's prospects. Smiling Bob reached a finger under his upper lip and stroked his gold tooth. It was a nervous habit, considered rude in most social circles but not so much that anyone wanted to risk the downside of pointing out the obvious.

"You know how I don't like change, don't you?" Smiling Bob remarked casually to an associate sitting at a nearby table. Bob was staring out the window at nothing in particular. It was not immediately clear to the associate whether his boss was talking about the sunshine which had replaced, temporarily at least, the usual clouds of black smoke or something else entirely.

"I don't like what's going on over at that rescue mission," the boss continued. Those people are fixing things up, and now they seem to think they can block us from passing through our own turf. Maybe they've fried their brains by spending too much time in this sun we're seeing a little more of these days. I don't know, but I don't like it at all."

There was no anger in Bob's voice, and the tone was relaxed, almost thoughtful. Perhaps this emboldened the associate to speak more freely than he otherwise would.

"I don't think you need to worry about that place, boss. It doesn't take us more than a couple blocks out of our way to bypass the mission. It adds less than 10 minutes of time to get to the bridge."

The associate grinned. "We haven't been late on a shipment in over two weeks," he added with visible pride.

Smiling Bob didn't say a word. He turned away from the window. He wasn't smiling. Carefully and without any hurry at all, he withdrew a thin, ornate case from his pocket. He folded a long blade into lock position, paused briefly to relish the sound of the click, and then abruptly slammed it down through the hand of his associate. The knife firmly pinned the hand to the table. A trickle of blood oozed out onto the skin.

There was a muffled scream from the associate as he immediately forced the fleshy side of his free hand into his mouth. He bit down slightly and tried to remain perfectly calm. It was, the associate had learned over time, the best way not only to minimize the current pain but also to prevent his boss from inflicting any more. Smiling Bob continued to hold a tight grip on the knife. He still had not said a word.

This lasted for several minutes, long enough for the blood to form a sizeable puddle on the table. Quiet, perfectly quiet, which served mainly to make the whole episode more menacing, more terrifying somehow than it already was. This was by design, of course. It was one way the boss liked to make sure everyone clearly understood his point.

Finally Smiling Bob broke the silence. He spoke softly, and he was smiling now. "Don't you ever tell me what to worry about or not to worry about. Understand?"

"Yes, boss," the associate stammered, having just removed the hand from his mouth. "I understand, boss!"

"Very good then," Smiling Bob replied. He was no longer just smiling now. He was flat out beaming across the full width and breadth of his face, showing off his prized gold tooth on purpose. It was a little hokey, he knew, but he liked doing something a little special to show his appreciation when someone learned something, even if it took some real pain to make it stick.

He pulled the knife out of his associate's hand. "You need to clean that up." Smiling Bob motioned towards the puddle of blood on the table. The associate nodded weakly.

The blood on the knife was still an unresolved matter though. With a rather sudden burst of inspiration, Smiling Bob laughed out loud and then whistled. Almost immediately, a large German shepherd bounded into the room, tail wagging, eager to please. Bob knelt down and nuzzled the animal's coat, presenting the knife at the same time. The dog quickly obliged by licking the blade clean.

"That's it. Good girl! You're such a good girl." The shepherd danced back and forth, looking for the next thing she could do to please her owner.

"Now give daddy a big kiss." Grabbing a handful of fur and collar, Smiling Bob drew his girl in close and puckered up. The dog eagerly lapped away at his lips and face.

"Okay girl," he chuckled after accepting several of those kisses, "that's enough now." He punctuated the command with a sharp blow to the animal's flank before getting back to his feet.

Smiling Bob carefully folded the blade of the knife back into its case. He looked over at his bloodied associate and laughed once again. Strange he had to admit, but the pain and suffering of others always seemed to have this kind of effect on him. He couldn't quite explain it himself — though he knew he loved it so, craved it like some dirty street addict. The ultimate rush: it made him feel so intensely alive, from the hair on his toes all the way to the very tips of his fingernails.

Bob was still smiling, and he was still laughing. It just felt too good to stop.

Louder, louder and more animated the laughter grew, a terrific energy roiling through the air and washing over the room. It came to an end, finally, only when Smiling Bob bent over to suck in a big gulp of fresh air. All was silent then, save the labored wheezing of one trying hard to catch his breath. He emerged thereafter, more subdued, and calmly wiped spit away from the corner of his mouth. Yet there was a savage glow in his eyes, something borne of a terrible bloodlust, something all too dark and unnerving.

The associate continued to hold pressure on his bloody hand. Somehow he still managed a response to his boss, an expression which was about midway between a grimace and a smile. Not that he really wanted to. Not that he really enjoyed his own pain.

He just knew better by now.

Sergeant White knew better too. He knew all about Smiling Bob. As father and son walked along the street on this bright sunny day, the old Marine figured it was just too damn pretty outside to worry about the enemy right now.

It was a short walk to the mission. Russell White knew the way well. On a normal day, he could cover that distance with his eyes closed and without really thinking. Today, however, he walked with his eyes wide open, seeing more, thinking more than he had in a very long time.

Maybe today wasn't a normal day. Then again, as Russell White pondered further, normal over the past month seemed to be entirely different from what used to pass for normal around this place anyway.

It wasn't just the sunlight or the absence of thick black smoke; everything felt different. Here he could see up close the faces of those people he had watched from the window before. There was no doubt now; they were indeed smiling and laughing. That was a definite change, and it wasn't the only one. Directly up ahead, Sergeant White could see two young men helping an elderly woman slowly make her way towards the soup line at the mission. He also noticed an older man on top of the mission roof barking orders to several younger workers, and strangely enough, the workers actually seemed to be listening and following instructions. In the new garden, both old and young, the crippled and the strong, were working together, all contributing what they could to bring green once again from the tired grey earth.

People were working hard, and they appeared to genuinely care about what they were doing. They all seemed to stand just a little bit taller, a little bit straighter now. They had something to work for. They had a purpose again. White could see that.

He could also see children, young men and women, and others gathered around Arthur at the front steps of the mission. It was unusual for the teacher to lecture outside. But it was such a pretty day, and the crowd seemed to be much larger than the normal class. Arthur read from his worn history book. The audience seemed to hang on each and every word.

"Give me your tired, your poor,"
"Your huddled masses, yearning to breathe free,"
"The wretched refuse of your teeming shore,"
"Send these, the homeless, tempest tost to me,"
"I lift my lamp beside the golden door."

Russell White recognized the poem immediately. It made him think of his brother once again. He remembered way back when they were kids, when the two of them first went to visit the Statue of Liberty. It was a clear sunny day like today. For a moment there, he could almost smell the salt water of New York Harbor.

Their father used to take the boys to historic sites, thought it was good that they saw the places where their country's history was actually made, thought it would make them appreciate their own freedom just a little bit more: Washington, DC, Mount Vernon, and Freedom Hall in Philadelphia along with countless battlefield sites. The old sergeant thought back and chuckled to himself. He remembered how he and his brother sometimes used to bitch about going, particularly when they were teenagers, but somehow they always ended up going anyway. After a while, they stopped complaining. Something must have sunk in along the way.

That was probably why, Sergeant White seemed to recall, both he and his brother had been so eager to join the Marine Corps in the first place. They wanted to take their place in the long line of proud, brave men who had fought for their country's freedom. He remembered too how his brother had died on some far flung desolate battlefield in defense of that freedom. Russell White missed his brother with all his heart, but he didn't shed any tears of sadness; he was far too proud of the memory. Looking into the eyes of Arthur's young charges and then back over at his own son, he thought he saw that pride once again.

It was the wry look in a young man's eyes, the look of a man who controlled his own destiny. It was the very glow of freedom.

White pulled the package out from under his arm and held it in both hands. He was glad he had brought it with him. He knew now for sure the time was right.

Slowly, carefully, and with great reverence, he removed paper and string covering. The triangle of cloth was tightly wrapped and had not been touched for a very long time. Sergeant White sighed as he examined the material. The stars in the field of blue, the bars of red and white, all looked as fresh and bright as they looked those many years ago when the flag was first presented by a grateful nation. The old Marine inhaled the fresh air and calmly allowed it to escape. He could see that day and hear it all still: endless rows of white headstones, the sharp staccato of gunfire, the mournful echoes of a lonely bugle. The sound of taps, he remembered so clearly now, faded gradually away, as if carrying off the soul of a good soldier to lasting peace in the heavens above. Silence then.

Dead silence.

A sacrifice though, he would never forget. White took a long look all around. The sounds of life, the sounds of liberty were here.

Today, in the bright sunlight of present day, past memories gave way finally to the current imperative. A proud brother knew now there was a better way to honor the fallen. Pulling and tugging at the tight folds of fabric, he set free the full body of something he considered almost sacred.

Just up ahead, an old flagpole stood tall and bare in front of the rescue mission. Bent at the top and swaying just a bit with the wind, the pole had not been used for as long as anyone cared to remember. Sergeant Russell White aimed to change all that. In a few powerful strides, he covered the distance to his objective. Then, holding his brother's flag tightly in one hand, he grasped and worked free the rusty cable with the other. He attached the flag to the cable and raised it quickly to the top. The cable made a grinding squeaky sound on the way up. It was the most beautiful sound Sergeant White believed he had heard in a long time.

At the top of the pole, just below the bend, the old flag caught a breeze and waved full and free in the early morning sun. The old Marine immediately snapped to attention and saluted. So too did the son, who by now had noticed just exactly what his father was doing.

It didn't take long for others to notice as well. Slowly and surely, whether it be memory stirring or simple curiosity, people began to gather around the flagpole — first the aged and infirm, soon however, followed by young men and young women and even children. Arthur gave up lecturing as his class had drifted completely away. A few of the older spectators, veterans of the armed forces possibly, followed the sergeant's lead and did their best to stand at attention and salute. It was a ragged line to be sure, really more a loose semi-circle of old warriors who still remembered their former flag. Russell White couldn't have been prouder if he had been standing that very moment on the old parade ground at Parris Island.

Barely noticed in all the commotion, a small boy worked his way through the crowd and joined the ragged line. He threw up a salute just like all the rest. Sergeant White couldn't help but notice the newest and shortest addition to his line at attention. White knelt down to the child's level. He recognized the boy as one of Arthur's younger students.

"Do you call that a salute, mister?" the sergeant asked, trying very hard to be properly stern and intimidating.

"Yes sir," the boy answered with a smile. His face was dirty, framed with hair thick and red and filled with curls. The smile seemed to light up that dirty face. "Teacher told me about that flag. Told me to honor it. Told me that it meant I could grow up to be anything I wanted to be."

Sergeant White couldn't help but smile himself. "You're absolutely right young man. If you work hard, you're absolutely right." He rubbed the kid's head in a friendly way, nearly getting his fingers stuck in those damned red curls.

Simon Anderson saw the flag too. He was approaching the rescue mission himself, much earlier than normal today. For the first time, he had also brought along his wife Holly. Over the past month, Simon had found it increasingly difficult to keep up the charade over what he did when he wasn't at the trade association. He was tired of living a lie with the woman he loved. He knew he couldn't tell her everything, but he could tell her about this place. The truth, or at least this small part of the truth, had been a double-edged sword though. He was truly relieved when Holly had accepted his reasons for helping these people, but then he had been equally terrified when she wanted to come along.

"Where you go, I go," she had said. There had been no room for negotiation, not that he had really expected any.

Almost by instinct, Simon reached down and grabbed Holly's hand; he wanted to keep her real close. She squeezed his hand back and smiled. Simon looked deep into those brown eyes. It was still the most beautiful smile he had ever seen.

"What's that?" Holly pointed at the flag ahead with her free hand.

"You'll see," Simon chuckled warmly. "You'll learn all about that soon enough."

The old flag was visible far beyond the Catholic Rescue Mission. Hector Gonzalez could see it from the window of the meth lab where he worked. He recognized the Stars and Stripes. He knew what they stood for. Gonzalez pulled down his face mask and shook his head.

He knew that flag meant trouble.

Chapter 21

Simon Anderson stared grimly at the blank computer screen directly in front of him. There was a steady flicker, the white glow of electronic life; otherwise the inbox was absolutely empty. He wasn't receiving many e-mails these days, a sure sign he was effectively out of the loop at trade association headquarters now.

Not that it really bothered him much; his heart and mind were elsewhere, far away from computers, quiet offices, and the like. It wasn't all about the career anymore for Simon. That career, the job which once provided wealth and material comfort, had asked far too much in return. Now it was just an all too painful memory. The nightmares, the guilt: he worked hard each and every day to keep all of it buried deep down inside.

There were newer memories, better memories. Simon thought of the sparkle in Holly's beautiful brown eyes, the soft touch of her skin, the excitement he felt when he held her close. She wanted him. She needed him. He thought of the lost souls on the wrong side of the bridge. They needed him too. He had recognized that the very first time he crossed the bridge those many weeks ago. In that time though, real progress had been made, and Holly had become part of it as well. He no longer had to keep it from her. She had come along willingly to be by his side, to work, to share in the danger if need be.

There was much to be done despite that danger. Owing to motherly instincts perhaps, Holly had been drawn to the little ones, children much less fortunate than their own daughter. She made sure they were fed, bandaged little wounds, and helped to teach them their school lessons. For some of them, she was truthfully the closest thing to a mother they really had. Simon smiled when he thought of their dirty little faces, the children who simply adored his wife.

Things were better on the far side of the bridge now. Simon knew that. People were making and selling things. They were eating better. They were building things back up from the ruins. People were starting to believe in themselves again.

Actually, they were starting to believe in something greater than themselves, something more than just living day to day now: a real home, a real community.

Simon closed his eyes but could see it all so clearly: amid the charred wreckage of broken bricks and stone, the garden green sprouted anew from the tired old earth, a rebirth inexorable as the dawning of a new day. It was a second chance — for many their last chance — all in that place across the bridge. A place where people cared, a place where hard work counted for something, a place where a man could change his lot in life, a place protected by an old flag which suddenly stood for something again.

Hope.

It was the simple, undying belief in a better tomorrow. The hopes and dreams of so many, there was great power in them, and that power was beating back finally the forces of despair, the scourge of malaise. The tired, the poor, the huddled masses: they had tasted the sweet succor of freedom, and they liked it. They liked it a lot.

Simon opened his eyes.

All the things Arthur had said once about America were no longer just words in a dusty old book. A people's history had been brought back from the dead to be passed on to the next generation, a proud history, a history of shared sacrifice for the common dream. The American Dream — with liberty and justice for all — was for real now, at least in the very small area surrounding the Catholic Rescue Mission. Simon could feel it. He could believe in it.

"God bless the United States of America," Simon mused. He leaned back in his chair and looked up at the ceiling.

The office was quiet still except for the soft hum coming from that blank computer screen. That was just enough to bring Simon firmly back to the here and now. He stared once again at the screen. He was worried. Blank wasn't necessarily a good thing; it didn't mean he was a forgotten man, just a resource who wasn't really needed at this very moment. He knew the trade association all too well. He knew how quickly things could change. He also knew that things were not going very well right now for the TAA.

The European Union was proving to be a much tougher nut to crack than Daniel Garcia had originally anticipated. Simple, quick terror strikes had not been enough to bring the EU to heel. Quite the opposite really. Blood and slaughter had only further inflamed the civilian population and stiffened resistance.

The TAA had upped the ante first with air strikes from off-shore vessels and then more extensive landings of security forces to take and hold military bases on the ground. In media reports of late, the escalation and additional manpower had been justified as necessary to more efficiently support continued operations. The Europeans were fighting back hard though and beginning to inflict significant casualties on the TAA. Men on the ground, even those in fortified positions, were simply easier to get at and kill than those in airplanes or helicopters.

Scores of people were dying, on both sides now, but the desired results were simply not being achieved. Bombs, bullets, and bloodshed: still no terrorist rings uncovered or much less defeated. Justice for the fallen, promised once with great fanfare, remained elusive as ever. That much was plainly evident, despite what attractive, well-heeled television anchors might be saying publicly. Some people were quietly calling the whole operation a waste of trade association resources, and Simon knew just how much Daniel Garcia hated waste — and people who questioned any of his policies. Simon feared that he might be called on to do more interviews to help shore up flagging public support for the war. He didn't know if he could face the cameras again — to lie — or if not to lie, at least not to yell out the truth.

He looked back up at the ceiling and sighed. He tried to visualize what was most important to him, to see Holly's face and the place across the bridge. There was a soft knock at the office door.

Chris Smith stuck his head in. "Are you busy?"

Simon didn't say a word. He just turned the blank computer screen around to face the door.

"Uh, I guess not," the I.T. man replied flatly. There was a sly smile on his face as he eased himself fully into the office and took a seat.

"I know you probably already know this," Smith continued, "but things are not going well for the trade association right now."

Simon frowned, still without saying a word.

The silence didn't seem to bother Chris Smith much. "And you know," he added without missing a beat, "what that might mean then."

Simon nodded in agreement, though his expression was clearly pained. He understood full well what that meant.

"Have you gotten that request yet?"

"No!" Simon answered firmly, as if the word itself could stop such a thing. He took a deep breath and clenched his fists. His eyes were dark, fierce almost. It was the look of a man who surely intended to try.

Smith paused, taking full measure of that response and the somewhat disquieting look in those eyes. The I.T. man leaned back in his chair. He had known Simon Anderson for several weeks now. They had talked many times about many different things; Simon was one of the few people who actually cared to speak to him at the office. Smith considered Simon Anderson a friend, but sometimes he wondered if he really knew the man at all.

The air was still. The silence was uncomfortable.

"Okay then," the I.T. man began again, this time with a bit of a nervous chuckle. "Let me tell you something you may not know."

"Like I said, things are not going well for the TAA right now, and there are plenty of people who aren't too happy about it. Some of these people are starting to speak up."

"And you know," Smith drawled on purpose, "how the CEO hates to hear anybody who disagrees with him."

Simon's facial expression softened just a little. His interest was piqued.

"The new Gettysburg Containment Center: you know the story don't you? The official public story, that is. According to the press, the place is there to treat flu victims in total isolation. The total isolation is the key of course. That's why it was built in the middle of the old battlefield park. Lots of land so nobody can get too close. It's supposedly the only thing keeping the big bad flu pandemic in check."

"Supposedly."

The last supposedly was deliberately sarcastic. Smith toyed briefly with the idea of adding a third supposedly but then decided two was enough, at least for the moment.

"You know all about the flu pandemic." He looked straight at Simon, waiting for some sort of reaction. There was interest still, but nothing overly dramatic. "It's amazing to me," Smith continued with a smile, "just how many of the people who are complaining about the war suddenly seem to come down with a case of the flu. And of course, they then have to be locked away at the Gettysburg Containment Center."

"All in the name of public safety … supposedly."

That was the third supposedly. The I.T. man shook his head. It really was better with three, he thought.

Simon felt a sudden queasiness in his stomach. He had not bothered to count the times supposedly had been used, and he didn't much appreciate Smith's penchant for sarcasm.

The revelation itself, though hardly a surprise given the current environment and the powers that be, was disturbing nonetheless and only added to Simon's dilemma. It went far beyond simple physical discomfort; it made him feel even more complicit, even more dirty somehow. Sure he may not have personally put those people into prison, but he could almost feel his hand pushing the cell doors shut. His stomach churned and knotted up further.

He knew the deal even if he sometimes didn't like to admit it. There was a cost for his continued silence, and it seemed to get just a little bit bigger every day. Simon put his hand to his temple and forehead and rubbed particularly hard. Deep down, he realized this was something he really needed to know, maybe just something he didn't necessarily want to know right now — particularly if he had to force himself in front of those cameras once again.

Chris Smith had a keen eye for people and all the raw subtleties of human behavior. He had been paid very well for this particular skill once — in the time before, when he had been somebody other than the I.T. man.

He took careful note now of Simon's reaction even though the latter had not so far added a single word to the current conversation. It was something very close to despair, and it was written all over Simon's face. To the trained eye, there was a certain pain in the way Simon held his jaw, not clenched so tightly, somehow not quite so strong or rock solid as before. A great sadness, the weight of a terrible burden, had settled in the eyes, replacing for the time being, at least, the burning intensity Smith had grown accustomed to seeing.

The I.T. man knew all too well about the pain. He felt it nearly every day he walked the lonely halls of trade association headquarters, and he didn't wish it on anyone, particularly the only friend he had in this godforsaken place.

And yet, despite the empathy and any internal misgivings, Smith suddenly smiled. He had to quickly turn away from Simon to conceal his expression. It felt so wrong and so right at the same time. Safely hidden though, he continued to smile, big and broad now. Smith found something strangely comforting about the pain in his friend's face, not the pain itself of course, but that there was pain at all. The pain, Smith knew, was a sure sign. It meant that Simon cared about something, that he cared about what was going on — that he was actually bothered by the injustice of putting innocent people in prison simply because they dared to criticize the party line.

Yes, the I.T. man recognized it clearly. And it was so very much different from the rest of the TAA where studied ambivalence, the immorality of pretending not to know, was the rule. The rule, some called it a culture of fear; others called it a culture of convenience. Either way, Simon didn't seem to be following the rule right now, and that made Chris Smith very happy.

"You know," Smith said finally. He had turned back around, still smiling, but definitely more subdued. "There's somebody else in that containment center, somebody important, somebody who's been locked up for a long, long time."

Smith paused. He wasn't really sure why he was about to share this fact with Simon. Maybe it was just the spur of the moment. Maybe he felt some sort of strange kinship, a shared bond with someone else who understood the pain.

"Have you ever heard the name Jim Harris?" He asked the question, not that he truly expected an answer from Simon. He wasn't so surprised then when he didn't get one.

"Congressman Jim Harris? Former United States Congressman Jim Harris?" Still no answer. Still no surprise.

"I guess not." Chris Smith shook his head, grinning energetically enough to be just a tad below laughing outright. He reached over and playfully cuffed Simon on the shoulder. "Anyway, if you don't know, I guess I can tell you."

"Congressman Harris was the end of era, if you will. He was apparently the last man in the whole country who still believed in government by the people, government for the people. Or at least, he was the only man still willing to say so publicly. Many years ago, when the United States Congress was preparing to vote itself out of existence in order to join the Trade Association of the Americas, he was the only representative to actually vote no. It didn't do any good, of course. It just made Harris a marked man."

"Funny thing," Smith continued. "The TAA didn't eliminate Mr. Harris, as in killing him. Maybe they didn't want a martyr on their hands at the time. They did eliminate him, however, as in locking him away … out of sight, out of mind for all these years."

"And now," the I.T. man added quickly, "they've moved Harris to the Gettysburg Containment Center. I guess the CEO likes the idea of all that land and isolation between the public and one of his favorite detainees. Must be another case of the flu, right?"

Simon didn't answer; he still wasn't much in the mood for talking.

But the new information clearly got his attention. His eyes were suddenly alert, and there was a renewed tightness in the jaw, something he didn't even try to hide from his very perceptive colleague. For the moment then, his mind drifted away from the current problem, his own conflict, his own guilt. Simon thought once again of men who had stood alone against the many, of men who had made great sacrifice when the Gods, or the times, had demanded it.

The images, the words, were a mixture of all he had known before and all he had learned over the last few weeks on the other side of the bridge. Simon recalled the story of the last Congressman from Arthur's history class. The teacher had mentioned it only in passing really, more like an old memory which had suddenly been triggered rather than an intended part of the lecture. He had not even bothered to tell the class the Congressman's name.

Now Simon knew a name. He wondered what kind of courage it had taken to vote no in the face of all that opposition, when there were known consequences for the man and his loved ones. In some respects, it seemed to Simon, casting that vote had been tougher than wielding a sword. Simon knew courage, admired it in a man. He could admire a man who had sacrificed for a principle even if that man had not slain a single enemy.

He also wondered what Arthur would say when he found out the Congressman was still alive.

Chris Smith looked away from the face he had been so carefully reading. Part of him was still excited to know things other people didn't. Part of him hated how and why he knew such things. Sure he knew the story. He knew what it meant too. He knew that any poor soul in the same prison with the Congressman wasn't going to be getting out any time soon. Smith looked down at the floor. Sometimes it really sucked to know what he knew.

The computer screen suddenly flickered back to life. Both Simon and the I.T. man noticed that. The tell-tale beep followed next, the only sound in the room. It was unmistakable; a new e-mail from the TAA had arrived. Simon shook his head. His right hand again clenched tightly into a fist.

The I.T. man got up from his chair and turned toward the office door. "It's always good to have these conversations with you, Mr. Anderson."

Chapter 22

The early morning sun warmed Arthur's face. Three small beads of sweat soon formed at the edge of his hairline but then seemed to stick right there, clinging stubbornly to a few wild strands of white hair. A little warm maybe, but Arthur believed it still beat the hell out of those days when thick black smoke used to cover up the sun almost entirely. Without another thought, he then forced his right hand through thinning hair and wiped away two of the three beads of sweat. The last droplet refused to budge somehow.

Arthur looked up at the flag of stars and stripes gently waving in the breeze. Framed against the clear blue sky, the colors seemed even brighter, even bolder — the red blood of patriots; the purity of white; the justice embodied in blue. The teacher knew them all well, and he was so glad to finally be teaching American history again, to be able to pass all this on to the next generation.

A member of the next generation approached the flagpole at just that moment, red curly hair bouncing with each and every step. There was a clear urgency, a tangible enthusiasm, in the way he moved. The face was dirty but otherwise bright and cheerful. Arthur recognized him immediately. The child stopped suddenly, looked up at the flag, and then saluted. It was a crisp, well-practiced salute, something Sergeant White would have been proud of. The child smiled at his teacher before turning and skipping away. Arthur smiled too. The little things, these little victories, seemed to make the long years of suffering worth it.

The teacher bowed his head and murmured a quiet prayer to himself, thanking the Almighty he had lived long enough to see this very day. He looked around at all the progress made over the last several weeks. Food growing in the garden: people working together to tend it. Buildings being repaired. A whole community being re-built from the ashes. People were walking with pride again, with a little bounce in their step just like the little boy. Arthur looked back up at the flag. He was grateful for the brave men and women who had defended the flag and the brave men and women who might defend it in the future.

At least now there seemed to be a future worth defending.

That flag above meant there could be heroes once again. Arthur could believe in those heroes, much like he used to believe in the heroes of the past. He thought back to a time when the flag flew over the entire nation, when a duly elected Congress used to meet — when a United States Senator stood up to the will of his party for the good of the country.

The teacher smiled. He remembered how that Senator refused to back a candidate his party wanted him to support. It was a matter of principle. The candidate lacked any real qualifications except for the notoriety and publicity of beating criminal charges on a technicality. All that mattered to the party was winning another seat to help them gain control of the Senate, and they figured this man could do it — to hell with the ethical considerations.

But the ethical considerations, the principle, did matter to Senator Harris as Arthur recalled. Not only would Harris not campaign for his party's candidate, he even stated in the media he would not welcome the man to the Senate if he was elected, that it would be a stain on the honor and integrity of the institution. This public repudiation enraged the party bosses. When their candidate then lost a very close election, the party went after Senator Harris with a vengeance and spent huge sums of money trying to defeat him in the primaries.

It didn't work. Senator Harris was re-elected easily. Arthur chuckled out loud. It felt good to think of a time when Americans actually voted for a man of principle, a single man who stood on his own merit — not a political party or some talking head the political party simply told them to vote for.

"A single man of principle," Arthur thought it and said it out loud at the same time, quietly enough though, so no one else would notice.

He thought of Harris' grandson, the Congressman. The younger Harris had been a man of principle as well, a real chip off the old block; he had spoken out at a time when the United States Congress was preparing to vote itself out of existence. Then, however, there had been no ground swell of support, no common outrage which caused the American people to rise up.

There was nothing at all.

Americans had become so jaded. They had lost the faith, Arthur remembered, and so they hung the young Congressman out to dry. Harris went down to defeat, hard, and then he went away. To where, Arthur never knew exactly. He did know the Congressman was not heard from again. A voice had been silenced.

It was the beginning of the dark times, as Arthur had often referred to these years past. Like most voters, he had never really known the Congressman, but even now it still bothered him on principle. Without principle, Arthur believed, there could be no freedom. Without freedom, there could be no America. And Arthur wanted so bad to believe in America again. Maybe, just maybe, now was the time. He could see it. He could feel it all around him.

While the teacher pondered, others stopped at the flagpole and saluted, or in some cases put their hands over their hearts. A few lines from the Pledge of Allegiance could be heard drifting over the wind. Some particularly friendly individuals waved before they moved on. Arthur noticed them too. He nodded back politely and then nodded twice more, just because it felt so right. Times were definitely changing. He wondered what the Congressman would make of all this, assuming of course the man was still alive.

"Nice day, isn't it?" Father Christopher put a hand on his friend's shoulder.

"It sure is," Arthur replied, waving his arm in a broad sweeping arc that seemed to encompass the flag, the rescue mission, the garden, people walking on the street — everything.

"Look all around you, Father. Can you see it?"

The eyes of Father Christopher did take it all in, following slowly the general path traced by his friend. Before the circuit was even finished, the priest had already broken into a noticeable smile. He didn't attempt to hide it. All the changes around this place: changes he never could have imagined a few weeks before. There was a steady hum of progress on the street now. There was pride. There was hope. Somewhere not too far off, children laughed and played. It was a miracle of sorts.

And it was the best kind really, the priest thought as he took special note of the garden. It was the kind that feeds empty stomachs.

Father Christopher looked skyward, past the flag, past the clear blue sky and bright sun, straining so hard to see past the far celestial boundaries of human existence. He couldn't see that familiar presence no matter how hard he tried or how much he wanted to, but he could feel it for sure. It had been far too long. A single tear rolled down the priest's face. He was smiling still.

In a room across town, Smiling Bob sat alone waiting for a phone call. His fingers tapped out a steady rhythm on a bare table. He wasn't smiling. He wasn't happy, not one bit, mainly because he hated having to wait on anything. Just like he hated having to divert his delivery men around the rescue mission and that goddamn flag. Given the choice between the two though, he knew which one he hated more. He was the boss, and the thought of having to go around anybody in his own neighborhood grated on his very last nerve. It didn't send the right message to the people who worked for him. It was a lack of respect pure and simple, and he wasn't going to stand for it.

So he waited.

Then he waited some more.

The phone rang. Bob picked it up before the second ring.

"I understand you have a delivery problem," the voice said.

"It's not a delivery problem," Smiling Bob quickly replied. "We haven't missed a single shipment."

"Then we don't have a problem," the voice continued, "and you certainly don't need my help."

Smiling Bob swallowed hard. He didn't like what he was about to do. It was only slightly less repulsive than the alternative. The very thought of a man of his stature having to stoop to this level....

Less was the key word though, and Smiling Bob knew it. No matter what, he could not and would not allow the status quo to continue.

"I do need your help," the boss answered softly, in a voice which almost seemed to be coming from someone else. Again he swallowed hard. "Yes, we've worked hard to meet our deliveries, but I need your help eliminating an obstacle, or there might be some problems in the future."

The voice didn't answer right away. Whether it was simple surprise or some small extra time taken to savor someone like Smiling Bob actually asking for help, it was impossible to tell.

"Really?" the voice chuckled. "You really need my help. Who is it you need me to eliminate? Who is it you can't handle on your own?"

"I really need to know."

There was an uncomfortable pause. "Or maybe it's simply more efficient," the voice continued, with no hint of humor whatsoever, "to eliminate you and put someone else in charge, someone who doesn't have to call me for help. How about that?"

This time, Smiling Bob held back for a moment. The muscles in the back of his neck tightened. He didn't like being talked to in such a manner. He didn't like being disrespected. People who attempted to disrespect him usually ended up dead. This was different though; the man on the other side of the phone was not someone you could just kill if you felt like it. Smiling Bob was angry, but he wasn't that stupid. He knew he had to pick his words carefully.

"I think my performance over the last few years speaks for itself," Smiling Bob answered firmly. "I do what needs to be done. We both make money, lots of it, and you don't have any embarrassing headlines on the news."

"Besides, who the hell are you going to get to replace me in this hellhole? This isn't the type of place you can just transfer new management into. They might get their pretty business suits dirty."

Pleased with the cold-blooded logic of his argument, Smiling Bob relaxed a little. It was simple really. He didn't mind killing people when he needed to, when there was money to be made; actually he kind of enjoyed it. He knew the people he was dealing with pretty much felt the same way.

The voice was silent. There were cold, hard calculations to be made. It didn't take too long.

"Okay, Bob, you got a deal. You pick out a rendezvous point, and I'll send in a team."

"That works for me," Bob replied casually. "I'll create a little diversion to make it easier on your team."

"Goodbye then." Smiling Bob hung up the phone and reached down to pet his shepherd on the head.

James Wilson hung up on the other end of the line and turned back to face his computer screen.

Chapter 23

Sergeant White checked his watch and then motioned urgently to his son in position at the edge of the factory building. The son frowned, not at all impressed with the gesticulations or the energy behind them. The father, undeterred, repeated the hand signals three times until he finally got a satisfactory acknowledgment. He wanted the kid to stay sharp just in case — just in case Smiling Bob's thugs tried to break through on his front. He had been a Marine for a long time. He had seen combat before; he had seen men die before. All that was small comfort this time around. It was his son, his own flesh and blood, on the skirmish line now. Over on the next block, there was a steady rattle of small arms fire.

Minutes passed, but still no hard advance. The old Marine checked the time again. He figured the factory made a good target if Smiling Bob was trying to break their spirits. Break up their trade. Eliminate their source of income. Eliminate the food, everything. It all made perfect sense. He just wished Bob's thugs would damn well get on with it.

There were others getting on with it, however. And they weren't where the sergeant expected anyone to be.

Armed men in black moved silently through the rubble toward their target. They could hear gunfire off in the distance.

The man on point threw up his right hand clenched into a fist. The rest of the group halted on his signal. In a hushed tone, he called out to his nearest teammate, "You know what that means, Mike?"

"I sure do, Chris. It's our signal."

Chris switched the weapon to his other hand and checked his watch. "You got it. It means we're right on schedule."

Up ahead, directly in the path of the advance, a single sentry stood guard. No fancy uniform, but he was there with a purpose, and he had a gun. The team could see that. He was also an easy target, totally unaware of their approach and a perfect silhouette against the backdrop of fading sunlight.

Mike took aim, but Chris proved a little quicker on the trigger, dropping the guard with a single shot.

"That's one for me," crowed the shooter, still in a well-practiced, hushed tone.

"Oh, I see we're keeping score, are we?" Mike chuckled. He was careful to keep it quiet though. "By the end of the evening, we'll see who has the top score."

"You're on, dude."

That being settled, the team moved forward again. The target soon came into view. Mike shook his head. It wasn't going to be easy. The area immediately around the building was fairly crowded. Men, women, and children: people just going about their business, tending to a garden, serving soup, talking, laughing. They all seemed so unaware, just like the guard. They had absolutely no clue what was about to happen to them. Mike knew this would clearly work to his advantage. Still, he was concerned: there were just too damn many potential targets. He wondered if the team had brought enough ammunition.

It was a nice garden. Chris could tell that from his vantage point. He saw all those targets too. He had the same concern as his teammate, but only for a moment. He figured it would all work out in the end, one way or the other. Things didn't bother him much. Killing didn't bother him — no matter who, no matter how many. It was all about accuracy, all about keeping score, and challenging himself to do better each and every time. It was a game, and he was good at it. That the Trade Association of the Americas paid him very well for what he enjoyed doing just made everything so much better.

As he gradually increased pressure on the trigger of his weapon, Chris smiled.

This time Mike got the shot off first. An older man at the edge of the garden fell. He never knew what hit him.

"We're tied up now." Mike scanned the field for another target.

"Not so fast, partner," Chris replied with a hint of sarcasm. "You call that a kill! That was a crippled old man who was standing still besides. That's no challenge at all."

"Now," Chris continued, "I'll show you how it's done." He took aim at a little boy with bright red curly hair running away from the garden. "Keep going kid," he whispered to himself. "It's not going to help you."

The first shot missed.

"Damnit!" Chris re-focused and leveled his weapon again. "Hold still you little bastard."

The next shot found its mark.

"Now that's the way it's done," he laughed. He gave a quick thumbs up sign to Mike who simply frowned in return.

Arthur watched in horror as the little boy fell. He tried to reach his young friend but was quickly driven back by a hail of gunfire.

The competition, the killing, was in full swing now. Mike and Chris moved forward with the assault team, firing as they went. Bullets hit their targets again and again, each time a thud followed immediately by a burst of crimson. For the poor souls in the line of fire, death came quickly, and it played no favorites. Men, women, and children fell. Chris particularly liked to get the little ones. They were faster, smaller targets. They really tested his skills, he thought.

Many, at least those who could still move, fled the bullets.

But others didn't.

They fought back — with sticks and stones, with rakes, with their bare hands. They weren't soldiers. Some had been soldiers once, a long time ago. Some were old, infirm. They had known better times before, and over the last few weeks, they had come to recognize the future in this place. Maybe that future was worth fighting for.

Maybe those who had tasted freedom again saw their world differently now. They had a choice. They controlled their own destiny, their own life or death.

Mostly they were tired of running, of being pushed around. Mostly they cared about saving friends and family. Mostly there were no good options left.

They had absolutely no chance at all, but they struck back at the assault team anyway.

"Goddamnit," Mike yelled as he dodged a swinging rake. "This is like being attacked by a gang of skeletons."

"Almost like a video game, isn't it?" Chris laughed. He dropped one of his attackers with a shot to the gut. "At least you don't have to shoot them in the head like zombies!"

Mike laughed too. "I guess you're right about that." He immediately pivoted and leveled his weapon at a charging old man with a stick.

The attacker suddenly dropped the stick and slowly raised his hands in the air. He struggled a little with the left arm due to a gaping wound in that shoulder. There was a pained look in his eyes, frustration and anger all mixed up together with the resignation of absolute defeat. The old man began to sob uncontrollably

Mike hesitated.

Chris didn't. He emptied the rest of his clip into the old man. "We're not in the prisoner taking business," Chris said as he calmly loaded a new clip.

"Besides, I'm way ahead right now. You better get your act together, or you'll never catch up."

"Don't worry about me," Mike replied tightly. "I've got plenty of time to catch up." He began to move forward again, firing in small bursts as he went.

Arthur glanced back at the killing fields only briefly. He knew exactly what was happening, and he knew he couldn't help the dead or the brave souls who were trading their lives for time. That time was precious, and Arthur realized there was no point wasting it on tears right now. He could only try to gather up as many of his young charges as possible and hopefully get them to safety.

"Come on children. You have to follow me so we can get you out of here." Arthur motioned with his hands.

There was crying and terror all around as the children huddled together near the entrance to the rescue mission. They had seen parents fall. They had seen friends, brothers and sisters fall. They didn't understand why, and some of them didn't exactly understand how. All they understood was that people dear to them were down on the ground and not getting back up. The blood and carnage only made it all so much more terrifying. Somehow though, amid the chaos, the horror, the children responded to the calm, soothing voice of their teacher. They stopped crying and began to cluster around Arthur.

"Goddamnit to hell! I'll kill them all!"

Arthur looked up to see young Matt Carson shaking his fist and preparing to run out to meet the men with guns. The teacher had to move quickly to grab the erstwhile hero before he charged to almost certain death.

"It's pointless," Arthur yelled at the struggling teenager. "It's just a waste of your life! You can't stop what's going on out there. You're going to end up dead for absolutely nothing."

The gunshots, the screams, the death continued, not so far away now. Matt Carson stopped struggling. Deep down inside, he knew. He buried his face in the teacher's shoulder and cried. Keenly aware of the time slipping away, Arthur comforted the teen only for a moment.

"No-one questions your personal courage," Arthur said quietly. He pushed Matt back gently and looked him straight in the eyes. "But there's a difference between personal courage and senseless waste — the difference is whether or not your effort counts for something."

"Matt, I need you to do something for me," Arthur continued, more firmly than before. He didn't have the time to do otherwise. "I need you to live to fight another day. I need you to run. I need you to run away as fast as you can!"

His eyes narrowed almost all the way to tight slits, Matt Carson was just about to violently disagree when the teacher interrupted him.

"I need you run as fast as you can to find Sergeant White and his men. You have to understand. You can make a difference. You can bring back help."

There was no room for argument. There was no time for argument. Matt nodded twice, slowly but with clear purpose now. He had a slight smile on his face. Without hesitation then, he turned and ran away as fast as he could in the general direction of the old factory building. He was going to get help.

"God be with you, Matt Carson," Arthur mumbled as he watched the teenager leave. "I pray you can find the Sergeant and his Marines in time. They're the only ones who can save us now."

At that very moment, through the smoke and haze, Arthur saw Father Christopher near the soup line.

"And God be with us," the teacher added without really thinking.

Father Christopher stood in the center of everything, the nightmare swirling around him in all its terrible fury. Time itself seemed to slow down in this hellish vision, to mark in particular every single second of chaos. Every single second brought only more horror and more death. People ran, the priest could see them, but they were not fast enough to escape the bullets. And when they surely fell, they fell for what seemed like an eternity; as if it was somehow pre-ordained he should have to look into the cold, lifeless eyes of each and every poor soul. The sounds of gunshots, of screams, filled the air but were somehow muted all the same.

It was not real, could not be real, Father Christopher had to believe. He closed his eyes tight and prayed that he could open them again and make it all not so.

The priest opened his eyes. He could see the terrible reality still, and he could hear the screams clearly now. He looked directly at Arthur. He saw the incredible sadness in his friend's face. The bloodshed and the death. Hope, the promise of this place — the hard work of so many was all lost.

But then Father Christopher saw something else.

He saw Arthur gathering children together, calming them, trying to lead them out of this horror. He saw a grim determination to save those who could still be saved. He saw too that his friend needed more time.

By now, the men with guns had completely broken through the brave men and women who had tried to stop them near the garden. Sticks and stones and raw courage were no match for bullets. Broken bodies littered the ground. Here and there, any wounded who still moved were quickly being dispatched. It was all so horrible and all so methodical. It was the work of men who killed because they could, because it came naturally to them. They were men who had no value for human life, or at least no value for the people in this place. Father Christopher could see it in their eyes, and it made him very angry. If he had possessed a real weapon, he would have used it right then and there. He would have killed for the greater good, without any remorse.

No matter that it might break his own vows.

Maybe it would have been a great moral or spiritual dilemma. Maybe — if there had actually been a weapon within reach. As it was, Father Christopher was unarmed and a realist above all else. He knew he could not prevail, or even delay the inevitable, by meeting violence with more violence. He knew there had to be another way.

As the killing machine approached, the priest did then the only thing he could do. He did what came most natural to him. He kneeled down on the ground, clasped his hands together, and shouted out at the top of his lungs.

"Our Father, which art in heaven,"
"Hallowed be thy Name."

And just then, the shooting, or most of it, stopped. Hell on earth had stumbled upon a pause button.

"Thy Kingdom come."

The frail woman who had been serving up soup instantly comprehended what Father Christopher was trying to do. She moved quickly to the spot and kneeled down beside him. The priest smiled and grabbed her hand. Together their voices rose, powerful and pure.

"Thy will be done in earth,"
"As it is in heaven."

Chris and Mike, along with most of their team, approached the kneeling pair. They were angry and a little confused.

"What the hell are you two trying to do?" Chris yelled. He gestured with his weapon but didn't exactly point it at anyone in particular. "Do you think this is somehow going to save you or your friends?"

"Do you think God is going to show up all of a sudden and save you?"

"Give us this day our daily bread."
"And forgive us our trespasses,"

"Stop that shit right now!" Chris pointed his gun this time. Mike aimed his weapon as well and then fired a shot directly into the priest's shoulder. It wasn't meant to kill. It was meant to scare, to simply get them to stop.

The priest barely flinched though the pain was surely great, and he didn't stop. With no more than a soft groan, his voice rose again.

"As we forgive them that trespass against us."

Arthur couldn't bear to watch anymore. He knew what was going to happen in the end, and he understood why. He understood the nature of sacrifice — even when it involved his best friend in the whole world. It was incredibly brave and tragic all the same, but it had to mean something. These precious seconds: he already knew they could not be wasted. The teacher turned away for the last time and hustled the final children on their way to some place safe.

"And lead us not into temptation,"

It had always been about power for Mike. He loved having it. He loved using it. Killing was just a natural extension of that power. While he did enjoy testing his marksmanship and competing with Chris in missions like this, what he really enjoyed more was the moment just before he pulled the trigger, the moment when the victim realized he was going to die. The fear in the eyes, the look of someone totally helpless: it really jazzed Mike up. He knew he could do that to people. It made him feel powerful.

"But deliver us from evil."

There was a problem though. Mike didn't feel very powerful right now, just like his moment of hesitation with the sobbing old man before. He wasn't about to repeat that rookie mistake here, and he knew only one way to restore the balance. No messing around this time. He sprayed several rounds square into the chest of the kneeling priest. Chris did the same to the frail woman.

"That'll shut them up!" Mike laughed. Chris laughed too, mainly because he had just screwed his friend out of a chance to close the gap a little in the body count race.

The priest slumped down, but he didn't fall. He tried hard to hold onto the woman's hand. Her eyes were beginning to glaze over, yet there was still a certain sparkle to her face, a grateful smile almost. The blood soaked his shirt, making it feel so terribly heavy, and it hurt like hell just to breathe. He wasn't ready to give up though. He knew every single second counted. His voice was weaker now but still pure.

"For thine is the kingdom,"
"The power, and the glory,"

The two gunmen shook their heads. The rest of the team waited impatiently.

Father Christopher paused to suck in some air and tighten his grip. The end was near. He knew it. He felt the blood and strength drain out of the woman. She had been so frail and only weighed a little. He tried again to squeeze harder, but his own physical strength was failing; he could not hold her any longer. As his hand and fingers gave way finally, she slid down slowly to the ground.

The priest took one last look at her face. A single tear rolled down his cheek.

"For ever and ever," he whispered.

"Aw will you look at that," Chris chuckled. "Priest, you're all alone now!"

"No God. Not even your lady friend here anymore."

Mike didn't say a word. He leveled his weapon.

"I am not alone." The priest smiled.

"Amen," he finished.

Father Christopher never felt the last bullet. His essence was far away by then.

Some distance from the rescue mission, a small child walked hand-in-hand with his teacher. The child was sobbing softly, as were several others, but he was alive. They were all alive. The teacher looked down at his young friend. Though the old man's eyes were wet with tears, he tried to force a smile.

Chapter 24

Simon knew something was wrong as soon as he approached the bridge. There were no guards, and there was no routine shuffling of passenger traffic back and forth. That was a first, and not necessarily a good first, he suspected. He also thought he could hear the faint sound of gunfire even with the windows rolled up in the car. Simon looked over at Holly in the passenger seat. He suddenly felt very sorry that he had brought her along this time.

Holly knew that look and wasn't having any part of it. "I know what you're thinking," she said in the most threatening voice she could muster, "and the answer is no! You can't take me home. I'm staying with you, no matter what."

Her husband didn't immediately reply.

Holly smiled and gently squeezed Simon's hand. She had figured pretty quickly the threats weren't working at all. The touch of skin on skin, however, was having a decidedly different effect. Simon looked back into the most beautiful brown eyes he had ever seen still and then squeezed his wife's hand too. It was a terrible worry to risk her safety, but he couldn't bear to leave her behind. He would have to protect her from whatever waited for them on the other side of the bridge. He was strong, and he was ready. That he didn't have a clue exactly what they might run into was the part that bothered him the most.

"I think we need to stay in the car," Simon answered firmly as he turned the wheel and accelerated over the bridge. "It will provide some protection." He tried to smile, but it didn't work really. Holly did appreciate the effort nonetheless and leaned over to kiss Simon on the cheek.

Driving wasn't easy once they crossed the bridge. There were still rusted cars and other debris blocking the streets. But it was possible, if slow going, and Simon was determined. Driving over and around bricks, wood, and anything else in the way, even driving on what once passed for sidewalks; it didn't matter. As they neared the mission, the sound of gunfire was no longer so faint. Simon didn't need to roll down the window to know that something bad was happening just up ahead. He squeezed Holly's hand again, harder this time.

That something bad soon came into view.

Still nothing could have prepared him for what he saw next, absolutely nothing. Not the experience of battlefields over the ages. Not the experience of a warrior's battle up close and personal. It was all different this time. He saw the bodies. He saw the slaughter — men, women, and children. He didn't have to count; there were just far too many.

He saw the men in black too, the men with guns. Worse yet, they saw him. They saw Holly. The men closest leveled their weapons and fired on the car. Splinters of glass flying, bullets tore through windshield and metal. Instinctively, Simon pushed Holly down in the seat. Instinctively, his muscles tightened, and his eyes sharpened to a steely gaze. The rage had returned. Battle had returned. Visions filled his head, visions of brave men in magnificent bronze armor and bright red tunics. He would not disappoint such men. With a great and terrible war cry then, Simon floored the car straight toward the shooters.

The charge: it was sudden and unexpected. One of the shooters jumped clear. The other didn't move fast enough and was crushed by the oncoming vehicle. There was a loud crash and a violent jolt as the car skidded to a stop. Simon shook his head forcefully back and forth to clear the side effects of collision and ready himself to fight. He stopped only for a moment to check on Holly before getting out of the car. Picking up the closest weapon, a broken pipe, he moved quickly on the second shooter. The man in black never had a chance to bring his weapon fully to bear. Simon crushed his skull with a single powerful blow from the pipe.

The rest of the assault team was stunned, not just by the car crash, or the sudden loss of two of their own, or the awesome power of that blow. It was all these and more. The team had not expected any real opposition, certainly not someone like Simon. They had been fighting and killing women and children and skeletal old men who swung at them with sticks and stones. Now they knew they faced a man of substance, a man of singular courage. No matter that he didn't even have a gun; he still scared the living hell out of them.

And he wasn't done yet.

Swinging and clubbing and stabbing, Simon advanced again totally without fear. He struck totally without mercy. He broke automatic weapons. He broke bones and heads. He shed blood and sowed great terror among the men with guns, who soon found themselves too panicked to properly aim and use their weapons. Their training was of no use; the fearsome and bewildering fog of war had descended upon them. It was so much harder, they realized now, to shoot at somebody who moved so quickly, at somebody who fought back so savagely.

Men broke and ran. Men who had once admired their own bravery ran from the first real fight they had ever been in.

A short distance away, Chris didn't have to worry yet about running. He coolly watched the unfolding melee with a mixture of trepidation and frank admiration. He had only seen such power and violence in a video game, never in one of his real missions. It was mesmerizing. It caused Chris to hesitate, and that was something he just didn't do. Even as he leveled his weapon and brought finger to trigger, Chris was genuinely conflicted. Part of him wanted to work with the fighting machine he saw wading through his own assault team; part of him longed for the challenge of killing such a man.

"You know dude, it's really too bad," Chris mused. "We could have made beautiful music together." He took careful aim at his target.

"I know you're a real beast in hand-to-hand combat," Chris continued, his voice barely above a whisper now. He was really trying to concentrate on the shot. He wanted it to be a clean kill. He wanted it to be absolutely perfect.

"I wouldn't dare mess with you one-on-one, but I have superior firepower, and that's always been the great equalizer." Chris smiled and gently increased the pressure on the trigger.

At first, Chris didn't feel it. He had been concentrating so hard on his own shot. But then he saw the blood on his shirt, and he suddenly felt his arm go weak.

"What the fuck?"

Chris did feel the next four shots hit his chest in rapid succession. They drove him back a couple of steps. They burned like hell too. Blood oozed from each wound. Struggling to stand and even breathe now, he found he couldn't hold his own weapon anymore. It seemed way too heavy. The gun discharged when it fell to the concrete pavement.

"That was my kill, damnit," Chris mumbled. He finally looked up in the direction of the shots. The shooter was a ragged man, and he moved stiff-legged. But the man could definitely handle a weapon. Chris could see that. He could also see the shooter re-loading.

The very last thing Chris saw was the flash from the next bullet.

The shooter, pivoting on his stiff leg, took aim and dropped another man in black. This one took only two rounds, both to the head.

"So you little bastards at the trade association thought I was useless," the shooter yelled, "all because I lost a leg. Well, how do you like me now?"

Simon heard the shots. At first, he didn't realize those shots had saved his life. Then he heard the yelling, and he knew for sure. He was surprised, but only a little, to see Bill handling a weapon so well. Simon understood better than anybody there were things which some people kept hidden until circumstances forced them out. Right now was one of those times — for a lot of people. Right now, Simon just appreciated the help. He waved to Bill who took time out to return the gesture before opening fire again.

Mike had seen Chris fall. The assault team was taking heavy casualties and beginning to fall back in confusion. It wasn't supposed to work out this way. No way, he thought to himself, could two guys fighting back cause this much damage, particularly when one of them was a cripple. Mike shook his head. He wasn't going to run himself. He knew what he had to do to eliminate the two threats in front of him.

Then things suddenly got a whole lot worse, and the problem wasn't just in front of him anymore. Mike could hear now more gunfire coming in from the right flank. He could see more members of his team falling, some of them hit from two different directions at the same time.

Mike didn't really know what to do next.

Firing first in one direction and then spinning back to fire in the other direction didn't help matters much. He wasn't aiming; he was just shooting. It was all so much bravado and a terrific waste of bullets. He was also standing out in the open, inviting return fire. Mike felt the first hit in his leg. He almost crumpled to the ground right then and there. He managed to stay on his feet though until the second bullet struck him in the neck just above the collarbone.

His weapon dropped to the ground as he fell backwards. Mike looked up at the sky. It was calm, peaceful. The last of the daylight was fading, and he could just make out the faint glow of the first star of the evening. He could hear the firing still. He could hear the voices moving closer. He could hear, but he couldn't do anything about it. Mike felt powerless.

That was the most painful wound of all.

"Stay low and keep firing in small bursts," Sergeant White yelled out to his son. "We've got the bastards on the run!"

Matt Carson stood behind the Marines covering up his ears. Real combat, real war, real bravery, was a whole lot louder than he had ever imagined. He also wondered if all this had come a little too late. He could see the bodies of friends and others covering the ground. It made him sick to his stomach.

It was all over soon enough. The firing subsided. The assault team, or what was left of it, had retreated, leaving their own dead and wounded spread among their earlier victims. Revenge, retribution, whatever it was; it still wasn't pretty. And it didn't bring back all the poor souls the men in black had murdered.

Sergeant White realized as much. He had won, but he had lost. As he moved slowly towards the ruins of the rescue mission, he had to be very careful to step over the bodies. He had seen fields of battle where soldiers fell. This place, this tragedy was so much worse. Soldiers, he knew, at least had a chance to defend themselves. Women and children and old men did not.

The old Marine shook his head, and tears of frustration fell. He had simply been too late. He had failed to defend these people; he had failed to defend his people.

And most of all, he had failed to defend his friend. Sergeant White looked down at the bodies of Father Christopher and the frail woman. He stood there quietly and almost perfectly still, moving only to wipe his eyes once or twice. It took a while before he even noticed that he had been joined by Simon and Bill.

"You know," the sergeant said softly, "despite all of this, despite a horrible death, they look somehow at peace." Simon and Bill nodded.

"I hope to God they're in a better place now."

Simon was angry, ready to fight still, but he had absolutely no doubt about the better place. He remembered how he had first met the frail woman. She had been so alone then. He was thankful at least she had not died alone here. Simon knew too she and Father Christopher would never be alone again. He thought to tell White that, perhaps to ease his pain, but then decided against it. He wasn't quite sure the sergeant would believe him anyway.

"The trade association did this," Bill broke the silence. Simon and Sergeant White thought so too, but they didn't repeat it out loud. For the moment, both men were more interested in what their new-found ally had to say.

"I know the trade association did this. I know...." Bill hesitated. He looked up. He looked down. He drew in a deep breath and then exhaled slowly. "I know because I used to be one of these guys."

"I used to do missions. I used to kill for the TAA."

Simon and Sergeant White didn't say a word. They listened, maybe just a little more uneasy than they were before.

"Yeah, I was good at it too," Bill continued calmly. "I was real good at it ... at least until I lost my leg."

"Then they didn't need me anymore."

"But I wouldn't do stuff like this," Bill seemed to add at the last minute. His voice was harder, more bitter now. It was hard to tell whether the bitterness was tied more to the lost leg/lost job or to the current tragedy. Simon and Sergeant White weren't exactly sure either.

Bill stopped talking. Neither of his two companions was quite ready to respond. The lull, the silence, was not comfortable at all.

"Help me." All three men were startled to hear a strange new voice, weak though it was. At first, they weren't sure where it was coming from.

"Help me, please." Faint from blood loss, Mike had lost nearly all of the bravado. He wasn't the tough guy, the hotshot anymore. He wasn't living in a video game; he was bleeding out in real life. And he was powerless to stop it. That had surely changed his perspective. He feared death now more than asking for help.

Not that anyone was exactly eager to help him. Sergeant White certainly wasn't too keen on the idea as he looked down at the bleeding man in black.

"You know son," the sergeant said, trying hard to contain the anger in his voice, "I hear only God can grant mercy."

"The problem is that you sons-of-bitches just killed the man here who had the most direct line to God. He was a good man too, a good priest who also cared for the rest of the poor people you killed today."

"You see son," White continued hotly, "there's simply nobody left to talk to God on your behalf."

"What about me? Are you asking me?" The old Marine touched his finger to his chest and grinned. "I'm not the guy who talks to God for you."

"I'm typically the guy who arranges the meeting!" He pointed his gun at the wounded man.

Mike closed his eyes and waited. White really, really wanted to pull the trigger.

He couldn't do it. He couldn't finish a wounded man, even a brutal killer. It was something about honor and dignity and the ideals he had fought for as a United States Marine. Americans were the good guys, he had always believed, and the good guys just didn't do things like this.

But he didn't have to help the man either.

Sergeant White pulled back his weapon and turned to walk away.

Mike opened his eyes again. He wasn't so happy to see the sergeant and his companions leave, yet he didn't have the strength anymore to protest. He looked back up at the sky again. There were a few more stars he could see now. He tried several times to count them but kept getting stuck at three or four. He gave up soon enough. Mike could feel his breathing slow down, and every sound in the world seemed to disappear all at once. The stars faded gradually away.

His last thoughts were of a pretty girl he knew at work.

The shooting having been over for a while, other survivors were just beginning to emerge. They came out of hiding places in the ruins, dirty and shaken but alive. Others drifted back in from places they had fled to when the attack started. Arthur was walking toward the mission, trailed by nearly a dozen small, crying children. Holly was out of the car by now doing everything she could do to help. As soon as she saw the children with their teacher, she immediately headed that way.

Here and there and everywhere, there was a collective outpouring of grief. People searched frantically for loved ones, more often than not finding them among the dead. A light rain began to fall. It was as if the heavens above shared in the grief and wept also. Amid the sobs, the moans, and the early evening mist, the survivors began the solemn work of collecting the fallen for burial.

Sergeant White watched and listened. He didn't blink. He didn't move. He held his weapon at the ready, squeezing the barrel tight until his knuckles lost all color. He couldn't crush cold steel, but he also couldn't feel any pain right now. That the physical effort was not accomplishing anything didn't seem to register. Only when he turned to face Simon and Bill did White finally relax his grip enough to allow the blood to flow back into his hand and the feeling to return to his fingers. He didn't notice that either.

"I know Smiling Bob is behind this," the old Marine said. Simon and Bill nodded in agreement. Though he knew the responsibility truthfully went much higher, Simon chose not to say as much just yet.

"Times have changed, and Smiling Bob couldn't push us around anymore," Sergeant White added with some pride. "He couldn't handle us on his own so he called in for help from the trade association."

"I skirmished with his thugs at the factory. I see it now though for what it was. It was all just a diversion to leave the rescue mission undefended so those killers could crush all our hopes and dreams. Smiling Bob was willing to kill all these people here just to get us out of his way."

"And I allowed it all to happen. If I had just been here….."

White lowered his head. He started to squeeze the gun barrel again but stopped almost immediately.

"This place, these people," he continued firmly, "won't be safe until that man is out of the picture for good." He looked directly at Simon and Bill.

Bill calmly replaced an empty clip in his weapon. Simon tossed aside the pipe and picked up a gun dropped by one of the men in black. He checked the weapon over and then kneeled down to retrieve a couple of extra clips.

"I didn't think you actually used one of those things," Sergeant White chuckled as he pointed at Simon's gun.

"I told you before I'm older than I look," Simon replied with a smile, "and I've picked up a lot of valuable experience over the years."

The old Marine grinned. "Let's go evict the neighbors."

The trio of armed men marched out with a purpose. They were met right away by Holly Anderson.

"Where do you think you're going?"

Simon didn't answer. Neither did Bill or Sergeant White.

"You're going out to take revenge for all this, aren't you?"

Holly didn't wait for an answer this time. She knew the answer. "You know it's not going to bring back all these people. It's only more bloodshed, and there's a risk you might get killed!"

She looked straight into Simon's eyes. "I want you to be with me. I want you to be with our daughter." Tears welled up in Holly's brown eyes.

It was hard to resist those tears, but Simon knew what he had to do this time. He knew what he had to do from now on. He just didn't know how to tell Holly yet. For now, he put down his weapon and swept up his wife into his arms. He held her tight.

"Don't worry, I'll be back," Simon whispered into her ear. "You have to trust me, honey, this is the only way to protect these people and all that we have done here. I have to do it."

"It's what I was sent here to do."

Simon reluctantly let go of his wife. She tried to hold on just a little longer as he pulled away. She tried but couldn't hold back or delay what was going to happen, even for a few more seconds. Simon retrieved his weapon and re-joined Bill and Sergeant White. He didn't look back.

Holly watched the men walk away until they were completely out of sight. She wondered what Simon's last words really meant.

Chapter 25

The music had ended. Smiling Bob was puzzled.

He had been tracking the action earlier this evening by the sound and movement of the gunfire. It was sort of old-fashioned in the modern digital age he had to admit, but he did enjoy it so much. The smooth rattle and rhythm of automatic weapons, the rising crescendo of the attack punctuated by the boom-boom of percussion grenades: it was always such a sweet melody to his ears. Throw in some screams on the side and it could be just about as good as a Sunday afternoon concert in the park with a full-blown symphony orchestra.

Things had started off well enough. The diversion at the factory went off as planned. The attack on the rescue mission started on time. He heard the tell-tale gunfire and explosions of battle. He heard the echoes of screams rising in the neighborhood, the very sound of slaughter. Bob had been brimming with self-satisfaction at the time, wondering just how long it would all take — until everyone at the mission was dead and out of his way. Though hoping it wouldn't take too long, he was still keen to enjoy the festivities while they lasted.

And he had surely savored it, his favorite tune: the music of discord, death, and destruction.

Then the music ended.

That was nearly 40 minutes ago. Smiling Bob wondered still. He didn't know exactly what the quiet meant.

But then he was struck by a sudden inspiration. There had to be a logical explanation. Maybe the attack was simply over. Maybe they were all dead. Maybe the plan had worked to perfection. Yes, that had to be it. Bob chuckled. No matter that he hadn't heard anything official from the commander of the assault team yet. It was all just a matter of time he was sure.

"You know what, puppy: your daddy is a goddamn genius!" Bob reached over and roughly rubbed the head and face of his German shepherd. The animal responded with a low, playful growl.

"Yes sir, a certifiable genius." Bob was almost convinced.

But he had to see for himself to be absolutely sure.

There was a window at the far end of his room. It faced the Catholic Rescue Mission. It had a perfect view. Bob had his swagger going as he strolled over to the window. He took his time because he had the time, and there was nobody there to tell him otherwise. When he was good and ready then, Bob did look out that window. He saw it immediately. It wasn't supposed to be there. The assault team was supposed to take care of it. He knew he had been very clear on that point. Slowly and without any swagger at all, he stepped back from the window.

The flag was still flying over the Catholic Rescue Mission. Now Smiling Bob was worried.

Hector Gonzalez stood outside Bob's building. He saw the flag too. He had heard the gunfire earlier as well. Unfortunately he knew what that probably meant. He quickly made the sign of the cross on his chest.

"In the name of the Father, and of the Son, and of the Holy Spirit," Hector said softly.

"Amen." He thought of those poor souls at the rescue mission. He knew it didn't have to be that way. He knew it didn't have to be Smiling Bob's way.

He just didn't know what was coming next — after things had been done Bob's way.

Smiling Bob didn't know either, but he wasn't taking any chances. He dialed one number right after another on his cellphone, trying desperately to pull together his scattered security guards as quickly as possible. He wanted all his men back at the building. He needed some firepower. He needed protection. Until they got there, he wouldn't feel safe. Bob reached up and stroked his gold tooth. It was a nervous habit, crude in front of other people who were too scared to say so, just plain nervous when he was by himself. And right now it wasn't helping him relax at all.

Many of Bob's men wouldn't reach the building. The trio from the rescue mission had seen to that already. And they had been very quiet about it.

A phone rang. Hector heard it. The guard at the front door of the building picked up and mumbled something in the affirmative that he would keep an eye out for anything unusual. Hector could tell the guard was young, way too young to be carrying a weapon almost as big as he was. He could also see that the kid was scared. It made Hector think of his own young son. He wondered what the guard's father, if the man was still around, thought of his son working for and potentially defending Smiling Bob. All Hector knew was that Smiling Bob wasn't a man worth dying for.

After the phone call, all was quiet once again. Not the pleasant kind of quiet though, more the unnerving kind of quiet. Hector felt it. It made his skin crawl. And for a minute there, he also wondered if it made him imagine things. Over in the general direction of the rescue mission, Hector could swear he saw movement among the ruins. At first, it was just shadows which appeared suddenly in the flickering lights and then just as suddenly disappeared — only to re-appear again somewhere else. Maybe it was something playing tricks on his eyes, Hector thought, but then again, the shadows weren't so random and so scattered. They seemed to move with a purpose. They seemed to be getting closer too. Then Hector saw it: the outline of a gun barrel. Now he knew for sure. These shadows were packing heat, and they were coming for Smiling Bob.

Payback was going to happen soon.

The only question was how many people were going to have to die besides Bob. Hector didn't want to think about it, but he had already decided he wasn't going to be one of them. As he turned to leave, Hector took one last look over at the door, at the young man guarding it. Hector hesitated. He wondered. Maybe he could save at least one kid tonight.

"Hey boy," he called out to the guard, "I just got word from the Boss. There's been a change in plans. You need to come with me to help guard the lab."

The guard was confused now and didn't move. Being polite wasn't working.

"Come on kid," Hector yelled again, this time much more aggressively. He could see the shadows closing in. There wasn't much time left. "Come on kid, we have to go!"

"We have to go right now!"

The words were threatening, and the last now in particular had a great deal of force behind it. It was meant to scare the hell out of somebody — and fast. It worked too. The kid didn't protest. He simply turned away from the door and followed Hector without saying a word.

As he watched the young guard leave, Simon breathed a sigh of relief. He was glad they weren't going to have to go through a child to get to their target. The guard looking out the second story window, clearly an adult male, wasn't nearly so lucky. Simon dropped the man with a single shot.

That was the signal. Sergeant White rushed the front of the building. He kicked in the door but then quickly drew back to the cover of the outside wall. Instinct and training: the old Marine knew there had to be someone on the other side of the door. Sure enough, the guard on the inside opened up immediately. And just as immediately, those shots fell harmlessly in the street. The return fire from Bill and Simon wasn't quite so harmless. The guard fell. White peeked into the doorway now, weapon at the ready, and straightaway dispatched another gunman coming down the stairs. He signaled the all clear. Bill and Simon joined the sergeant.

They were in.

Smiling Bob knew it too. He had heard the gunfire. And he had already made a decision. He wasn't going anywhere.

Calmly and without any hurry at all, Bob put a clip in his favorite handgun and stuffed it in the front of his pants. He picked up something a little heavier from the table. He loaded a fresh clip in that one as well.

There was only one thing though. Smiling Bob reached down and petted his German shepherd. The animal twisted her head so she could lick her owner's hand. Bob laughed out loud, playfully pulling his hand back but not so far as to be out of range. For the moment, as the dog continued to share her affections, he almost forgot all about the men coming to kill him.

Almost.

"You're a good girl," Bob said quietly, "but I think you'll be in the way here. So I really need you to go now." He rubbed the shepherd's head one last time and then shoved her roughly through the pet door, latching the door so she couldn't get back in.

That was it. Now he was ready.

"Okay mother-fuckers, come and get me!"

Smiling Bob leveled his weapon and sprayed the door from top to bottom as well as the drywall all around the doorway. The sound was deafening. Bob didn't even try to yell over it. Splinters of wood and plaster flew off in all directions. Brass cartridges, spent and hot, bounced on the floor. No-one could live through that; he was absolutely, positively sure.

He stopped shooting. He turned his head just enough to spit to the side. He breathed in deep and let it all out, nice and easy.

Instinct and training: it had always kept Sergeant White alive in the past. It had gotten him past guards tonight, past men who were trying to kill him, all the way to this door where he could do the killing, where he could take his revenge. No, the instinct and training didn't let him down now. When the bullets came through the door and surrounding walls, the old Marine simply wasn't there. He had pulled back and away from the line of fire. He was waiting until the time was right.

Now was the time.

If Smiling Bob could shoot through walls, so could other people. White stepped up to the wall where a hole had conveniently been blasted out, shoved his weapon through, and immediately opened fire into the room. Bob tried to move but wasn't quick enough. He felt the impact first, the very sudden and violent jolt of multiple hits. Then there was the sharp burning pain in both legs and his right arm. He fell backwards, dropping his weapon in the process. Sergeant White kicked in the door while Simon and Bill covered him.

"Goddamnit, that stings!" Smiling Bob had never spent much time contemplating his own pain, and he sure as hell didn't like it much now.

"I'm sorry," the old Marine said calmly, "I bet that hurts." He approached cautiously, weapon at the ready. "But I bet it doesn't hurt any worse than what the people at the rescue mission felt — you know, the people you ordered killed."

Bob laughed. He was the boss. He did what needed to be done, when it needed to be done, and he wasn't going to start apologizing for it. "Yeah, you're right," he answered with a smile, "I had them killed. It was all business, baby."

"They were just in my way."

That wasn't the answer the sergeant wanted to hear, though it didn't surprise him much. He prepared to pull the trigger.

"You know Bob," White continued, "those people in your way were my friends, and you need to pay for each and every one of them."

"I only wish I could kill you over and over again.…"

Shots rang out in the hall, first from one of Bob's thugs and then the return fire from Simon and Bill which quickly dropped the man in his tracks. It lasted only a few seconds, but Sergeant White did pause at the sound. Smiling Bob saw his chance and reached for the handgun in his pants.

Instinct and training again: the sergeant was quicker on the draw.

There were only two more shots, both to Smiling Bob's head. The handgun never made it out of his pants.

"But I guess once will have to do," the old Marine finished.

It was done.

But it wasn't over. Simon knew that.

Killing Smiling Bob may have satisfied the immediate thirst for revenge. What it didn't do, however, was make the survivors at the rescue mission really any safer. As the trio worked their way back to the mission, Simon was thinking just how he was going to break that news to the sergeant and the rest of the people who had buried the dead, who might still believe in the possibilities. They had been trying to create their own little place in this hell-hole based on some of the best ideals of the old American dream. People had fought for it, died for it. Now Simon knew he had to tell them they would likely have to fight again, and very soon at that.

Simon and Bill and Sergeant White made it back soon enough. Holly immediately jumped up to hug her husband. There were some scattered cheers, more like a spontaneous sigh of relief though rather than a real celebration. It was hard to celebrate much when so many good people had died. Revenge, necessary as it was, provided only some small measure of comfort; it didn't bring back loved ones. Simon should have been happy, at least to hold his wife again, but he couldn't quite manage that either. Holly could tell as much. She pulled back from the hug and looked straight into Simon's eyes. She saw what she needed to know right there, just like always.

"What's wrong?" She touched Simon gently on the face. He pulled away and shook his head.

"It's not over," he said quietly.

Holly didn't say a word.

"It's not over," Simon repeated, this time much louder.

Now others heard it too.

"What do you mean it's not over?" Sergeant White was the first to speak up.

Simon sighed. He didn't want to say, but there was really no choice.

"The killers who did this," Simon began, "weren't just some of Smiling Bob's thugs. They came from the trade association security force. Do you really think you can just kill men like that without any consequences?"

"Do you?" Simon scanned the crowd that was beginning to gather. He tried to make eye contact with each and every one of them.

Bill nodded. He knew. So did others. It was suddenly very quiet around the rescue mission.

"The TAA will come back again," Simon continued. "Next time, they'll come back harder, with more men, with more firepower, with more of everything."

There was a steady murmur now, the quiet rumbling of a multitude of side conversations among friends and family, among total strangers who just happened to be close by. People were worried. People wanted to talk, had to talk. They just weren't so ready to talk loud enough to be heard.

"And we won't be able to stop them."

Sergeant White didn't say it out loud either, but he knew. He was a realist, especially in military matters. He had been in large battles. He had been in small battles. He knew what fighting men could do, and he knew that most of these people here were not fighting men. For sure, he knew the odds, and that scared the living hell out of him.

"Okay smart guy," White replied finally, "what do you suggest?"

It was the most straightforward question asked in the most straightforward way. No sarcasm. No anger. No emotion at all. Sergeant White had just asked the question. They all just needed the answer.

When the answer came, surprisingly quick at that, it was just as straightforward as the question.

"We have to get them before they get us." If it sounded simple, what came next clearly did not.

"We have to take down the Trade Association of the Americas." Simon didn't flinch when he spoke.

Dead quiet. It wasn't quite the answer people had expected. In fact, it was an answer most people didn't even want to contemplate.

Sergeant White wasn't most people. Arthur, who had by now worked his way through the crowd, wasn't most people either. Both men were more intrigued than scared. Again the old Marine was the first to break the silence.

"Just how are we going to take down the trade association?"

"To kill a snake," Simon answered without any hesitation at all, "you have to cut off its head. To topple an empire, you have to remove the king."

There was no outright gasp of shock or anything else, but the murmur of a whole host of hushed conversations, among very worried people, had suddenly returned. They knew exactly who the king was.

"Okay, I'm not ready to say such a thing is possible," White continued with a grin, "but I have to admit you have certainly made me curious. Now I do have to ask: How can you even get to the CEO, let alone take him out?"

"I can get to Daniel Garcia," Simon replied. "Remember I still work for the TAA, and I think I can get some help on the inside. Besides, I don't necessarily have to take him out. To take away his power base, I just need to take out his image. I know some very damaging things about our CEO."

Simon paused, unable for the moment to say what he wanted to say next.

"And others," he added finally. His voice was a little softer as if he still wasn't so sure he wanted everyone to hear it. It wasn't much; it certainly wasn't the whole story. But he had said it out loud, and for now, that had to be enough.

"You mean using the power of the press to expose the truth? You could bring back freedom of the press, just like the good old days!" Jan Carson was excited. She had been hugging her son ever since they had re-united after the shooting stopped. Now she hugged him a little harder. Matt Carson protested, but to no avail.

"Yes, I guess I'm talking about exposing the CEO for what he really is," Simon answered confidently. Deep down, he wasn't so sure it would work. He knew, however, he couldn't let these people see there was any doubt at all. He knew they had to try.

The crowd bit. An audible buzz of excitement rippled back and forth and all around, moving from person to person like a fast moving fire. Arthur listened to the conversation, to the excitement. He liked where it was going, but he realized they all needed to know more. He wasn't ready yet to ask his own questions. For the moment, he was willing to leave that to others, like the sergeant.

"So you might be able to make trouble in the press for some big-shot, and I have to stress you might," White spoke up loud enough to be heard above the crowd. "Even if you can get rid of the CEO, there are others in the trade association who will take over, and they'll be just as bad."

"What if someone from the TAA doesn't take over?" Simon shot back quickly.

The buzz among the crowd stopped abruptly. Even the sergeant was too surprised to say anything.

"What if we helped put someone else in power?" Simon continued. "What if we tried to bring back government by the people, for the people?"

"How? How can we do that?" It came as a low, steady rumble of many voices. It came as shouts here and there.

The question came from no one in particular and from everyone at the same time. It was a collective expression of surprise, shock — but most importantly, it was not an outright rejection of the idea. There was a shred of optimism in those very few words, the hope that the man doing the talking just might have a real answer to how.

"When the people find out what I know about the Trade Association of the Americas — when the people find out the truth — they'll want something different for sure. They'll want a new way of running things, or maybe an old way of running things that is new to many of them."

Simon paused for effect. "We just need to give them somebody to lead the way."

"Who?" The crowd chanted almost in unison, satisfied for the moment, it seemed, with the how.

"There is someone," Simon went on. "There is former United States Congressman Jim Harris."

That caught Arthur's attention. "It can't be," he mumbled to himself. "It just can't be." Arthur shook his head. "No one has seen him or heard from him in years. Harris must be dead by now."

He had convinced himself. He couldn't afford to hope for too much, not after what had happened this evening.

"He's probably dead!" Arthur blurted out. It was the only logical conclusion. The crowd heard it and seemed to agree, or at least no-one disagreed enough to say so out loud.

"He's not dead," Simon replied firmly. "Congressman Jim Harris is not dead," he repeated even louder, just to make sure everyone heard.

"The Congressman is being held at the Gettysburg Containment Center along with a lot of other political prisoners who supposedly came down with the flu. The whole flu pandemic is a lie manufactured by the trade association. It's just an excuse to put away people who don't agree with the CEO or his policies."

"If we want to make this place safe," Simon continued, eyes aglow and his voice clear, strong, "if we want to have a chance to bring back some form of government by the people — for the people — we have to break Jim Harris out of that prison!"

"It can't be," Arthur mumbled again, unwilling yet to believe.

"It can be. I promise you it can be," Simon said softly. He looked straight into the eyes of the old teacher and smiled.

Those old eyes moistened, and a single tear trickled down Arthur's face. He was all alone in a crowd of many, totally oblivious to the general hub-bub around him. Not a sound as far as he was concerned. He was totally focused now on the man doing the talking. He could believe in Simon Anderson.

And he could believe in Congressman Jim Harris.

"The single man of principal," Arthur answered quietly and with a smile no one was really meant to see. It was the answer to a most important question even if someone had not actually asked it. Arthur needed to know. Arthur needed to believe. Jim Harris, if he was still alive, could be that single man, a man to inspire others. It just might work. It was certainly worth a try, Arthur thought.

"Holy shit!"

Sergeant White's response was a bit louder and much less cerebral. It did, however, get more directly to the point, and it did seem to more closely reflect what the rest of the crowd was thinking. The old Marine had just said it first, as usual.

Simon Anderson heard the expletive, and it didn't surprise him much. He pointed to the flagpole with the flag still waving in the evening sky and began to speak once again.

"See that flag up there. That's the flag of the United States of America. For so many weeks around here, we've created something special. We've thought of ourselves as Americans."

"The Americans I remember dared to dream big, dared to try big things. The Americans I remember didn't play it safe; they were willing to make sacrifices in the name of freedom. On the bloody fields of Gettysburg, Americans from both sides fought for their own vision of freedom. And as President Abraham Lincoln said of the Union dead, they gave the last full measure of devotion so that government by the people, for the people, might live."

"The men who landed on the foreign sands of Omaha Beach weren't playing it safe. We could have stayed at home, but we volunteered in droves. We were fighting and dying on that hellish beach to topple a tyrant and give the sweet gift of freedom to others."

There was a hushed pause as Simon took a deep breath. For just a moment then, he could hear again the sounds of the past, of bullets and explosions and the terrible screams of men dying in the surf and sand. Simon clenched his jaw and held it tight. The chorus of death and sacrifice faded slowly away.

"It was all worth it," he added quietly.

Holly had been watching and listening to her husband with an equal mixture of absolute surprise and frank admiration. She saw the passion, the fire in his eyes, so much like when he looked at her in their private times. It was mesmerizing. She also noticed the sudden shift to the first person, the use of "we" instead of "they". She wondered if anyone else had picked up on that.

"Americans understand sacrifice," Simon continued. "It is left to us, the living, to make sense of that sacrifice. It is left to us to make sure that this sacrifice is not in vain. This is how we can honor the brave souls who gave their lives here. This is how we can honor men like Father Christopher."

"Americans don't give up!" Simon's voice was louder and more passionate now. He balled his hand into a fist and pumped his arm into the air. "We're not going to disappear quietly into the night. We're not going to be exterminated. We're going to take the fight to the trade association. We're going to take back our freedom and take control of our own destinies."

"We're all Americans here. We're the good guys, damnit. It's time for the good guys to win one again!"

Simon pointed at the crowd. "Who's with me?"

Everything made sense now, at least to Sergeant White. The old Marine, by his nature, much preferred to attack rather than just sit back and wait to get slaughtered. He stepped forward.

"I'm in."

Others soon stepped up to join the sergeant, including young Matt Carson who had to pull away from his mother's grasp. Bill shook his head and laughed, but he stepped forward as well.

Simon smiled and looked up to the heavens above. Holly wiped away a tear running down her cheek. She was proud and terrified all at the same time.

"Get hold of a truck and meet me here tomorrow at midnight," Simon said to Sergeant White. "I've got to prepare for a meeting with the CEO."

Chapter 26

For Holly and Simon, the ride home was very quiet, awkwardly quiet. After the events of this evening, Holly was too scared and confused to say much of anything. Simon, on the other hand, was just praying that their battered vehicle could stay together long enough for them to get home. With a smashed front end, holes in the windshield, and damage from automatic weapons, he knew it was going to be close.

The drive seemed to last forever.

By the time husband and wife finally did pull into their neighborhood, it was well past the hour when the neighbors might take notice of the car turning into the driveway. They were both glad to be home and genuinely relieved they weren't going to have to explain to anybody why the car was full of bullet holes. Simon pulled into the garage and closed the door, all the better to hide the evidence. The car shuddered to a halt.

Home at last. Holly breathed a sigh of relief as they entered the house. It was quiet inside too. Suzie was spending the night with a friend. Without saying a word, Holly abruptly turned back around to face her husband. She threw her whole body into Simon, wrapping her arms around him as tightly as she possibly could. She had never in her life held onto something or somebody harder. She could feel every muscle, every breath, every heartbeat. Simon smiled and gently stroked Holly's hair.

He scooped his wife up into his arms and carried her back to their bedroom. He looked deep into her eyes the whole way. The only sound was the opening and closing of the bedroom door.

Morning came much too soon for Simon. As sunlight filtered through the blinds, he let out an audible groan. It came so quickly and so naturally even though he was really trying not to wake Holly. It didn't matter; she was awake already. The giggling gave her away. Simon proceeded to trace with his finger, ever so slowly, the contour of Holly's thigh. He was very serious and intent on the effort, lost in thought as he felt the smoothness of her skin. Holly giggled again and turned over to face her husband. Simon smiled. He always smiled when he looked at the woman who meant everything in the world to him. He didn't want to leave her ever.

The giggling had stopped. The bedroom was silent. Husband and wife had not spoken a word since they left the rescue mission. That was hours ago. Simon looked back into those beautiful brown eyes. He knew what he had to do.

It was time to talk.

Holly knew as much. She just couldn't bring herself to ask the first question.

"I can't begin to tell you how much I didn't want last night to happen," Simon said slowly. "All the bloodshed, so much death and destruction: I tried so damn hard to prevent that. I tried so hard to help those people without things getting violent. I wanted things … to be different this time."

Simon shook his head. A terrible sadness settled upon him, seizing his brow, his eyes, his entire facial expression in its iron grip.

"You know now there are things I have to do." He paused and cleared his throat.

Holly nodded. She struggled to manage a weak smile. Part of her didn't want to hear what came next. Part of her had to know.

"There is a place, a most beautiful place," Simon continued. "There are peaceful fields where brave men rest, men who have three times served the greater good."

"We all try to get there someday." Simon looked upward, lingering for the moment as if he fully expected at any second to see those peaceful fields. "But we have to earn our way in with the deeds we do."

"I was sent here, to this place, at this time, to do these deeds."

"Sent here? What do you mean sent here?" Holly had recovered just enough of her composure to ask the question. There was no doubt now she wanted to hear more.

Only Simon wasn't quite so ready to give her more. He turned away from Holly's eyes. He breathed in deeply and exhaled slowly. He stood up from the bed. He shifted his body weight from one leg to the other and then back again. He slowly rotated his head and neck muscles. He did everything but speak.

Holly couldn't wait any longer. "What do you mean sent here?" she repeated. She got up from the bed as well and touched Simon on the shoulder.

"I'm not your husband," he answered softly.

Holly didn't say a word. She couldn't say a word. She wasn't even so sure what she had just heard.

"I'm not your husband," Simon continued, his voice clear and firm. "Your husband died in the bombing. I was placed in his body. I have his memories. I have his — I have my love for you and our daughter."

Simon turned around quickly and tried to grasp Holly's hand, but she pulled away. She knew Simon had been so different since the bombing; he was really better in many ways, she had to admit. On many occasions, she had even suspected this man was not her husband. Yet she had allowed herself to love him anyway. She knew. Deep down, she knew. Maybe she had always known. But now she still pulled away. Maybe now she just couldn't bear to hear it said out loud.

Simon had said it though, and it could not be taken back.

It was all quiet again, the type of quiet which might last awhile, mainly because neither party knew exactly what to say next. Simon for sure didn't. For Holly, it was going to take some time to sink in. She needed something to do, and it clearly wasn't going to be talking.

Cooking was something; it was an easier something, a safer something. Holly immediately turned her attention to making breakfast. That suited Simon too. He was hungry anyway. The smell of fresh bacon filled the air. Grease popped in the frying pan.

Sometime between scrambling a few eggs and toasting the bread, something easy suddenly became something not quite good enough. Things had sunk in. Holly had another question, the most obvious question of all.

"If you're not my husband, who are you?" It was all very matter of fact. She didn't even look up from the eggs.

The man who was not Holly's husband shook his head. He was hungry, but he knew he wasn't going to be eating for a while yet. He knew he had to answer Holly. He owed her that much.

"My name, the name my mother and father gave me many ages ago, is Dienekes. I am a son of Sparta. I was born to defend her."

To hell with breakfast. Holly turned around immediately. Simon grimaced. He had really been hoping she wasn't going to burn the eggs.

"You mean to tell me that you're some sort of ancient Greek warrior or something?"

Simon nodded awkwardly. "I have served the Gods," he said softly. "I have served them over the ages."

Holly didn't respond. She looked at Simon. She looked deep into his eyes, deep into the place where she had always seen the truth.

The eggs were burning by now.

Suddenly Simon wasn't so hungry anymore. He looked back into the eyes of the woman he loved.

"I have lived — and died — under many names: Dienekes, Captain John Miller. And now I live again as Simon Anderson. I have always fought for what the Gods led me to believe was right. In my homeland, I fought alongside my brothers at a narrow mountain pass against an invading army of 100,000 men to protect the freedom of our people. Later, I came ashore with an army storming the beaches of France to conquer tyranny and free a whole continent from the clutches of a mad man."

"Now I fight to topple a corrupt and immoral organization, an organization of unchecked power, an organization that lies to its people and kills whoever it wants to. I fight to give freedom back to poor people who have forgotten what the word means, to give hope to people who have none. I fight to help people remember a proud history of their own homeland."

"I fight for a dream and a place, a place where a flag waves, a place we used to call the United States of America."

Simon smiled. It felt good. It felt liberating to tell the truth — most of the truth at least.

"I fight because I was born to be a warrior. That I have lived many lives, that I have the memories of many people, only makes me stronger."

Holly managed a weak smile of her own. It seemed the right thing to do. She still wasn't sure exactly what to say. Simon reached forward and touched Holly's hand. She didn't pull away this time.

He thought about pulling her close but was interrupted by two messages which came into his cell phone one right after another. Simon sighed heavily. On any other day, he wouldn't even consider letting go of the woman he loved. Today wasn't any other day though. Time was short; things had to be done. With much regret, he drew back slowly from Holly's hand and clicked on his phone.

The eggs were beginning to smoke in the frying pan. Holly turned without saying a word and promptly dumped the first attempt at breakfast into the trash. Soon enough, she was scrambling up more eggs. Simon sniffed the air again. He really hoped he might get to eat this time.

Both messages had been short and about what he expected. The first was an answer from Chris Smith. It was good news; it confirmed that the I.T. man would help Simon with his plan. The second put the final piece of that plan into place. It was a request for a meeting after work — from the CEO himself. Simon nodded. There was a sly grin on his face. No, it wasn't a surprise at all. Apparently the extra-curricular activities from the night before had not gone unnoticed.

No burning. No smoke. Breakfast was ready now, and Simon was ready to eat it.

Suzy was back from her friend's house. With blonde curls bouncing and all the energy in the world, the child giggled and gave her father the biggest hug she could muster. Simon smiled and playfully ran his fingers through those curls. He held her tight; just about sure he could smell bubble gum. It was a good smell. It was a happy smell. He wasn't in any hurry right at the moment. Eating could wait just a few more minutes.

Suzy's mother laughed as she put the plates on the table. The Andersons sat down to eat as a family. Despite all that had been said and all that was now known, breakfast was exceedingly relaxed. There was more laughter, more smiles, more good food. Simon leaned back in his chair and looked around the table. It was the little things for sure, he thought, the small intimate moments like this, which made a family. And he had learned to treasure that family and all those little moments. Loved ones were worth fighting for. It wasn't just about crushing the enemy anymore. He wondered if the beautiful fields had anything quite as wonderful as what he had at this table right here, right now.

Simon smiled again. Holly noticed that.

When breakfast was over, Simon was in no hurry to leave the house. He played with Suzy and otherwise tried to entertain Holly. He knew what waited for him at the office. He knew what he had to do. He just wanted to enjoy the right here and the right now — for a little bit longer.

His wife noticed that too. It was a small thing to take this time, but it was real, and it meant everything.

A simple honesty and decency and caring: it showed in the eyes. She had seen it there since the very moment Simon came home from the hospital, the very moment the man she had lived with started to become something so much more. Maybe she didn't quite understand it, and maybe she never would. Still she could feel it in the very depths of her soul.

A little bit longer did finally end. Simon checked his watch. It was time to leave.

"Honey, I'll need to take your car to work today," Simon said matter-of-factly. "Obviously," he added with a chuckle, "the bullet holes in the other car might attract some attention."

"However, I do promise to switch out cars with you after work. I can take the wrecked car with me over the bridge to the rescue mission."

Simon picked up the car keys and headed towards the garage.

Holly suddenly threw her arms around Simon and squeezed him tight. "You are my husband," she whispered into his ear.

"You're the very best part of him."

Chapter 27

Daniel Garcia had a few minutes to kill. It was near the end of the work-day, and there was still time before his last appointment. He didn't feel he needed the time to prepare for that meeting. On the contrary, he felt very well prepared. Daniel Garcia glanced down at his desk drawer and smiled.

He was ready, as he always was, and he could handle things all by himself, as he always had.

That being settled, Garcia returned to the issue at hand. No, he didn't ever like to waste time. Time, he believed, had to be put to good use, to do something that was value-added. He had built his career and the entire Trade Association of the Americas on this basic premise. He looked over at the plaque showing the guiding principles, his guiding principles:

1) All non-value added activity is waste.
2) Waste does not add to bottom-line profits.
3) Eliminate all waste.

Things were no different now. Not because of the continued conflict with the European Union. Not because of some subordinate who wouldn't follow orders.

There were e-mails in the CEO's inbox still, all of them about the real work he needed to get back to after he finished up with the appointment. He scanned through the list message after message, past suggestions for the sequel to the George Washington blockbuster, past the update on the Yellowstone condo project, past all the typical financial reports. Then there was something new. It was the latest recommendation to reduce the drag of healthcare costs on the economy, and it had a video attached. It piqued Daniel Garcia's interest; he decided to open the attachment.

The video opened with stark scenes of a haggard wife and children crying. The voiceover was solemn.

"Don't be a burden to your family. Don't take food out of your child's mouth. Don't prolong your own suffering."

"There's a better way."

"If you're seriously ill, the medical bills can be staggering. The cold hard truth: even if you manage to survive, you'll be bankrupt, and your family will be out on the street."

The voiceover suddenly became more upbeat. An energetic tune played in the background.

"A new program from the Trade Association of the Americas can change all that now. We call it *A Managed Death*: it allows you, and you alone, to control how you exit this world. Death by your own hand, however you choose, whenever you choose."

"It's very simple," the voice continued as the music grew louder. "Call this toll free number on the screen, and we'll make all the arrangements. We'll supply the gun, the pills, whatever you want. If you need someone to pull the trigger, we can do that too."

"And best of all — we provide safe and secure clean-up afterwards. No having to worry about your family finding you."

The video cut quickly to a new scene. It was a funeral. The same wife and the same children were there, all dutifully dressed in black. The sun was shining, and birds were singing.

"Your family will be taken care of financially," the voice added. "Your savings will be intact. Under the guidelines of this new program, you may even be eligible for a partial payout of your life insurance. We have several insurance companies in the program who have agreed to waive their standard suicide clauses and allow payment up to 30% of the policy face value to beneficiaries."

The wife at the funeral turned around to face the camera. A single tear trickled down her cheek. She hugged her children and then smiled. The camera pulled slowly back, capturing leafy green trees at the cemetery, the blue sky, and the bright sun above. The music faded away. The toll free number flashed once more before the screen went black.

According to the e-mail, the attachment was a proposed commercial to help sell the new program to the public. The financial justification was all there as well. Private insurance companies who offered both health and life insurance were particularly excited about the program. They had done their own calculations, figuring that a small settlement on a life insurance policy was still a whole lot cheaper than paying for extended hospitalization or treatment.

Daniel Garcia was pleased. He appreciated innovative solutions to nagging problems, and he really liked young, ambitious executives taking cues from his own leadership. He took mental note of the name of the executive. He was going to keep an eye on that young man.

After responding with supportive words to the healthcare proposal, Garcia processed through several other e-mails. He was determined to handle as many as he could before the appointment. He read some. He answered some. He deleted some. About three-quarters of the way down through the list, he was suddenly interrupted by the meeting reminder on his electronic calendar. Garcia exhaled a deep breath and pushed back from the computer screen, quite pleased that he had gotten through so many.

The CEO glanced back over at his desk drawer again. Yes, he was ready to see Simon Anderson.

And Simon Anderson was ready to see him.

As he approached the office of the CEO, Simon only hoped that Chris Smith had gotten everything in place. Simon noticed that Mary, Garcia's secretary, had already left for the day. That was most fortunate, he thought.

There would be no witnesses.

The door to the office was heavy. Simon didn't notice. He opened it easily and without knocking. Now was not the time to worry about protocol. Daniel Garcia was waiting behind his desk. He wasn't much worried about formalities either.

"I see you're on time at least," the CEO said with a chuckle. "I worried you might still be in bed after your exploits of last night. You know I've seen the reports from the surviving members of our security team. Swinging a pipe around and busting heads — I hear it's pretty exhausting work."

"Not really," Simon replied with a smile. "Not when you're good at it — and I've had plenty of practice over the years. Sorry about breaking so many of your hired killers though. I don't think you'll get much use out of them now."

"Oh, don't worry about that. We have plenty more where those came from." Daniel Garcia nonchalantly waved his left hand in the air. His right hand was close to the desk drawer.

"You know Mr. Anderson," the CEO continued, "you used to be such an ambitious little shit. You wore the right clothes. You traveled with the right people. You said the right things. And most importantly, you took on the right jobs."

"I understood you so much better back then."

Garcia sighed and forced a hand through his thick black hair. He sounded almost nostalgic for days gone by, for something lost.

"But now...."

"Now you spend your free time hanging out at a broken down rescue mission with a bunch of poor people who don't add any value at all to our trade association. They're scum, waste that needs to be eliminated — yet — you defend them. I don't understand it, not one damn bit."

"You're quite the changed man, Mr. Anderson." Garcia sighed again and shook his head.

"Oh, you don't know the half of it," Simon quickly replied. There was a fierce glow in his eyes now, and Simon made no attempt to hide it.

The CEO recognized that look immediately. He had seen it before. It was unnerving then, and it was unnerving now. He shifted in his chair, careful to be sure that his desk drawer was still within reach.

For a moment then, Garcia contemplated his decision to make this a private meeting. Only contemplated, not questioned, or even re-considered. And it was only for a moment at that. Daniel Garcia never re-considered his decisions. He got to the top by being decisive, and when necessary, adapting to changing circumstances.

Yes, Daniel Garcia knew what to do. He leaned forward, opened the drawer, and pulled out his Glock semi-automatic. The weapon fit his hand perfectly; it made him feel strong, in control. He stood up and pointed the gun at Simon.

Suddenly that look wasn't quite so disturbing anymore. "I knew it would come down to this," the CEO said with a smile. "You've served your purpose quite well, but I'm afraid we won't be needing your services anymore."

"You mean after I planted the bomb for you at the trade conference." Simon didn't flinch when he spoke. He didn't flinch as he looked down the barrel of the gun either. He was tired of flinching or playing it safe. He was tired of keeping secrets.

"I'm so glad to see you've fully regained your memory. It just warms my heart. It really does." Garcia laughed.

"Only one thing about that bomb though," Simon continued calmly, "that bomb wasn't supposed to kill anybody. It was just supposed to scare the European Union into making the deal. If I remember correctly, the bomb wasn't supposed to go off until after I had gotten all of the delegates out of the conference room for the break."

"But then that bomb explodes early." Simon looked directly at Daniel Garcia. He felt his muscles tighten, the rage building in the very depths of his soul. "I wonder why that would have happened."

"Oh that." Garcia again saw the intensity in those eyes. He was decidedly less comfortable than he had been a few minutes before. "It was just a change in the plan," Garcia replied cautiously, "that I simply forgot to tell you about."

"You do have to understand, Mr. Anderson, I don't do anything half-assed. How can you throw a perfectly good terrorist bombing without having massive casualties? It's just not good form."

"Besides, and this is very important, you need to have all that blood and gore in order to get the best possible ratings on the evening news. It's all about winning the time slot. It's value-added you see."

Simon didn't respond with either words or action. He wanted to so very badly; every muscle and fiber of his being wanted to strike a powerful blow. At the moment, however, there was a greater good to be served here. He needed to be patient. He needed the whole truth to come out.

He needed most of all for the CEO to continue talking.

Daniel Garcia wasn't going to disappoint. After all, the CEO did very much like to talk about how his decision-making process really worked. The talking, the teaching: it came so naturally to him in his position as a leader. Lower level executives needed it, he had always believed. They needed to understand his genius for fitting together individual decisions or activities into a broad, cohesive strategy for achieving the desired goal. It would serve to inspire them. It would make them better.

"I needed that blood and those ratings to push through my plans to strike at the EU. The Europeans were never going to come to their senses and join us; more aggressive negotiating tactics were clearly needed. In my opinion though, the bombing wasn't absolutely necessary — we might have gotten the same effect with a couple of well-staged assassinations we could've blamed on the EU."

"But there are so many damn bleeding hearts out there. And they were always so insistent about things. Not only must we be attacked first, but we must be attacked in a very big way before we can retaliate or take any sort of military action."

"You see, my friend, I just gave the people what they wanted. They wanted lots of blood; I gave them lots of blood!" Garcia smiled. He was suddenly very comfortable again. He really enjoyed talking about himself, and he still had the gun, which ensured he had a captive audience too. He was in control. Yes, life was good.

"I see the plan," Simon answered, "but I'm not so sure it's working." He couldn't hold back his words anymore.

That got Daniel Garcia's attention. He didn't like it when anyone dared to question his decision making. Coming from a subordinate at that, merely the hired help, it was surely an insult.

And yet, at this very moment, it just didn't seem to matter. Garcia didn't even stop smiling. He could afford to let this one go. It was all a matter of control really, and he still had it. He pointed the gun directly at Simon's head.

This wasn't going to last much longer anyway.

"Your war isn't going so well," Simon continued tartly. "You're killing lots of people but getting no results. Now you're even starting to see resistance at home, and you're having to pack away protesters in the new Gettysburg Containment Center."

"It sure doesn't look like an unmitigated success to me." Simon smiled through gritted teeth.

"That's where you're wrong." The response was sharp and quick. Garcia still had his gun pointed at Simon's head, his finger tight on the trigger. He was tiring of the insults. "You really don't understand, do you?"

Not that Daniel Garcia expected an answer from his subordinate. He was quite prepared, actually eager, to answer his own question. For the moment, nothing else mattered but that answer.

For the moment, Garcia did not bother to question why Simon knew anything at all about the Gettysburg Containment Center.

"It's not a war," the CEO chuckled. "Nobody fights wars anymore." He shook his head and frowned. "Wars are a relic of the past, just like the nation-states who used to justify them with all that patriotic fervor. Wars, dying for somebody's flag: it's all bull-shit, much too expensive and not very efficient."

Simon thought of the flag of red, white, and blue waving over the Catholic Rescue Mission. He thought of the brave men in green who wore the same flag on their uniforms and landed on that hellish beach many years ago. He knew there were still brave men willing to die for that flag.

"No, it's not a war." It frustrated Garcia that others did not see what was so obvious to him. He wondered if he had misjudged Simon Anderson's intelligence in the first place.

"It's all business," Garcia added with clear disdain. "We're just in a rather extended negotiation with the EU. The shooting and killing is just a negotiating tactic. And as with any negotiation, patience is the key. The Europeans will come to their senses soon enough. They won't be able to stand the pain forever. If more members of our security forces have to die in the meantime, that's not a problem; those guys are cheap enough."

"You see, Mr. Anderson, you just have to give these tactics time to work."

"Oh, I see," Simon replied, nodding at the same time. "We all just have to wait a little bit longer, and only a few more people have to die." He pressed the thumb and index finger close together on his left hand, leaving only a small gap. The sarcasm was obvious, and Simon didn't care.

"And while we're waiting for your plan to work, Mr. Garcia, I'm wondering just how many more protesters you're going to have — and I bet all those protesters will suddenly come down with the flu too. Maybe you're going to have to build another containment center to hold all those new flu cases."

The containment center again: this time, it registered very clearly. The CEO didn't miss a beat though. If his subordinate wanted to talk about the containment center, he was fully prepared to talk about that as well. He figured it would be a short conversation anyway.

"You're a real funny guy, Mr. Anderson. Once again, you have no appreciation of the big picture, and you just don't understand the brilliance of my plan."

"The Gettysburg Containment Center actually serves two purposes." Daniel Garcia had a smug smile on his face. He paused briefly on the outside chance that Simon might actually make a guess.

No such luck.

"Sure, the facility at Gettysburg allows me to put away people who make too much noise." Garcia laughed out loud. "But I bet you don't realize how good that center is for the economy. Just think, the bigger the containment center gets, the more people worry about the flu pandemic. All these people then go out and buy lots of disinfectant wipes and disinfectant soaps. The companies that make these products are making a fortune. We're making a fortune."

"Face it; the flu is good for business! Putting people away in prison helps us sell the flu and increases profits. It's all very value-added."

Simon didn't say a word. He just smiled. He savored the victory. The fire glowed in his eyes. All that needed to be said had now been said.

Daniel Garcia felt prepared to celebrate victory as well, a different sort of victory. He was ready to finish things. He just didn't quite understand the smile on the face of the guy who was about to get shot.

"You never really understood the guiding principles, did you Mr. Anderson? You never really accepted my principles. That's too bad." The CEO leveled the gun squarely at his target. He wasn't going to miss.

"But I guess that's all academic now."

The office was quiet, totally still and not disturbed even by the sound of breathing. It was the CEO thought, the proper environment for an execution.

"I always thought you talked too much." Suddenly there was another voice in the room. Startled at the interruption, Daniel Garcia pulled his weapon back and immediately turned in the direction of the voice.

"And personally I think you come off like an arrogant ass." Chris Smith stepped out from the shadows. "But hey," Smith grinned, "that's just me."

"When this gets streamed out across the globe, we'll just have to let the people decide for themselves."

"What do you mean?" It was a logical question. It was also the first and only question that popped into Daniel Garcia's head. He was surprised, confused now. Big strategic thoughts and statements weren't so forthcoming.

"You know exactly what it means," Smith replied sharply. "It means we got your confession on tape. It means all your goddamn lies have been exposed. You're going to have to pay for all this."

Things were not going according to plan anymore. Garcia was no longer in control, and he didn't like that at all.

He knew only one way to change that, but he was going to have to move quickly. Two threats needed to be neutralized now.

In the pale light and quiet stillness, there was movement. No words, no sounds, just movement, sudden and decisive.

Garcia had made his move.

He wasn't quick enough. As he brought his weapon to bear on Chris Smith, Garcia was struck from the side by a powerful blow. He never got the chance to fire. With lethal speed and agility, Simon had cleared the chief executive's desk and interrupted the shot. Daniel Garcia held onto the gun still — barely — but now Simon held it as well.

A terrific struggle ensued for control of the weapon. The CEO was driven by a certain quiet desperation, something he had never known before, something he hoped would make up for his lost focus, his lost control. Simon had the strength of the ages, the strength of truth and honor mixed together in equal parts with justice and cold, hard revenge. Simon saw the eyes of the dead, at the bombing, at the rescue mission — all of them — as he forced the gun back and up tight against Daniel Garcia's chin.

The barrel of the gun made a cold touch to the skin. Garcia felt it and shuddered. He looked into the eyes of his assailant and saw that terrible glow once again. He knew now for sure. The fear began to take control of the body, sickening his stomach and racing his heart. He tried to call out for help but the words, the sounds, would not come. His knees shook and buckled finally, no longer able to support any weight. The CEO slumped down into his chair, feeling very much like a beaten man. The gun was still stuck under his chin.

For all the awesome power of his position, Daniel Garcia lacked the power, the strength he needed right here and right now to save his own life.

There had been a plan all along: a plan which would have guaranteed success, if properly executed, a plan flexible enough to cover every possible contingency. It wasn't supposed to be like this. It wasn't supposed to end like this. Garcia could barely comprehend that the plan, his perfect plan, had failed. In his final moments, the CEO wondered just where his subordinates had gone wrong, just how these people could have failed him.

Using Garcia's own finger on the trigger, Simon applied pressure enough until the weapon fired.

The office was quiet, again. Unlike the aftermath of the massacre at the rescue mission, there was no collective outpouring of grief, no heartfelt moans or mourning for the dead. There was silence. There was just death, pure and simple. The most powerful man on the continent had died as he had lived. No feelings, no compassion: it was all just business. Kill or be killed.

Chris Smith broke the silence. Ever the practical man, Smith pointed out the obvious.

"Well, that certainly takes care of one problem, but it just as certainly creates others."

Simon didn't say a word. He was well aware of the problems.

"Then again...."

The I.T. man had an idea.

"The scene here almost looks like a suicide. If I edit the tape a little before release, get rid of the struggle in particular, we might be able to perpetuate that for a while. They'll find the body in the morning. We just might be able to throw them off at first. They'll have a hard time tracking you while they're dealing with the massive PR nightmare of the truth about the bombing and the camp along with the apparent suicide of their great leader."

"But I stress you won't have much time. If you're going to hit the containment camp, you have to hit it early tomorrow morning and then get out of there."

"The attack is scheduled for dawn," Simon replied flatly. Smith nodded.

All that needed to be said had been said — almost.

"Thanks for your help," Simon added. Smith nodded again.

"You better leave now." The I.T. man smiled. "Take care of yourself, my friend."

Simon turned and pushed through the office door. He knew he was leaving the headquarters of the TAA for the final time. It felt good. It felt right. It felt like freedom.

The ride home was a blur. Simon knew who he wanted to see, but he knew it had to be quick. He didn't have the time to explain everything.

As he pulled into the driveway, he could see Holly waiting for him at the front door. She rushed out to greet him when she saw the car door open. Simon was eager for the embrace too. Then Holly stopped dead in her tracks. She had seen the blood on her husband's shirt.

"Oh my god, are you hurt?"

"No, it's not my blood." Simon looked down at his shirt and frowned. "I'll have to change, but I'll take it with me and get rid of it later when I get to the rescue mission."

"Why, whose blood is it on your shirt?" Holly had that look again: a healthy dose of stubbornness that said she fully expected an answer to her question. There was also just a touch of fear in those eyes. Maybe she hadn't fully digested everything that had happened over the last 24 hours. Simon recognized it all immediately.

He didn't have time for any of it.

"I told you there were things I had to do." Simon reached forward and gently, yet firmly, placed his hands on Holly's arms. "And I have to do everything on a tight schedule."

"I came here to see you. I don't have time to explain everything."

Holly nodded slowly. She didn't say a word, but that look in her eyes was gone. No fear, no stubbornness; just those beautiful brown eyes again softened suddenly around the edges. Simon smiled and pulled his wife close.

There was so little time. Simon tried to use it wisely. He ate a quick dinner. He changed clothes. He tucked his daughter into bed. Mostly he tried to spend time with Holly. These were the things he had grown to value. These were the things he was prepared to go into battle to defend.

By now, it was late enough to switch vehicles and bring out the bullet ridden car without fear of the neighbors seeing it. Simon started the car; he was glad it did. There was one last thing though. He got back out of the car and took Holly into his arms.

"Honey, there are some things you may hear over the next few days. There are some things you'll hear about me — about Simon."

Only a day ago, Holly would have been mightily perplexed by the third person reference. Not so, not now, not after things had changed so much. She had come to believe the unbelievable. She had come to believe in mythical gods and ancient souls who occupied the bodies of the fallen. She had come to believe in real-life heroes, warriors of flesh and blood, who battled great odds for the greater good. Yes, Holly had come to believe in lots of things she never could have imagined before. In truth, she also wondered at times if she had absolutely lost her mind.

She shook her head. Holly tried now to block out everything else and just listen to the man, the hero, she had come to love.

"Trust me when I tell you this," her hero continued. "Simon got involved in something bad. He got in way over his head and never dreamed things would go so far. He got double-crossed. Others took advantage of his youth and yes, unfortunately, his blind ambition."

"But I know, in his own mind, he was also trying to secure the future for you and Suzy. He didn't always show it, but I know he loved you very much."

"I love you very much."

The man who was Simon now pulled Holly close and kissed her before she could say anything. He kissed her long and hard, and she kissed him back with every ounce of strength in her body and every single fiber of her being.

If he could, he would have gone on kissing her forever, but that was not his destiny. That was not what he was sent to this place to do. He did let her go. It was time. He pulled away, slowly, reluctantly.

"I'll love you forever, Holly Anderson." Simon opened the door and got back into the car.

Holly couldn't speak. Tears rolled down both cheeks.

He looked back once more before pulling out of the garage. "I'll see you again," he yelled.

"I promise."

As he drove away into the night, Simon wiped first one eye and then the other. There was an unusual amount of wetness in both eyes.

"I'll see you again," he mumbled to himself, "in this life … or the next."

Chapter 28

Hector Gonzalez looked out his apartment window at the quiet streets below. It was dark, peaceful, no movement at all down there. More importantly, there was no shooting. No screams either. No dying tonight.

There had been too much bloodshed. Hector knew that all too well; it made him appreciate this bit of quiet so much more now. He was content really, or at least as much as someone in his profession could be. His family was safe, and Smiling Bob was gone, which bode well for some future stability in the neighborhood. Maybe, Hector wondered as he glanced up at the stars, it could be simple again. Maybe they could just go back to making money around this place — without all the killing.

"Live and let live," he mumbled to himself.

It could work. It had to work. Yes, Hector believed it. He smiled rather suddenly at the thought and then, still absorbed in that thought, casually reached down to scratch the head of the dog at his side. The shepherd immediately returned the affection. With a low, playful growl, she quite happily licked her new master's hand. Hector didn't seem to mind all the slobber.

It was a new day after all. No matter that it was night and pitch black outside. A minor distinction, Hector thought.

He was still smiling when he looked back down at the streets. This time though, he noticed movement — two or three figures scurrying about in the darkness, darting back and forth between several parked delivery vans. Hector strained mightily to see, and it did become clear soon enough. He thought he could just about make out one of the figures. It sure looked and moved a lot like an old Marine he knew. The old Marine and the other two figures, Hector noted, had just worked their way into one of the vans and gotten it started.

Hector toyed with the idea of what to do for only a moment. He knew what Smiling Bob would have done. However, he wasn't Smiling Bob, and he never would be. He didn't know why the Marine and his buddies wanted the van, and he didn't care that he didn't know. In the end, Hector did the only thing he could do.

He did absolutely nothing.

It just seemed like the right thing to do. It was the least he could do for those guys over at the rescue mission. Hector watched the van drive away.

"Live and let live," he repeated.

Simon was on the move too, just not where Hector Gonzalez could see him. Like the sergeant and the others in the van, he was headed towards the rendezvous point. It was almost midnight. It was time to execute the plan.

As he nursed his battered vehicle to a stop just outside the Catholic Rescue Mission, Simon breathed a heavy sigh of relief. He had made it — on a wing and a prayer maybe — but he had made it on time. Better yet, he could see a large cargo van parked there as well. Sergeant White had apparently kept up his end of the bargain.

"I see you made it back here in that shot-to-shit car," the old Marine said with a grin. Sergeant White was glad to see that Simon had kept up his end of the bargain as well.

"Of course I made it," Simon chuckled as he extracted himself carefully from the vehicle, moving deftly around twisted metal and jagged glass. "I'm very dependable. We have a job to do."

Once he had cleared all the hazards, Simon tried to close the car door; it wouldn't stay shut. He tried a few more times out of habit before finally giving up. Shaking his head, he laughed and kicked the tire one last time for good measure.

"I bet our long-lost friends at the trade association will be really surprised by our visit tomorrow," Simon continued. "They'll never be expecting us to come in and relieve them of some of that waste, the human kind, they've been holding onto all these years. You know we might even add some real value to the place in the process."

The sergeant didn't say a word. He just kept smiling. He didn't quite understand everything Simon had just said, but it sounded confident and loose. That was a good thing right now he figured.

"But we don't have much time if we're going to get to that containment center before dawn." Simon was suddenly serious. "Do you have all the firepower we'll need?"

White nodded. "Already in the van."

"We better get loaded up then," Simon replied tightly.

Men around the rescue mission understood. They began to step forward, pushing their way through the crowd, pulling away from a loved one here and there. They moved with a purpose. They were all sorts — young, old, some with a limp or a stiff leg, others wearing bandages to cover wounds. It was quite the collection, ragged and battered as they were, but to a man, they all had that certain fire in their eyes. Simon recognized it immediately.

Matt Carson finally managed to pull away from his mother and stepped forward with the rest of the group. Proving that he was good on his word from the night before, Bill joined them as well.

Slowly and surely, and very quietly, those who had made the commitment filed one after another into the van. When they were all done, Sergeant White slid into the driver's seat. Simon put his hand on the passenger door. It was time to go.

There was just one last thing to do though.

Simon turned around and scanned through faces in the crowd until he found Arthur. He saw pain in the old man's face. He saw doubt too. It didn't really surprise Simon. So many had died at the rescue mission in the last 24 hours; they had just finished burying the last of them. And now, still more were putting their lives on the line: fathers, sons, husbands, brothers. It was a highly risky raid at this place called Gettysburg, and some of them were going to die. Simon knew it. Arthur knew it. Simon had always known it would come to this. Arthur had only suspected as much, until tonight at least.

"We'll bring back the Congressman," Simon yelled out. "We'll bring back your single man of principle." Under the circumstances, it was the first thought which came to mind. It was really the only thing Simon could do. He had to tell the old teacher something, had to reassure him somehow.

They were powerful words. Deep down inside, Arthur thought of what that single man of principle might be able to do for the people in this place. He dared to hope. It was a long shot he knew, but it was hope indeed. It didn't take away all the fear or all the worry; it helped though. Arthur smiled, throwing up his hand as well to wave a small farewell and to wish good luck. For his part, Simon wasn't much for smiling on the eve of battle. He nodded to the teacher, quite simply and rather quickly, and then turned back around to get into the van.

Arthur understood. He didn't really expect any more than that.

Now it was definitely time to go. Sergeant White started the van and pulled away from the Catholic Rescue Mission. It was just about half past midnight.

There were less than six hours until dawn, and plenty of miles to go before then.

As it had always been since the beginning of things, time moved forward — inexorable, inflexible, and totally indifferent to the schedules of men. Dawn would arrive exactly on time. The sun would rise. The night would retreat. Whether or not the men from the rescue mission would be in the desired place by the time dawn came was quite another matter.

The miles passed by quickly. Simon slept through most of them. It was the old Marine's job to keep the team on schedule. So he pushed on. Then he pushed on some more. And just as the first hint of light appeared on the eastern horizon, the van pulled into the sleepy town of Gettysburg.

Simon was awake by then. Actually he hadn't really been asleep for some time. His eyes closed, his ears had still heard the muffled sounds around him. It wasn't just that. It was hard to sleep when he thought of Holly: her beautiful brown eyes, the sweet smell of her perfume, the soft touch of her skin. It was harder yet to be so far away from her and from their daughter. Simon had to remind himself that this was all for them, that real freedom for all, rich or poor, was worth the sacrifice. He believed it. The men from the rescue mission believed it. Together they could make a difference now, in this very place, even if meant making the sacrifice. Simon looked out the window as the streets passed by.

No, he had never really slept at all.

The van pulled off the main roads of the town onto narrow lanes choked by weeds and lined with weathered statues and toppled, broken monuments of stone. Here and there too, the odd rusty cannon dotted the road. They moved slowly past a bronze man sitting astride a great horse. There was a gaping hole in his chest, and he was missing most of his left leg. Yet he looked out still over ragged and lonely fields, a silent vigil uninterrupted by time, destruction, or even neglect. Sergeant White suddenly tightened his grip on the steering wheel. He knew exactly where he was. It just didn't look at all like he remembered it those many years ago, back on warm sunny days when his entire family used to come here to remember history and honor courage. Lots of people came here back then. That had been in the time before the trade association.

The old Marine wiped a tear away from his eye as he looked at it now. The men in the van who were old enough to remember shook their heads.

"We're here," the Sergeant said flatly, his voice choking back a bit. The van rolled to a stop right before a long double row of barbed wire. Remains of the original split rail fence were tangled in the wire, making the entire barrier look somehow sadder and more formidable at the same time. There were no warning signs, but it was clearly meant to keep anyone and everyone out. White stepped out of the van and touched his finger to one of the twisted barbs.

"Brave men died here, on both sides, fighting for what they believed in. Nobody believed in shit like this." The old Marine pulled his finger back. Simon and the rest of the men had climbed out of the van. Several of them stretched and rubbed their eyes. It was just possible now, in the grey mists of the dawn, to make out the rough outline of the containment camp sitting on the far side of an empty field.

"We don't have much time," Simon snapped. "We have to cross that field before the sun is fully up. It's our only chance to surprise the guards."

Sergeant White nodded. "Gentleman, let's lock and load." Under the circumstances, he couldn't yell it out. It was, nonetheless, a strong and very forceful whisper. And he didn't have to repeat it either. Men moved, and they moved quickly.

Some began to cut a path through the barbed wire.

There was plenty of locking and loading too. Gun cartridges clicked and clattered as they slid fast into position. Men stuffed extra ammo clips along with the odd grenade or two into vests. They checked out weapons, and their eyes had a steely gaze. They were armed. They were dangerous. They were ready.

Simon watched it all intently. "I am honored to share this field of battle with you today," he said quietly. No one said a word. They didn't have to.

"We are standing on sacred ground here," Simon continued firmly. "We are standing in the place where Americans once gave the last full measure of devotion so that their nation might live — so that America might have a new birth of freedom."

"We're here today to retrace their steps. We're here today to once again give the United States of America that new birth of freedom. "

The way through the wire was clear now.

"Let's go save some of our fellow Americans."

They trotted out into the field all at the double-quick, Simon and Sergeant White in the middle with the rest of the men spread out on both wings. The lines were ragged, not even close to a standard military formation. Old men. Young men, some not more than boys really. A couple with a definite limp. They all moved at their own pace, but they all moved forward together. Simon looked left. He looked right.

He was proud.

This tiny army, this band of misfits, was nothing like the fierce, disciplined warriors whom he had fought beside at a narrow mountain pass a millennia ago. Nor were they anything like the well-equipped army which had stormed the beaches of France. Ahead too, a heavily armed enemy and very long odds awaited them in the camp. It was near suicide to move against — to charge such a position.

But charge they did.

Onward, the few carrying the hopes and dreams of so many, to save those who had suffered and longed to be free.

Through the field of tall weeds.

Into the valley of the shadow.

Following in the footsteps of the brave men who had sacrificed before.

Onward they came, to victory or to death.

They reached the camp and the guard towers just as the sun climbed fully above the eastern horizon and kissed at last the storied fields of Gettysburg. The sunrise was blinding to those who had to look out over the fields and aim their guns. It gave the men from the rescue mission their chance. Sergeant White was the first to open fire. Simon and the others followed suit. Guards fell from the towers, and the gates were forced open.

But men from the rescue mission fell also.

Simon didn't look back. There was no time to grieve. The action, the mission, was straight ahead. He had known there would be losses. He had always known the Gods would demand a high price for victory.

Men who had made it through the gate closed up with Sergeant White and Simon at the camp headquarters building. They knew the most important or most valuable prisoners would be there. White motioned with his hand towards the other buildings.

"You and you," he pointed to Bill and young Matt Carson, "go to the next building over and start releasing prisoners." The old Marine repeated the same instructions to others and sent them off in different directions.

He turned back towards Simon. "We need to create some chaos out here. We need a few more distractions for the guys shooting at us." Simon nodded in agreement just as he cut down another guard with a short burst.

"Let's go get the Congressman now," Simon said with a grin.

Sergeant White smiled and kicked in the door. He tossed in a grenade for good effect before entering. It worked as planned. Guards near the door scattered. Simon and the old Marine were quickly in the building and took out many of the gunmen before they could recover. Moving steadily down the hall, the duo checked corners and covered each other. More guards fell. Simon and the sergeant stopped to check each cell. They released grateful prisoners but had not found what they were really looking for.

A female prisoner made a break for the door. She was shot down by a guard before she made it outside. Sergeant White immediately turned and dropped the guard in his tracks.

"You keep checking cells," White yelled to Simon. "I need to provide some cover for these poor people so they have a chance to get away!" Simon moved on alone, his weapon at the ready.

The last cell in the hall was dark and quiet, so very different from the rest. No shouting. No banging. No people begging to be free. Simon peered through the bars. He could just make out the rough figure of a man slouched at the end of a cot. The man wasn't moving at all.

It wasn't immediately promising, but something told Simon he had found his target at last.

"Congressman," Simon called out. Still no movement from the prisoner.

"Congressman Harris," Simon tried again as he shot off the lock and entered the cell.

"Congressman Harris!" Simon put his hand on the prisoner's shoulder. It was a firm grip to be sure, and it seemed quite natural, quite inevitable under the circumstances, that he should shake the man. Yet Simon resisted the urge. There was a definite frailness about the man sitting on the cot: bowed head, thinning brown hair speckled with white, drab grey clothes which all but swallowed him whole. He was breathing; Simon could tell that but not much else.

The seconds passed. There was screaming and shouting and shooting outside the cell, absolute chaos. Inside the cell, there was silence — for what seemed like an eternity. Simon was rethinking the whole not shaking thing when the man at the end of the cot finally stirred.

"No-one has called me that in a very long time," he said quietly. He looked up, and for the first time Simon could see the face of Congressman Harris. The face was gaunt, unshaven, with pale blue eyes sunken back almost entirely into the cheekbones. It had been a long time, and the prisoner on the cot looked nothing like a potential leader of men.

Nothing at all, except for the faintest glow in those blue eyes. Simon noticed it. It reminded him very much of the dim glow of freedom, the same freedom which was being contested on this field right now. Both needed to be nurtured. Both needed to be fought for.

"We're here, Congressman Harris, to get you out of this place."

"Why?" the Congressman asked blandly. He had not moved from the cot.

Simon didn't answer right away. For just a moment, he feared they had come to this camp for nothing, that men were dying out there for nothing. He heard more shooting and screams outside.

He felt the fear; he felt the doubt; he felt the anger, and then that moment passed. He knew they had simply come too far to give up now.

"We're here," Simon continued firmly, "to fight for freedom. We're here to fight for the United States of America."

"We need you, Mr. Congressman, to help lead us. We need you to speak out for us. We believe you are the one man who can make a difference."

"I tried that before," Harris replied sharply. "The people wouldn't listen back then. So forgive me if I seriously doubt they would listen this time around." The glow was stronger in his blue eyes now. Simon saw that too. Maybe it was just anger, but it was something at least.

"Besides, young man, I don't believe that one man can make a difference anymore."

This time, Simon shot right back. "Pardon me, Congressman, if I disagree with you. But there are brave men who just made the ultimate sacrifice out there in that field because they believed very strongly that one man could make a difference."

"And they all believed that one man is you."

Now Simon had a real glow in his eyes. It was intense. It was fierce. He pointed straight at Harris.

"They died for you!"

Congressman Harris stood up immediately and straightened himself. He didn't say a word. He saw that look in Simon's eyes. Frankly it scared him a little. Maybe it convinced him just a little bit too. Maybe somebody did give a damn, Harris thought. Either that or this crazy son-of-bitch was going to kill him right here, right now.

Simon motioned with his gun towards the open cell door. It was time to go.

The best course, the Congressman quickly decided, was to go with the crazy son-of-bitch and just hope the guy and his friends really did give a damn. If not, he was at least counting on the death being a quick one.

Harris and a man who just might be crazy walked out of the prison cell together. They were quickly met by Sergeant White.

"It's getting pretty hot out here," the old Marine yelled. He didn't have time for pleasantries, and he needed to be heard above the terrific din of battle. "We have to go."

"Right now!"

That much was obvious.

No one paused to agree or even nod. They just went.

Amid smoke and sporadic gunfire, the trio carefully picked their way back down the hall. The wreckage of conflict, blood on the floor, bodies here and there: it wasn't exactly a walk in the park. Harris cringed. Simon and Sergeant White simply moved on, always mindful to cover their package. They made their way to daylight soon enough, but that was only part of the challenge.

Outside in the courtyard, there were more bodies — plenty more — friend and foe alike, along with lots of innocent people, prisoners before, who had just been trying to get away. The guards had not discriminated when they started shooting.

And they were still shooting.

Now with the element of surprise gone, the sheer weight of numbers was beginning to tell. The guards were many; those opposing them were a pitiful few. Men from the rescue mission, the bloodied handful who were still on their feet, kept up the contest. Here and there, prisoners picked up weapons and fought back as well. It was all very brave, but it wasn't enough.

Bill and young Matt Carson were making their way back to the gate, firing as they went. Even as more guards fell, the volume of return fire did not slacken much. Bill was hit first in the shoulder and then in his artificial leg. He stumbled. More bullets shattered the leg entirely. His weapon dropped, and Bill crumpled to the ground. Matt Carson stopped in his tracks.

Bill waved him away. "Go on kid, get out of here! I'm done for."

Matt Carson would hear none of it. "The hell you are," the kid snapped back, "not today, not on my watch!"

Carson picked up help from Sergeant White's son. The two of them worked their way back towards their fallen comrade. The young Marine laid down covering fire as Carson reached Bill and helped him up. Bill tried to hop on his good leg, but it was slow going.

Across the courtyard, a father's heart ached. Sergeant White could admire the singular courage of not leaving a man behind, particularly in those so young. He could also see, all too clearly now, that an injured man and his support made awfully good targets. White quickly turned to Simon.

"I hate to say it, my brave friend," the old Marine said calmly, "but I don't see both of us making it out of here. You make sure the Congressman gets to safety. I have to take care of someone else."

Sergeant White broke away from the cover of the building. He headed hard towards the gate where his son was desperately trying to hold back the enemy long enough so Matt could get Bill to safety. Along the way, White cut down several guards who were too intent on the easy prey in front of them to watch their own backs.

Simon was ready to move as well. "Congressman, we have to get across this courtyard. I'll cover you, but you're going to have to run."

Harris nodded. Simon dropped an approaching guard with a short burst and then pushed the Congressman forward.

The old Marine reached the gate and crouched down beside his son. There was a brief smile between the two before the father opened up as well, adding his weapon to the covering fire. More people, prisoners mostly, were flooding through the gates and into the field beyond. At least they were trying to; not all of them were making it. Too much heavy gunfire aimed at one spot. Too many bullets: all with an equal chance of hitting a random somebody.

Nonetheless, the cold, harsh mathematics of war and death was clearly turning in their favor now. More blood would spill, and more poor souls would surely perish getting through that gate. But there were simply too many people — too many targets — for the guards to kill them all.

It was a numbers game which Sergeant White understood better than most. He knew some would live. He also knew way too many would still have to die. He changed out a clip and fired again at the guards, dropping two men and forcing some others to keep their heads down.

He was determined to change the odds in the game.

He was determined to save one person in particular.

"Son," the father called out, "I need you to fall back into the field and work your way to the van. People will need some cover from there."

"I'm not leaving you, Dad." The son kept firing.

"That's a goddamn order," the father yelled again. "Now get the hell out of here!"

The son squeezed off a few more rounds before beginning to slowly fall back. He cleared the gate and moved into the open field, turning to fire short bursts every few steps. He was following orders because that was what good Marines did, and his father had raised him to be a good Marine. He stopped only briefly to reload and wipe the tears from his eyes.

"I'm proud of you, son," Sergeant White mumbled as he kept up the fire. He did hope, maybe against all odds, to have the chance after all of this to say that to his son's face. Right now though, he couldn't worry about that. Right now, he had to kill more guards so others might live.

There were too many.

He knew bullets alone weren't going to be enough.

White pulled back his weapon and retrieved a grenade from his vest. He stood up tall and straight among the bullets flying. In one smooth motion, he removed the pin and made a mighty heave towards the wall where the heaviest fire was coming from.

The grenade exploded. There was a blinding flash behind the wall. Body parts and weapons flew. Guards died. The shooting stopped. Survivors lay on the ground, moaning and groaning, dazed and confused.

All was quiet now to Sergeant White. The smoke of battle had cleared. Rays of sunlight danced off the steel barrels of silent guns. The old Marine thought to celebrate his victory, their victory. He tried to yell out, to tell the whole world, but no sound would come. He so much wanted for everyone to hear, but no sound would come. He reached down to grab his chest and felt his soaked shirt. He saw the blood. His weapon dropped.

He didn't feel the ground when he hit. The sunlight had gone away. The blue morning sky was suddenly black. There was so much still he wanted to say.

But no sound would come.

Simon saw the blast. He saw the sergeant fall. He saw the final act of a very brave man. He saw his friend die. A single tear rolled down Simon's cheek and dropped quickly to the hard clay below.

The blast had killed several guards and stunned others. The sergeant's sacrifice, however, had only brought a few precious moments. Even as Simon and the Congressman made their break for the gate, the guards were already recovering and beginning to open fire again. With

Sergeant White no longer blocking the way, gunmen were also starting to focus their attention on the open field where helpless prisoners still struggled to get away.

The people in that field, the innocent, the defenseless: Simon could not allow them to be slaughtered — not as long as he still had a weapon and the strength to fight. He reached the gate and pushed the Congressman through.

"Stay low but keep moving Congressman," Simon yelled. "Get to the van on the far side of the field. Men from the rescue mission will get you out of here. I've got to try to hold back the guards at this gate."

"Remember, you have to be the voice of freedom." Simon looked straight into the eyes of Congressman Harris. "You can make a difference!"

Harris nodded slightly, still unsure and a little bewildered. He tried to say thank you, but Simon had already turned back around and starting shooting again. There was no point in trying to say anything else. Harris knew that. He also knew that other men, brave men, wanted him to live so he figured right now he needed to at least try. Harris moved into the field, tentatively at first, and most of all tried to keep his head down.

The fire was hot and heavy coming at Simon. He had succeeded in drawing fire to himself and by default, drawing attention away from the field outside the gate. Simon returned the fire. More guards fell. More time for others to escape.

But there was a high price for more.

Simon had been hit twice and was bleeding heavily from a leg wound. Still he fought on. Still he kept up the fire. Still he held the gate. As the bullets flew all around him and the blood flowed, Simon thought back across the ages. He thought of a narrow mountain pass, of brave men in bronze armor and bright red tunics. He could see their faces even now. The courage in their eyes, their willingness to sacrifice for the freedom of an entire people: it had been worth it then.

It was worth it now. Simon gritted his teeth. He felt his strength renewed.

The shooting increased. Wood splintered, and a portion of the gate collapsed. The guards were concentrating all their firepower on his position. Simon felt another bullet enter his side. It burned like hell, but it didn't stop him. He wouldn't let it stop him, not yet. Simon changed out an empty clip and returned fire. It was his last clip.

The shooting increased again, this time coming from behind. This time the bullets were aimed at the guards. Simon pulled back his weapon and turned around, slowly and painfully. He had to see who was trying to help. Matt Carson, Sergeant White's son, or whoever it might be: Simon intended to tell him to get out the hell out of here. Then Simon saw.

It wasn't at all what he expected. He saw the man. He saw the crooked half-smile, and he knew.

Simon bowed his head. "My King," he said simply. Simon took in a deep breath even though it hurt. He wanted to look proud, erect.

"I am honored to see you on this field of battle. It has been a long time, my King."

The King tried to wipe the blood from his shirt. It didn't work. "My loyal Dienekes," the King replied, "it is I who am honored to be here with you on this glorious, sunny day."

During the brief lull in the firing, two guards had worked their way up to the remains of the gate. They now cleared the obstacle and were about to shoot when they too saw the man in the bloody shirt. They hesitated, not believing who or what they were seeing. Simon didn't hesitate. He dropped both of them with a short burst.

"My King," Simon continued, "you cannot stay here."

"Why not, my friend? It is like the narrow mountain pass. We can hold back the enemy here together."

The King began firing again. He did not totally understand the weapon he was holding, but his hands seem to know exactly what to do with it. The guards stopped advancing and began to fall back to better cover.

"No, my King," Simon replied firmly. "This is but one battle in a long struggle. They will need heroes for this struggle. The people have always needed heroes." There was a clear urgency, and just a hint of desperation, in Simon's voice.

"My own strength is fading," he said quietly. "I can no longer be their hero. You, my King, can be their hero. You can teach another how to be a hero, and you can teach him how to lead the people."

"You cannot die here on this field today. They need you." Simon managed a weak smile. His eyes were almost pleading.

"You must go now." Simon pointed at his king. Blood dripped from his shirt sleeve to the ground.

"You must cross the field and get to the van where brave men are waiting for you. You will know these men when you see them. You will know too the man you are to help — the Congressman — when you see him."

The King nodded. As with the gun, somehow he just understood, without asking any questions, without saying a word.

The firing from the guards picked up again. They were preparing to rush the gate.

"I can only hold them here for a short time longer." Simon motioned again toward the open field and the van on the far side. The King began to back slowly away from the gate.

"My King," Simon's voice was tight with emotion. "Go tell the Spartans that obedient to their laws here we lie."

The King smiled. It was a moment, an understanding which only such men could share. He turned and quickly moved off into the open field.

Simon fired over the gate. He dropped one guard and then another, but the rest kept coming. He fired again. A third guard fell. The enemy was closer now. Simon took aim at the nearest threat. He squeezed the trigger. There was a sickening click but nothing else.

Nothing.

No bullets left. No way to stop them.

The sun was bright, the sky clear and blue. Simon looked up at the heavens above. A beautiful day he thought — calm, peaceful. A moment when it seemed he had the world all to himself. And time, for that instant only, waited patiently on just one man. All quiet it was too, as if to help him choose between heaven and earth, between life and death.

There was only one choice. Once again, he heard the sound of automatic weapons. Simon struggled to his feet and looked over at the men coming to kill him. He was not afraid. He would not try to make a break across the open field. He would stand tall. He would fight until he could fight no more.

Bullets flew. They flew hard. They flew fast. One struck Simon in the arm; he didn't flinch, not at all. He sucked in a big gulp of air; then let out a great and terrible war cry which echoed across the field. Others heard it. The first guard who reached the gate heard it too. It startled him and made him hesitate for a single precious second. Simon didn't hesitate. He swung his empty weapon with all his might, breaking the gun and crushing the guard's skull.

The second gunman came over the gate firing at will. Simon felt a bullet hit him square in the stomach. There was great pain, but he had strength still. He swung the broken weapon again and knocked the gunman off his feet. Simon grabbed the man's gun and quickly finished him with two rounds to the chest. Turning back to face the enemy head on, Simon fired again and again. Guards fell.

But enough of them kept firing back. Simon was hit multiple times. Each time, he felt the burning. Each time, he felt blood and strength drain out of his body.

One man, one warrior, against the many: he had held them back for as long as he could.

His iron will endured, but his body at last was giving way. Simon tried hard to keep standing. He tried hard to hold his weapon, but it was so very heavy now. He tried but could no longer....

As the weapon fell from his hand, Simon saw again the faces of the brave men in bright red tunics. Their bronze armor shined brighter than ever before. They were strong. They were proud. They seemed to speak directly to Simon this time. He could not so much hear their words as he could feel them in every fiber of his being and in the very depths of his soul. The words took away the pain. They seemed to be telling Simon he had done enough.

It was time.

Simon's legs buckled, and he slumped to the ground. His breathing slowed. The sounds of the day, the shooting, disappeared all at once. The light was suddenly brighter, almost blinding. Slowly Simon turned and looked, through the white light, across the open field. He saw a great emptiness: no struggles, no terrified stragglers. He saw the far side of the field and the great mass of people moving away. They were free now. They were moving to safety. They were moving to life.

Simon smiled.

He didn't feel the last bullet enter his back. The force though shook his whole body, and he fell over, landing face down in the dirt. With a last bit of strength, Simon pulled his arms back towards his body and dug both hands into his vest. He moved, and then he moved no more. The bright light began to fade away to black. There was one final image of Holly and her beautiful brown eyes. As the darkness settled over him, Simon prayed he might somehow see her again.

Just once more.

"Holly," he said softly, "always my love." A whisper, if only she could hear....

Eyes closed, and he lay still.

Stepping over the bodies of fallen comrades, the guards approached cautiously. They had lost far too many men to take any chances. The captain of the guards wasn't happy at all.

"Goddamnit, how could one man do all this?" The captain nudged the nearest body with his foot. The man didn't move, which only seemed to piss off the captain even more.

"Shit!"

"Just how the hell are we going to explain this?" the captain continued hotly. "We lost all our prisoners, along with most of our men to a rag-tag bunch of rebels. Tell me how we're going to explain that?" He pointed at two of his men. They promptly hung their heads.

"Shit!"

The captain looked across the open field at the former prisoners moving away from the camp and beginning to work their way into town. He knew he was powerless to stop it.

"Now everyone will know," he mumbled to himself. "There'll be hell to pay."

"Shit!"

"Okay then," the captain shook his head and pointed again at the same two men. "How about turning over this son-of-a-bitch here so we can at least see the face of the man who killed a lot of our guys?"

Putting aside their weapons, the guards reached down and roughly grabbed Simon around the shoulders and legs. They turned over the body; it landed in the dirt with a thud. The hands hit too and opened. A grenade rolled free from each hand. The pins were already gone.

The captain and his guards froze. They saw. They couldn't speak.

Someone else would have the last word.

There was one final moment which yet separated life from death. Simon opened his eyes. He couldn't see, but he knew. He knew for sure. Choking back the blood, Simon yelled out his defiance, one last great roar.

"May the Gods bless the United States of America!"

The King was working his way through the crowd to the cargo van when he heard the explosion. Many in the crowd gasped. A few even screamed. They were surprised mainly, not knowing exactly what it meant. The King bowed his head. He knew. He knew a brave warrior had made the sacrifice.

He knew also there was much still to do. He saw the men at the cargo van. Dienekes had been correct, the King had to admit. He did seem to recognize all their faces. The men at the van seemed to recognize him as well.

They saw the blood on his shirt too.

None of them knew quite what to make of that. Certainly none of them were prepared to ask about it. A strange mixture of relief, fascination, maybe even a little bit of fear: whatever it was circulating among the group, it wasn't exactly the recipe for a joyful reunion or even a casual conversation.

The silence was awkward.

Matt Carson fidgeted even as he leaned against the van. He had seen a lot over the last few days: a lot of blood, a lot of death. It had given him a different perspective. One more bloody shirt wasn't going to bother him now. He just didn't have the time or the patience to wait, particularly when he had a question.

"Simon, what about Simon?" Young Matt Carson looked directly into the eyes of the man in the bloody shirt. "Did you see him?"

"Is he still in the camp?"

"Is he still alive?"

The King shook his head. He looked at Matt Carson and then the others. "You heard the explosion. Our friend held the enemy at the gate and sacrificed himself so others might make it across the field, so others might live."

No matter what Matt Carson had seen over the last few days, this news still hurt, and it hurt bad. He couldn't bring himself to say anything else.

The other men just bowed their heads, including Congressman Harris.

The King turned his attention to the Congressman. "I'm glad to see you made it out of the camp. I understand you're an important man."

"We have much to discuss, you and I."

Harris nodded, somewhat weakly.

That was good enough for now, the King quickly decided. He smiled and nodded back to the Congressman.

"For the rest of you," the King bellowed, "I think it's time we loaded up the van and got out of here."

Again there wasn't a lot of conversation from the group. That also meant there wasn't a lot of argument either. In any case, people started to move, something about the tone of voice: familiar but just scary enough to make the point. One after another, men dutifully climbed into the van: Matt Carson, Bill who needed a little help, Congressman Harris, and the rest. They were all done in a matter of minutes — all except for one. The young man with the blonde hair and crew cut stood outside the van, still carefully eyeing the bloody shirt.

The King took notice. He wasn't angry or impatient for the order to be followed; he simply stared right back at the young man. There were no words. For a few seconds, the older man and the younger man just stared. It wasn't really so uncomfortable for the King; it just didn't seem to be quite as easy as using the gun. Suddenly something popped into his head, and just as suddenly, it became easy. The King smiled again and said what now seemed to come so naturally to him.

"I'm proud of you, son."

Sergeant White's son smiled back. He didn't say anything. That would have to come later. But for the moment, he wasn't so worried about the bloody shirt anymore. The son joined the rest of the men in the back of the van while his father slipped into the driver's seat.

As the van pulled slowly away from the fields of Gettysburg, Congressman Harris looked around at the collection of men seated near him. They were a bloodied lot. They had suffered, and they carried the wounds to prove it. It was more than bandages, shattered limbs, and physical scars. They had lost friends, brothers, or even fathers coming to this place — coming to rescue him.

Harris grimaced. He looked again at the men, really looked into their eyes this time. He saw tears. He saw pain. He saw loss. But he also saw something else, something indescribable but something very real all the same. He knew it well, or at least he had known it well at one time.

Hope, faith, a belief in something greater than yourself: whatever one called it, Congressman Harris saw it now in the eyes of the men looking back at him. He also knew these men were putting their faith in him.

It was a heavy burden. Harris felt it deep down inside, burning and churning in the pit of his stomach. A wave of nausea washed over him, and he felt a sudden weakness in each of his limbs. The Congressman hung his head. He wasn't so sure he had it in him anymore to be what these people needed.

The miles ticked by. It was quiet in the back of the van. No talking, just the steady hum of the tires riding on the road.

A time of reflection.

A time to mourn the fallen.

A time for some, just possibly, to find what had been lost.

Morning sunlight filtered in through a small hole in the top of the van. Harris reached forward into the beam to touch it, to feel it. He felt the warmth. He closed his eyes and smiled. For a moment then, he was transported back to another warm, sunny day many years ago. It was his first day in the United States Congress. He remembered his pride, his ideals. He remembered the flag of red, white, and blue, the stars and stripes, which flew proudly over the capital in those days. He had come to the capital to serve his fellow Americans.

Harris opened his eyes. He was back in the here and now, in a van with men who had sacrificed to free him. One of those wore an old uniform, torn and blood-stained, but sporting still a ragged patch, a small flag of red, white, and blue. Yes, Harris knew for sure. He was riding in this van with his fellow Americans.

Blood had been spilled in the name of freedom.

There was an intense glow in his pale, blue eyes now. Congressman Jim Harris had decided. He would speak out again — long and loud to anyone who would listen — no matter what the cost. He would speak for freedom.

Epilogue

It was mid-morning. Holly had just turned on the television and now she understood.

She had felt something earlier, something sudden, something strange. She swore she had even heard her name whispered right out of thin air, as if on the wind itself. A whisper by nobody and in a voice she could not totally understand. Whatever this something, it wasn't her imagination. It hurt like hell too, and it brought an indescribable, almost unbearable sadness crashing down upon her entire body. She had soon found herself crying and then crying some more. She could not bring herself to stop, and she didn't know exactly why.

Now she knew why.

The television told her, not directly but in so many words — a lot of words actually. It was all over the news: anything and everything, all about the trade association. The CEO was dead. Early reports suggested a self-inflicted gunshot wound. There was even a video circulating around where the CEO supposedly admitted to staging the bombing at the trade conference. To top that, now the news was reporting on a battle at some containment camp in a place called Gettysburg where political prisoners had been freed.

It was absolute chaos. Nobody knew anything for sure, but Holly knew.

She listened to stories from survivors of the camp battle. They told of a few ragged men who raided the camp and freed them. Some of these ragged men laid down their lives to defend the defenseless prisoners who were being gunned down by the guards. In particular, they told the tale of a single man who stayed behind and held the prison gate against all odds so that people could escape across the field. He held back the guards. He fought them to the last. There was a terrific explosion at the end according to eye-witness reports.

He had died so that others might live. It was what heroes did.

It was all over TV, and Holly knew for sure.

Simon was dead.

Her husband, her lover, her hero, was gone. Gone forever. Holly suddenly felt a great emptiness. The part of her soul that loved and belonged to her husband had died with him. Holly began to cry once again.

If things were chaotic on TV and over the airwaves, things were far worse still on the ground at trade association headquarters. With the death of the CEO, James Wilson, head of security, was nominally in charge, and he had big problems. For one, the TAA had lost control of the networks, at least temporarily. The stories were simply too big, too juicy. It was a feeding frenzy, and Wilson sure as hell didn't feel like the shark.

But the networks didn't know everything. The head of security knew the tape of the CEO's confession leaked to the public had been heavily edited. So far, he had not been able to piece together everything that had been edited out, but he knew Daniel Garcia had not been alone when he died. He knew Simon Anderson had been in that office. Whether or not Anderson had actually pulled the trigger, James Wilson didn't know just yet. And right now, Simon Anderson was nowhere to be found.

Not that Wilson was really surprised.

The security chief guessed that where Anderson was now had a whole lot to do with where he had been. Wilson wasn't a betting man by nature, but he'd bet the farm that Simon Anderson had been part of the raid on the Gettysburg Containment Center. The rag-tag group which attacked the camp matched the description of the armed men who nearly wiped out the trade association assault team sent to liquidate the old Catholic Rescue Mission. He knew Anderson had been at the mission with those armed men.

He knew Simon Anderson was dangerous. He had never trusted him from the start. Daniel Garcia just wouldn't listen, thought he could handle things all by himself.

James Wilson slammed his fist down hard on the desk. He had known it all along, but nobody believed him.

Now he would have to handle things — his way. If he couldn't immediately locate Simon Anderson, Wilson figured he would start with the next best thing, or at least the next closest thing. He knew Simon's wife and child lived not so far from headquarters. He could be at the house in a little over 30 minutes.

Maybe, maybe not....

The situation was still chaotic at the TAA. Someone needed to take charge. Someone needed to provide calm leadership in order to salvage something out of this mess. Wilson knew all that. He even supposed he was the guy. But this was personal. Besides, after this little job had been handled, he fully intended to get back in time to deal with the media.

He had always believed you just had to deal with first things first. The security chief holstered a pistol under his jacket and stuffed an extra clip in his pocket. He walked out the office door and headed towards his car.

Holly Anderson had no idea what was coming her way. She looked out the window at the bright sunny day. She was tired of listening to all the talk and the theories on TV. It wasn't just news anymore; it was so much more personal to her. She had to figure out a way to go on living without the man she loved. She had to figure out a way to tell her little girl that the man she knew as her father was never coming back. Holly looked back out the window and wiped away a tear. She had been able to hide the tears from her daughter so far, but she couldn't do that forever. Maybe it would just be better, she decided, if she took Suzy out for a walk around the neighborhood.

A few minutes into the drive, James Wilson found he was rather enjoying himself. It was pretty outside and kind of relaxing to be away from headquarters for a bit. More than that, it just felt good to be in the field for a change. He had been giving orders to other people for so long, too long really. Wilson glanced up at the clear blue sky and smiled. He was actually looking forward to pulling the trigger himself this time.

It wasn't too much longer before his target destination came into view. The leafy green suburb where the Anderson family lived: it was the perfect place for an executive of the trade association, or at least it had been once. All tree-lined streets and manicured lawns: the security chief appreciated the ambiance. But there was something else too. Something sudden, something bright that Wilson noticed just in the corner of his eye.

And then it was gone.

A little perplexing maybe, but it wasn't enough to slow him down. James Wilson had a job to do.

As he took a sharp left turn into the neighborhood, he saw it again. Not so much a light as it was a shiny object, some sort of bronze figure really. It moved, and it moved fast. It cut across his field of vision, crossing over to a neatly trimmed yard and then disappearing into some thick bushes. This time James Wilson turned his head almost immediately, but he wasn't nearly quick enough.

He stopped the car dead in the middle of the road. Now he was concerned, not worried so much, but definitely concerned. He didn't want any company. He surely didn't want any witnesses. For a few seconds, James Wilson did nothing, just sitting and waiting — for what, he didn't exactly know. It was totally out of character for the head of security to hesitate at all. He looked again. He didn't see anybody or anything else for that matter.

Then his luck changed suddenly. It was a beautiful day, a good day to be outside, a good day for a mother and daughter to walk. He saw his target now, heading down the street right towards him.

No more waiting; it was now or never. Wilson pulled out his gun and hit the gas.

Tires screeched. The engine roared. Holly Anderson saw the car and instinctively pulled Suzy back to shield her.

But she saw something else as well. It was bright and bronze-colored, and it moved directly in front of the on-rushing car.

The security chief saw it too. It made no attempt to move out of the way. The distance rapidly closed. James Wilson could see it very clearly now, though he didn't want to believe his own eyes. It was a definite figure of a man, a powerful man, a warrior in bronze armor and a bright red tunic. A plumed helmet covered the head and face, but Wilson could see the eyes. The eyes were terrible and fierce and seemed to glow blood red. The eyes most of all terrified the security chief.

It was some sort of nightmare. It wasn't real. It couldn't be real. Wilson tried to convince himself. Now time itself seemed to slow down for James Wilson, as if some all-powerful force had willed it so. His nightmare continued thus in small, painful increments. He saw the warrior draw a sword. He saw the scowl on the face through the helmet. And then he saw the sword come crashing down in one mighty blow.

Wilson screamed and immediately pulled the steering wheel hard to the right. The car jumped the sidewalk at full speed and smashed head-on into a sturdy oak tree.

It was a sick, absolutely unnerving sound, shocking in its suddenness too, as the metal crumpled and glass shattered. The tree shuddered and groaned. When it all stopped after no more than a few seconds, Holly was still shaking and still shielding her child. She had no intention of approaching the wreck.

Smoke and hissing steam escaped from beneath the twisted hood. Radiator fluid dripped steadily onto the sidewalk. In the car itself, there was no sign of movement. The airbags had deployed as intended, cradling the face and upper body of the head of security. He was dazed and bruised, but alive. He was breathing. He was thinking. He was aware. Nothing more than that: a body perfectly still. In truth, he felt like he couldn't budge a muscle no matter how hard he tried. He couldn't feel arms or legs or pain or anything at all. His mind sent one command after another to each and every part of the body, yet the body wouldn't answer. Nothing worked.

Nothing except....

The gun in his right hand: Wilson still held that. He didn't know what he could do with it, but he held it tight. Or at least he imagined he held it tight. He couldn't feel that either. His finger remained on the trigger nonetheless.

Then he saw the blood red eyes again — in the remains of the windshield, in the rear view mirror, reflected in the sunlight on mangled metal. The eyes were everywhere all at once. It was the nightmare again. It was real this time. Wilson couldn't decide.

Maybe it didn't really matter. He felt the same panic, the same terror either way. One thing he knew for sure: he couldn't just wake up and make all this go away. Heart beating out of his chest now, James Wilson was finding it increasingly difficult to get enough air. Still too, he could not will the muscles in his body to work.

The head of security for the entire Trade Association of the Americas was absolutely powerless. At this, his lowest moment, he closed his eyes. He prayed. He prayed from the very depths of his soul. He prayed for the blood red eyes to go away. He prayed to find the strength to move again. He prayed for his body to just feel something, anything at all.

He opened his eyes.

The blood red eyes, their terrible reflection, were gone from the windshield and the mirror. Wilson breathed a long sigh of relief. He smiled.

But it was not to be. Wilson saw that very quickly.

The warrior in the bronze armor and red tunic was not gone. With a terrible scowl and brandishing a glowing sword, the warrior lunged towards the driver side window. James Wilson could not hear himself scream. He could not feel his arm move. He could not feel anything until he felt the cold barrel of the gun touch the side of his head. He felt his finger pull the trigger.

The last thing James Wilson felt was the hot, burning explosion on his skin as the bullet did its work. Then darkness.

His prayers had been answered — in a way. In a way, justice had been served. Like his boss, the head of security had died by his own hand, fitting perhaps for men who had the blood of so many others on those same hands.

Holly heard the gunshot from the smoldering wreck. She didn't know exactly what to make of it. At the same time, she immediately felt different somehow. No longer fearful. No longer worried. She relaxed her grip on Suzy. A wave of calm, a wonderful feeling of serenity, washed over her entire body.

She saw the warrior too, clearly for the first time, and now she understood why. She didn't see blood red eyes. She didn't feel terror or fear. She felt safe.

The warrior in bronze slowly removed his helmet and held it in his powerful arms. He looked at Holly. He looked directly into her eyes, but didn't speak.

With long black curly hair, a rugged jaw, and piercing blue eyes, he was, Holly thought to herself, the most beautiful thing she had ever seen. She looked back into those eyes. She looked long, and she looked hard. She recognized something there. She saw the truth in those eyes — like she always had before.

The warrior smiled.

Holly smiled too. She knew. She knew for sure. A single tear rolled down her cheek.

The sun was still shining bright. Birds were singing, and a gentle breeze drifted through the trees on its way down the street. The smell of the wrecked car was soon taken away by the steady blowing of the breeze. The wind cleansed.

It brought peace.

Holly watched as her man in bronze began to fade away into the very elements of the day itself — sunlight, clear blue skies, the wind. He waved goodbye. It was the last thing she saw

Suzy tugged at her mother's sleeve.

"Mommy, was that an angel?"

"Yes, honey," Holly replied as she squeezed her daughter's hand. "Yes, it was."

www.ingramcontent.com/pod-product-compliance
Lightning Source LLC
Chambersburg PA
CBHW070742190726
48292CB00002B/386